ILLUSTRATOR
KIYO KYUJYO

AUTHO
SUNAO YOS

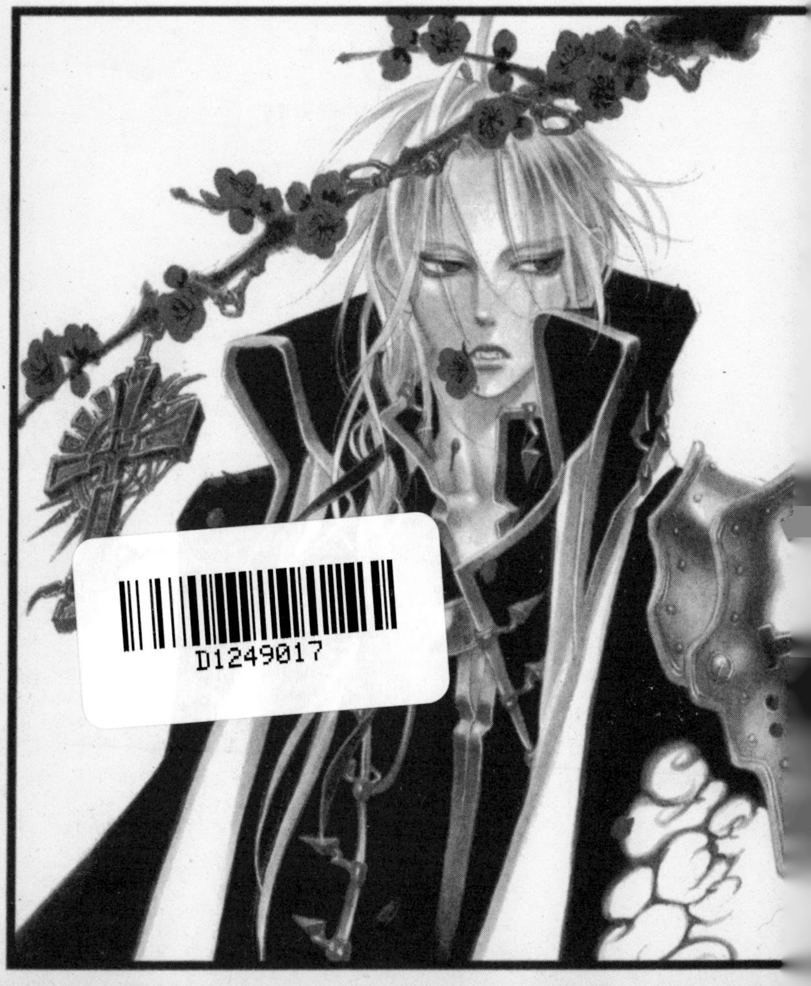

Trinity Blood Volume 6
Story By Sunao Yoshida
Art By Kiyo Kyujyo
Character Designs by Thores Shibamoto

Translation - Beni Axia Conrad
English Adaptation - Christine Boylan
Copy Editor - Shannon Watters
Retouch and Lettering - Star Print Brokers
Production Artist - Lauren O'Connell
Graphic Designer - James Lee

Editor - Lillian Diaz-Przybyl
Digital Imaging Manager - Chris Buford
Pre-Production Supervisor - Lucas Rivera
Production Manager - Elisabeth Brizzi
Managing Editor - Vy Nguyen
Creative Director - Anne Marie Horne
Editor-in-Chief - Rob Tokar
Publisher - Mike Kiley
President and C.O.O. - John Parker
C.E.O. and Chief Creative Officer - Stu Levy

A  Manga

TOKYOPOP Inc.
5900 Wilshire Blvd. Suite 2000
Los Angeles, CA 90036

E-mail: info@TOKYOPOP.com
Come visit us online at www.TOKYOPOP.com

ISBN: 978-1-4278-0015-2

First TOKYOPOP printing: May 2008
10 9 8 7 6 5 4 3 2 1
Printed in the USA

TRINITY BLOOD

VOLUME 6

WRITTEN BY
SUNAO YOSHIDA

ILLUSTRATED BY
KIYO KYUJYO

TOKYOPOP®

HAMBURG // LONDON // LOS ANGELES // TOKYO

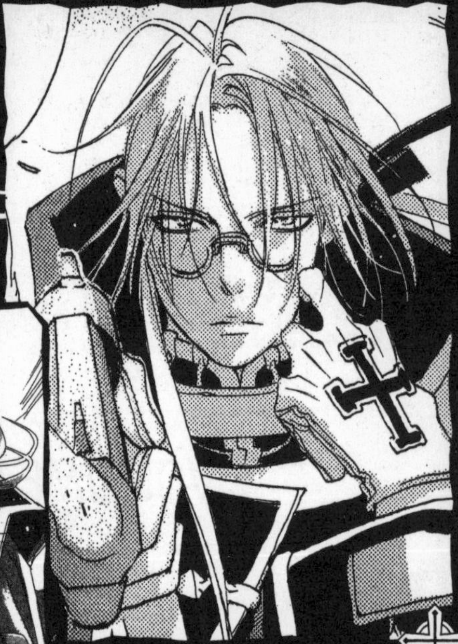

Becomes

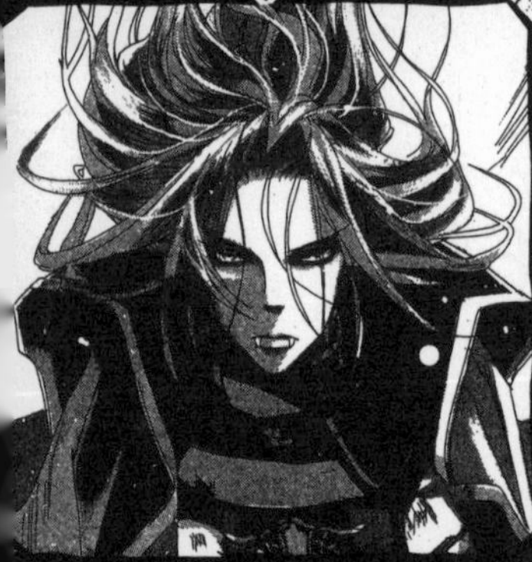

Crusnik

When Abel's threatened and left with no other means of escape, he transforms into a Crusnik, a mysterious vampire who drinks the blood of other vampires and possesses great power.

Abel Nightroad

An absentminded, destitute traveling priest from the Vatican's secret AX organization. His official title is AX enforcement officer. His job is to arrest law-breaking vampires. And he takes 13 spoonfuls of sugar in his tea.

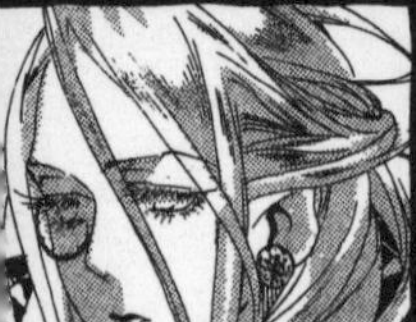

aterina Sforza

ne is Abel and Tres's perior, the director the Vatican Special rvices Annex.

Story

In the distant future, civilization has been destroyed by a catastrophe of epic proportions. Mankind is at war with vampires, an alien life form that appeared when the earth changed. The Methuselah Empire and the Human Vatican attempt to negotiate peace, but they are stopped by two forces: the betrayal of Ion, a messenger from the Empire, by his erstwhile best friend Radu, and by the martial intervention of the Inquisition. Meanwhile, Father Abel Nightroad is forced to activate the Crusnik, scaring away his companion, Sister Esther. The Iblis, a deadly weapon launched by the Rosenkreuz Orden, fast approaches the city of Carthage. Ion battles Radu, but cannot stop the weapon. Esther suddenly realizes that, even as a Crusnik, Father Abel is still Father Abel. She tears off into the dangerous underground waterway in pursuit of Father Nightroad, as the survival of the Vatican and two civilizations hangs in the balance.

Characters & Story

Tres Iqus

Like Abel, he is also an AX enforcement officer. His code name is "Gunslinger." He is more machine than human.

Esther Blanchett

A novice nun with a strong sense of justice. After she lost her church and friends in a battle with vampires, she chose action over despair and followed Abel when he said, "I am on your side."

Radu

He is Ion's best friend, the Baron of Luxor and an inspector from the Empire. He betrayed Ion to join the Rosenkreuz Orden.

Ion

A messenger from the Empire, a Noble of Moldova titled Earl of Memphis.

Petros

The Director of the Department of Inquisition also known as the strongest and most violent knight in Vatican. He cooperates with his enemy Ion to stop the

CONTENTS

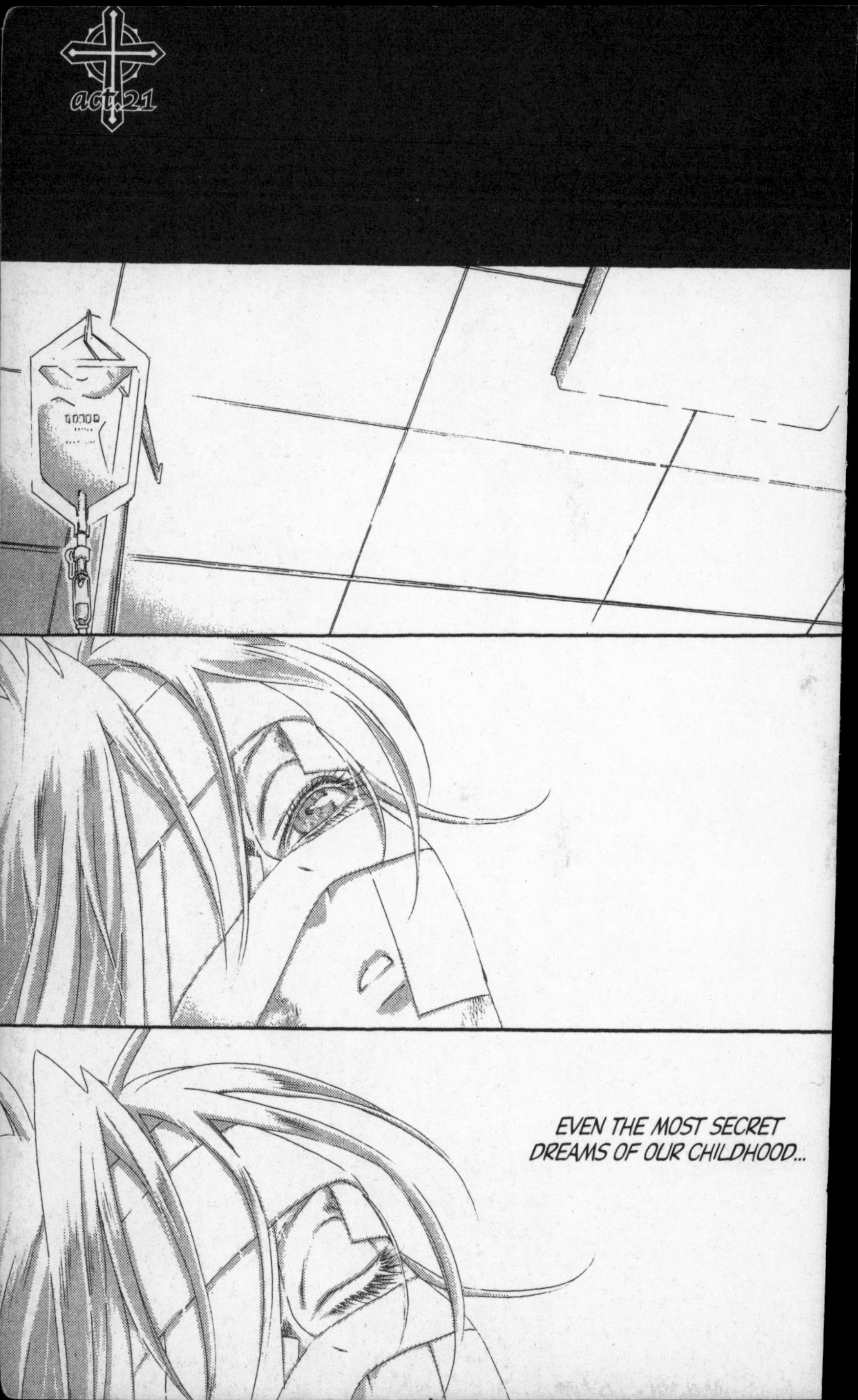
act.21
EVEN THE MOST SECRET DREAMS OF OUR CHILDHOOD...

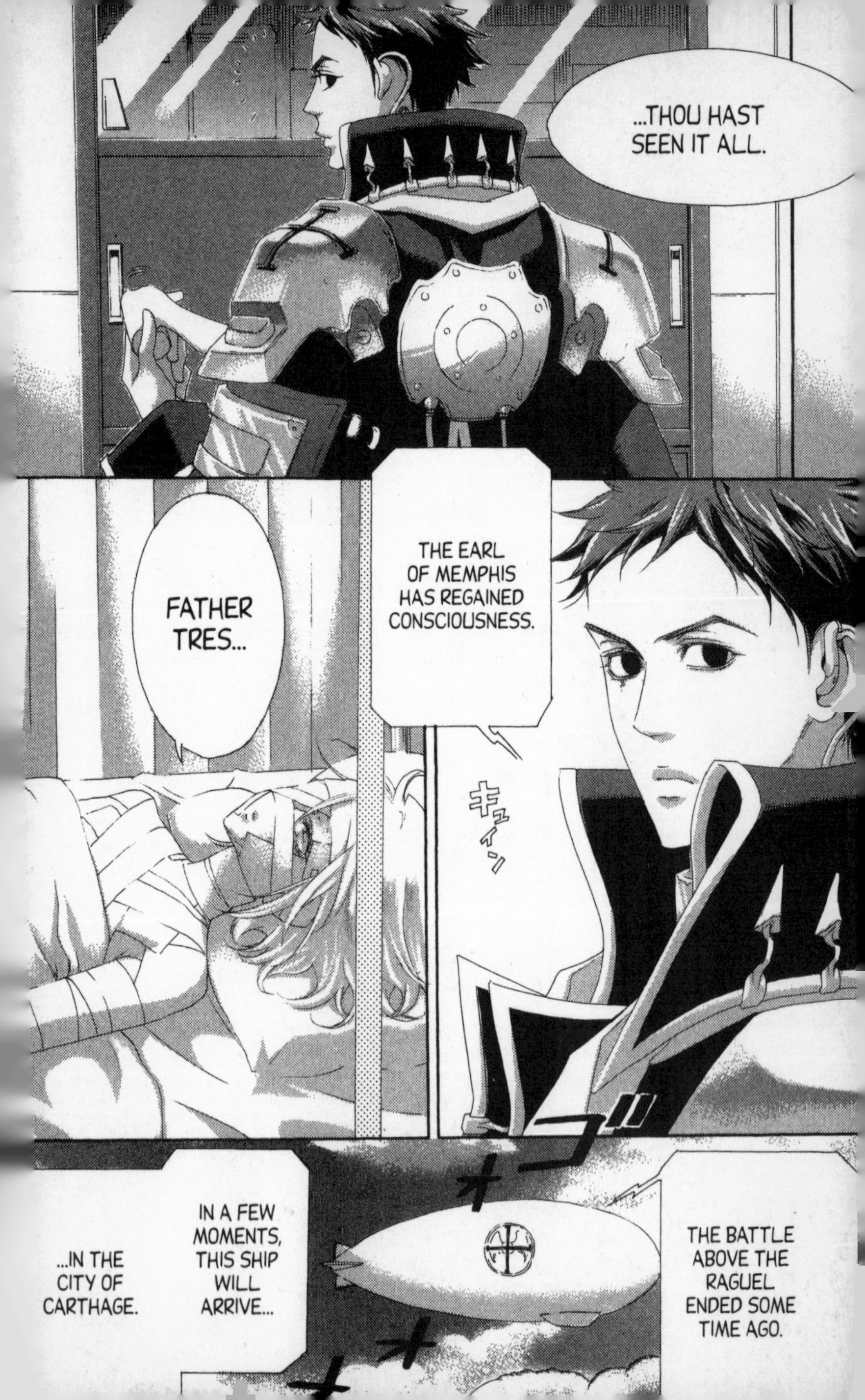
...THOU HAST SEEN IT ALL.
THE EARL OF MEMPHIS HAS REGAINED CONSCIOUSNESS.
キュイーン
FATHER TRES...
THE BATTLE ABOVE THE RAGUEL ENDED SOME TIME AGO.
IN A FEW MOMENTS, THIS SHIP WILL ARRIVE...
...IN THE CITY OF CARTHAGE.

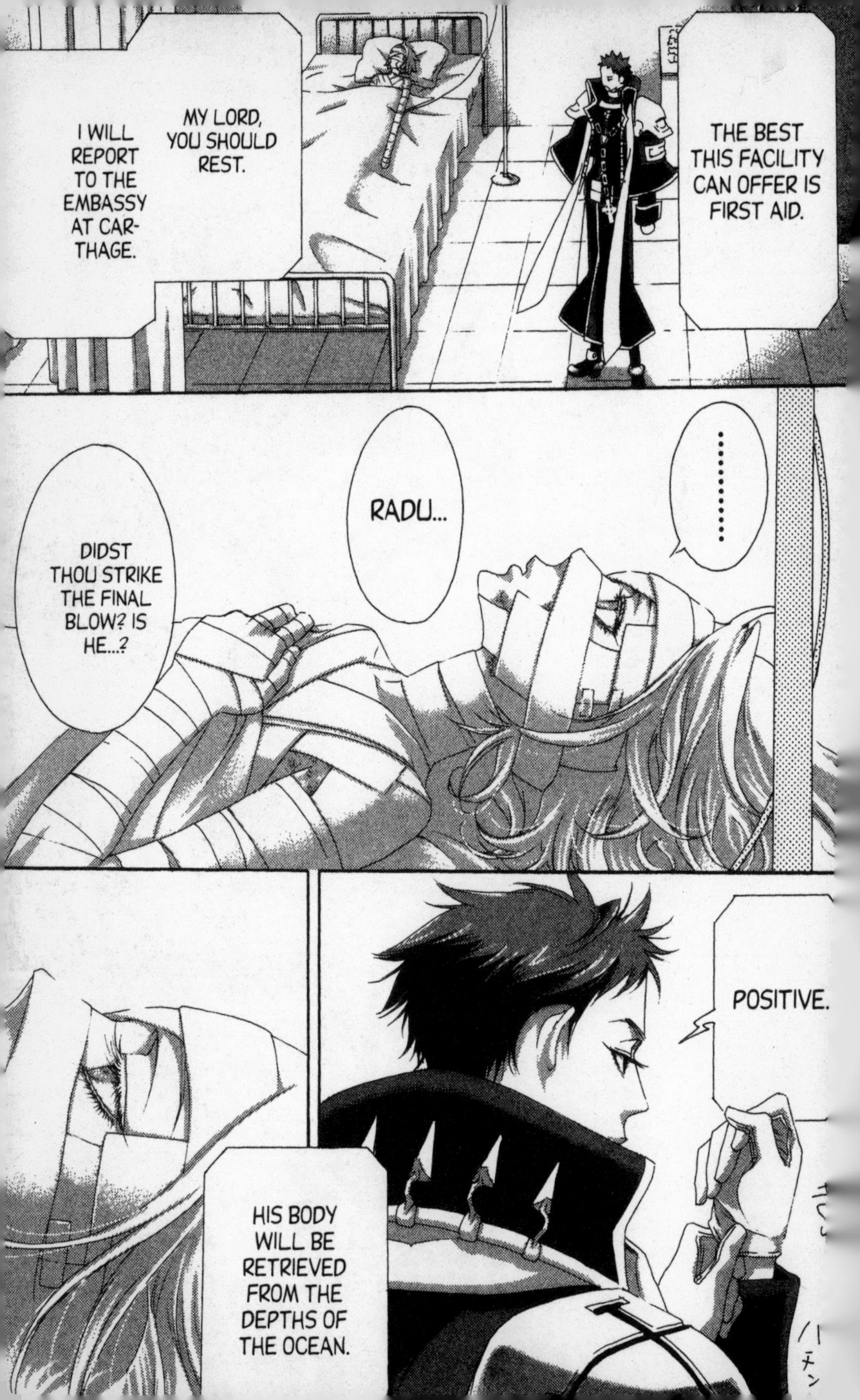
THE BEST THIS FACILITY CAN OFFER IS FIRST AID.
MY LORD, YOU SHOULD REST.
I WILL REPORT TO THE EMBASSY AT CARTHAGE.
....
RADU...
DIDST THOU STRIKE THE FINAL BLOW? IS HE...?
POSITIVE.
HIS BODY WILL BE RETRIEVED FROM THE DEPTHS OF THE OCEAN.

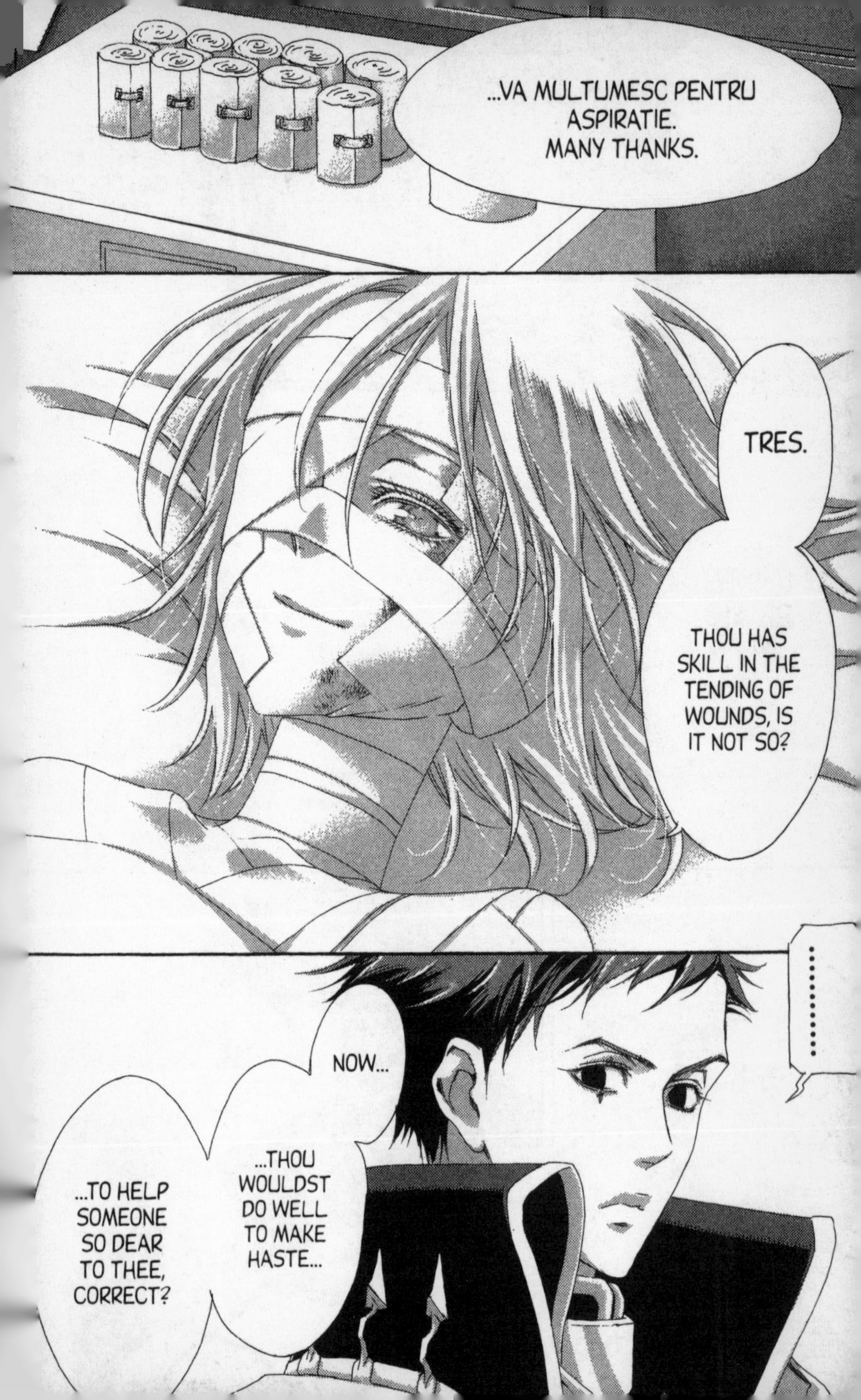
...VA MULTUMESC PENTRU ASPIRATIE. MANY THANKS.
TRES.
THOU HAS SKILL IN THE TENDING OF WOUNDS, IS IT NOT SO?
......
NOW...
...THOU WOULDST DO WELL TO MAKE HASTE...
...TO HELP SOMEONE SO DEAR TO THEE, CORRECT?

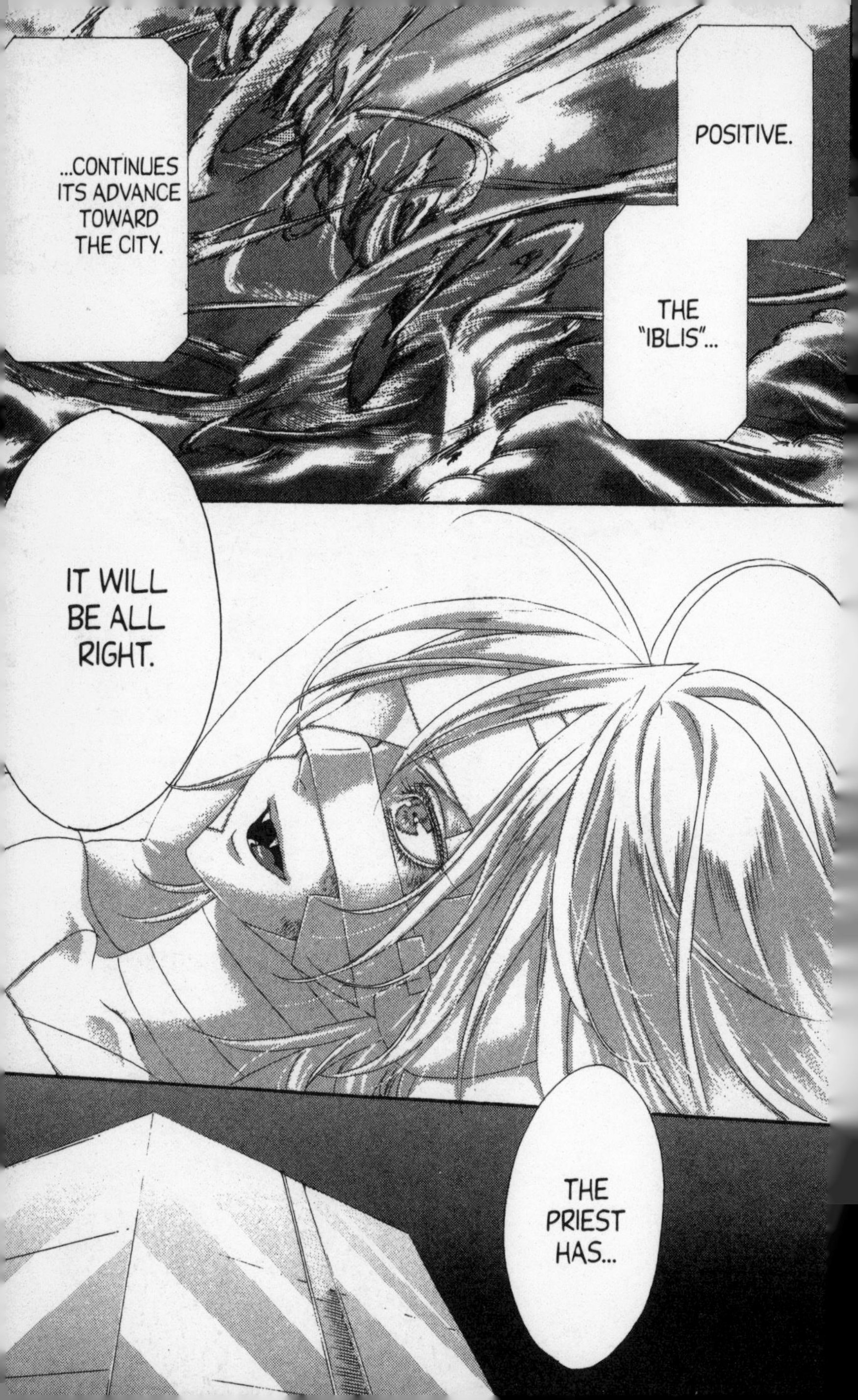
POSITIVE.
THE "IBLIS"...
...CONTINUES ITS ADVANCE TOWARD THE CITY.
IT WILL BE ALL RIGHT.
THE PRIEST HAS...

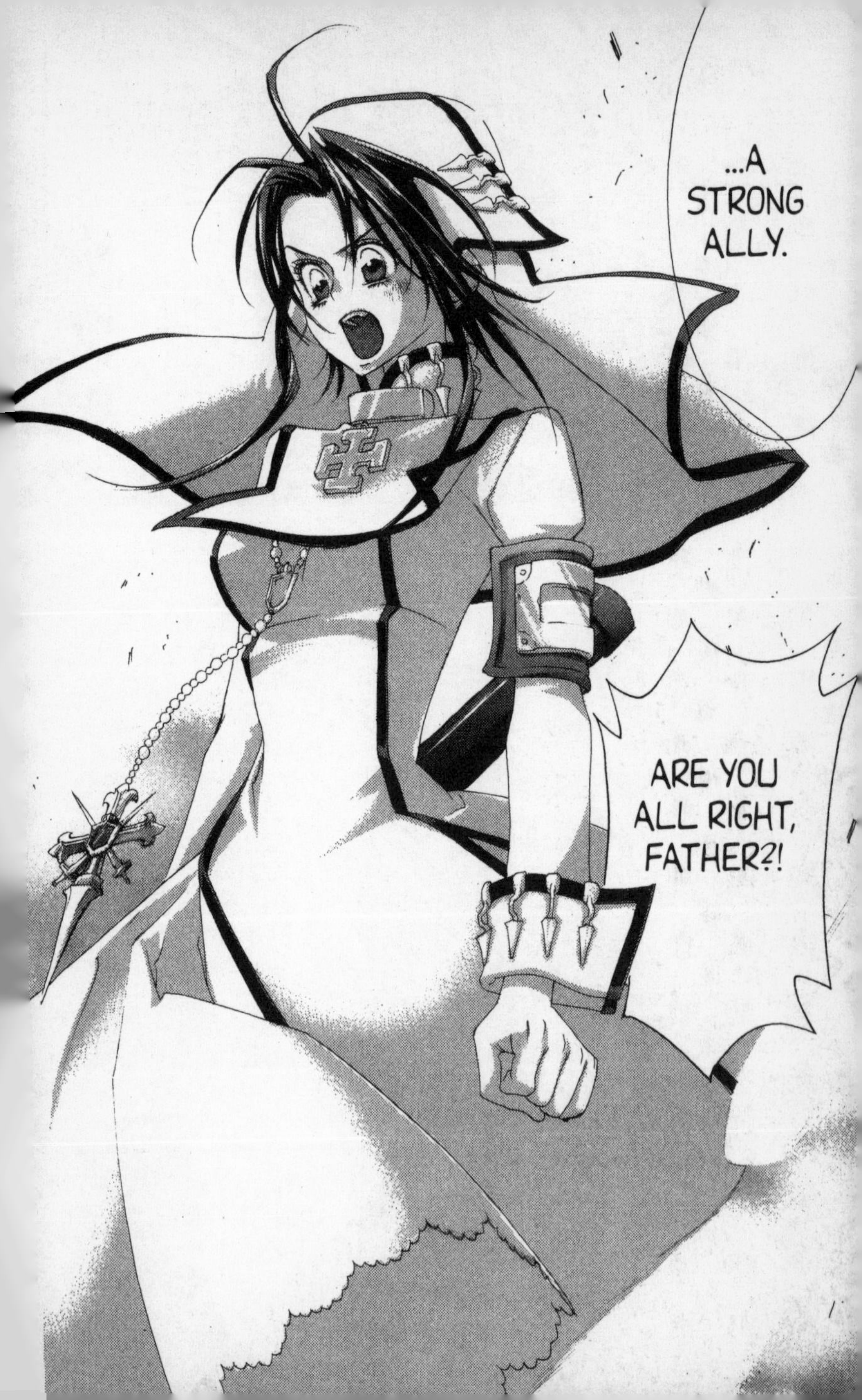
...A STRONG ALLY.
ARE YOU ALL RIGHT, FATHER?!

act.21 DAIJO-BU, MY FRIEND

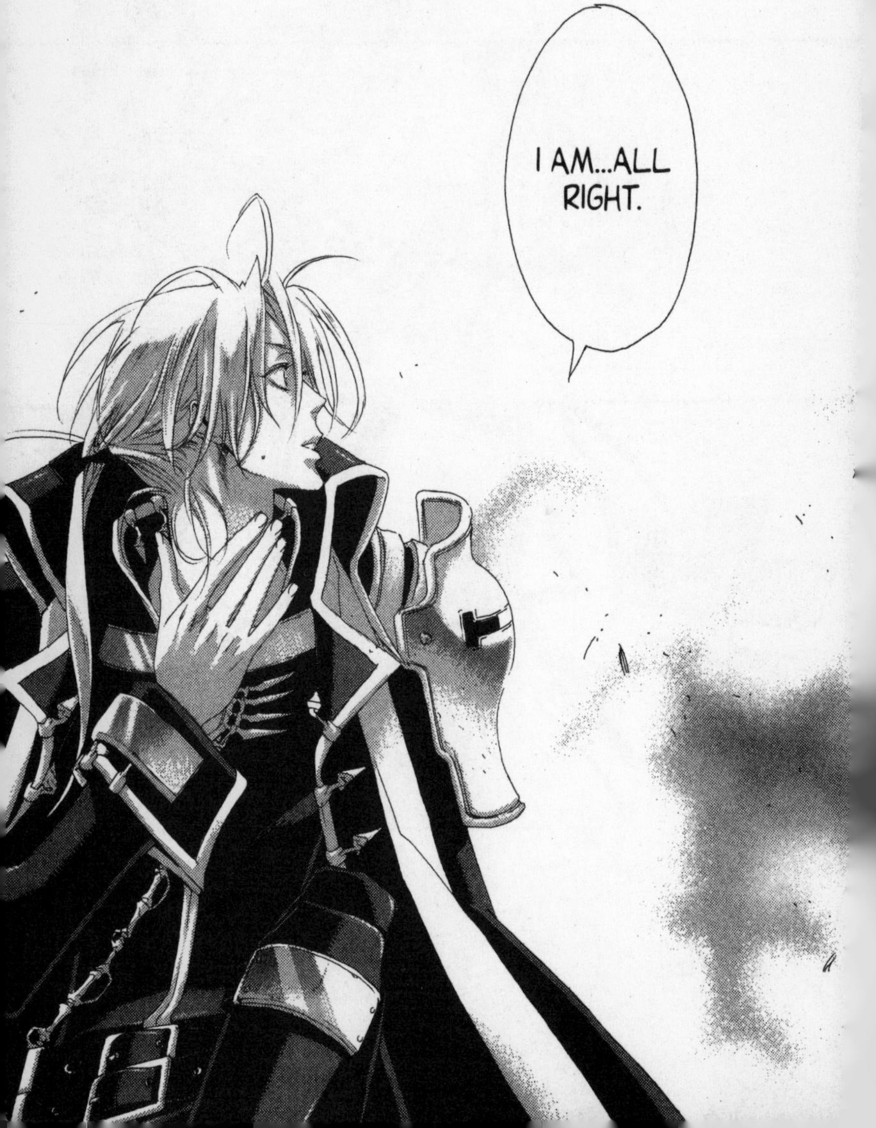
I AM...ALL RIGHT.

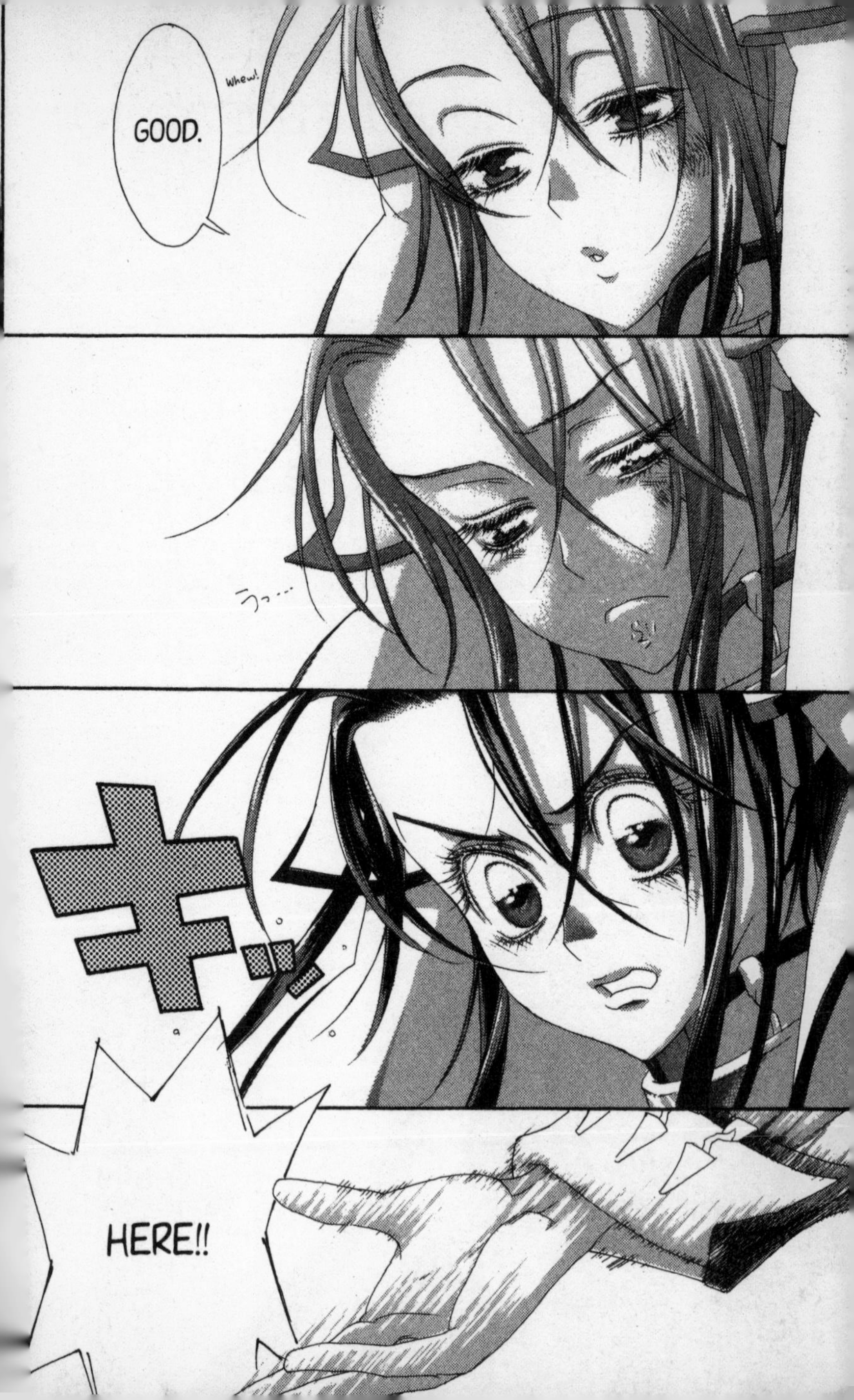
Whew!
GOOD.
ウッ…
ギュッ
HERE!!

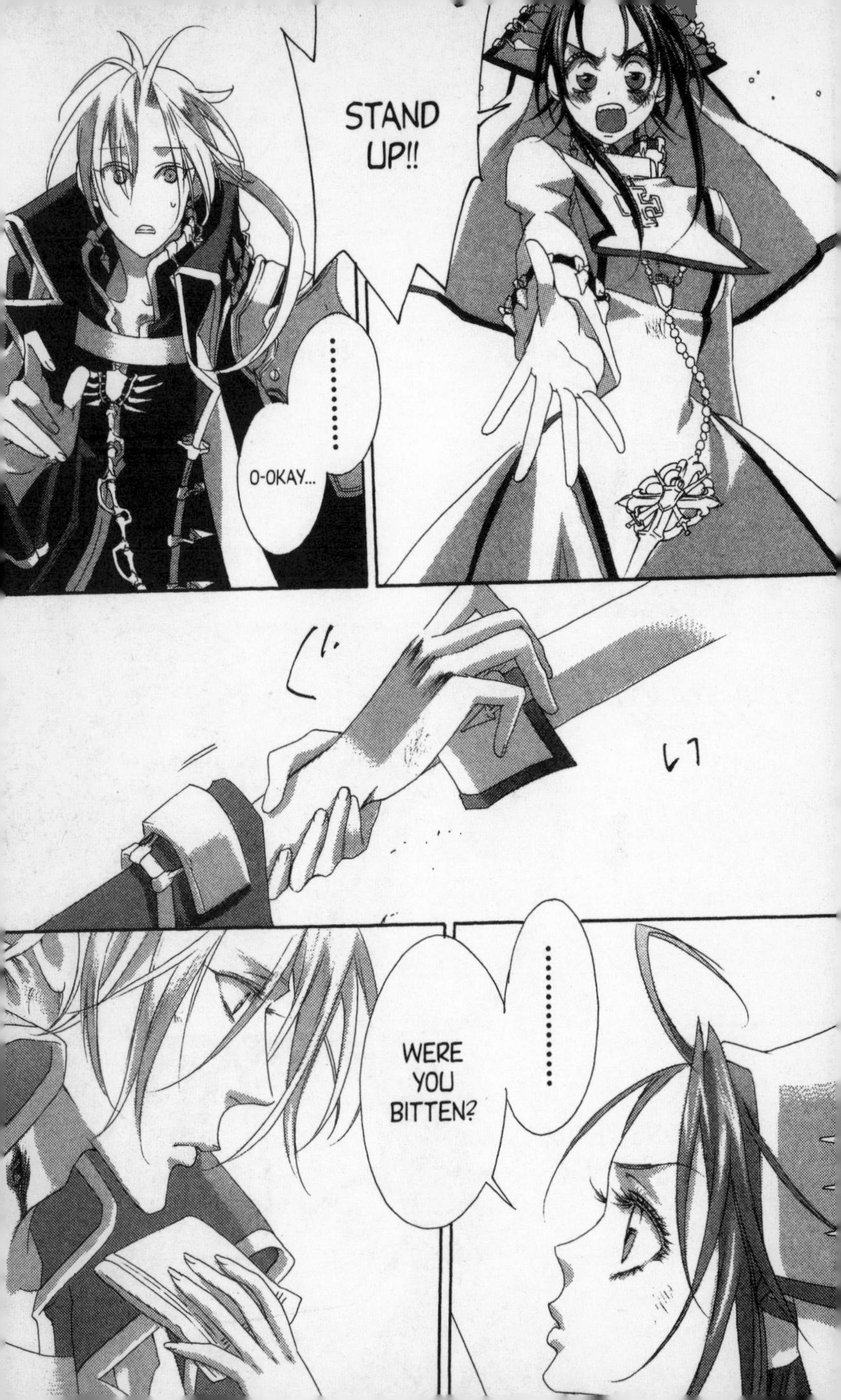
STAND UP!!
....
O-OKAY...
....
WERE YOU BITTEN?

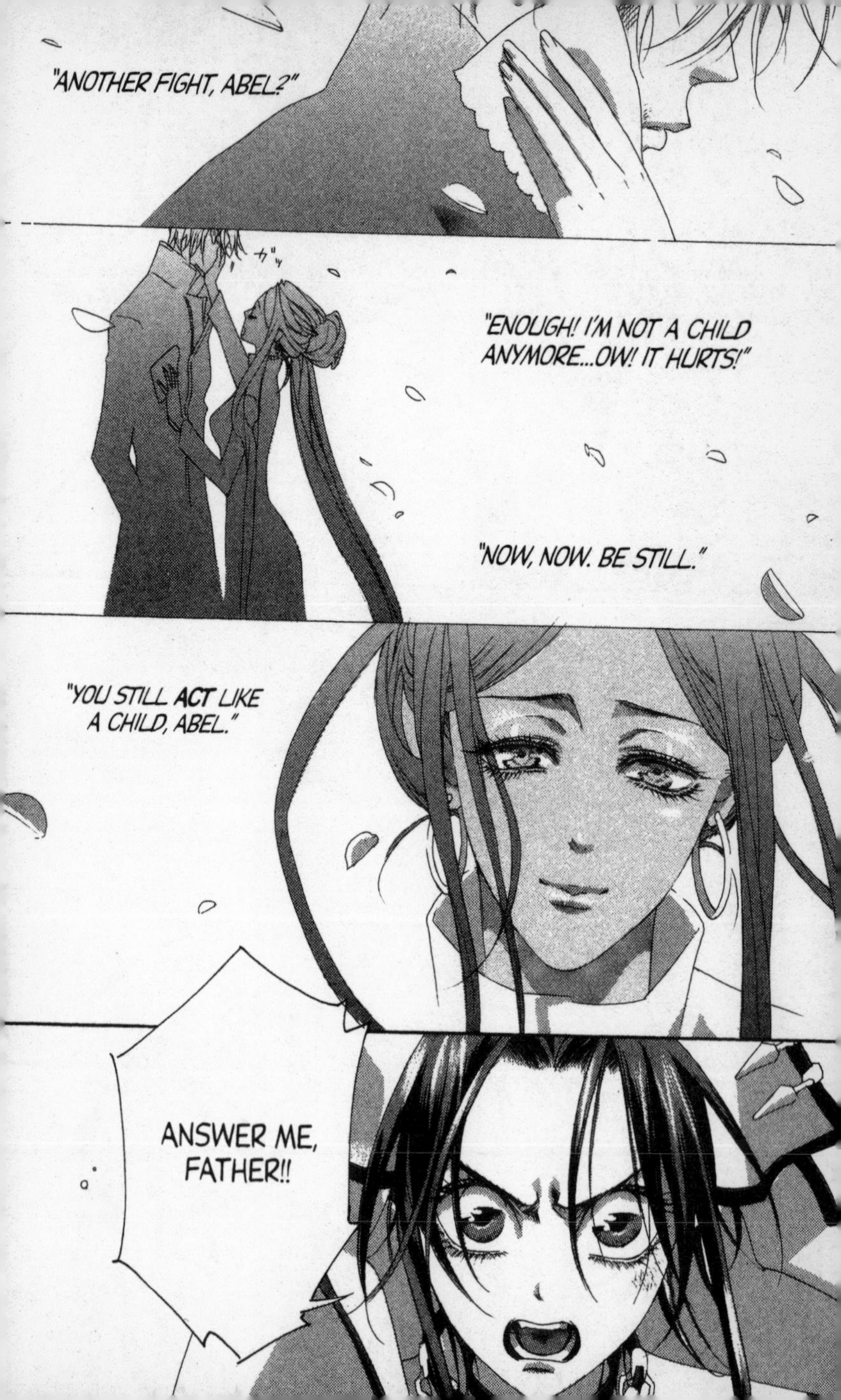
"ANOTHER FIGHT, ABEL?"
"ENOUGH! I'M NOT A CHILD ANYMORE...OW! IT HURTS!"
"NOW, NOW. BE STILL."
"YOU STILL ACT LIKE A CHILD, ABEL."
ANSWER ME, FATHER!!

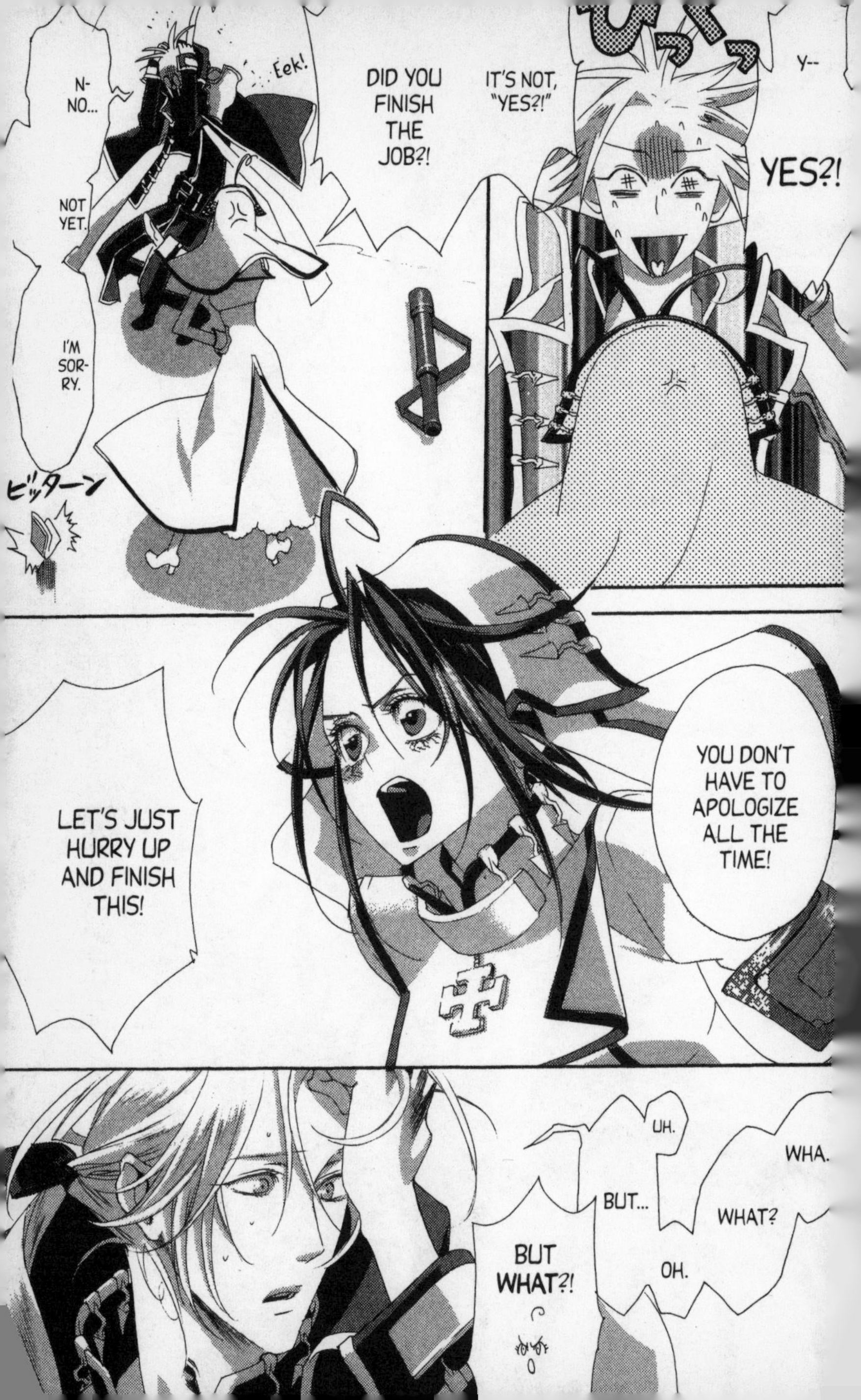
Y--
YES?!
IT'S NOT, "YES?!"
DID YOU FINISH THE JOB?!
Eek!
N-NO...
NOT YET.
I'M SORRY.
ビッターン
YOU DON'T HAVE TO APOLOGIZE ALL THE TIME!
LET'S JUST HURRY UP AND FINISH THIS!
WHA.
UH.
WHAT?
BUT...
OH.
BUT WHAT?!

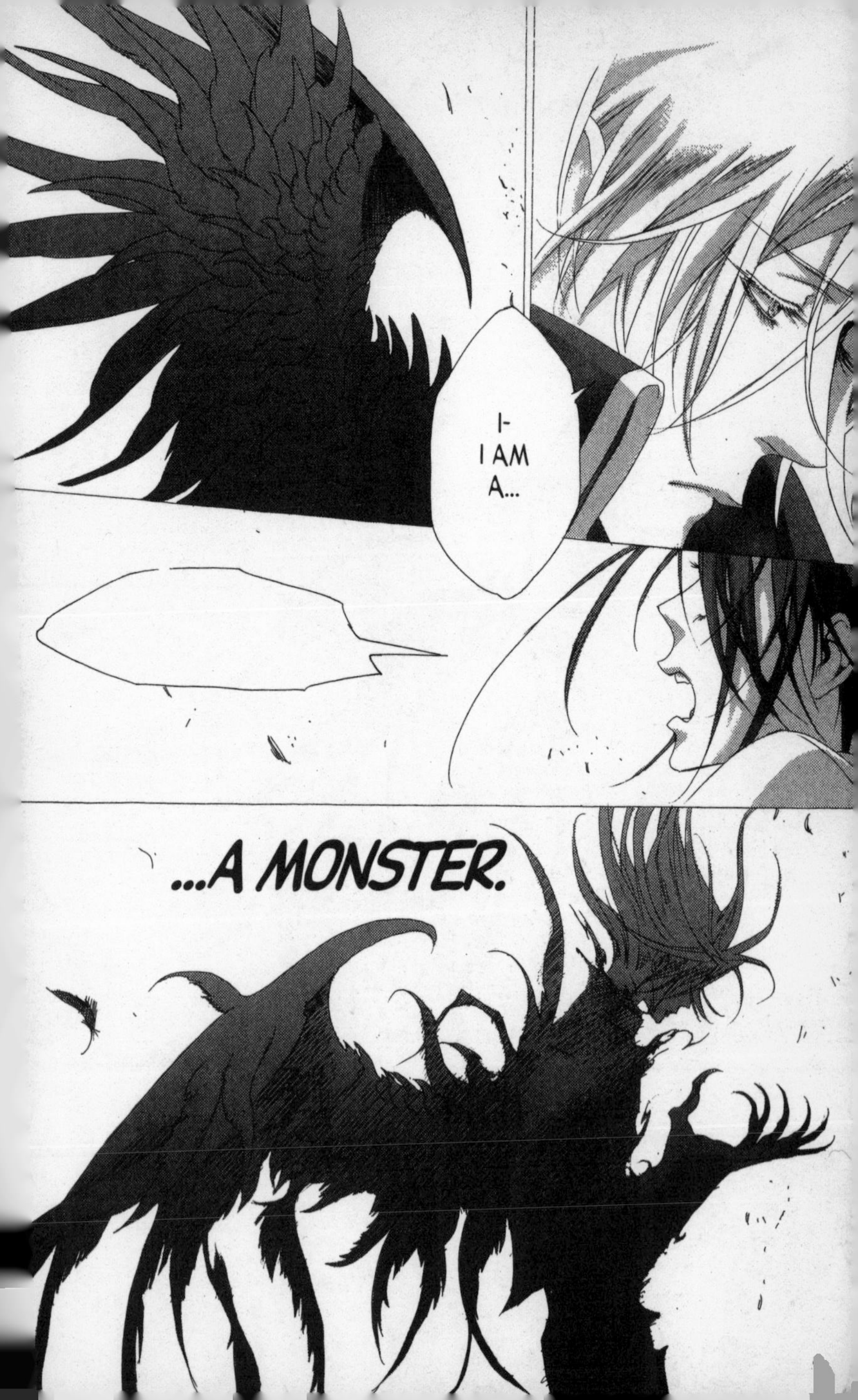
I-
I AM
A...
...A MONSTER.

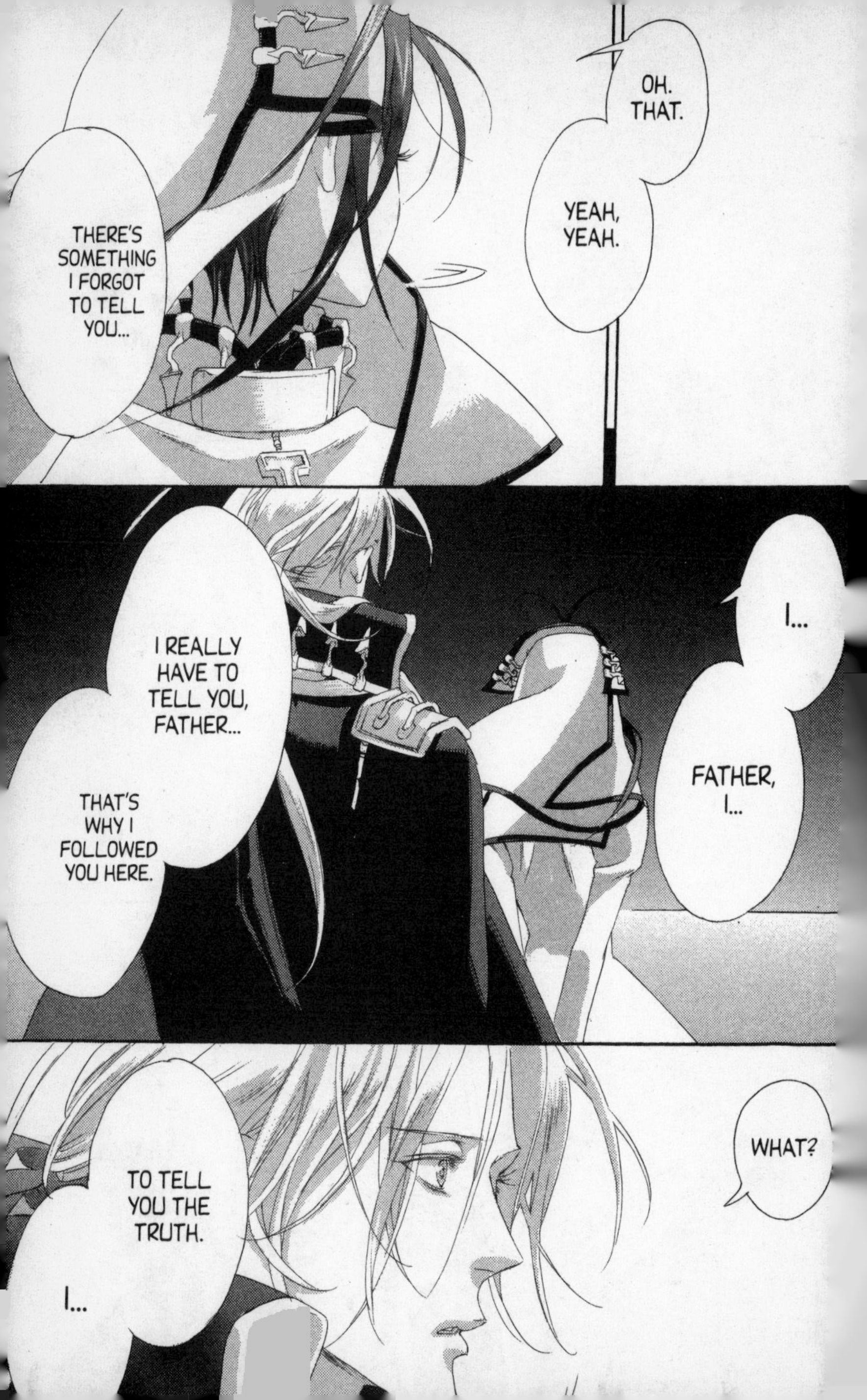
OH. THAT.
YEAH, YEAH.
THERE'S SOMETHING I FORGOT TO TELL YOU...
I...
FATHER, I...
I REALLY HAVE TO TELL YOU, FATHER...
THAT'S WHY I FOLLOWED YOU HERE.
WHAT?
TO TELL YOU THE TRUTH.
I...

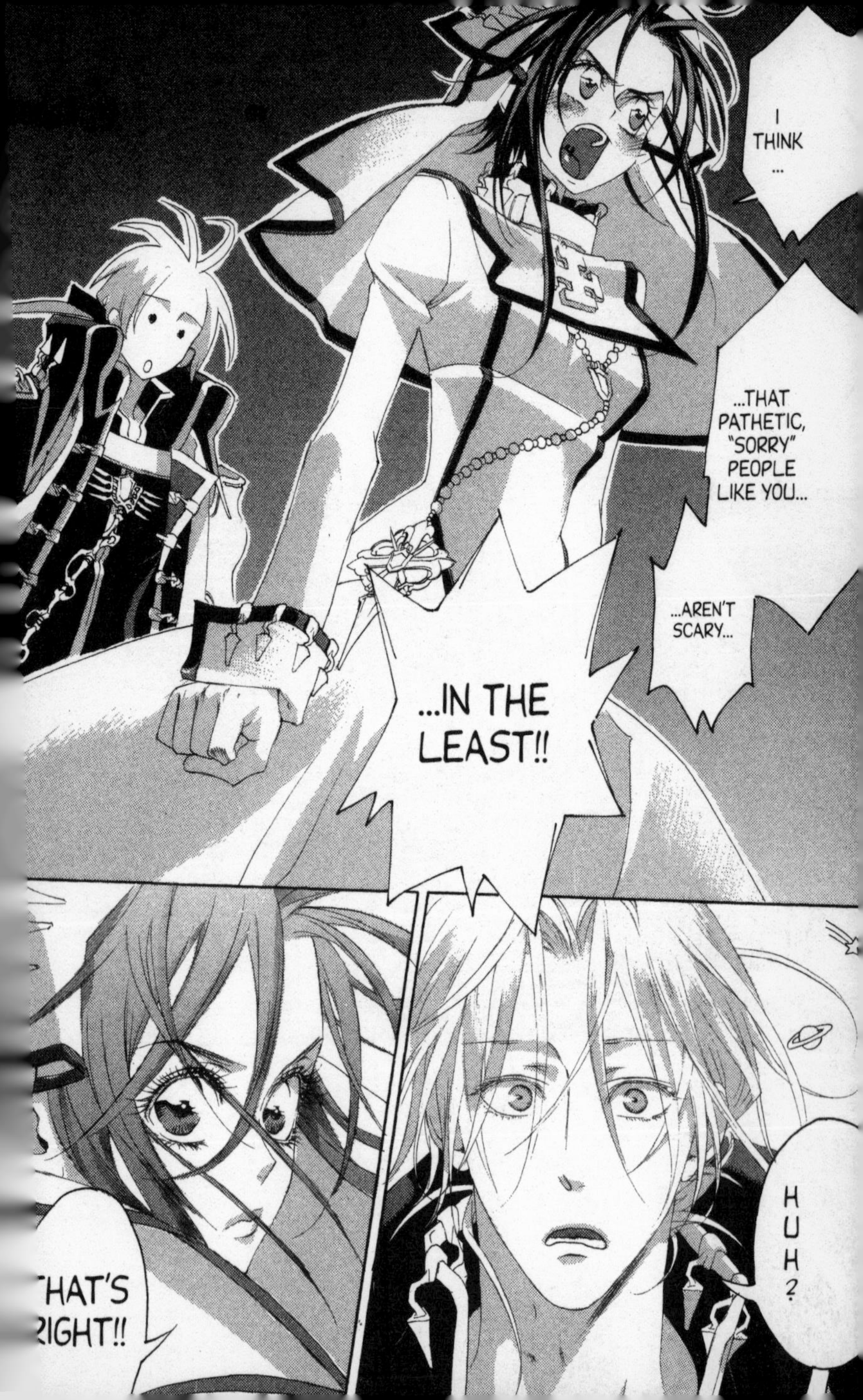
I THINK...
...THAT PATHETIC, "SORRY" PEOPLE LIKE YOU...
...AREN'T SCARY...
...IN THE LEAST!!
HUH?
THAT'S RIGHT!!

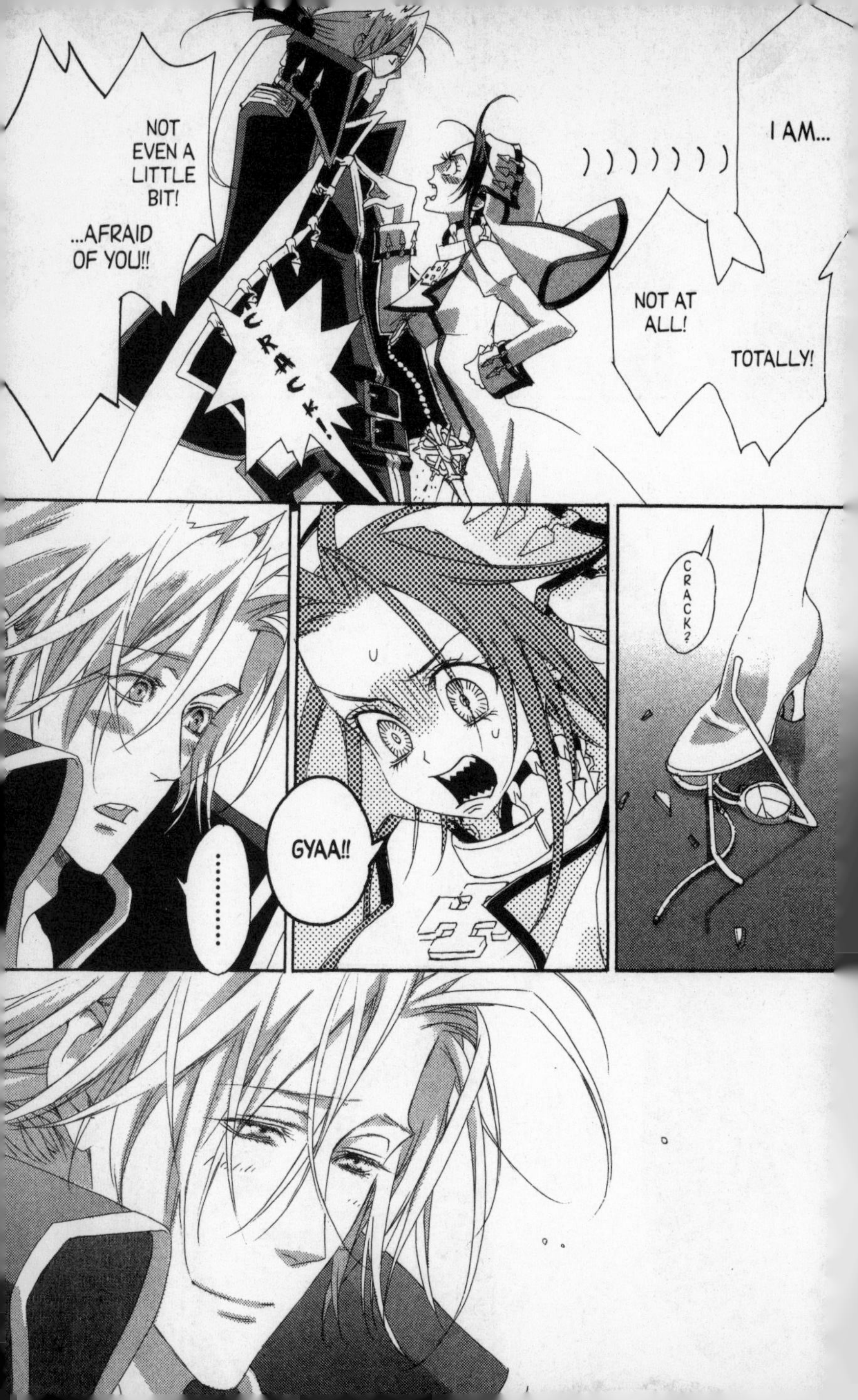
I AM...
NOT AT ALL!
TOTALLY!
NOT EVEN A LITTLE BIT!
...AFRAID OF YOU!!
CRACK!
CRACK?
GYAA!!
......

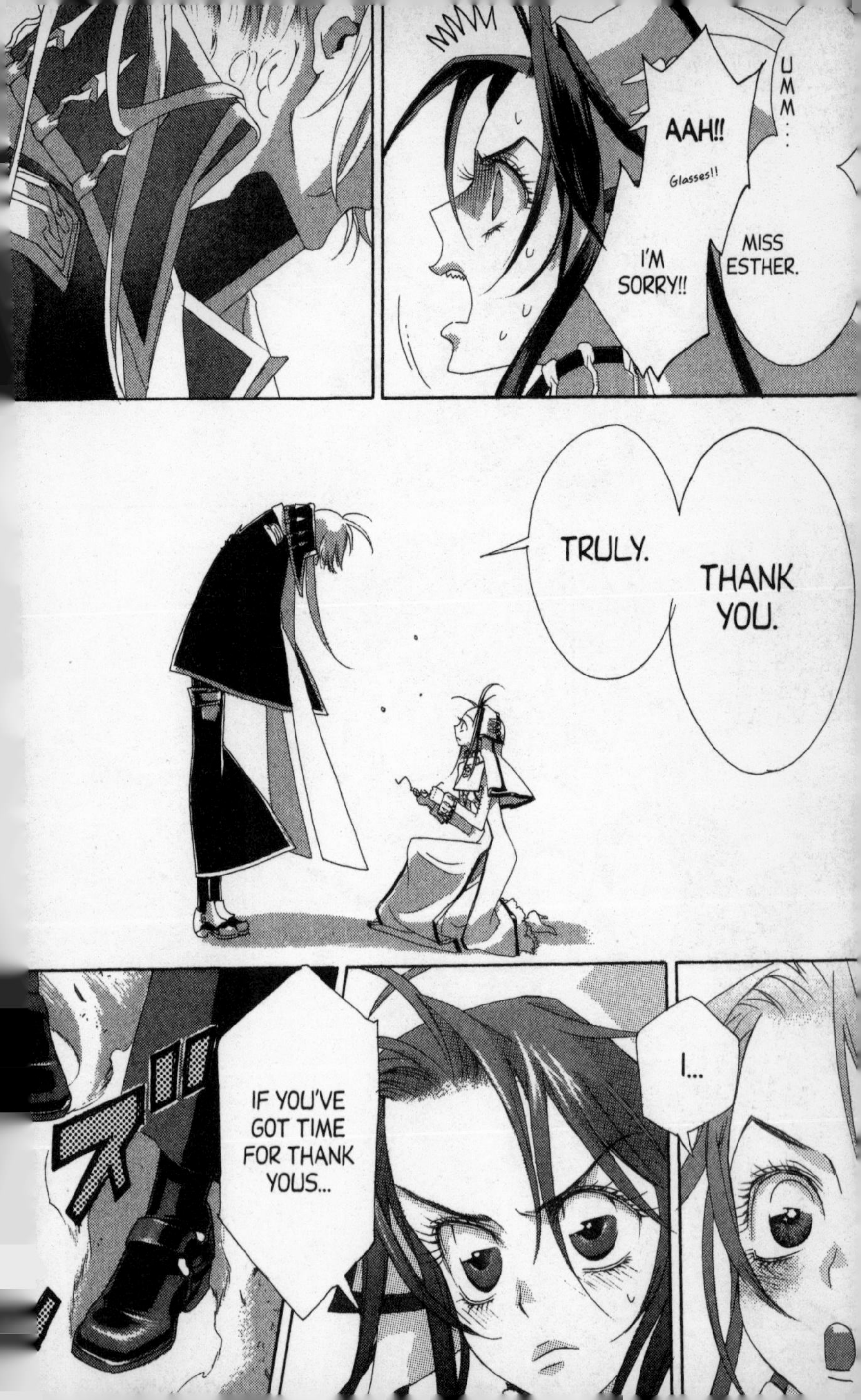
UMM...
MISS ESTHER.
AAH!!
Glasses!!
I'M SORRY!!
THANK YOU.
TRULY.
I...
IF YOU'VE GOT TIME FOR THANK YOUS...

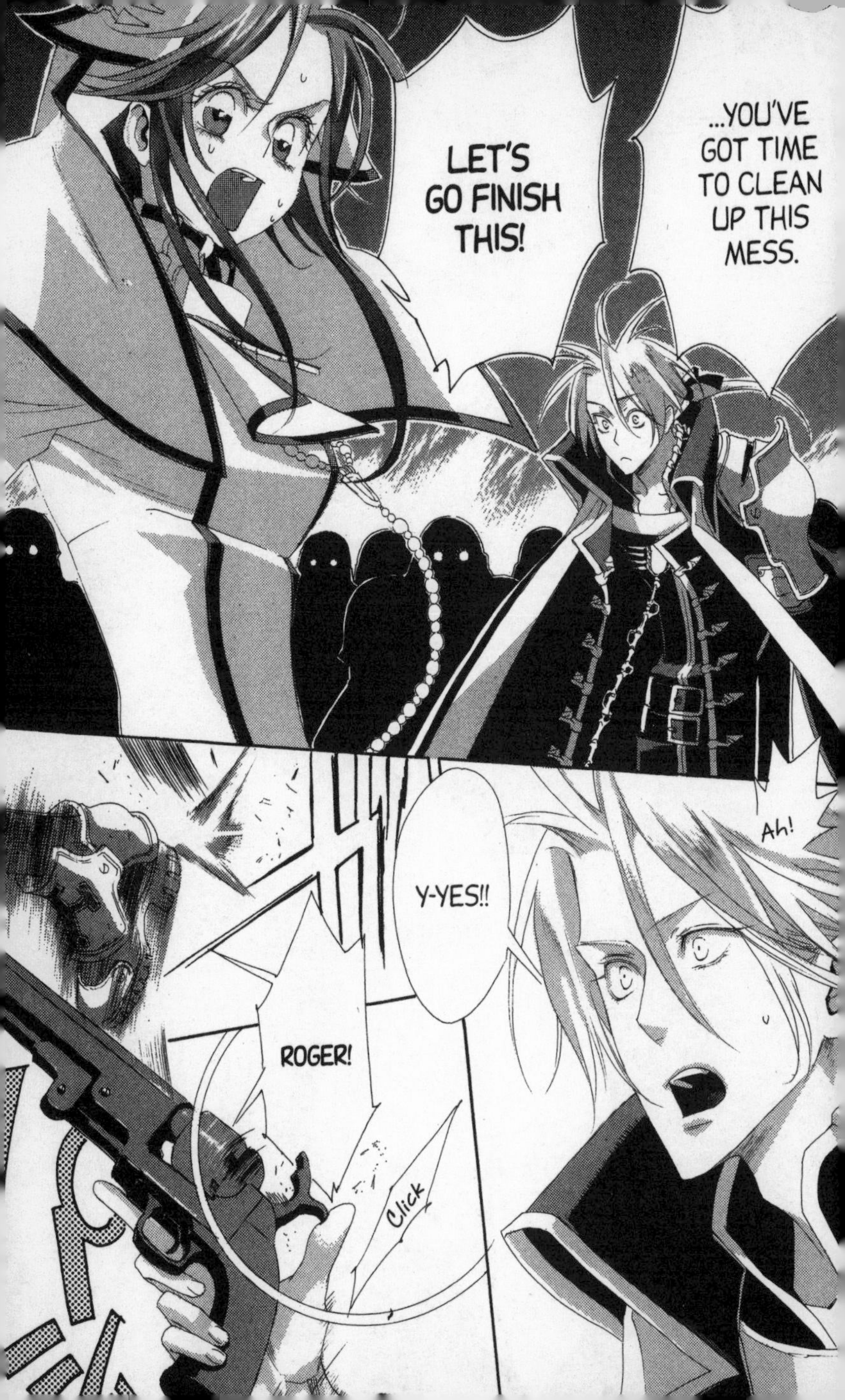
...YOU'VE GOT TIME TO CLEAN UP THIS MESS.
LET'S GO FINISH THIS!
Ah!
Y-YES!!
ROGER!
Click

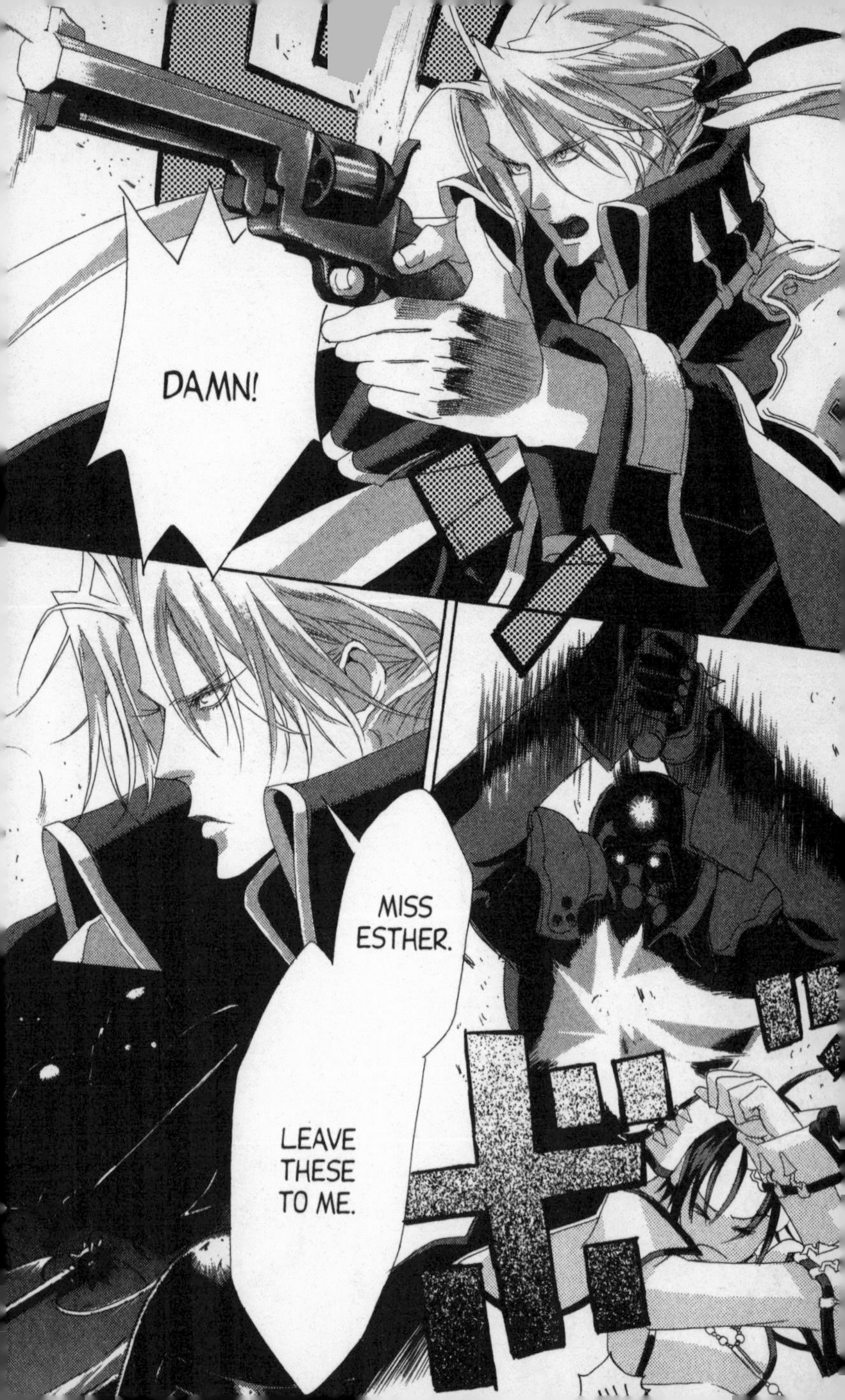
DAMN!
MISS ESTHER.
LEAVE THESE TO ME.

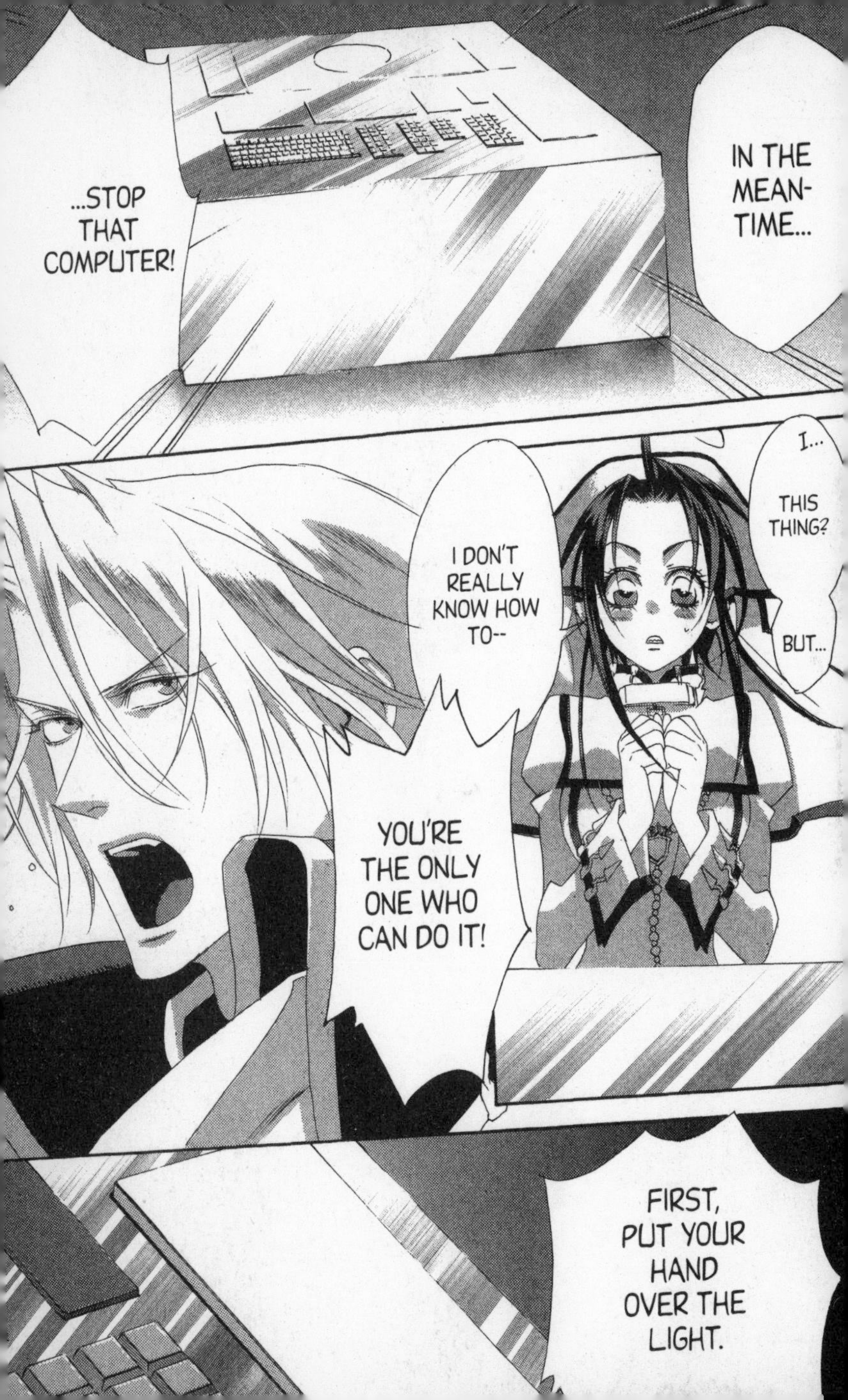
IN THE MEAN-TIME...
...STOP THAT COMPUTER!
I...
THIS THING?
BUT...
I DON'T REALLY KNOW HOW TO--
YOU'RE THE ONLY ONE WHO CAN DO IT!
FIRST, PUT YOUR HAND OVER THE LIGHT.

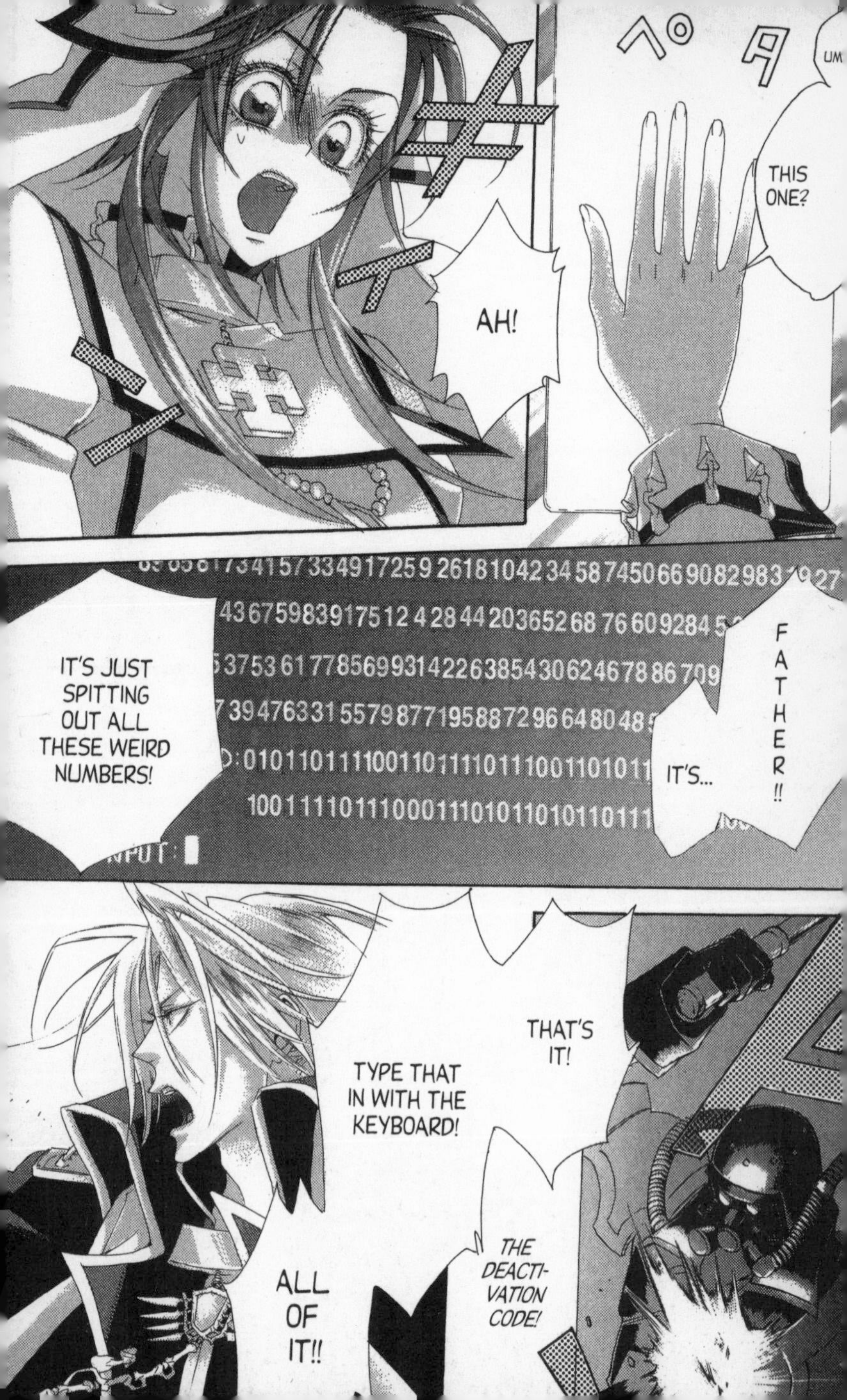
UM
THIS ONE?
AH!
IT'S...
FATHER!!
IT'S JUST SPITTING OUT ALL THESE WEIRD NUMBERS!
THAT'S IT!
TYPE THAT IN WITH THE KEYBOARD!
THE DEACTI- VATION CODE!
ALL OF IT!!

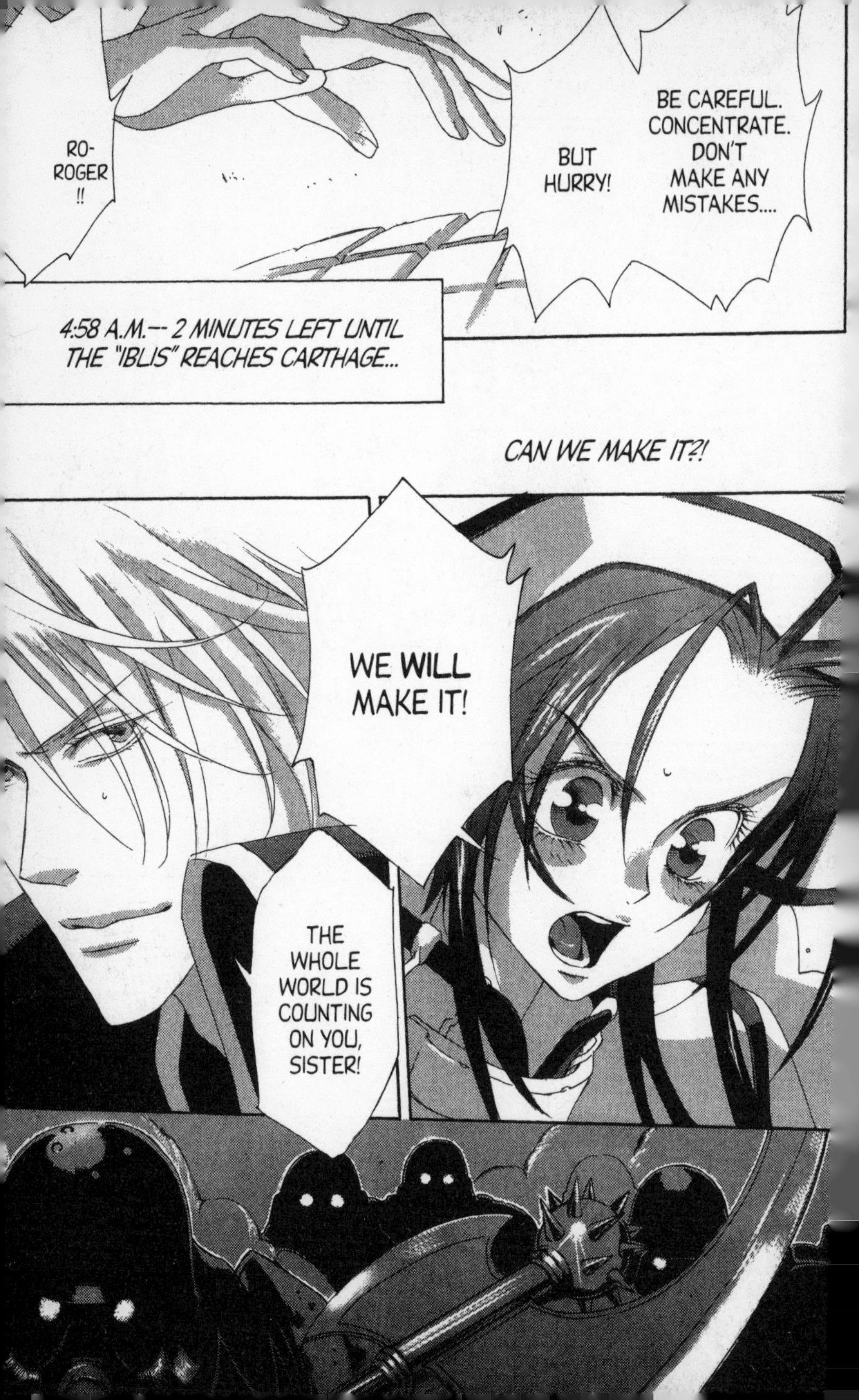

BE CAREFUL. CONCENTRATE. DON'T MAKE ANY MISTAKES....
BUT HURRY!
RO-ROGER !!
4:58 A.M.-- 2 MINUTES LEFT UNTIL THE "IBLIS" REACHES CARTHAGE...
CAN WE MAKE IT?!
WE WILL MAKE IT!
THE WHOLE WORLD IS COUNTING ON YOU, SISTER!

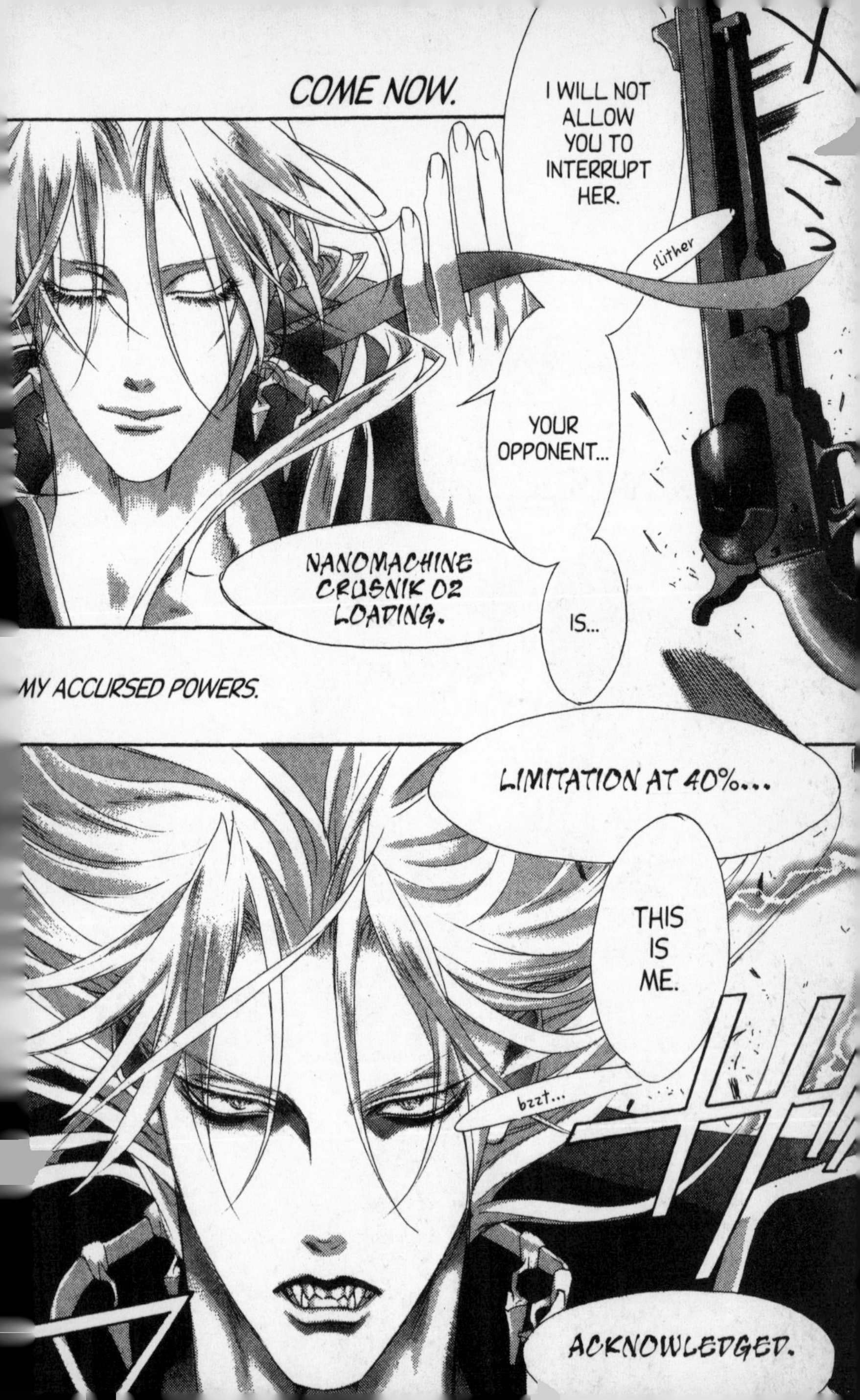
I WILL NOT ALLOW YOU TO INTERRUPT HER.
COME NOW.
slither
YOUR OPPONENT...
IS...
NANOMACHINE CRUSNIK 02 LOADING.
MY ACCURSED POWERS.
LIMITATION AT 40%...
THIS IS ME.
bzzt...
ACKNOWLEDGED.

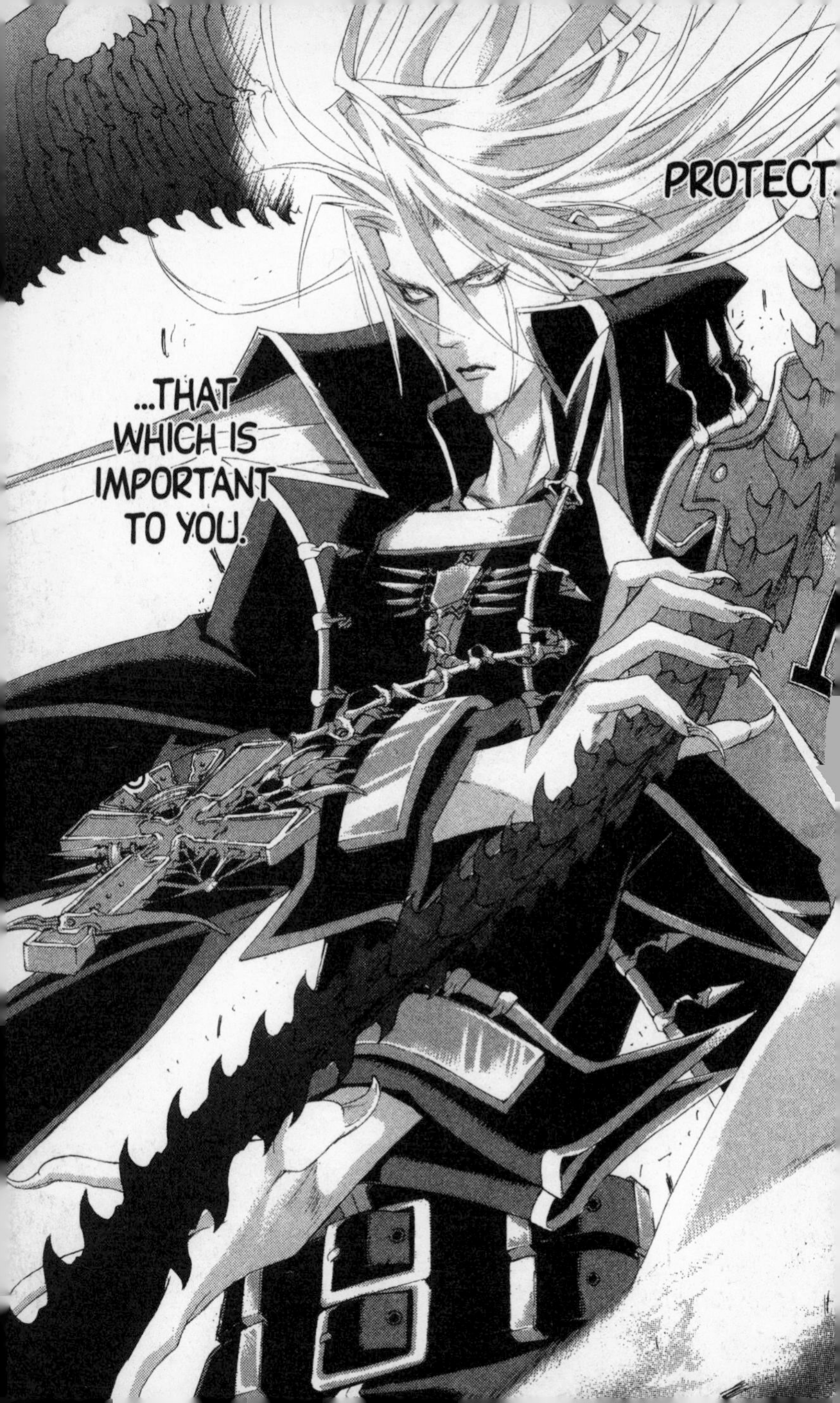
PROTECT
...THAT WHICH IS IMPORTANT TO YOU.

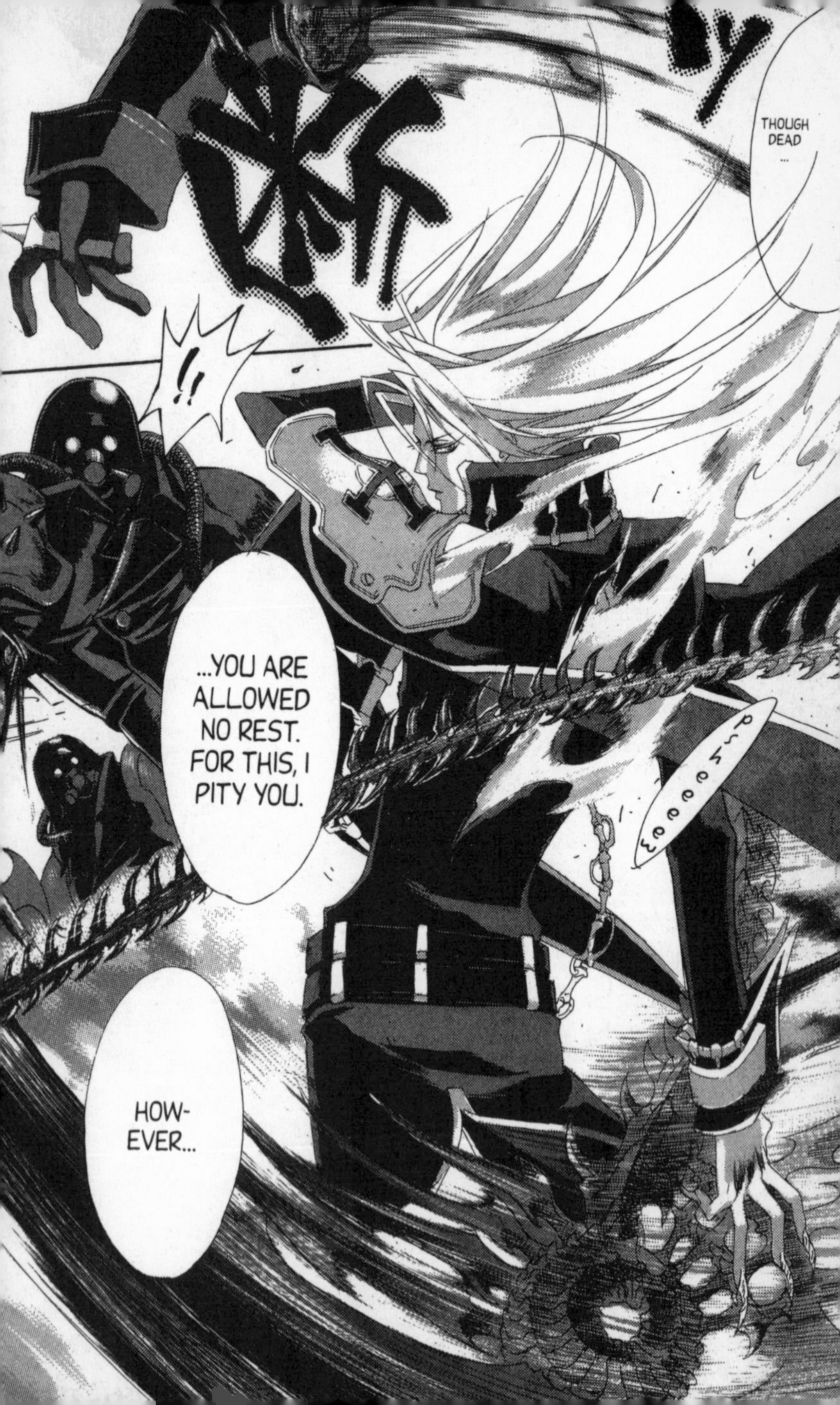
THOUGH DEAD ...
!!
...YOU ARE ALLOWED NO REST. FOR THIS, I PITY YOU.
psheeeew
HOW-EVER...

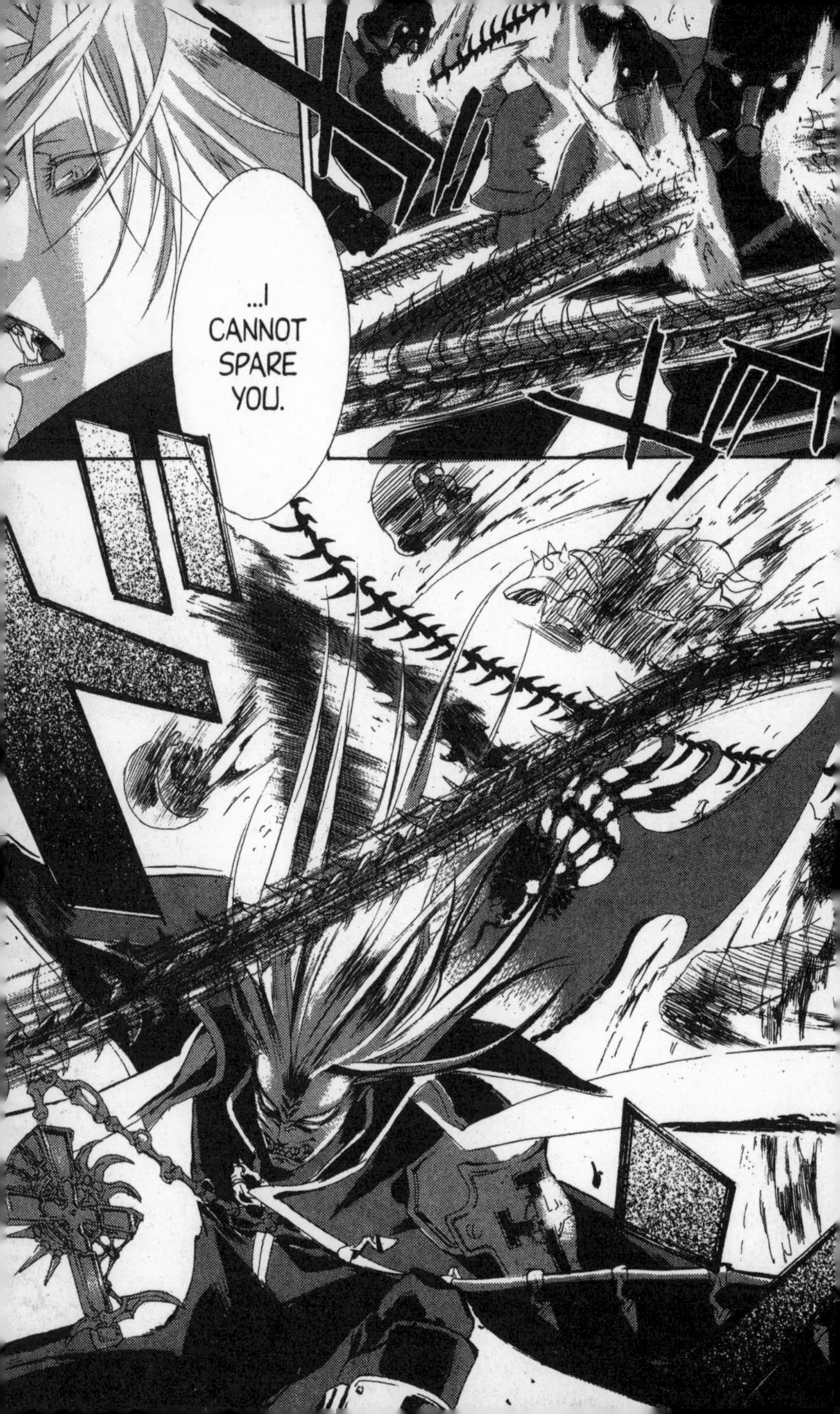
...I CANNOT SPARE YOU.

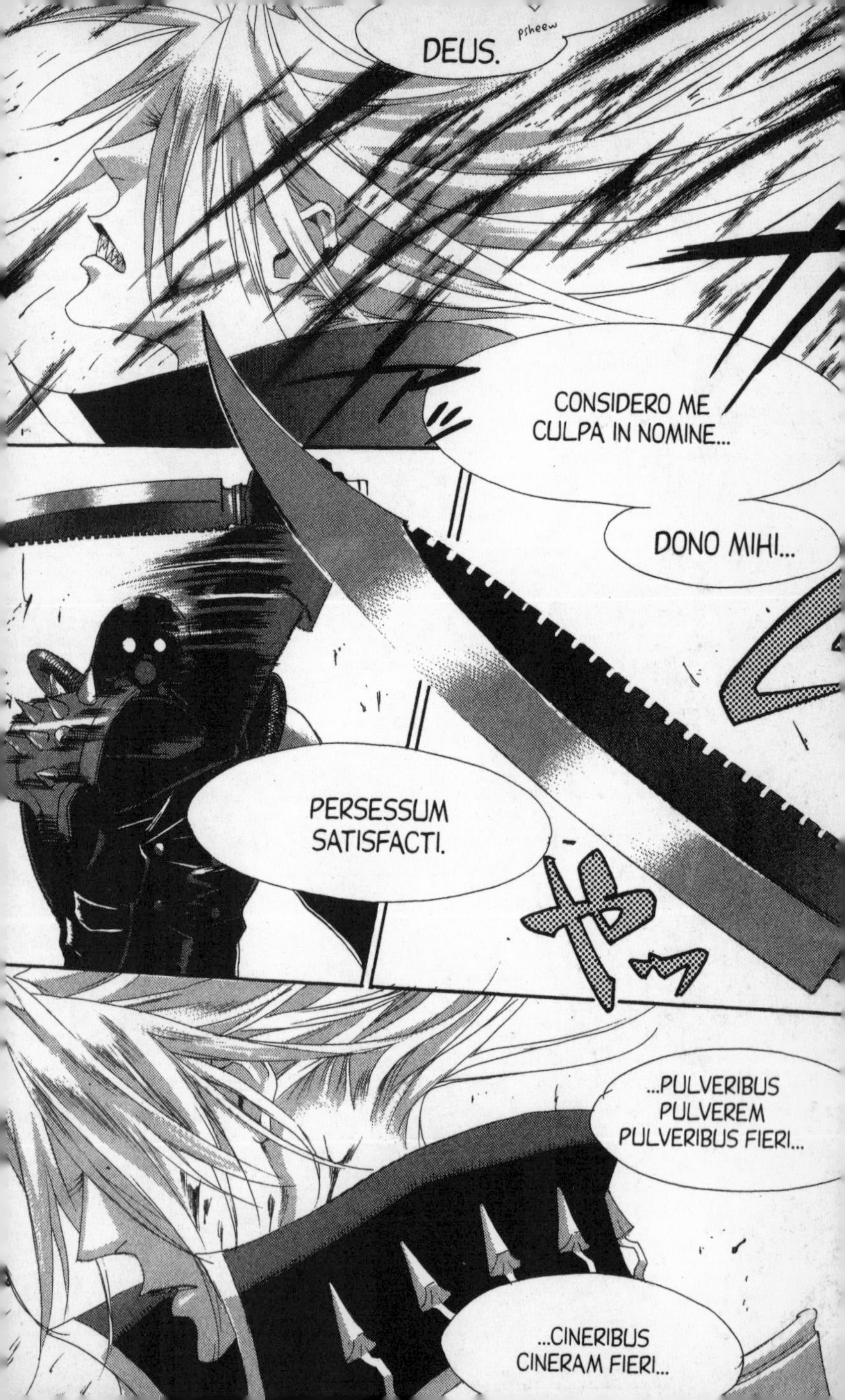
DEUS.
Psheew
CONSIDERO ME CULPA IN NOMINE...
DONO MIHI...
PERSESSUM SATISFACTI.
...PULVERIBUS PULVEREM PULVERIBUS FIERI...
...CINERIBUS CINERAM FIERI...

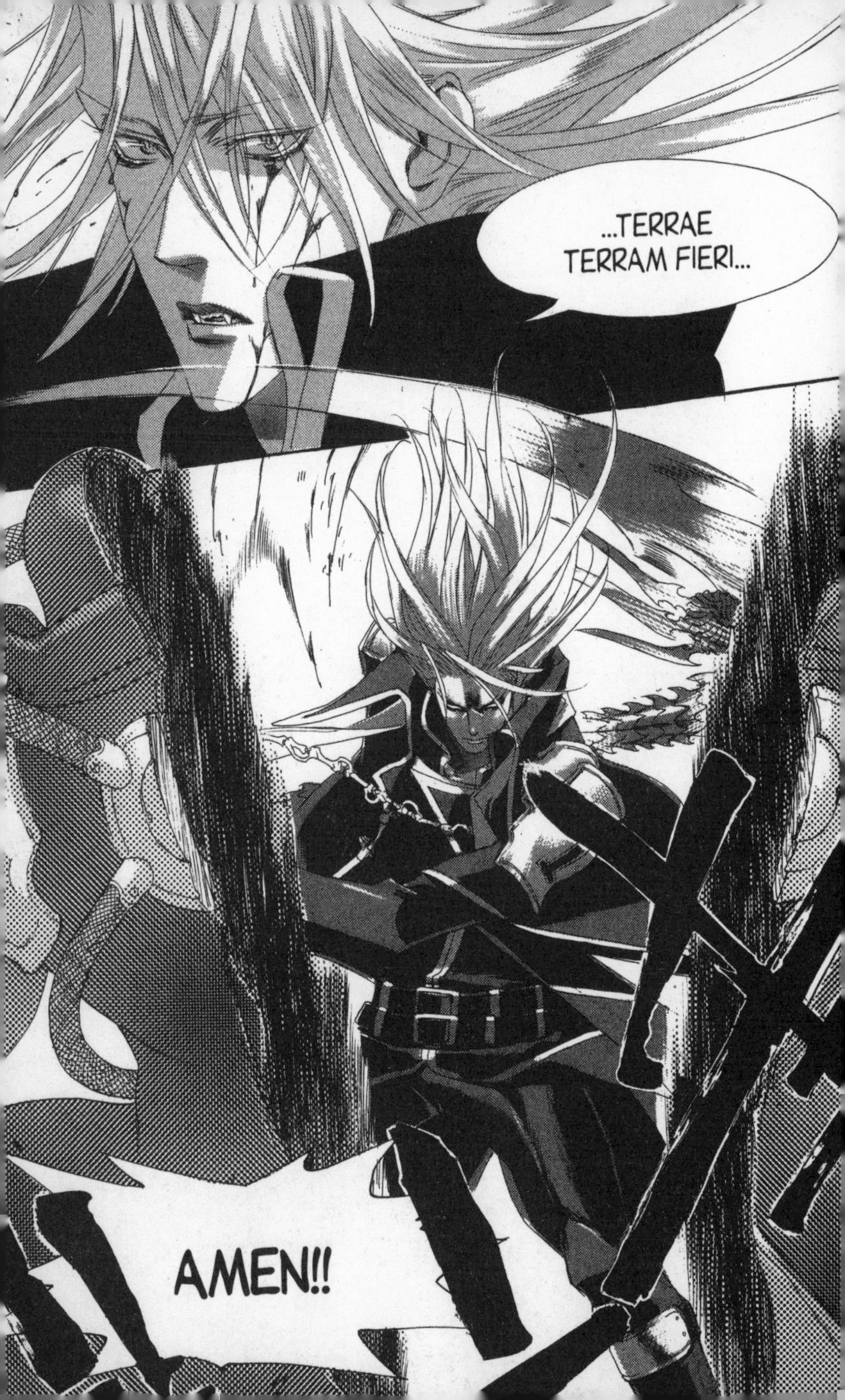
...TERRAE TERRAM FIERI...
AMEN!!

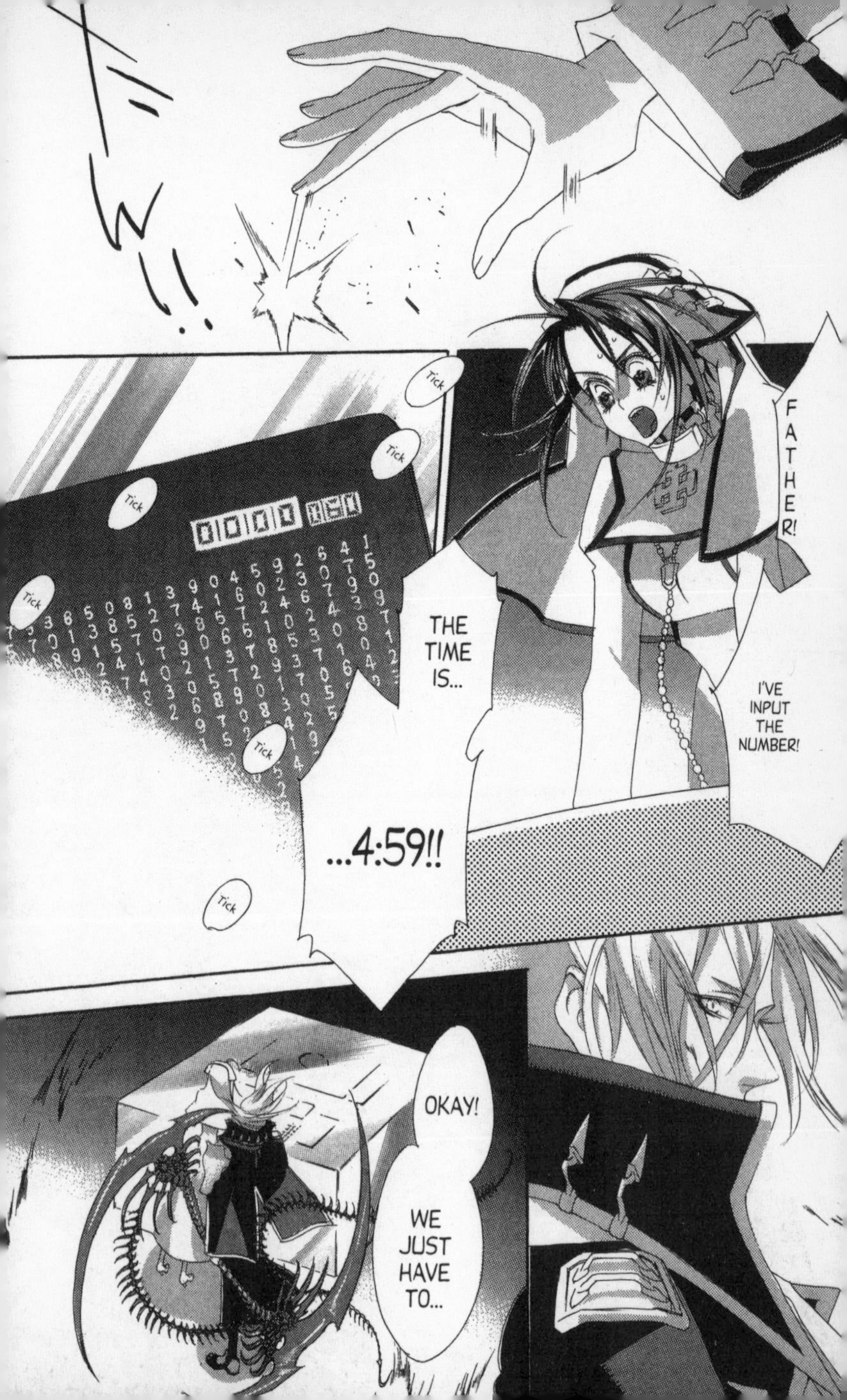
FATHER!
I'VE INPUT THE NUMBER!
THE TIME IS...
...4:59!!
Tick
Tick
Tick
Tick
Tick
Tick
OKAY!
WE JUST HAVE TO...

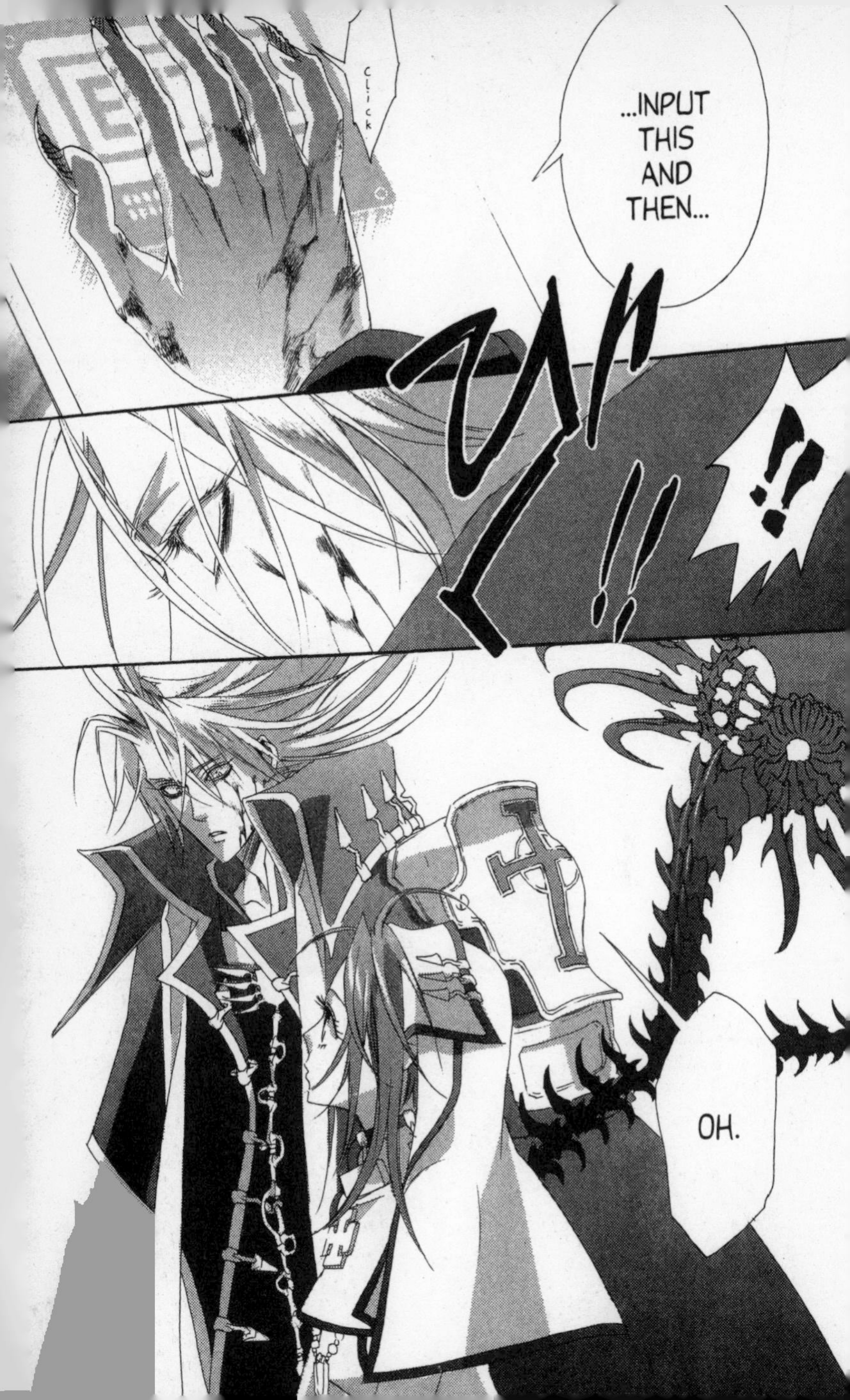
...INPUT THIS AND THEN...
Click
OH.

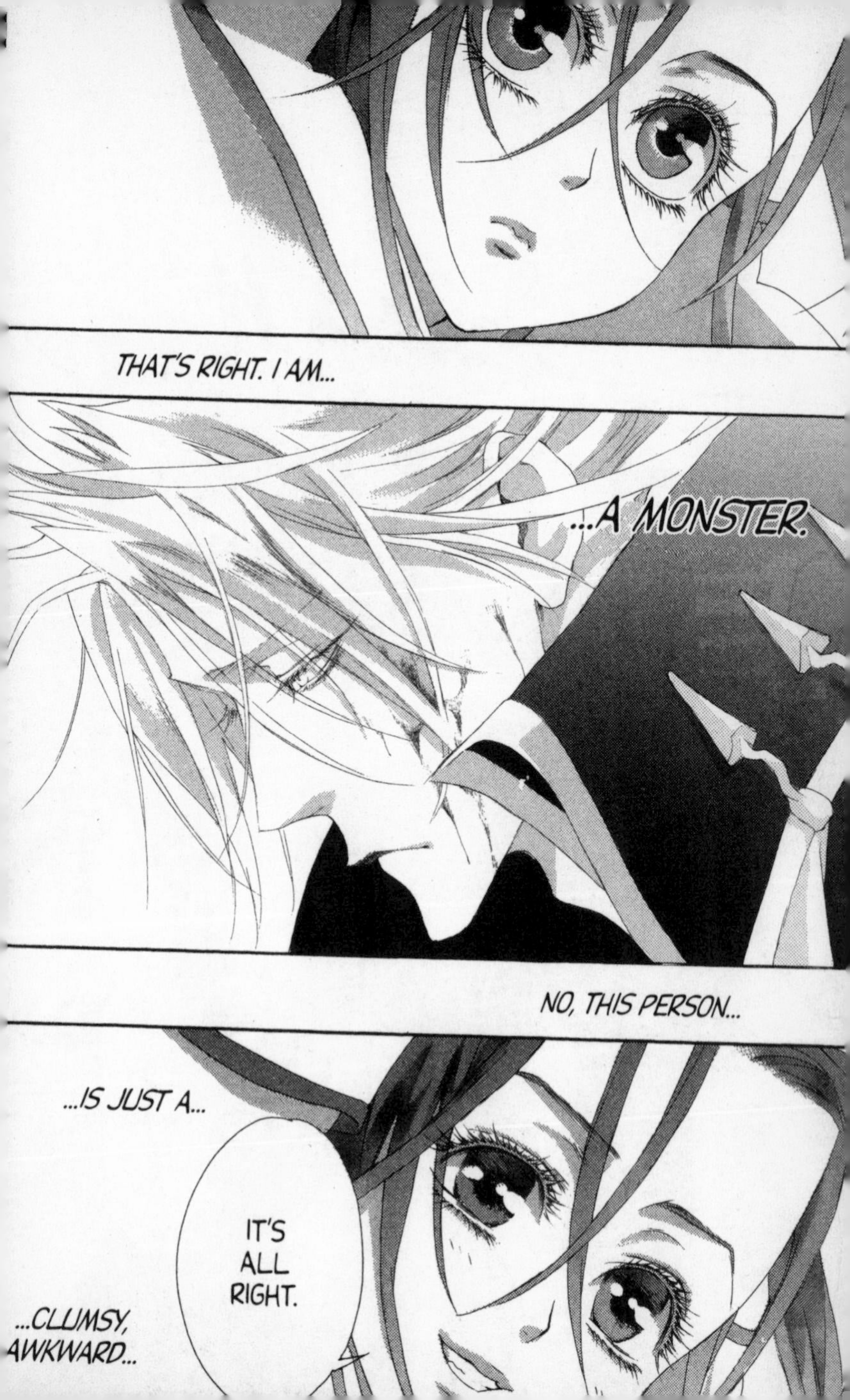
THAT'S RIGHT. I AM...
...A MONSTER.
NO, THIS PERSON...
...IS JUST A...
IT'S ALL RIGHT.
...CLUMSY, AWKWARD...

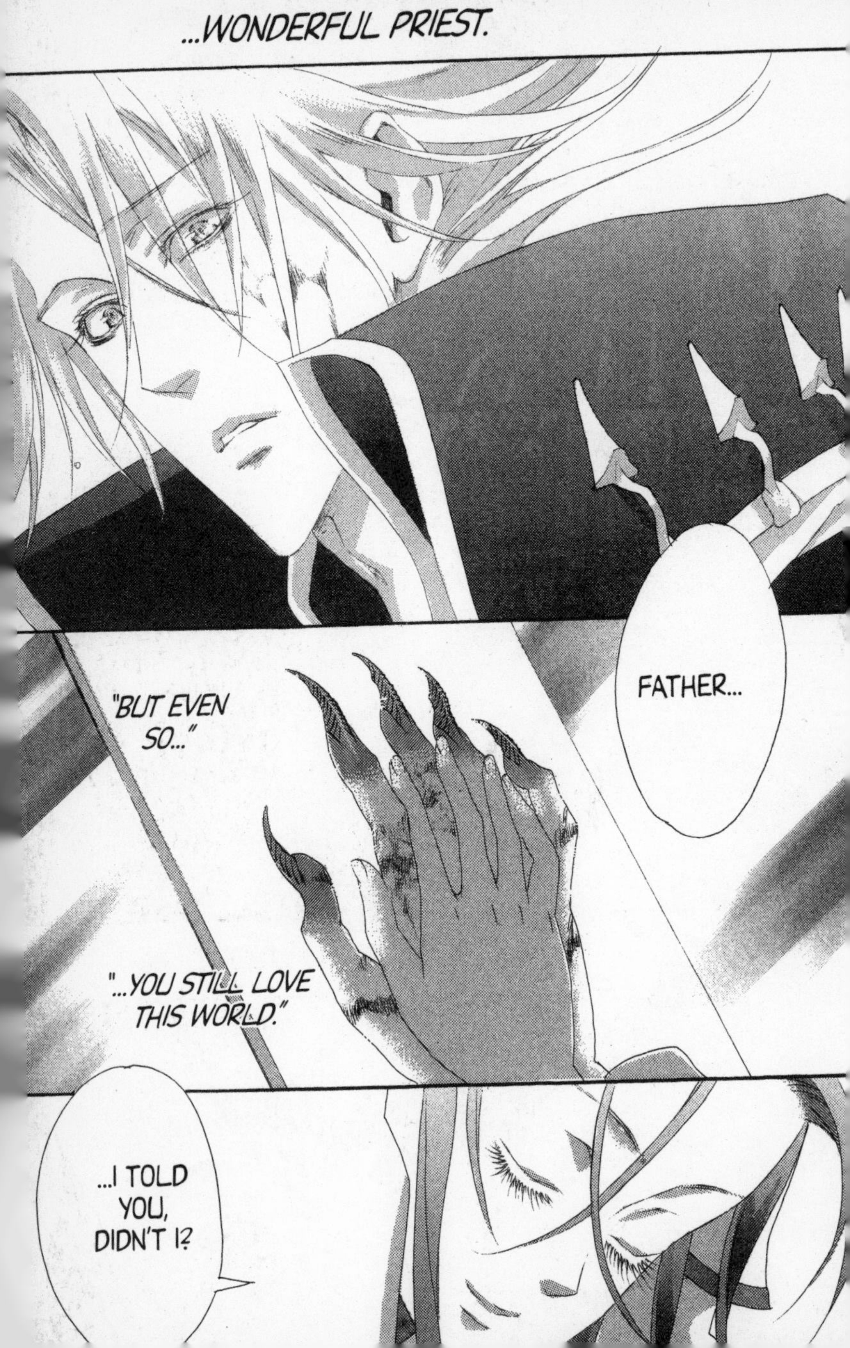
...WONDERFUL PRIEST.
FATHER...
"BUT EVEN SO..."
"...YOU STILL LOVE THIS WORLD."
...I TOLD YOU, DIDN'T I?

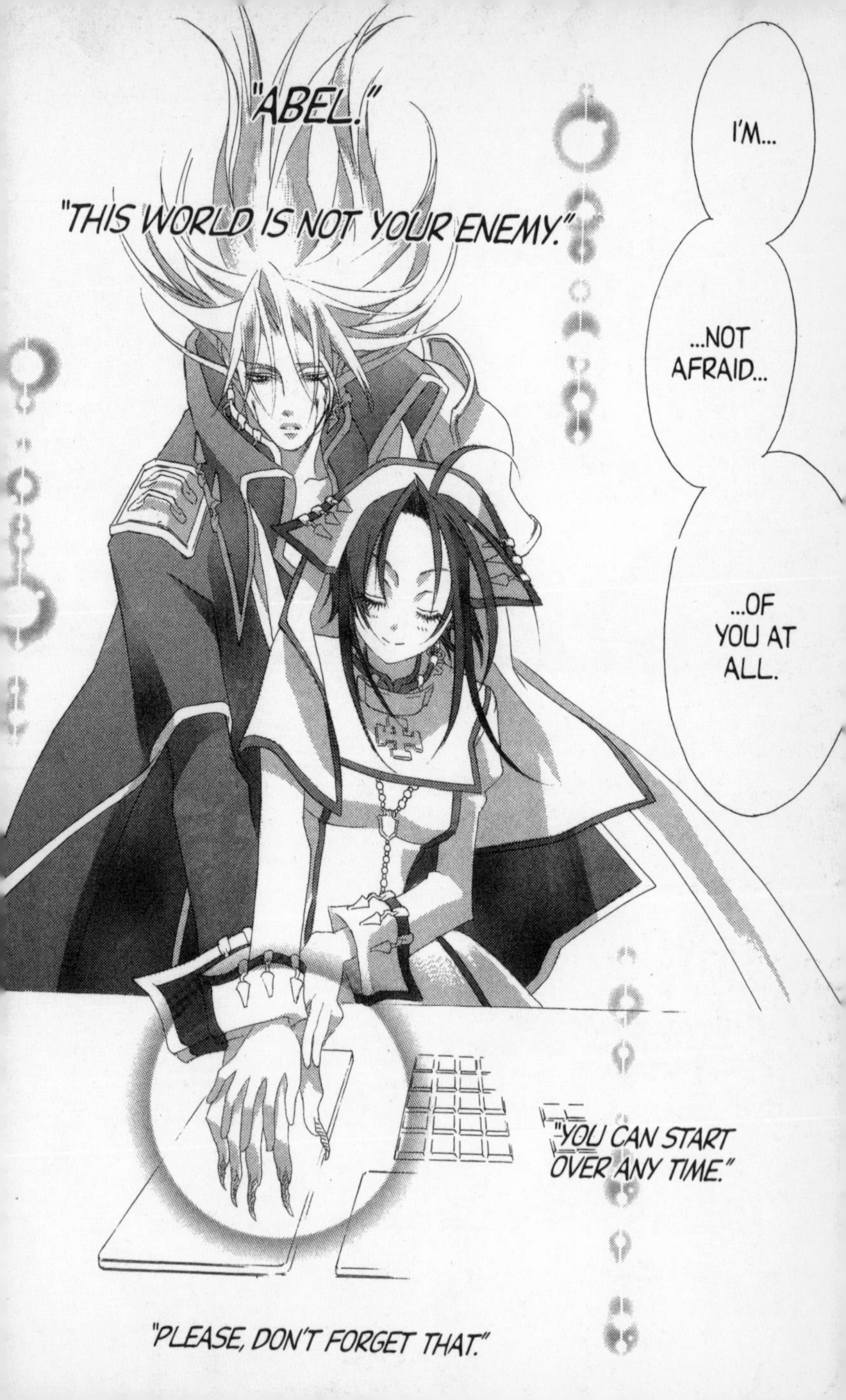
I'M... ...NOT AFRAID... ...OF YOU AT ALL.
"ABEL."
"THIS WORLD IS NOT YOUR ENEMY."
"YOU CAN START OVER ANY TIME."
"PLEASE, DON'T FORGET THAT."

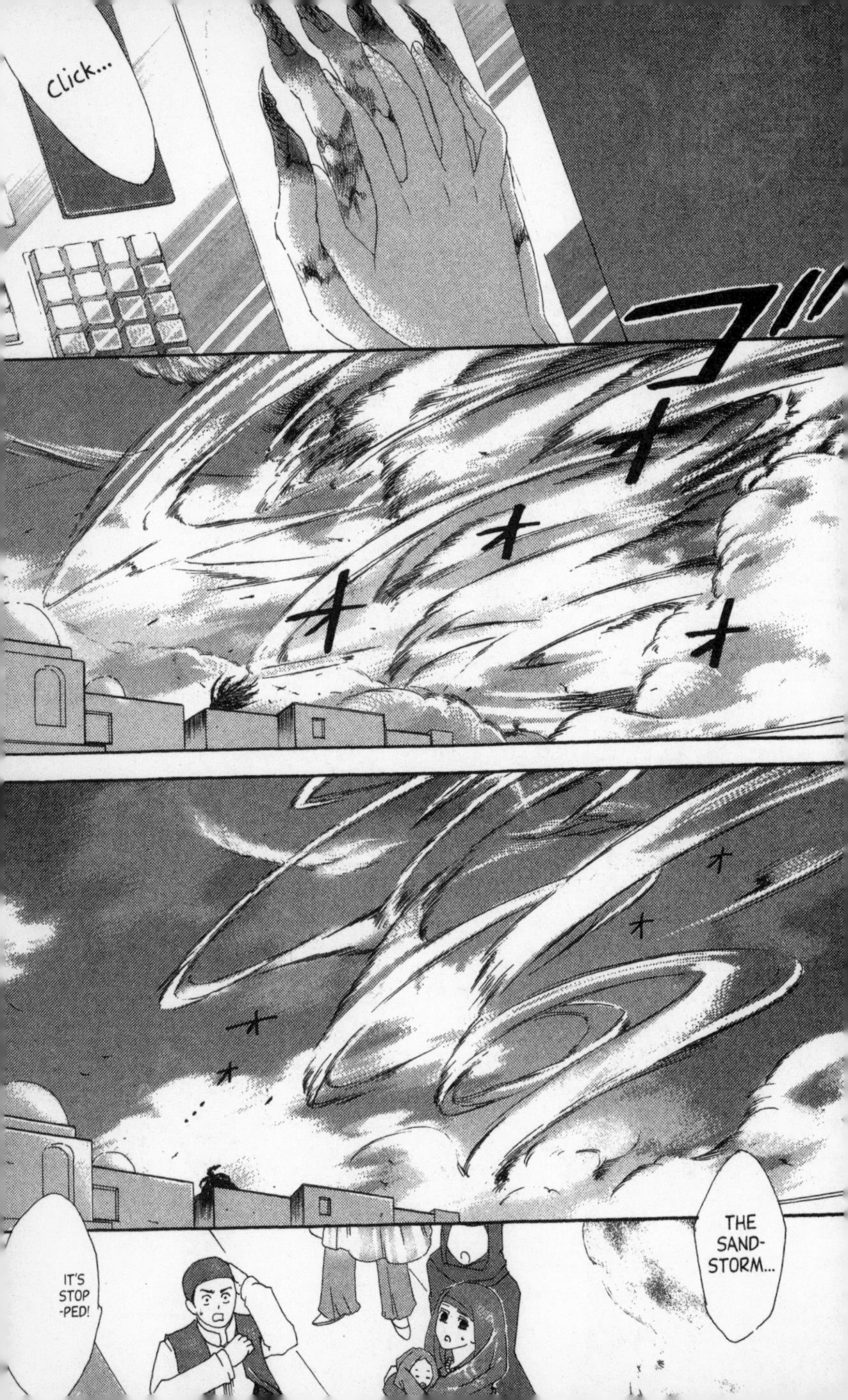
Click...
ゴォォォォ
THE SAND-STORM...
IT'S STOP-PED!

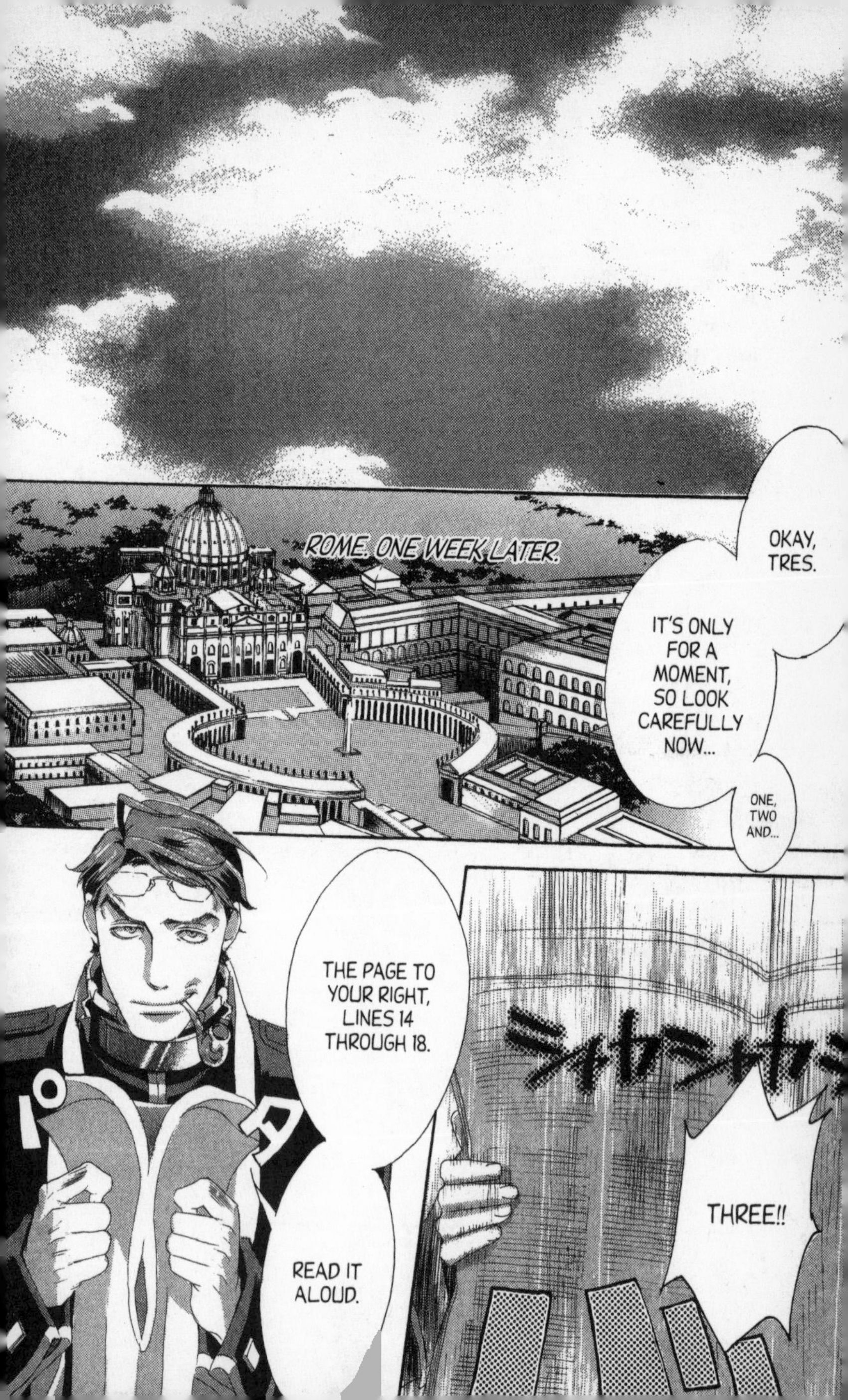
ROME. ONE WEEK LATER.
OKAY, TRES.
IT'S ONLY FOR A MOMENT, SO LOOK CAREFULLY NOW...
ONE, TWO AND...
THREE!!
THE PAGE TO YOUR RIGHT, LINES 14 THROUGH 18.
READ IT ALOUD.

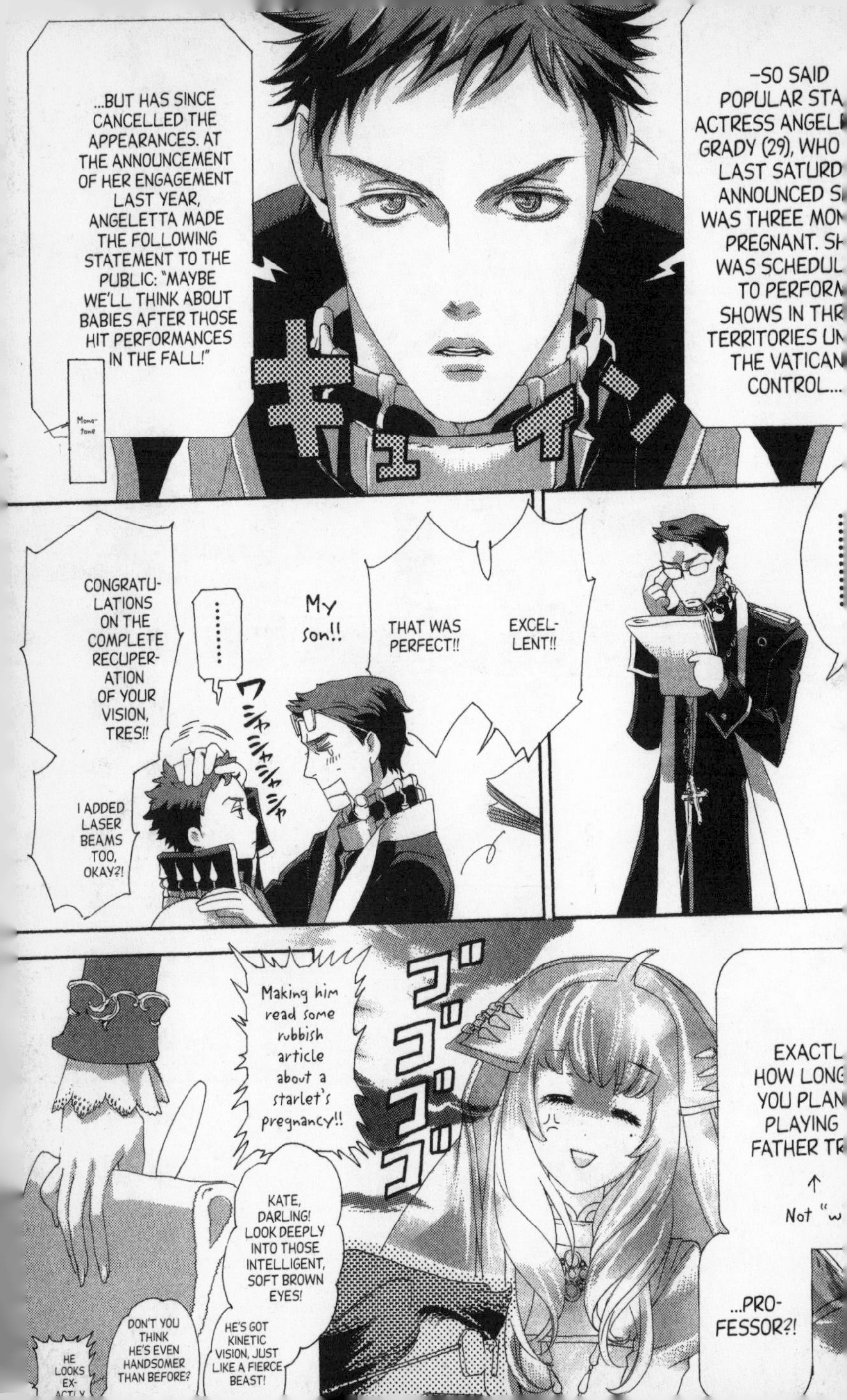
—SO SAID POPULAR STA ACTRESS ANGEL GRADY (29), WHO LAST SATURD ANNOUNCED S WAS THREE MON PREGNANT. SH WAS SCHEDUL TO PERFORM SHOWS IN THR TERRITORIES UN THE VATICAN CONTROL...
...BUT HAS SINCE CANCELLED THE APPEARANCES. AT THE ANNOUNCEMENT OF HER ENGAGEMENT LAST YEAR, ANGELETTA MADE THE FOLLOWING STATEMENT TO THE PUBLIC: "MAYBE WE'LL THINK ABOUT BABIES AFTER THOSE HIT PERFORMANCES IN THE FALL!"
Mono-tone
キュイーン
EXCEL-LENT!!
THAT WAS PERFECT!!
My son!!
....
ワシャシャシャシャ
CONGRATU-LATIONS ON THE COMPLETE RECUPER-ATION OF YOUR VISION, TRES!!
I ADDED LASER BEAMS TOO, OKAY?!
EXACTL HOW LONG YOU PLAN PLAYING FATHER TR
Not "w
...PRO-FESSOR?!
ゴゴゴゴ
Making him read some rubbish article about a starlet's pregnancy!!
KATE, DARLING! LOOK DEEPLY INTO THOSE INTELLIGENT, SOFT BROWN EYES!
HE'S GOT KINETIC VISION, JUST LIKE A FIERCE BEAST!
DON'T YOU THINK HE'S EVEN HANDSOMER THAN BEFORE?
HE LOOKS EX-

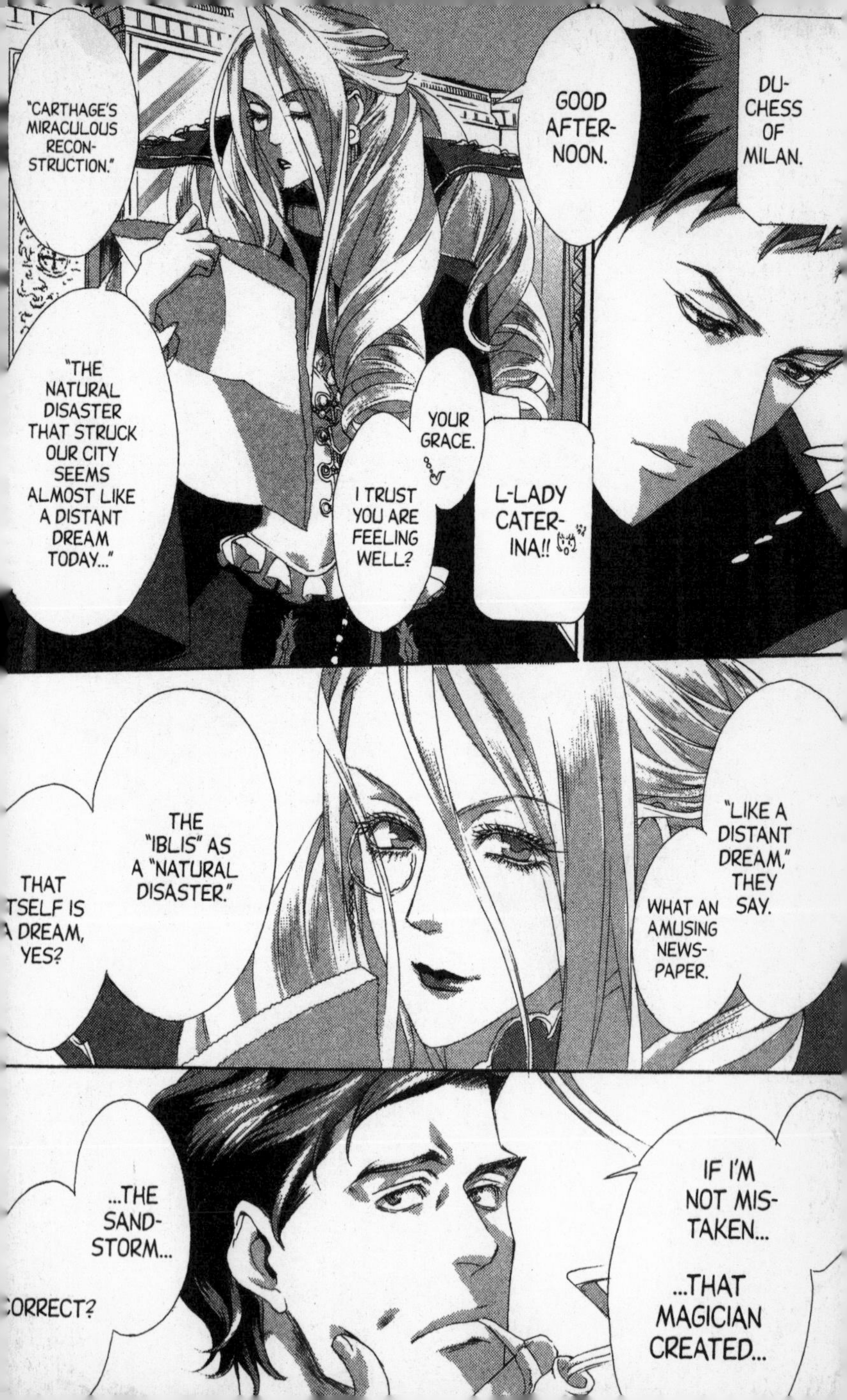
DU-CHESS OF MILAN.
GOOD AFTER-NOON.
YOUR GRACE.
L-LADY CATER-INA!!
I TRUST YOU ARE FEELING WELL?
"CARTHAGE'S MIRACULOUS RECON-STRUCTION."
"THE NATURAL DISASTER THAT STRUCK OUR CITY SEEMS ALMOST LIKE A DISTANT DREAM TODAY..."
"LIKE A DISTANT DREAM," THEY SAY.
WHAT AN AMUSING NEWS-PAPER.
THE "IBLIS" AS A "NATURAL DISASTER."
THAT ITSELF IS A DREAM, YES?
IF I'M NOT MIS-TAKEN...
...THAT MAGICIAN CREATED...
...THE SAND-STORM...
CORRECT?

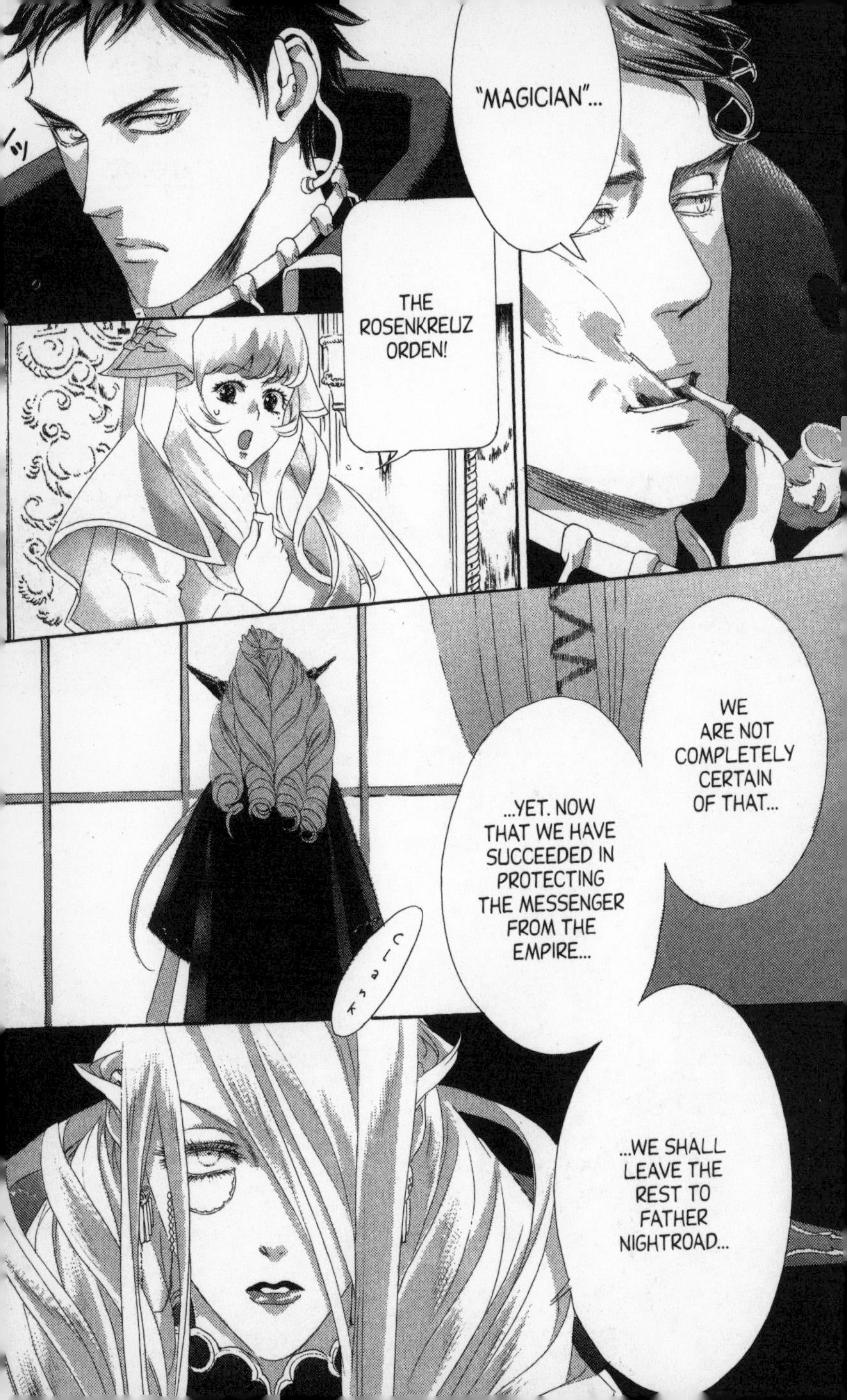
"MAGICIAN"...
ッ
THE ROSENKREUZ ORDEN!
WE ARE NOT COMPLETELY CERTAIN OF THAT...
...YET. NOW THAT WE HAVE SUCCEEDED IN PROTECTING THE MESSENGER FROM THE EMPIRE...
Clask
...WE SHALL LEAVE THE REST TO FATHER NIGHTROAD...

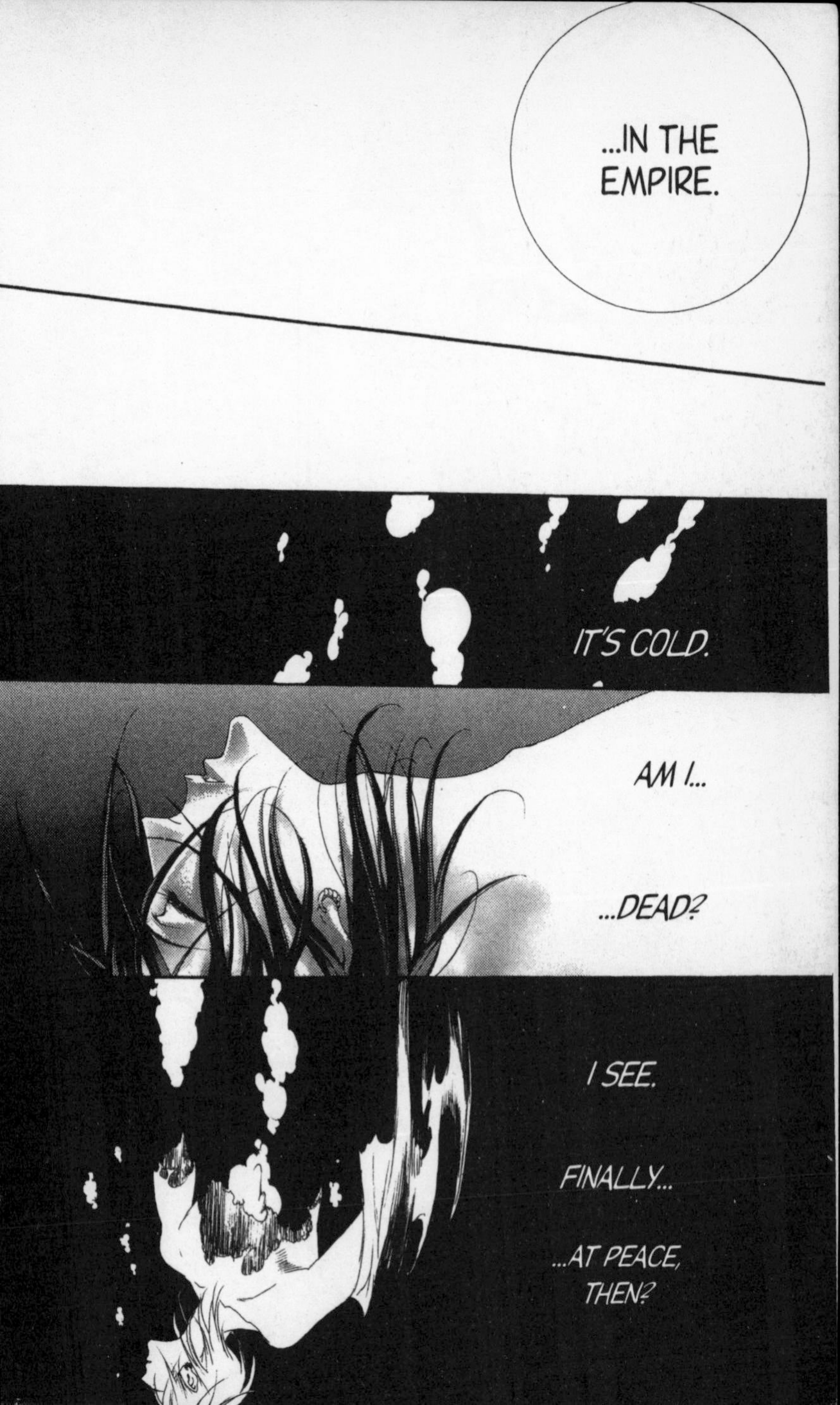
...IN THE EMPIRE.
IT'S COLD.
AM I...
...DEAD?
I SEE.
FINALLY...
...AT PEACE, THEN?

I'M SORRY, ION.

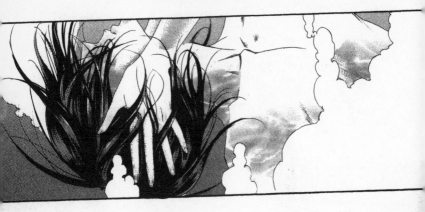

ION?

YOU'RE SMILING.

YOU'VE FORGIVEN ME

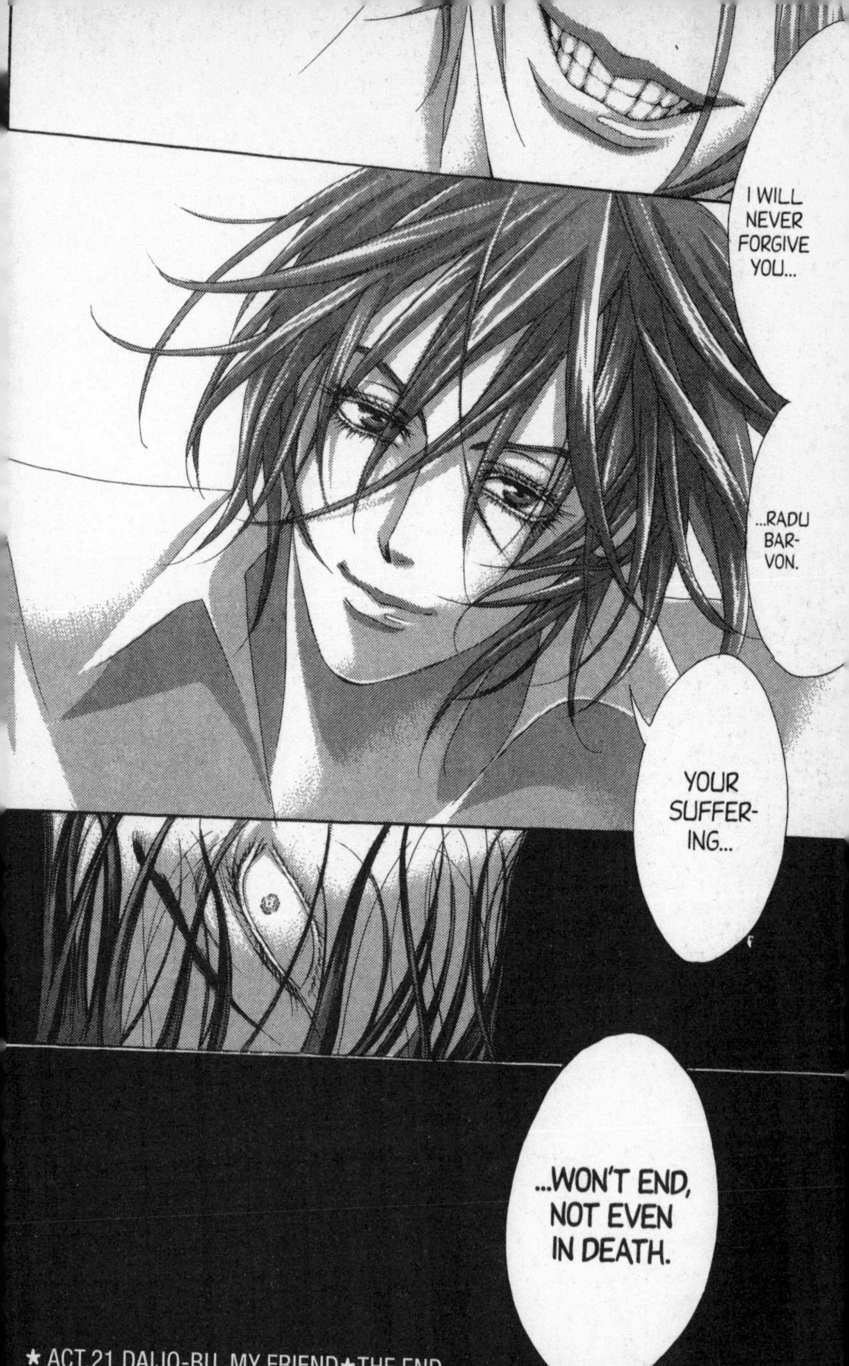
I WILL NEVER FORGIVE YOU... ...RADU BAR-VON.
YOUR SUFFER-ING...
...WON'T END, NOT EVEN IN DEATH.

★ ACT.21 DAIJO-BU, MY FRIEND★THE END

TRINITY BLOOD

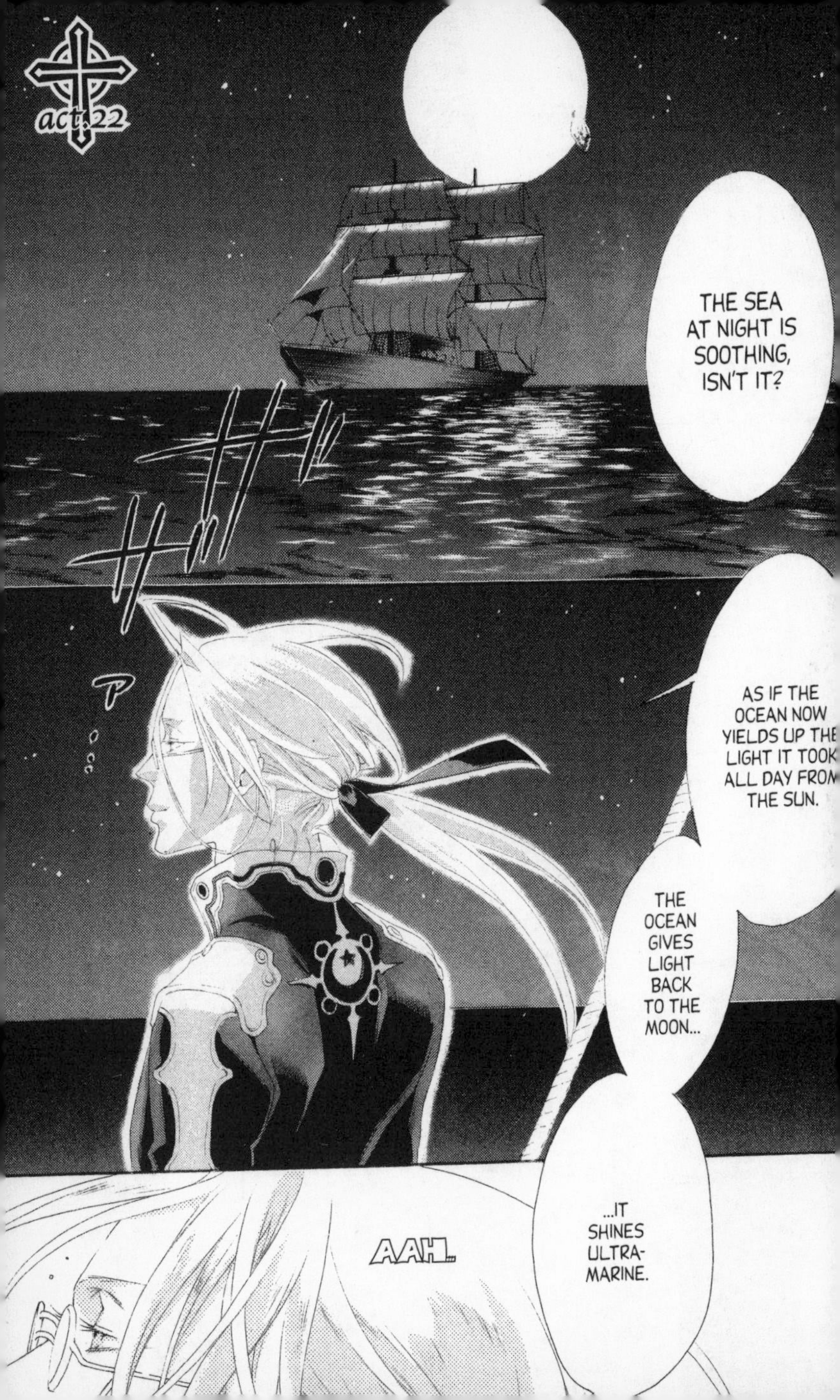
act.22
THE SEA AT NIGHT IS SOOTHING, ISN'T IT?
AS IF THE OCEAN NOW YIELDS UP THE LIGHT IT TOOK ALL DAY FROM THE SUN.
THE OCEAN GIVES LIGHT BACK TO THE MOON...
...IT SHINES ULTRA-MARINE.
AAH...

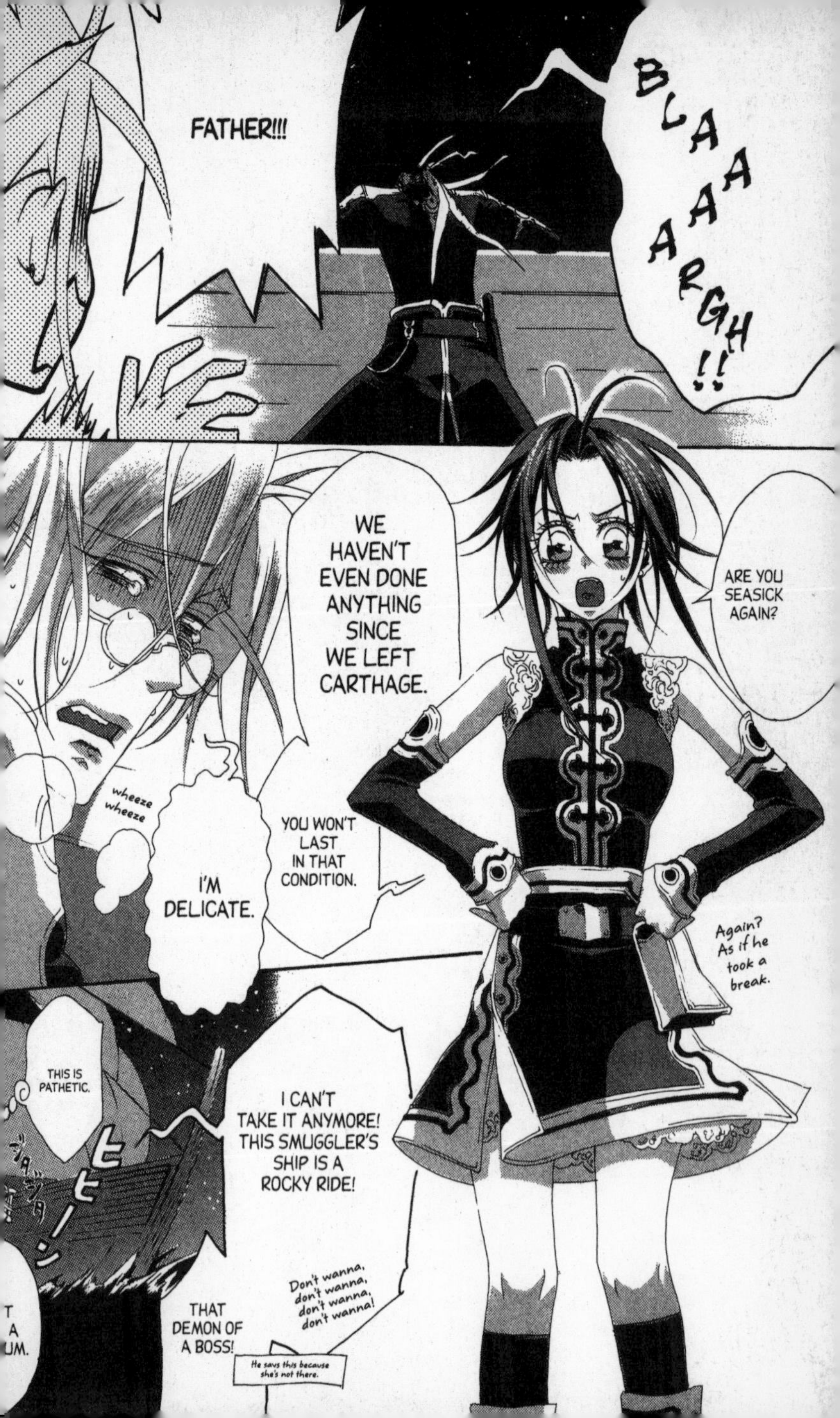
BLAAAARGH!!
FATHER!!!
ARE YOU SEASICK AGAIN?
Again? As if he took a break.
WE HAVEN'T EVEN DONE ANYTHING SINCE WE LEFT CARTHAGE.
YOU WON'T LAST IN THAT CONDITION.
I'M DELICATE.
wheeze wheeze
I CAN'T TAKE IT ANYMORE! THIS SMUGGLER'S SHIP IS A ROCKY RIDE!
THIS IS PATHETIC.
Don't wanna, don't wanna, don't wanna, don't wanna!
THAT DEMON OF A BOSS!
He says this because she's not there.

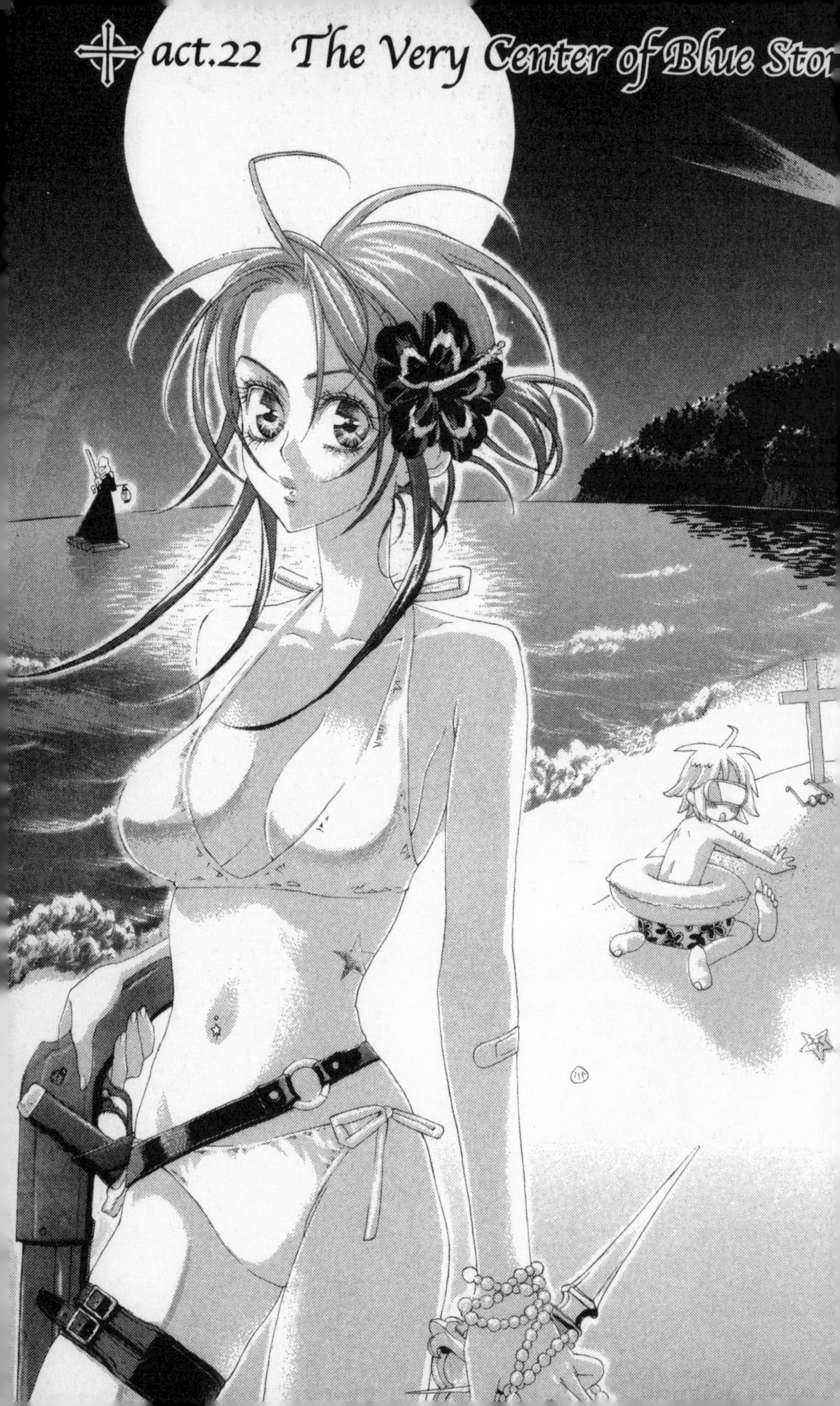
act.22 The Very Center of Blue Ston

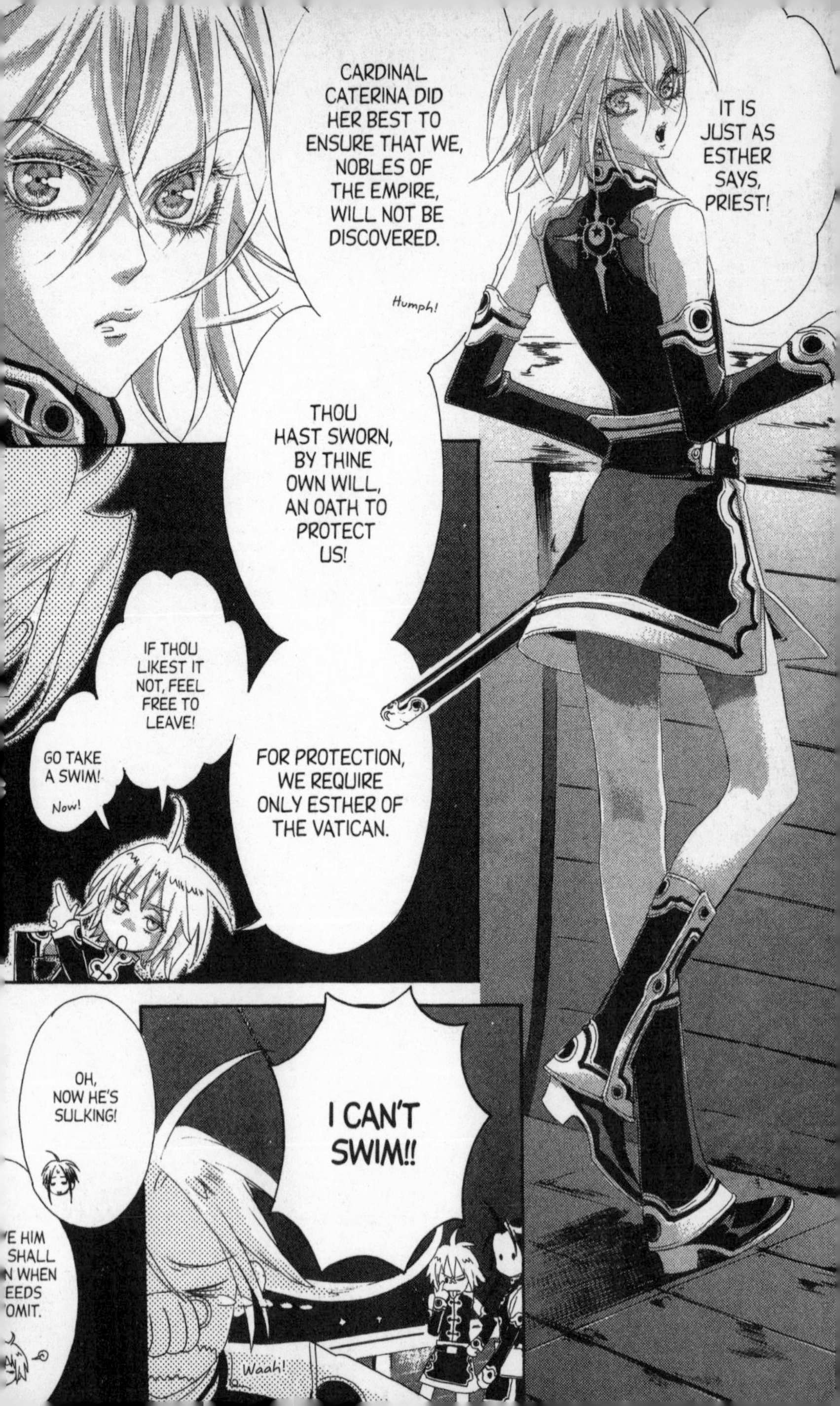
IT IS JUST AS ESTHER SAYS, PRIEST!
CARDINAL CATERINA DID HER BEST TO ENSURE THAT WE, NOBLES OF THE EMPIRE, WILL NOT BE DISCOVERED.
Humph!
THOU HAST SWORN, BY THINE OWN WILL, AN OATH TO PROTECT US!
FOR PROTECTION, WE REQUIRE ONLY ESTHER OF THE VATICAN.
IF THOU LIKEST IT NOT, FEEL FREE TO LEAVE!
GO TAKE A SWIM!
Now!
I CAN'T SWIM!!
OH, NOW HE'S SULKING!
Waah!

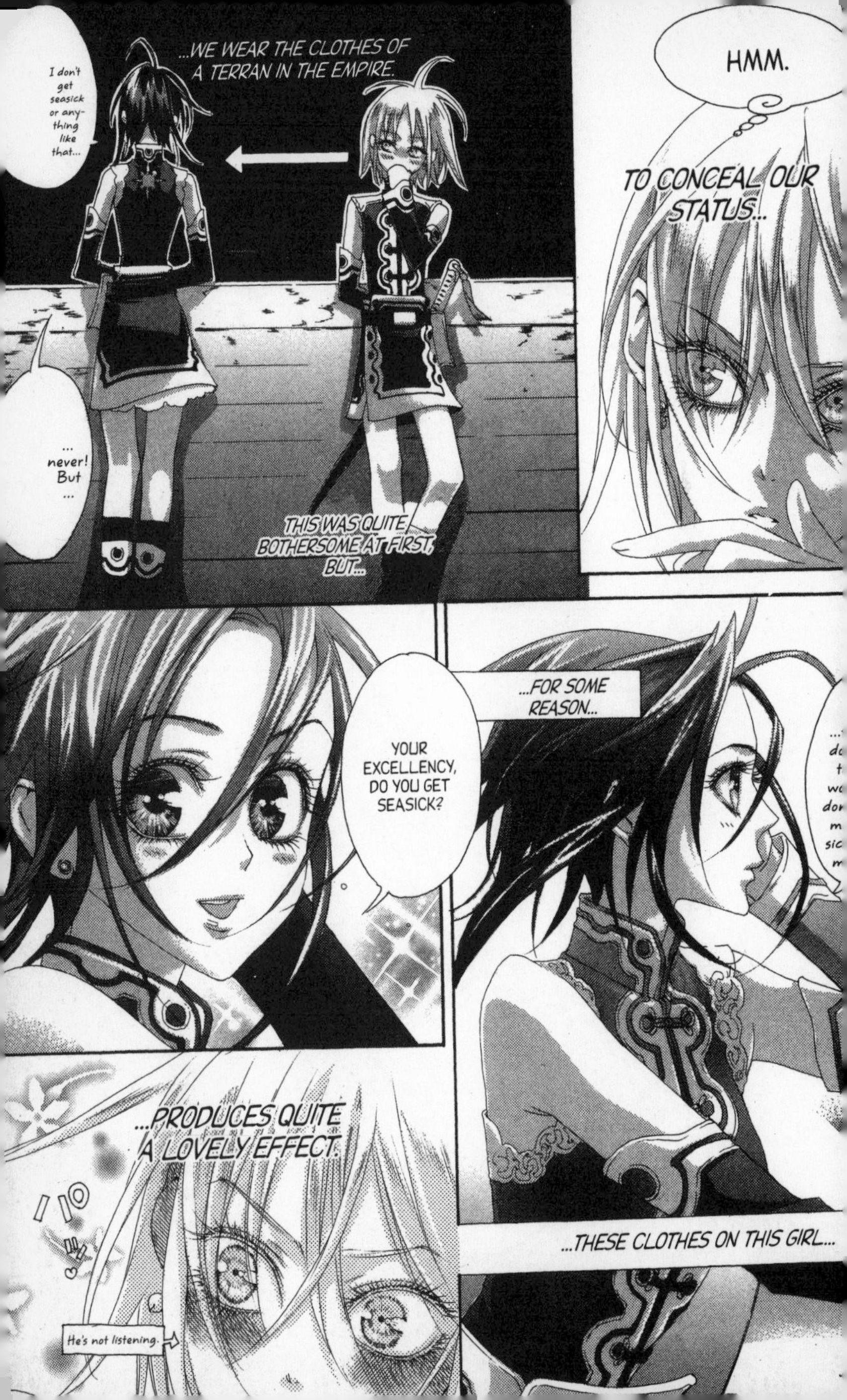
HMM.
TO CONCEAL OUR STATUS...
...WE WEAR THE CLOTHES OF A TERRAN IN THE EMPIRE.
I don't get seasick or anything like that...
...never! But...
THIS WAS QUITE BOTHERSOME AT FIRST, BUT...
...FOR SOME REASON...
...THESE CLOTHES ON THIS GIRL...
YOUR EXCELLENCY, DO YOU GET SEASICK?
...PRODUCES QUITE A LOVELY EFFECT.
He's not listening.

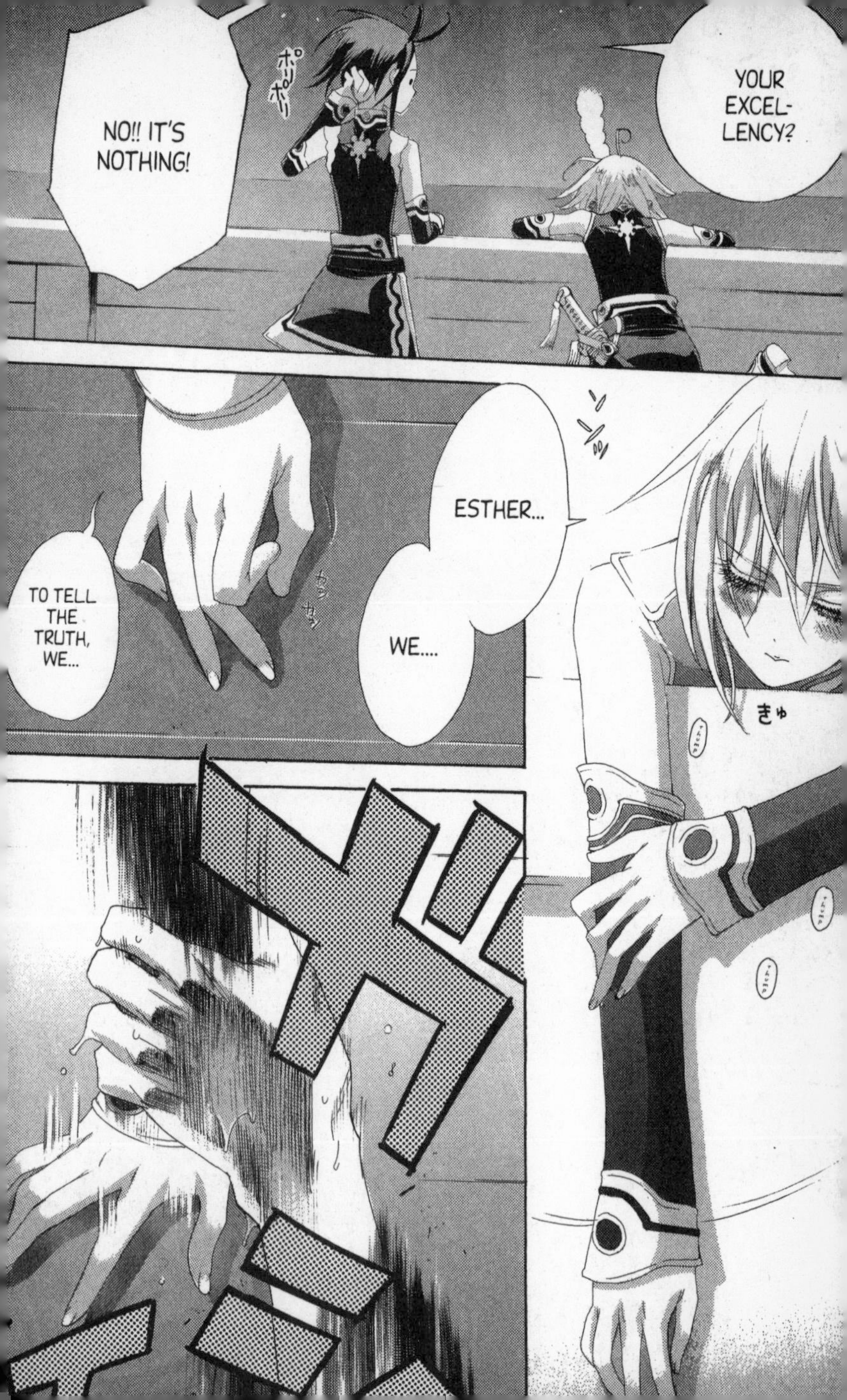
YOUR EXCEL-LENCY?
NO!! IT'S NOTHING!
ポリポリ
ESTHER...
WE....
きゅ
TO TELL THE TRUTH, WE...

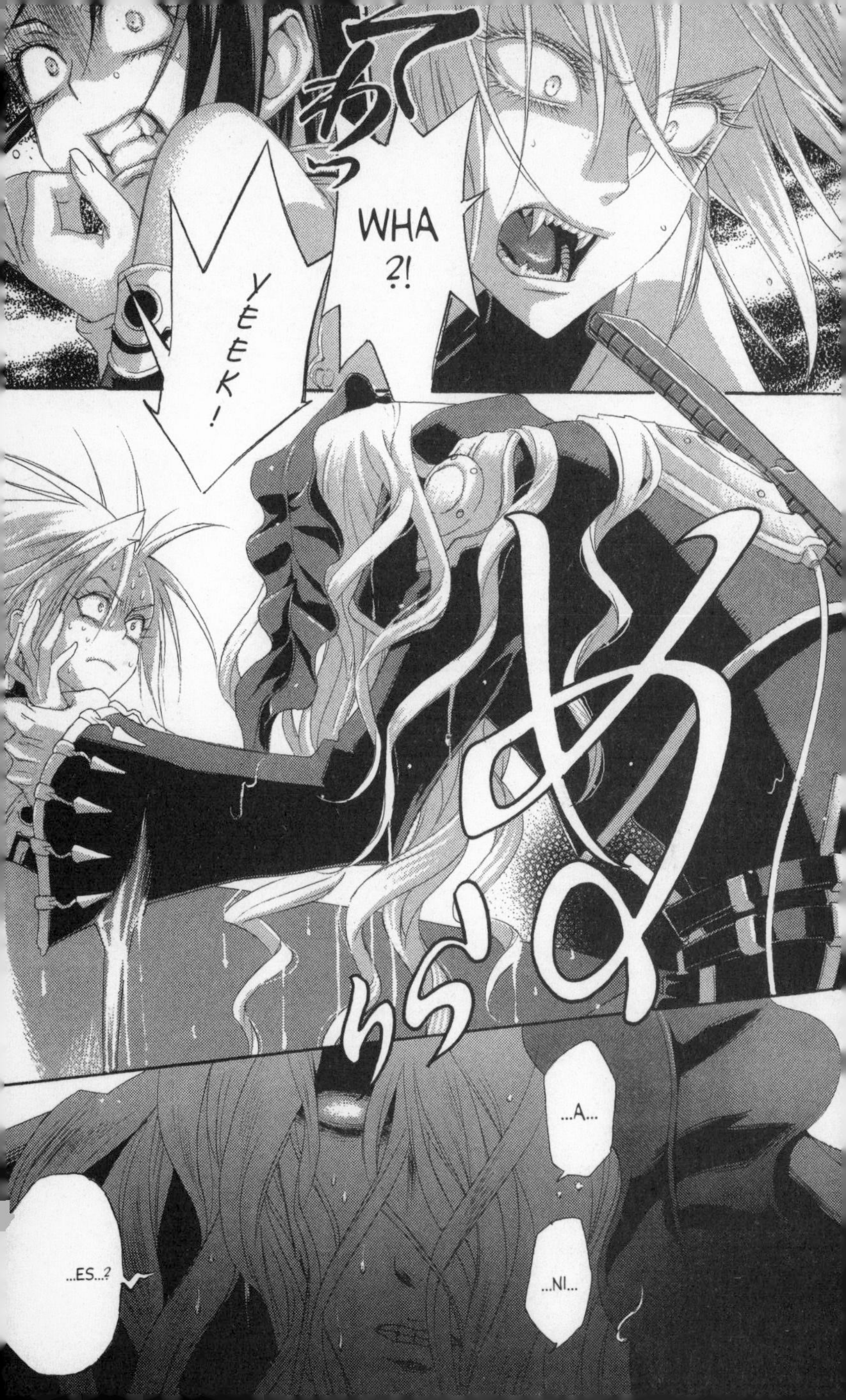
WHA ?!
YEEEK!
...A...
...NI...
...ES...?

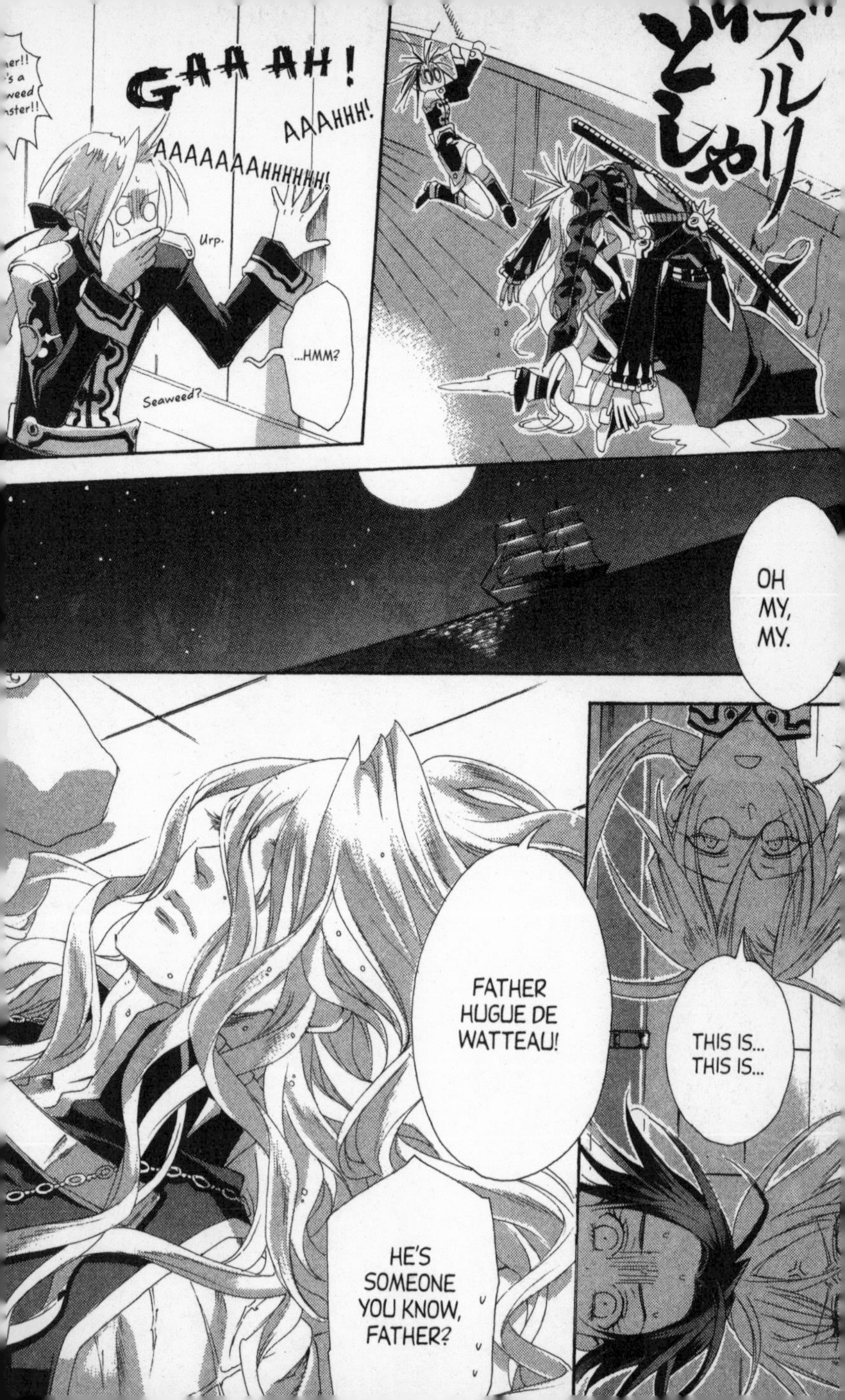
ズルリ
どしゃり
AAAHHH!
GAAAAH!
AAAAAAAAHHHHHH!
Urp.
...HMM?
Seaweed?
OH MY, MY.
THIS IS... THIS IS...
FATHER HUGUE DE WATTEAU!
HE'S SOMEONE YOU KNOW, FATHER?

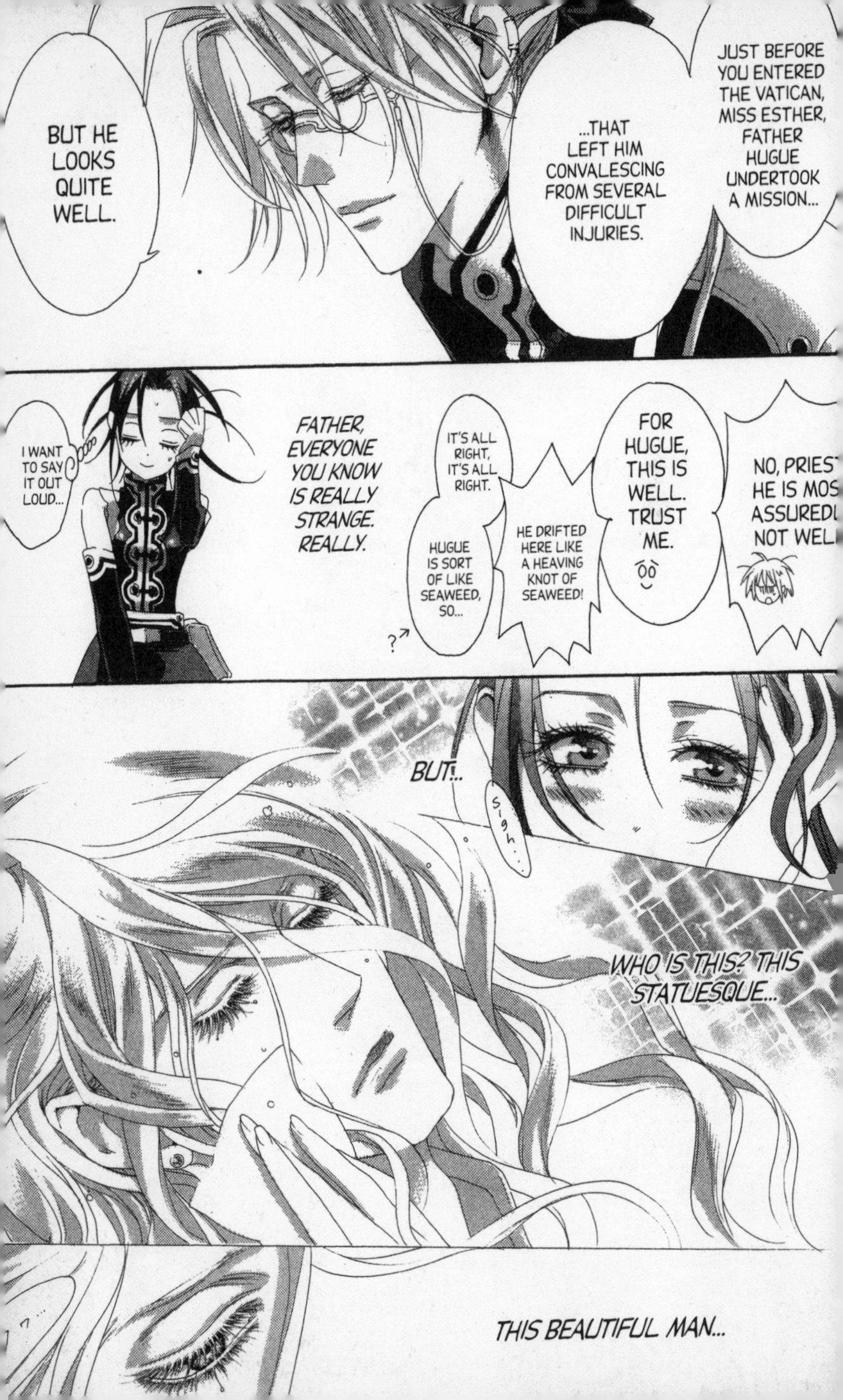
JUST BEFORE YOU ENTERED THE VATICAN, MISS ESTHER, FATHER HUGUE UNDERTOOK A MISSION...
...THAT LEFT HIM CONVALESCING FROM SEVERAL DIFFICULT INJURIES.
BUT HE LOOKS QUITE WELL.
NO, PRIES HE IS MOS ASSUREDL NOT WEL
FOR HUGUE, THIS IS WELL. TRUST ME.
HE DRIFTED HERE LIKE A HEAVING KNOT OF SEAWEED!
IT'S ALL RIGHT, IT'S ALL RIGHT.
HUGUE IS SORT OF LIKE SEAWEED, SO...
?
FATHER, EVERYONE YOU KNOW IS REALLY STRANGE. REALLY.
I WANT TO SAY IT OUT LOUD...
BUT...
Sigh...
WHO IS THIS? THIS STATUESQUE...
THIS BEAUTIFUL MAN...

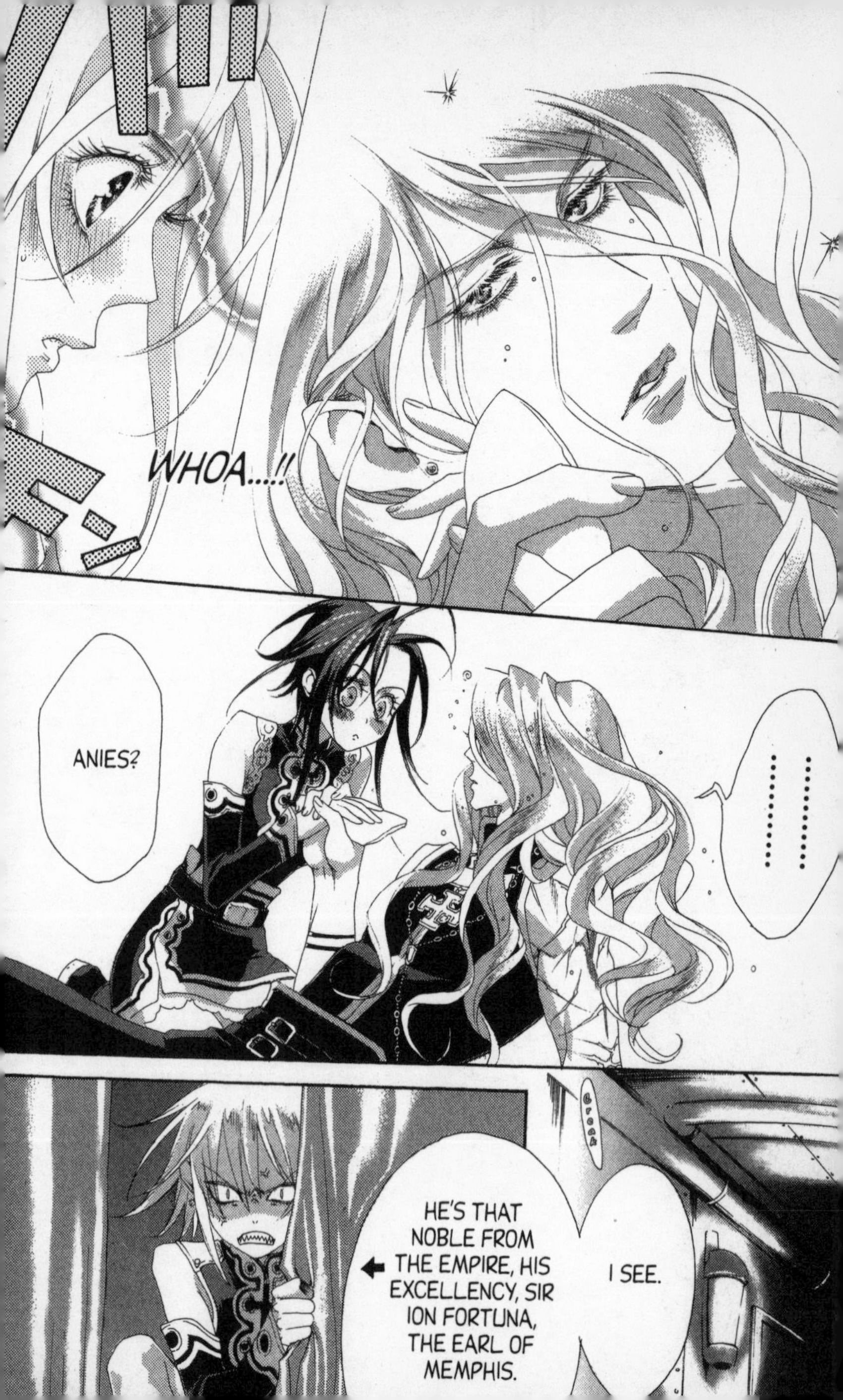
WHOA...!!
......
ANIES?
Creak
I SEE.
HE'S THAT NOBLE FROM THE EMPIRE, HIS EXCELLENCY, SIR ION FORTUNA, THE EARL OF MEMPHIS.

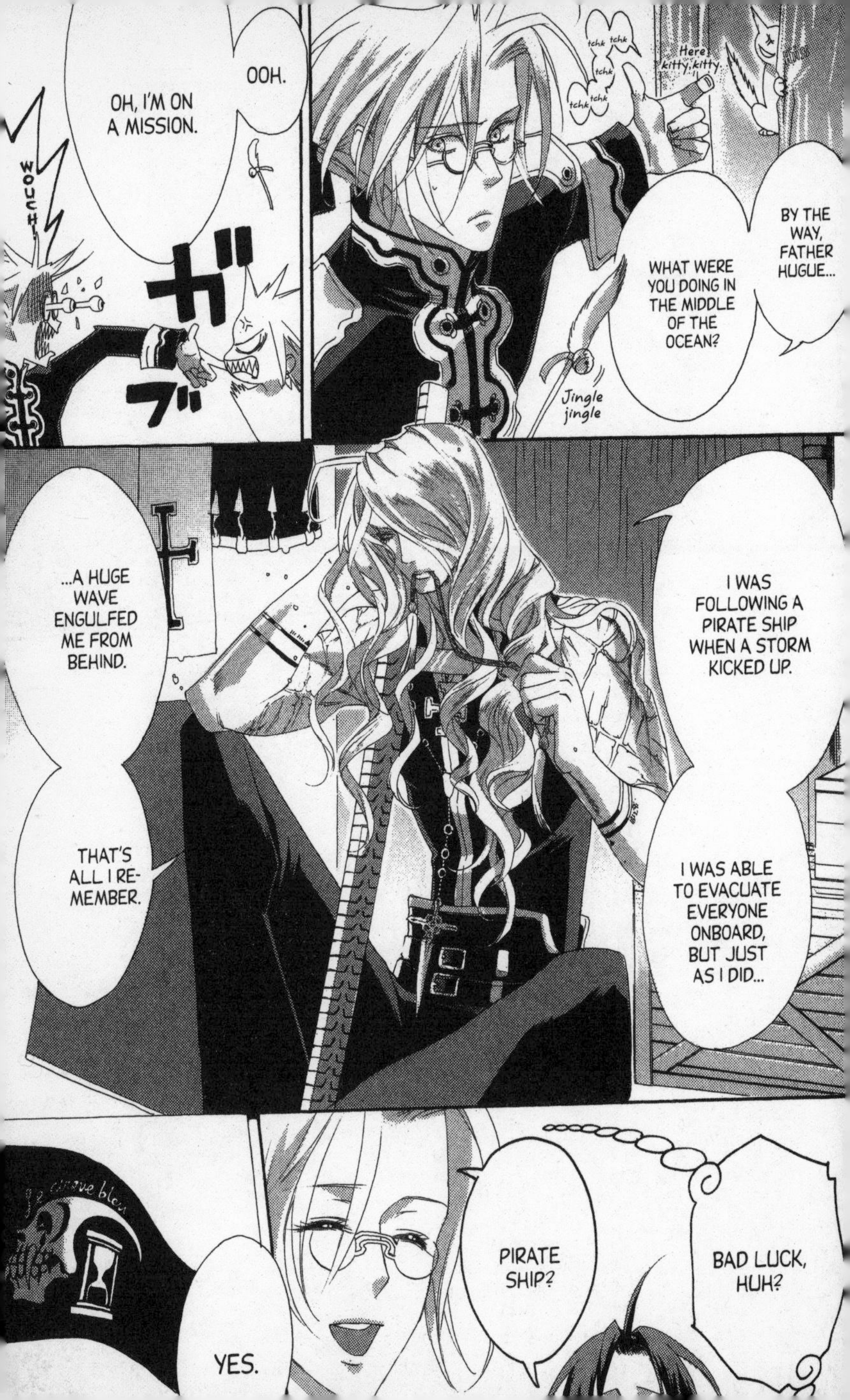
Here kitty, kitty.
tchk tchk tchk tchk tchk
BY THE WAY, FATHER HUGUE...
WHAT WERE YOU DOING IN THE MIDDLE OF THE OCEAN?
Jingle jingle
OOH.
OH, I'M ON A MISSION.
WOUCH!
ガブ
I WAS FOLLOWING A PIRATE SHIP WHEN A STORM KICKED UP.
I WAS ABLE TO EVACUATE EVERYONE ONBOARD, BUT JUST AS I DID...
...A HUGE WAVE ENGULFED ME FROM BEHIND.
THAT'S ALL I RE-MEMBER.
BAD LUCK, HUH?
PIRATE SHIP?
YES.

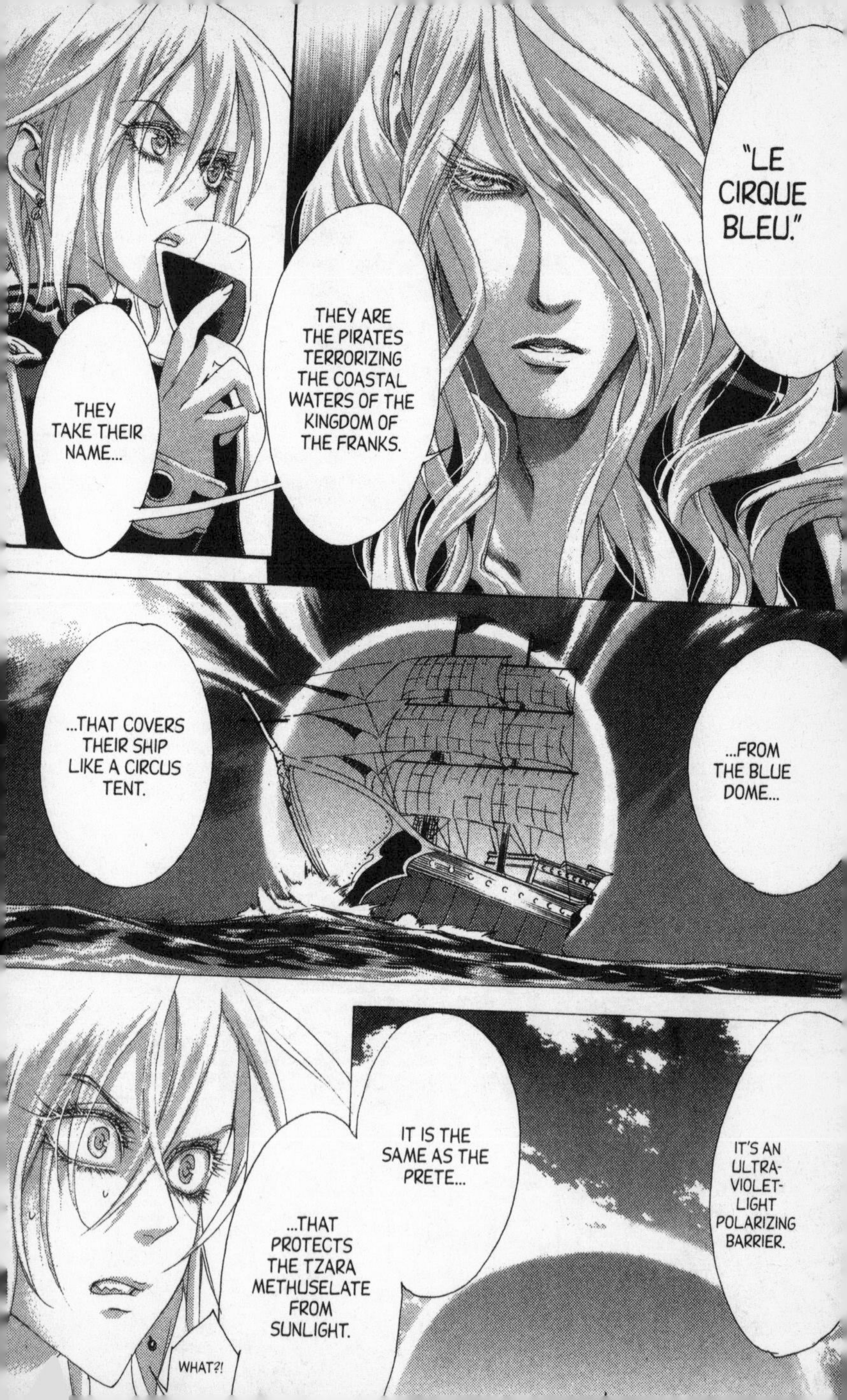
"LE CIRQUE BLEU."
THEY ARE THE PIRATES TERRORIZING THE COASTAL WATERS OF THE KINGDOM OF THE FRANKS.
THEY TAKE THEIR NAME...
...FROM THE BLUE DOME...
...THAT COVERS THEIR SHIP LIKE A CIRCUS TENT.
IT'S AN ULTRA-VIOLET-LIGHT POLARIZING BARRIER.
IT IS THE SAME AS THE PRETE...
...THAT PROTECTS THE TZARA METHUSELATE FROM SUNLIGHT.
WHAT?!

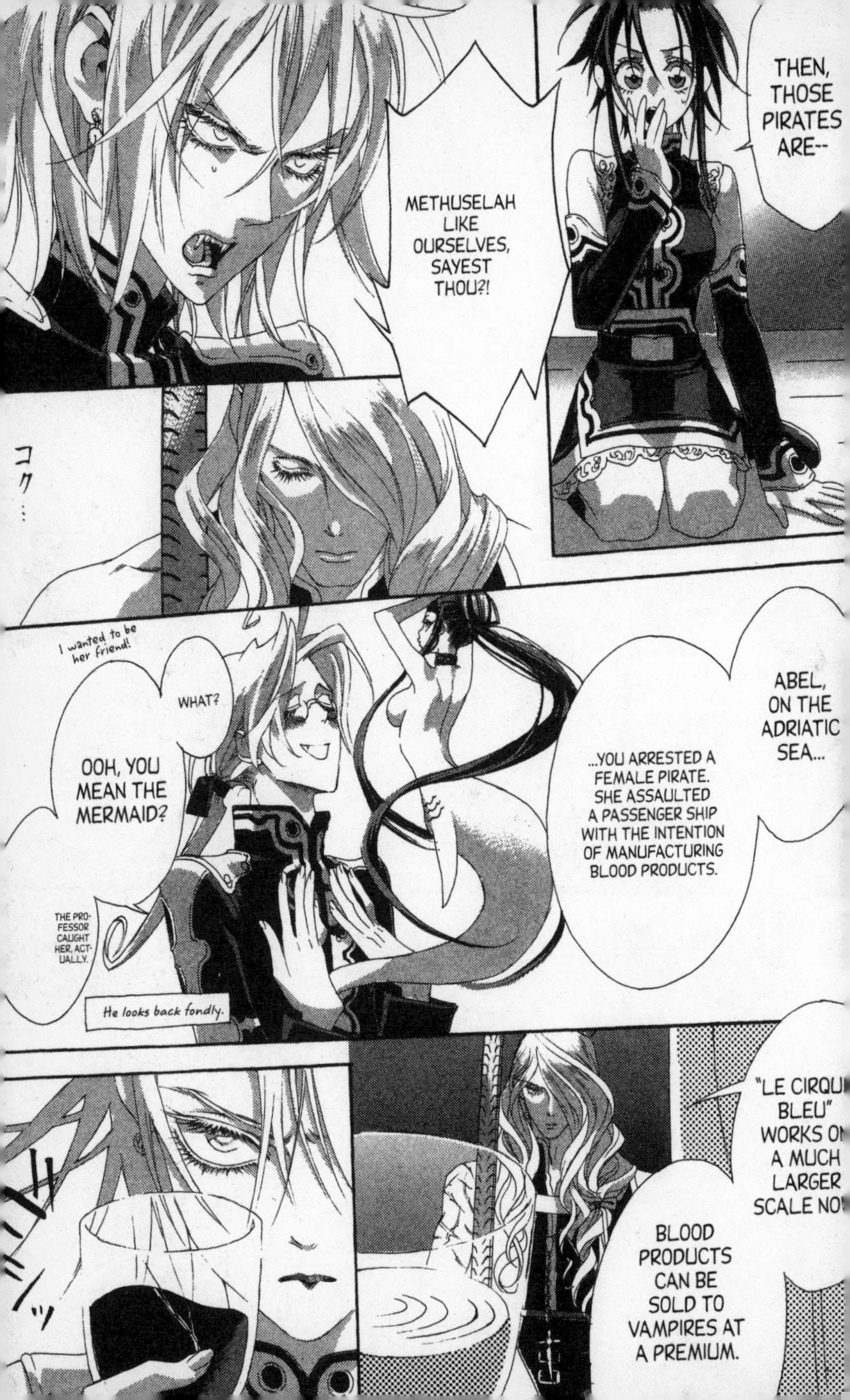
THEN, THOSE PIRATES ARE--
METHUSELAH LIKE OURSELVES, SAYEST THOU?!
コク…
ABEL, ON THE ADRIATIC SEA...
...YOU ARRESTED A FEMALE PIRATE. SHE ASSAULTED A PASSENGER SHIP WITH THE INTENTION OF MANUFACTURING BLOOD PRODUCTS.
WHAT?
OOH, YOU MEAN THE MERMAID?
I wanted to be her friend!
THE PRO- FESSOR CAUGHT HER, ACT- UALLY.
He looks back fondly.
"LE CIRQU BLEU" WORKS O A MUCH LARGER SCALE NO
BLOOD PRODUCTS CAN BE SOLD TO VAMPIRES AT A PREMIUM.

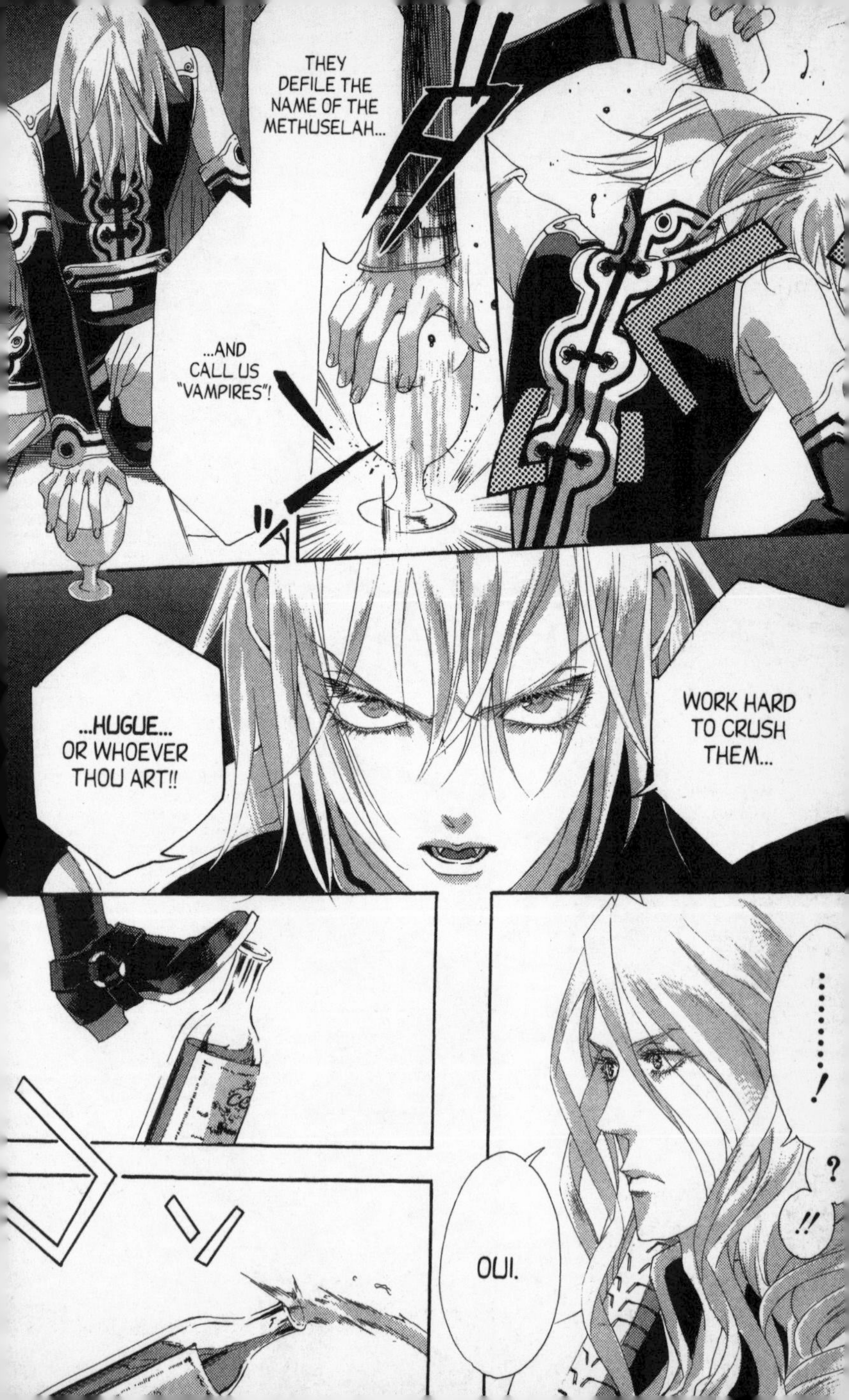
THEY DEFILE THE NAME OF THE METHUSELAH...
...AND CALL US "VAMPIRES"!
WORK HARD TO CRUSH THEM...
...HUGUE... OR WHOEVER THOU ART!!
......!
?
!!
OUI.

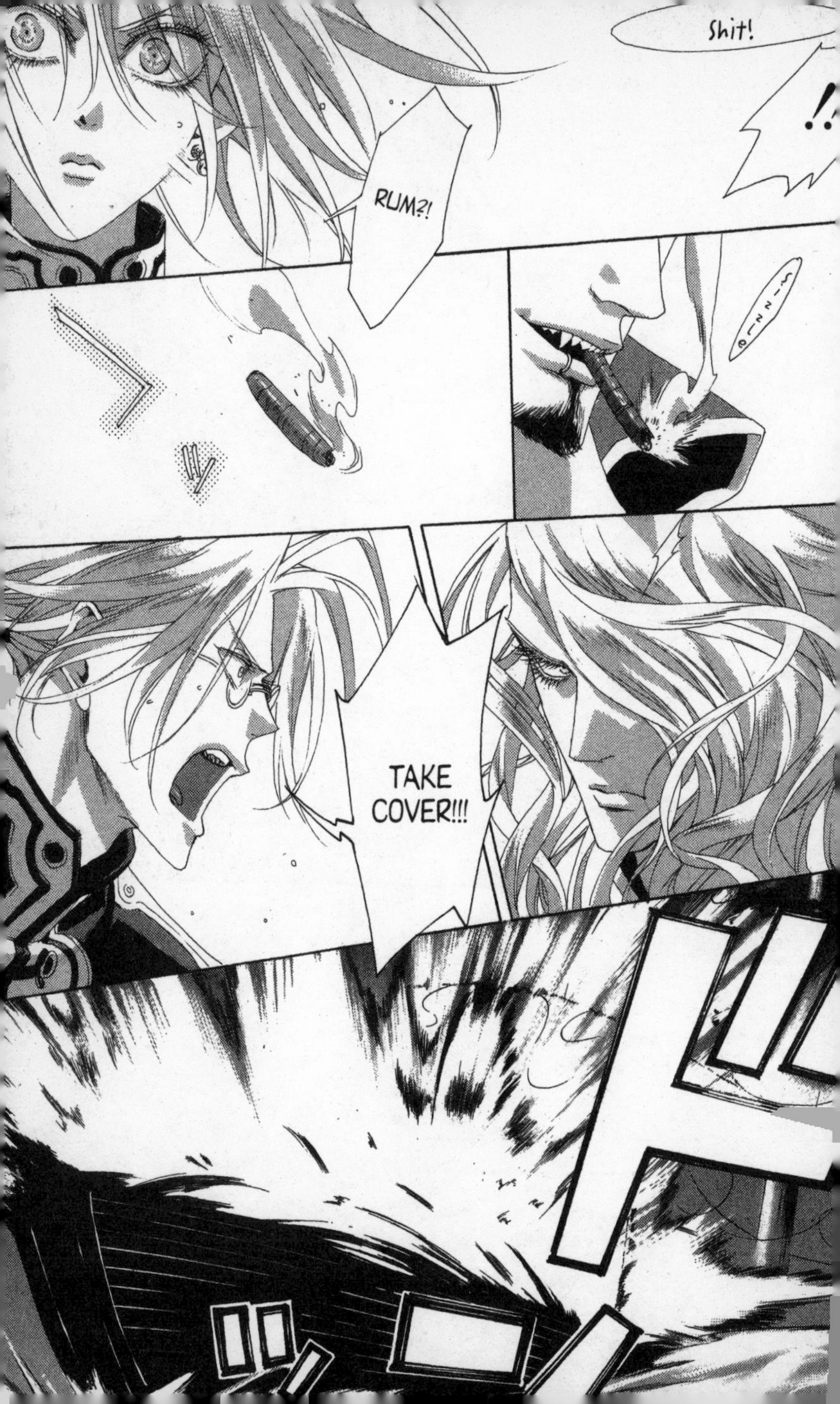

Shit!
!!
RUM?!
Sizzle
TAKE COVER!!!

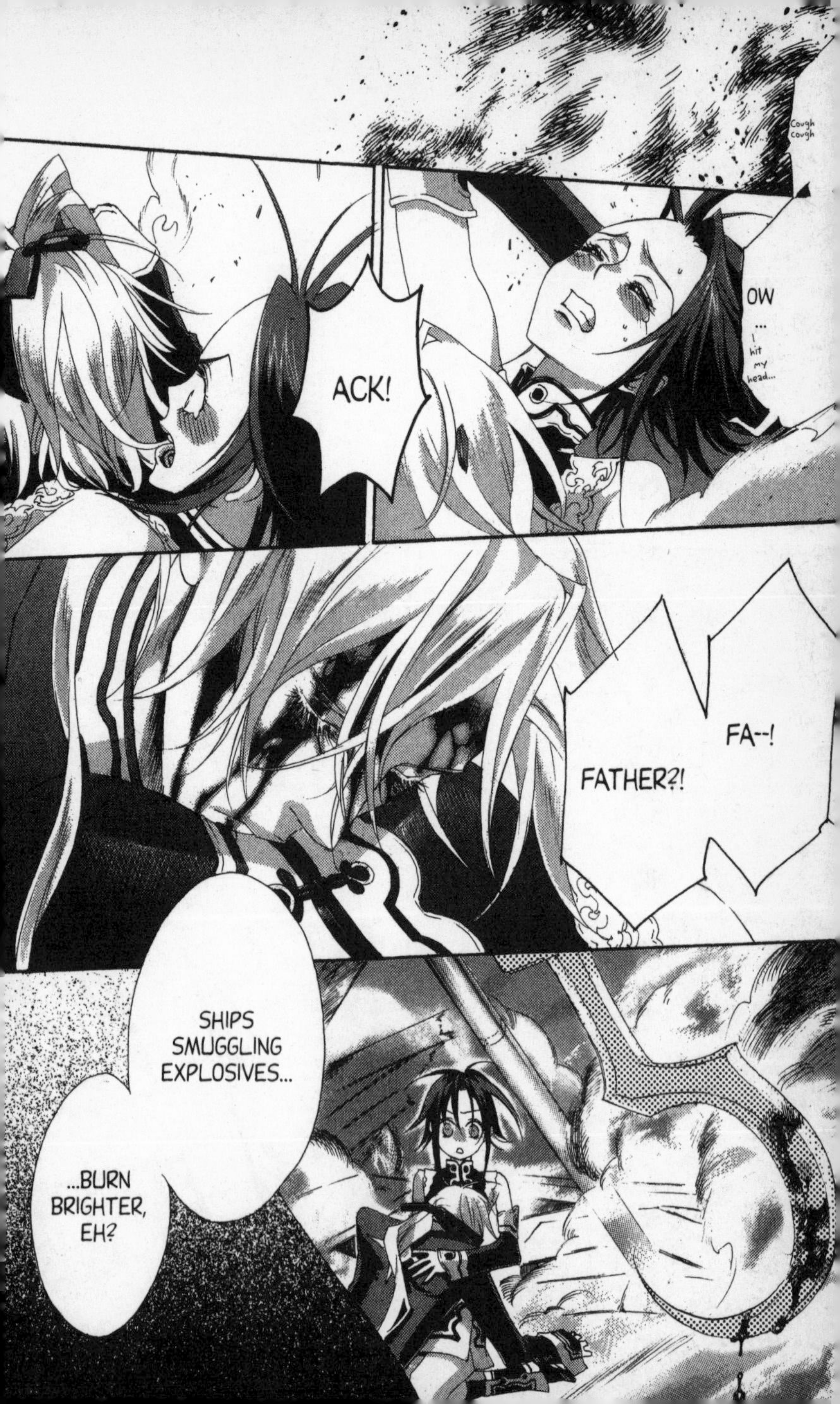
Cough cough
OW ... I hit my head...
ACK!
FA--!
FATHER?!
SHIPS SMUGGLING EXPLOSIVES...
...BURN BRIGHTER, EH?

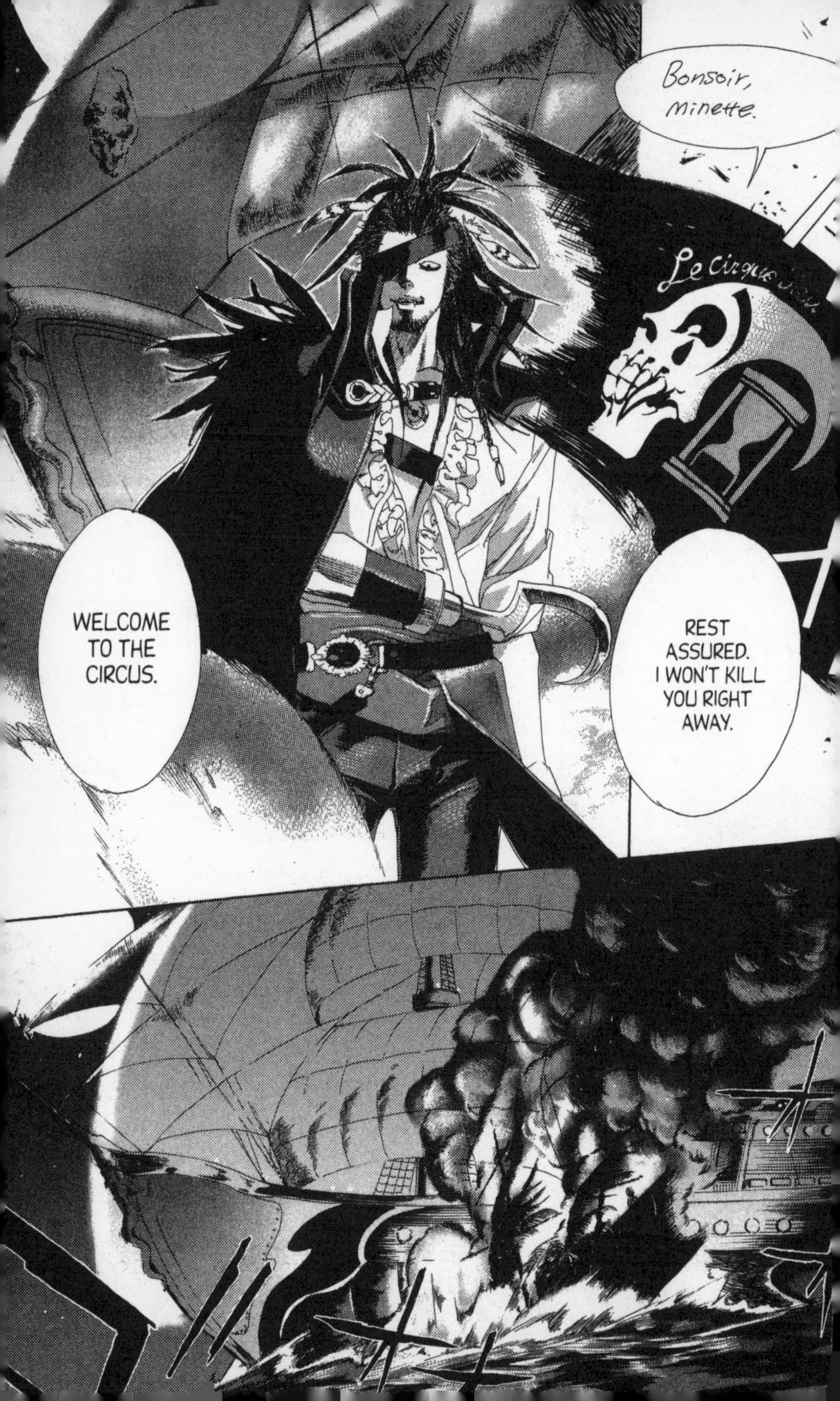
Bonsoir, minette.
Le Cirque
REST ASSURED. I WON'T KILL YOU RIGHT AWAY.
WELCOME TO THE CIRCUS.

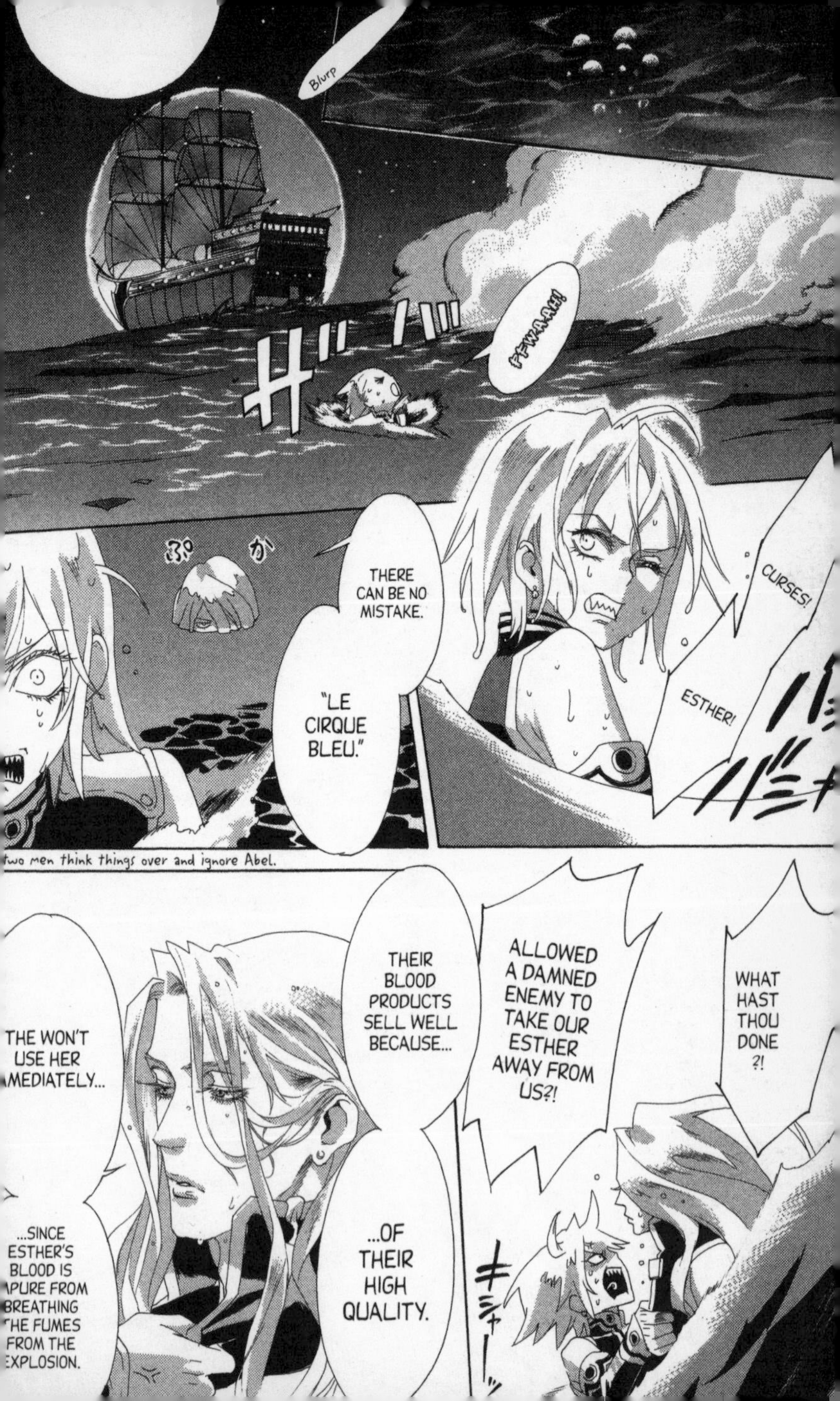
Blurp
PFWAAH!
CURSES!
ESTHER!
THERE CAN BE NO MISTAKE.
"LE CIRQUE BLEU."
ぷか
two men think things over and ignore Abel.
WHAT HAST THOU DONE?!
ALLOWED A DAMNED ENEMY TO TAKE OUR ESTHER AWAY FROM US?!
THEIR BLOOD PRODUCTS SELL WELL BECAUSE...
...OF THEIR HIGH QUALITY.
THE WON'T USE HER MEDIATELY...
...SINCE ESTHER'S BLOOD IS PURE FROM BREATHING THE FUMES FROM THE EXPLOSION.

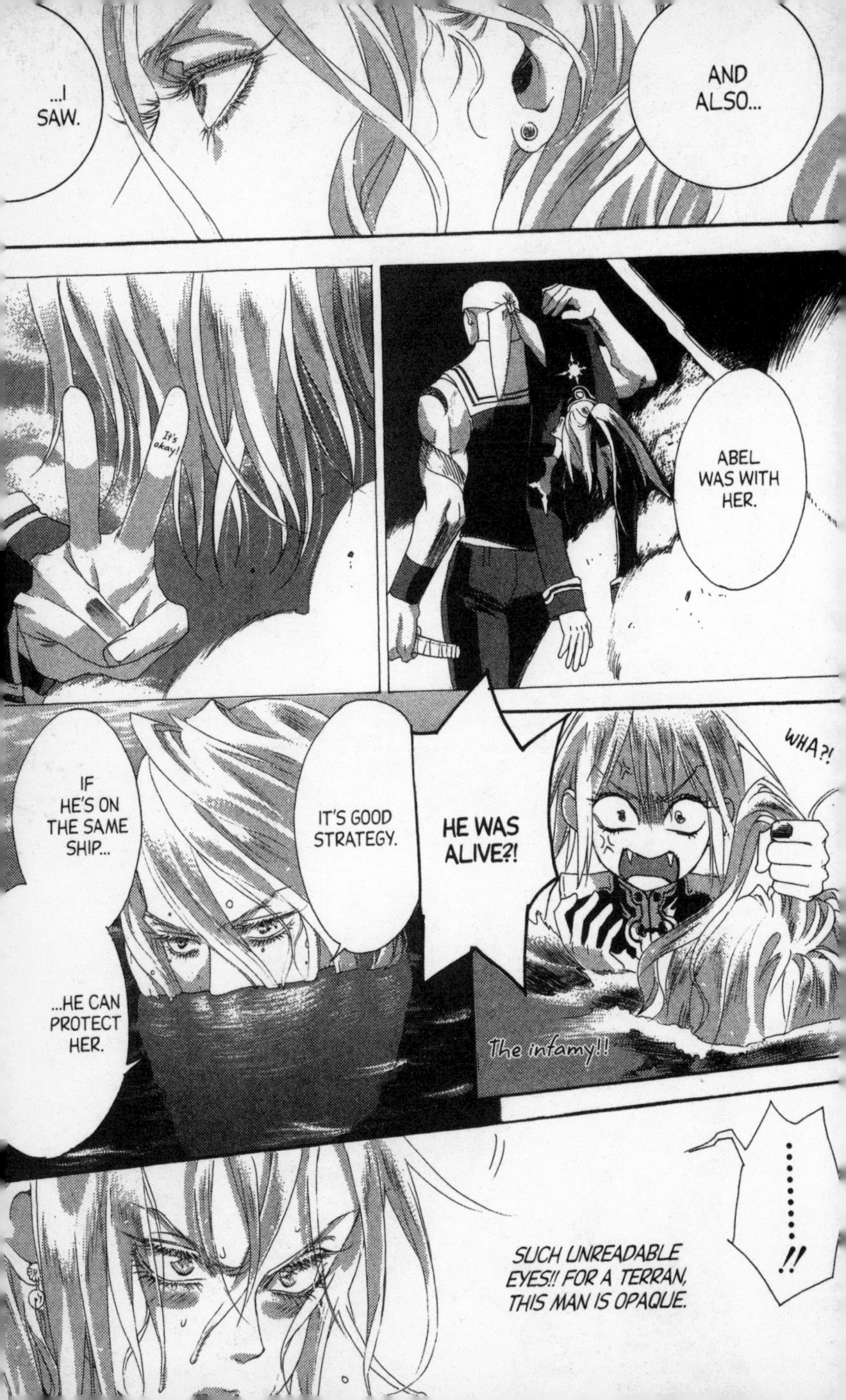
AND ALSO...
...I SAW.
ABEL WAS WITH HER.
It's okay!
WHA?!
HE WAS ALIVE?!
The infamy!!
IT'S GOOD STRATEGY.
IF HE'S ON THE SAME SHIP...
...HE CAN PROTECT HER.
......!!
SUCH UNREADABLE EYES!! FOR A TERRAN, THIS MAN IS OPAQUE.

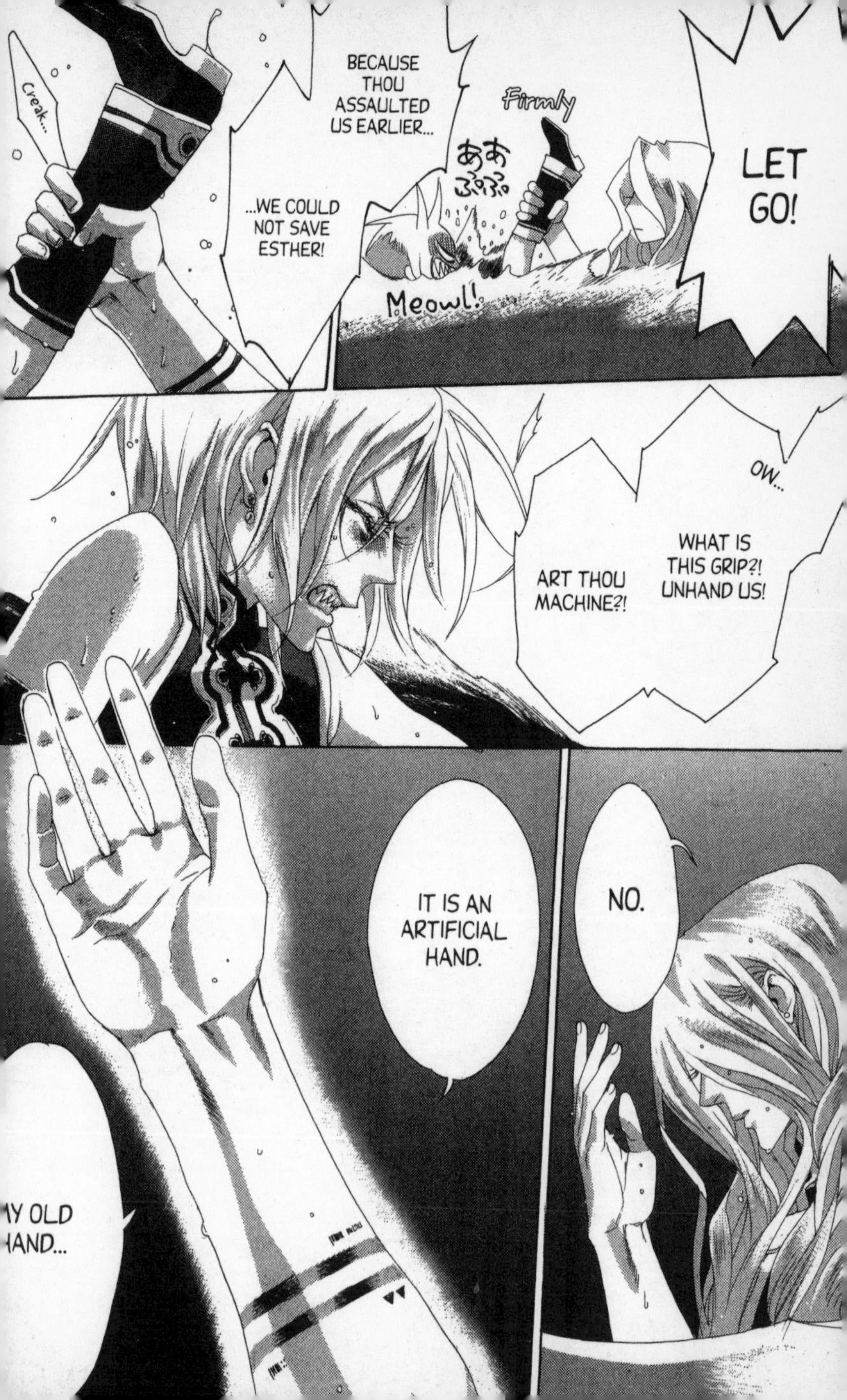

LET GO!
Firmly
ああぷぷ
Meowl!
BECAUSE THOU ASSAULTED US EARLIER...
...WE COULD NOT SAVE ESTHER!
Creak...
OW...
WHAT IS THIS GRIP?! UNHAND US!
ART THOU MACHINE?!
NO.
IT IS AN ARTIFICIAL HAND.
Y OLD
AND...

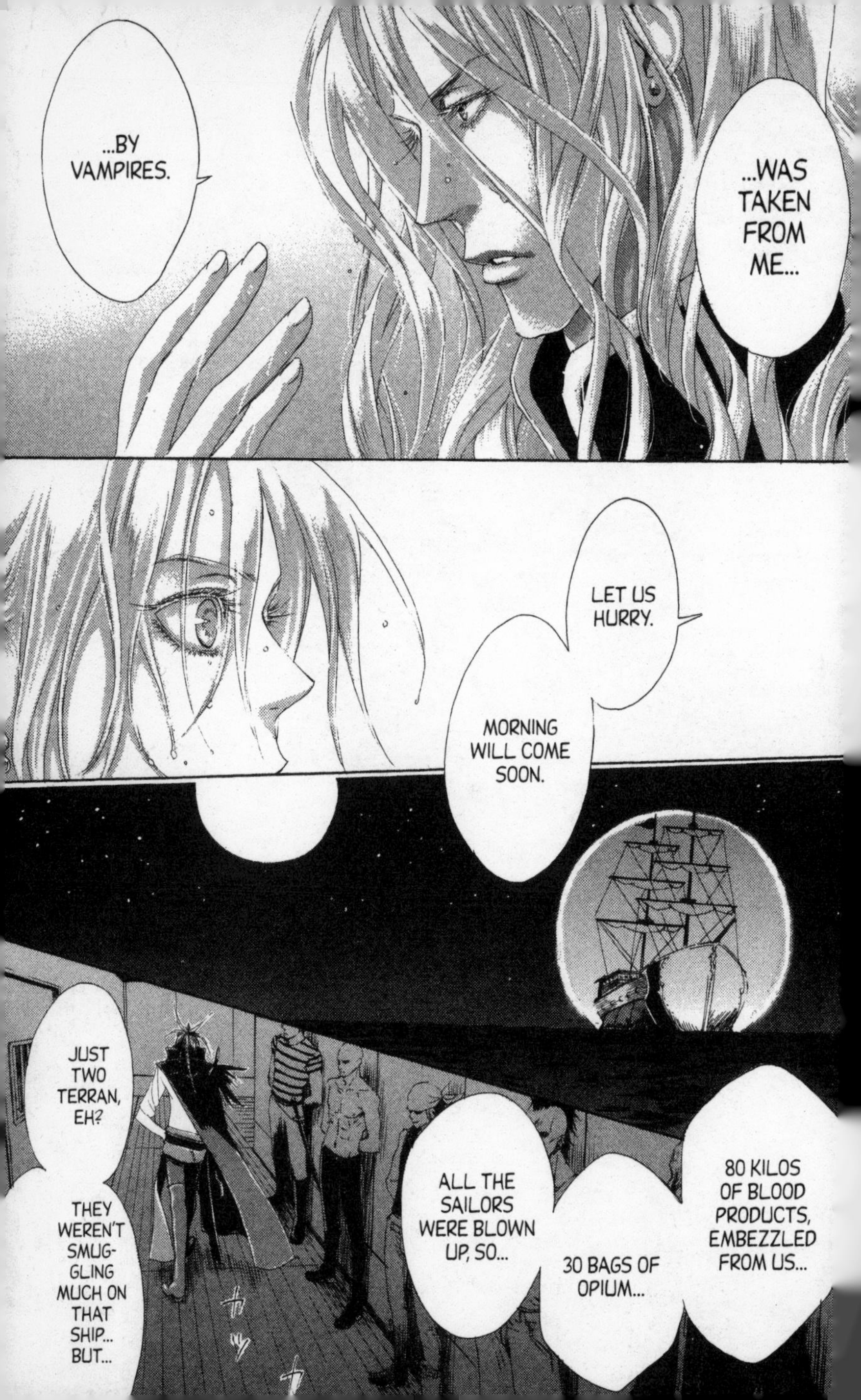
...WAS TAKEN FROM ME...
...BY VAMPIRES.
LET US HURRY.
MORNING WILL COME SOON.
80 KILOS OF BLOOD PRODUCTS, EMBEZZLED FROM US...
30 BAGS OF OPIUM...
ALL THE SAILORS WERE BLOWN UP, SO...
JUST TWO TERRAN, EH?
THEY WEREN'T SMUG-GLING MUCH ON THAT SHIP... BUT...

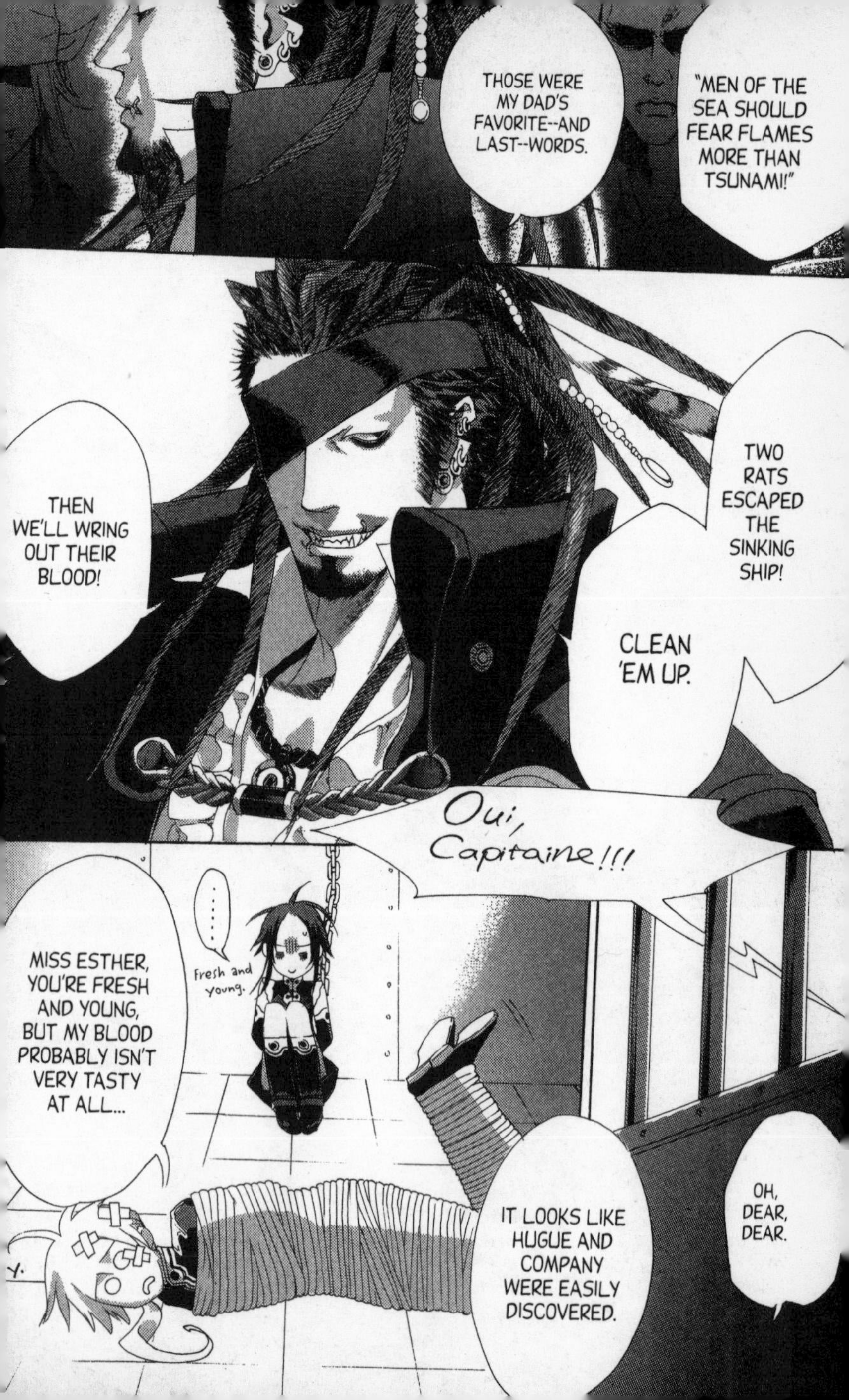
"MEN OF THE SEA SHOULD FEAR FLAMES MORE THAN TSUNAMI!"
THOSE WERE MY DAD'S FAVORITE--AND LAST--WORDS.
TWO RATS ESCAPED THE SINKING SHIP!
CLEAN 'EM UP.
THEN WE'LL WRING OUT THEIR BLOOD!
Oui, Capitaine!!!
OH, DEAR, DEAR.
IT LOOKS LIKE HUGUE AND COMPANY WERE EASILY DISCOVERED.
......
Fresh and young.
MISS ESTHER, YOU'RE FRESH AND YOUNG, BUT MY BLOOD PROBABLY ISN'T VERY TASTY AT ALL...

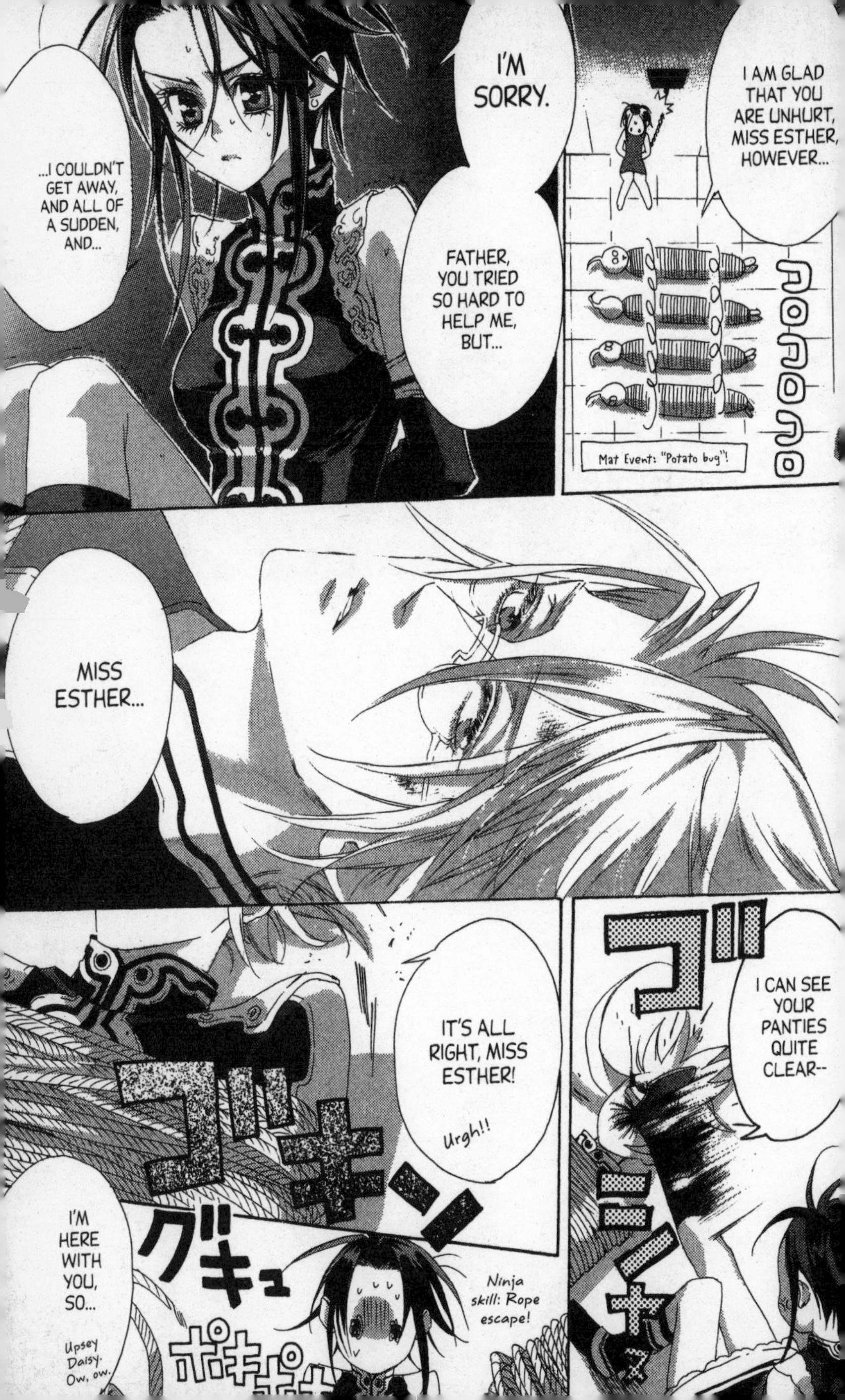
I AM GLAD THAT YOU ARE UNHURT, MISS ESTHER, HOWEVER...
Mat Event: "Potato bug"!
I'M SORRY.
FATHER, YOU TRIED SO HARD TO HELP ME, BUT...
...I COULDN'T GET AWAY, AND ALL OF A SUDDEN, AND...
MISS ESTHER...
I CAN SEE YOUR PANTIES QUITE CLEAR--
IT'S ALL RIGHT, MISS ESTHER!
Urgh!!
I'M HERE WITH YOU, SO...
Ninja skill: Rope escape!
Upsey Daisy. Ow, ow.

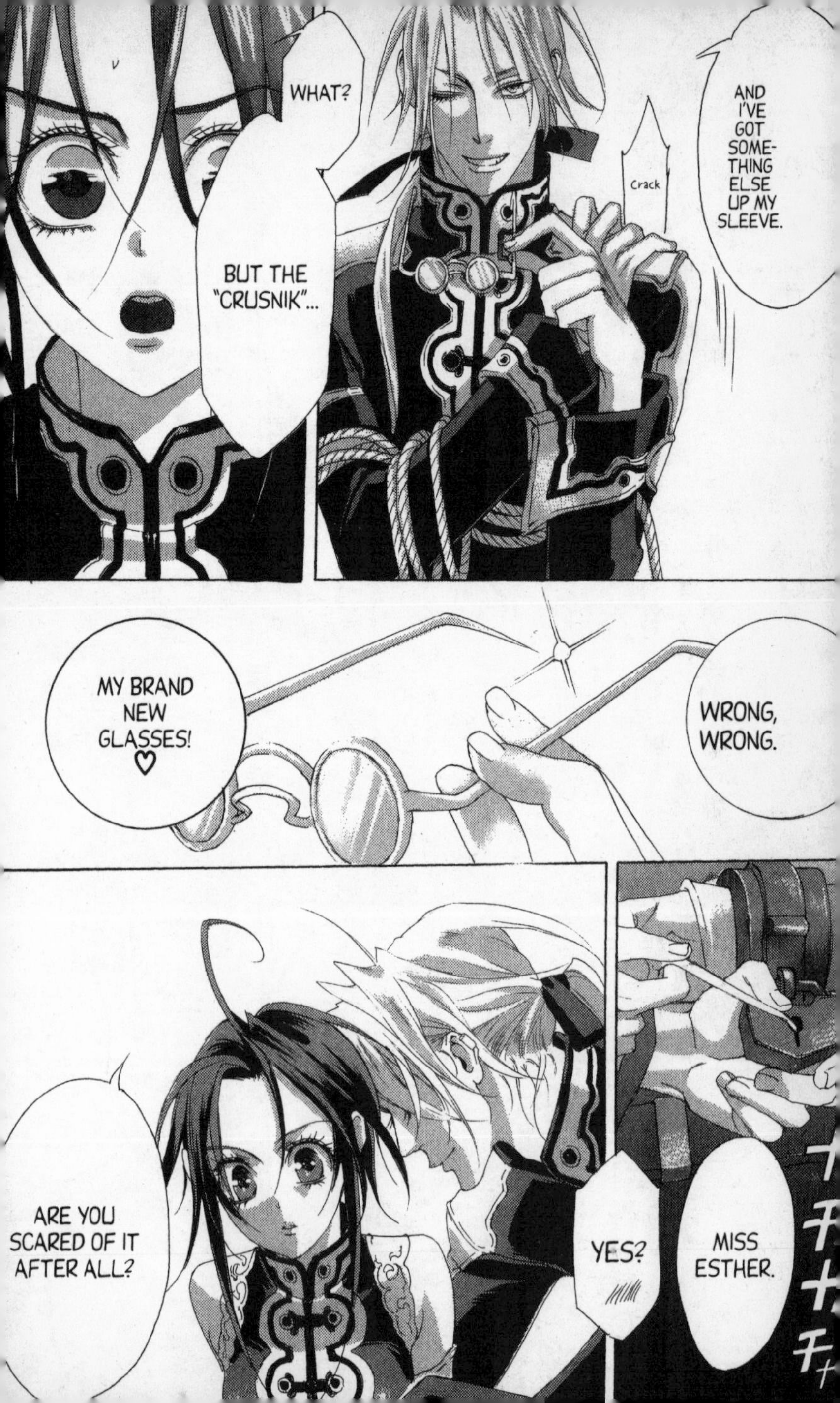

AND I'VE GOT SOMETHING ELSE UP MY SLEEVE.
Crack
WHAT?
BUT THE "CRUSNIK"...
WRONG, WRONG.
MY BRAND NEW GLASSES! ♡
MISS ESTHER.
YES?
ARE YOU SCARED OF IT AFTER ALL?

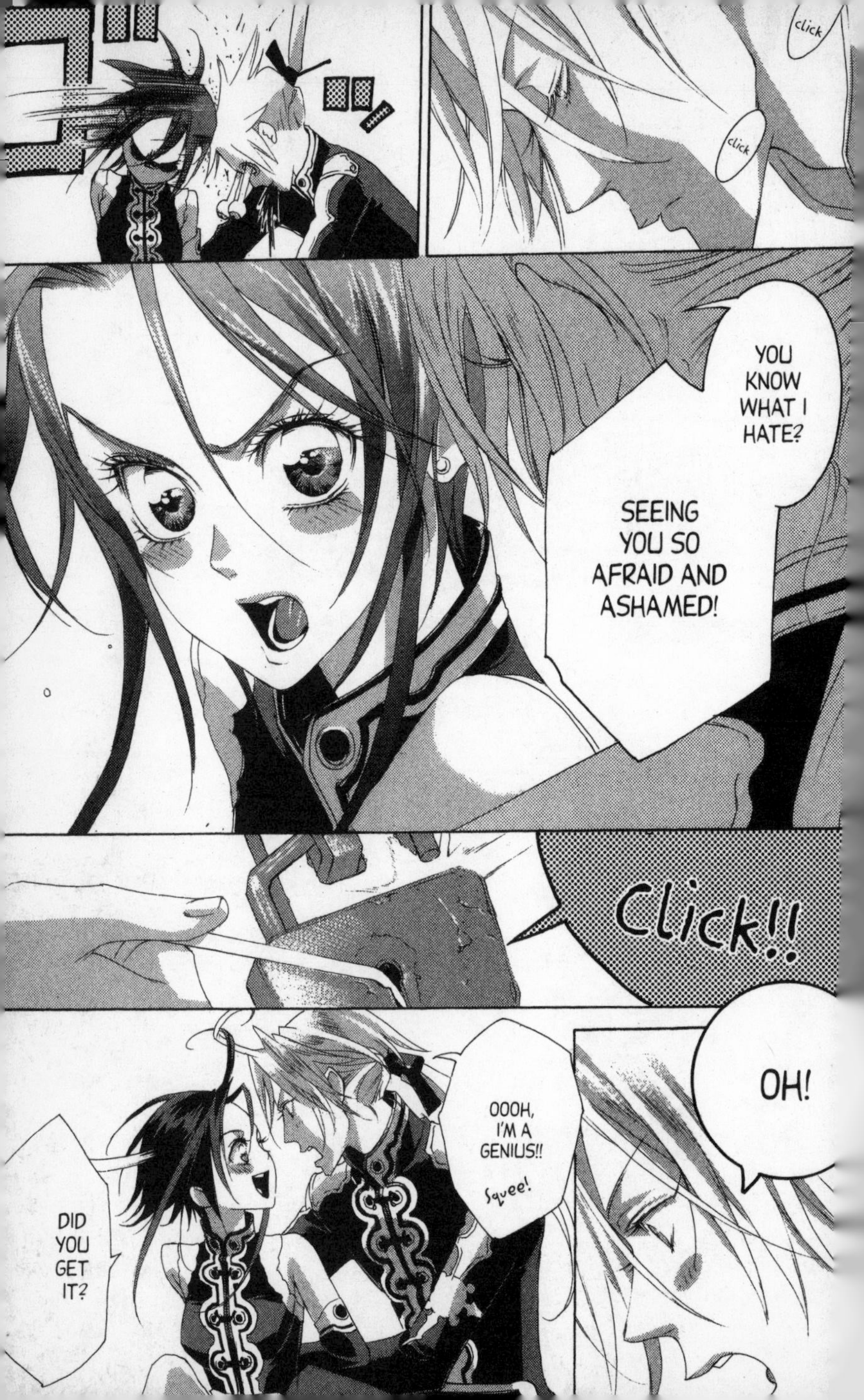
click
click
YOU KNOW WHAT I HATE?
SEEING YOU SO AFRAID AND ASHAMED!
Click!!
OH!
OOOH, I'M A GENIUS!!
Squee!
DID YOU GET IT?

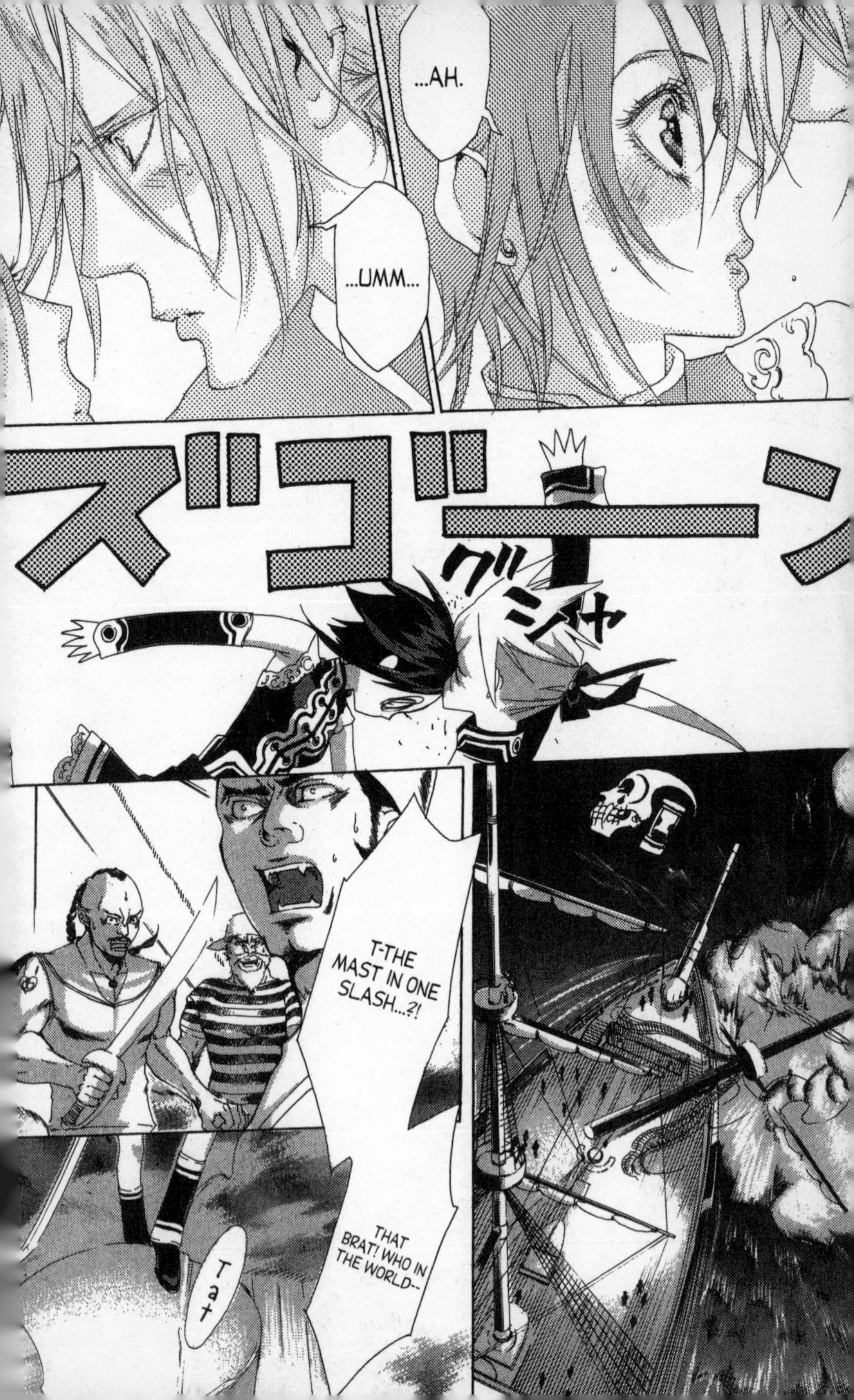
...AH.
...UMM...
ズゴーン
グシャ
T-THE MAST IN ONE SLASH...?!
THAT BRAT! WHO IN THE WORLD--
Tat

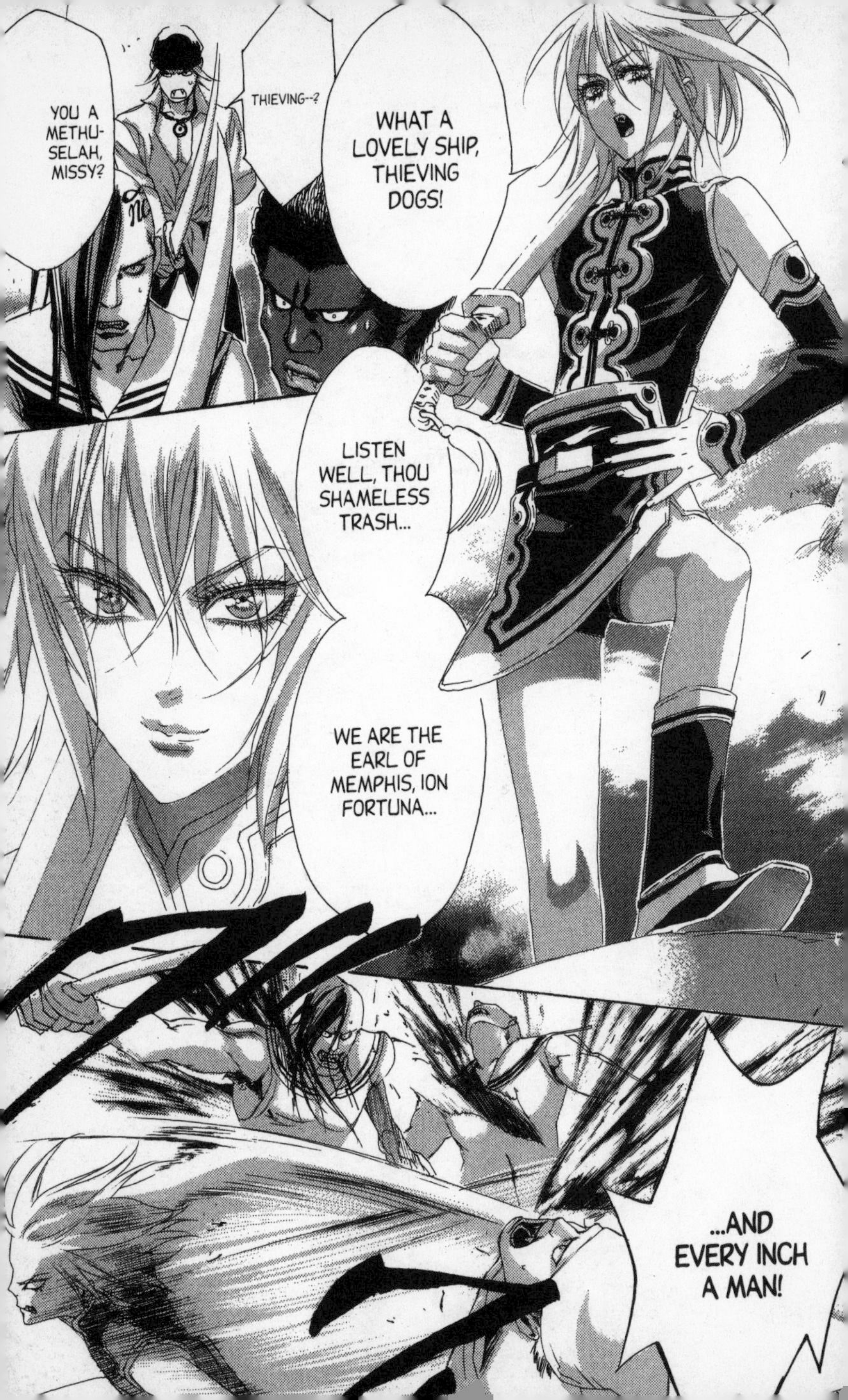
WHAT A LOVELY SHIP, THIEVING DOGS!
THIEVING--?
YOU A METHU-SELAH, MISSY?
LISTEN WELL, THOU SHAMELESS TRASH...
WE ARE THE EARL OF MEMPHIS, ION FORTUNA...
...AND EVERY INCH A MAN!

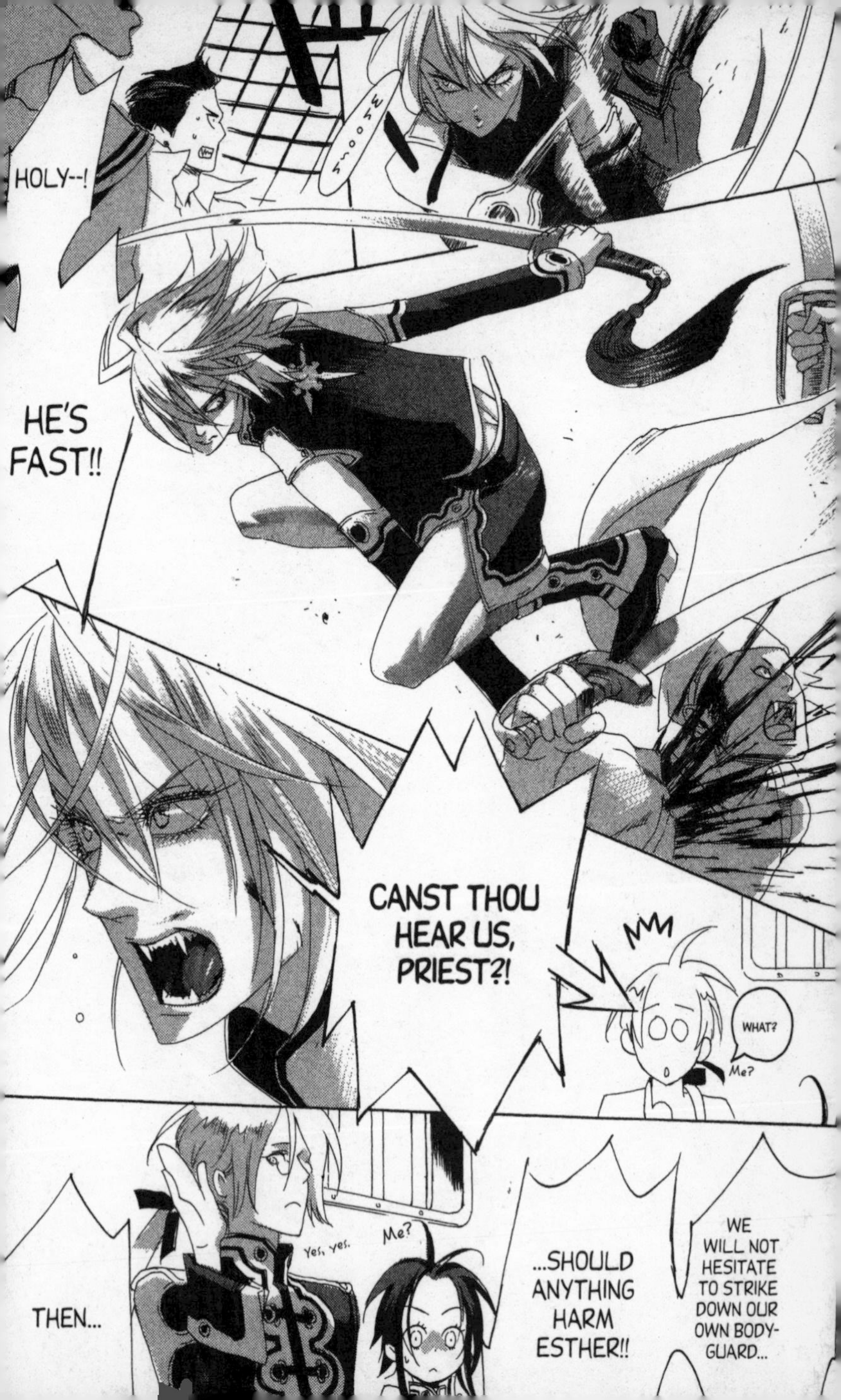

whoosh
HOLY--!
HE'S FAST!!
CANST THOU HEAR US, PRIEST?!
WHAT?
Me?
WE WILL NOT HESITATE TO STRIKE DOWN OUR OWN BODY-GUARD...
...SHOULD ANYTHING HARM ESTHER!!
Me?
Yes, yes.
THEN...

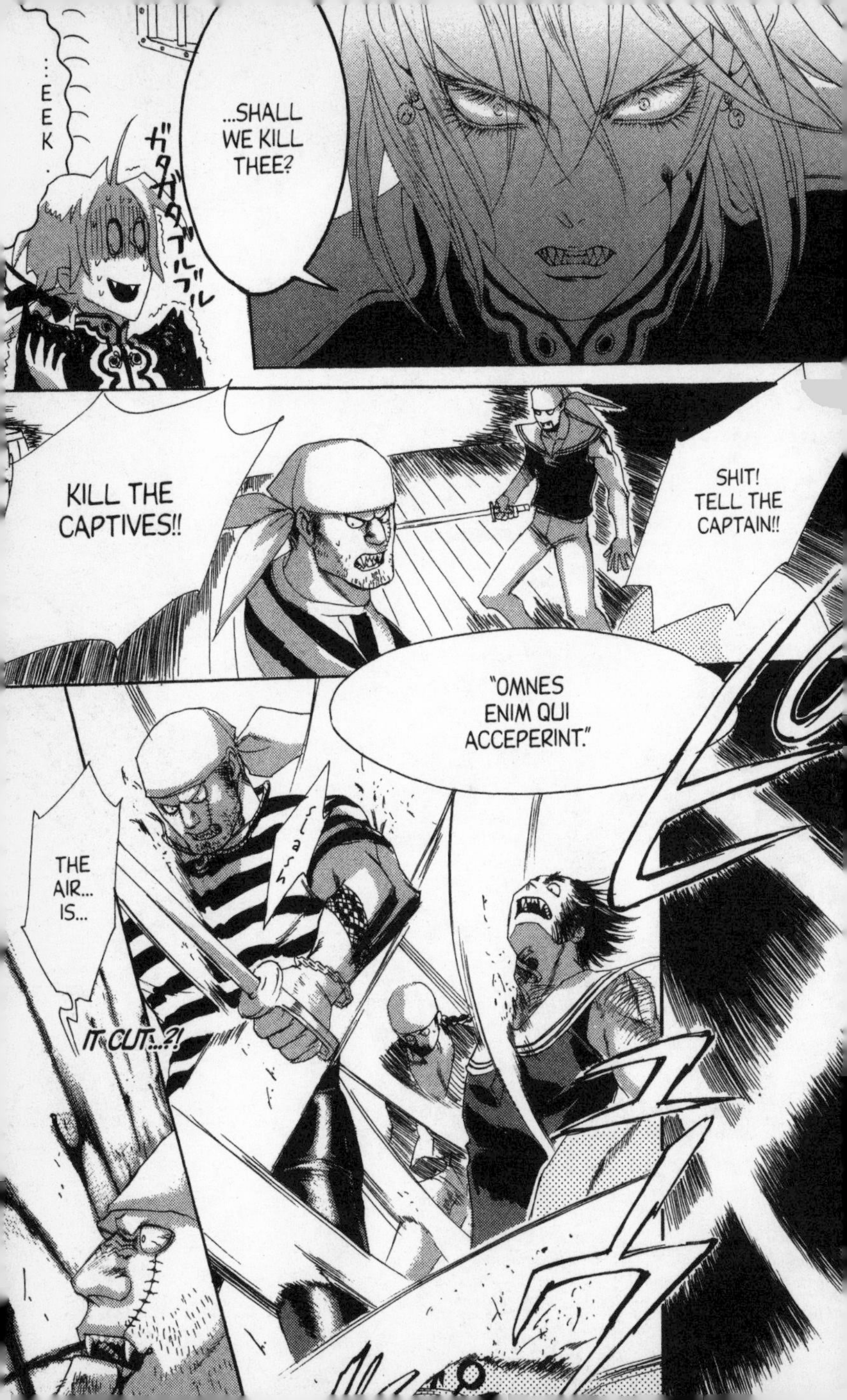
...SHALL WE KILL THEE?
...EEK ..
ガタガタブルブル
SHIT! TELL THE CAPTAIN!!
KILL THE CAPTIVES!!
"OMNES ENIM QUI ACCEPERINT."
slash
THE AIR... IS...
IT CUT...?!

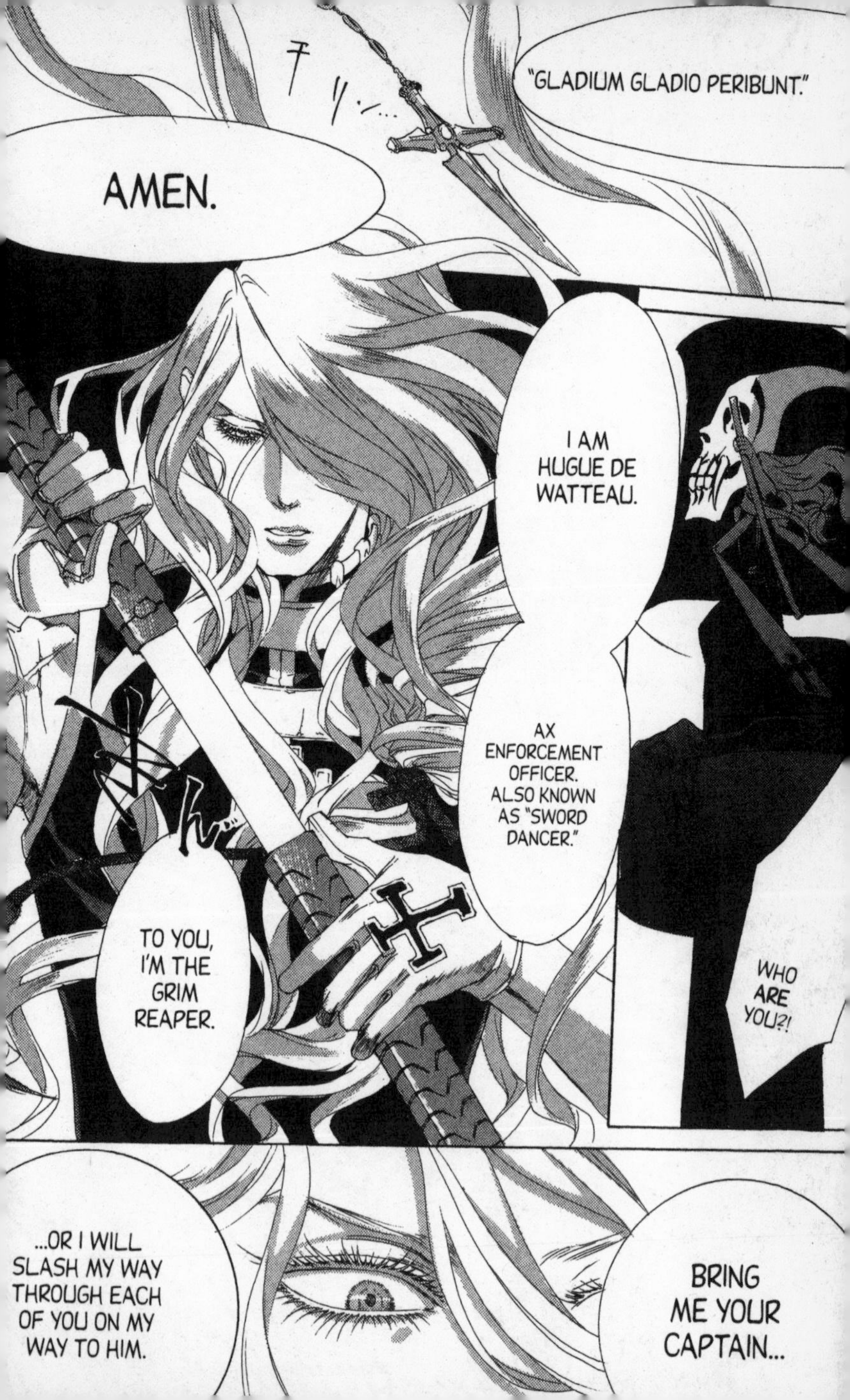
"GLADIUM GLADIO PERIBUNT."
AMEN.
WHO ARE YOU?!
I AM HUGUE DE WATTEAU.
AX ENFORCEMENT OFFICER. ALSO KNOWN AS "SWORD DANCER."
TO YOU, I'M THE GRIM REAPER.
BRING ME YOUR CAPTAIN...
...OR I WILL SLASH MY WAY THROUGH EACH OF YOU ON MY WAY TO HIM.

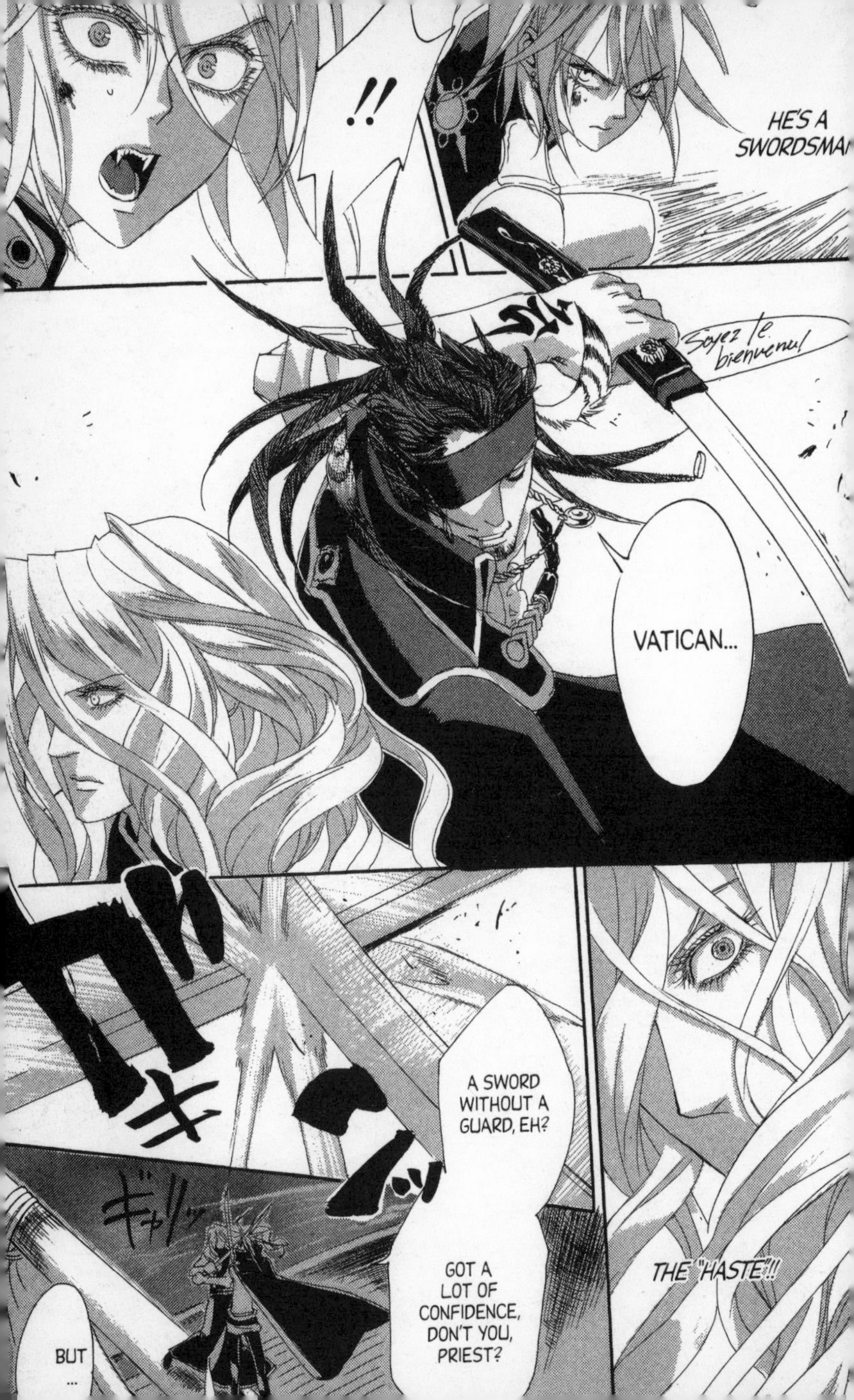
HE'S A SWORDSMA
!!
Soyez le bienvenu!
VATICAN...
THE "HASTE"!!
ガキッ
A SWORD WITHOUT A GUARD, EH?
ギャリッ
GOT A LOT OF CONFIDENCE, DON'T YOU, PRIEST?
BUT ...

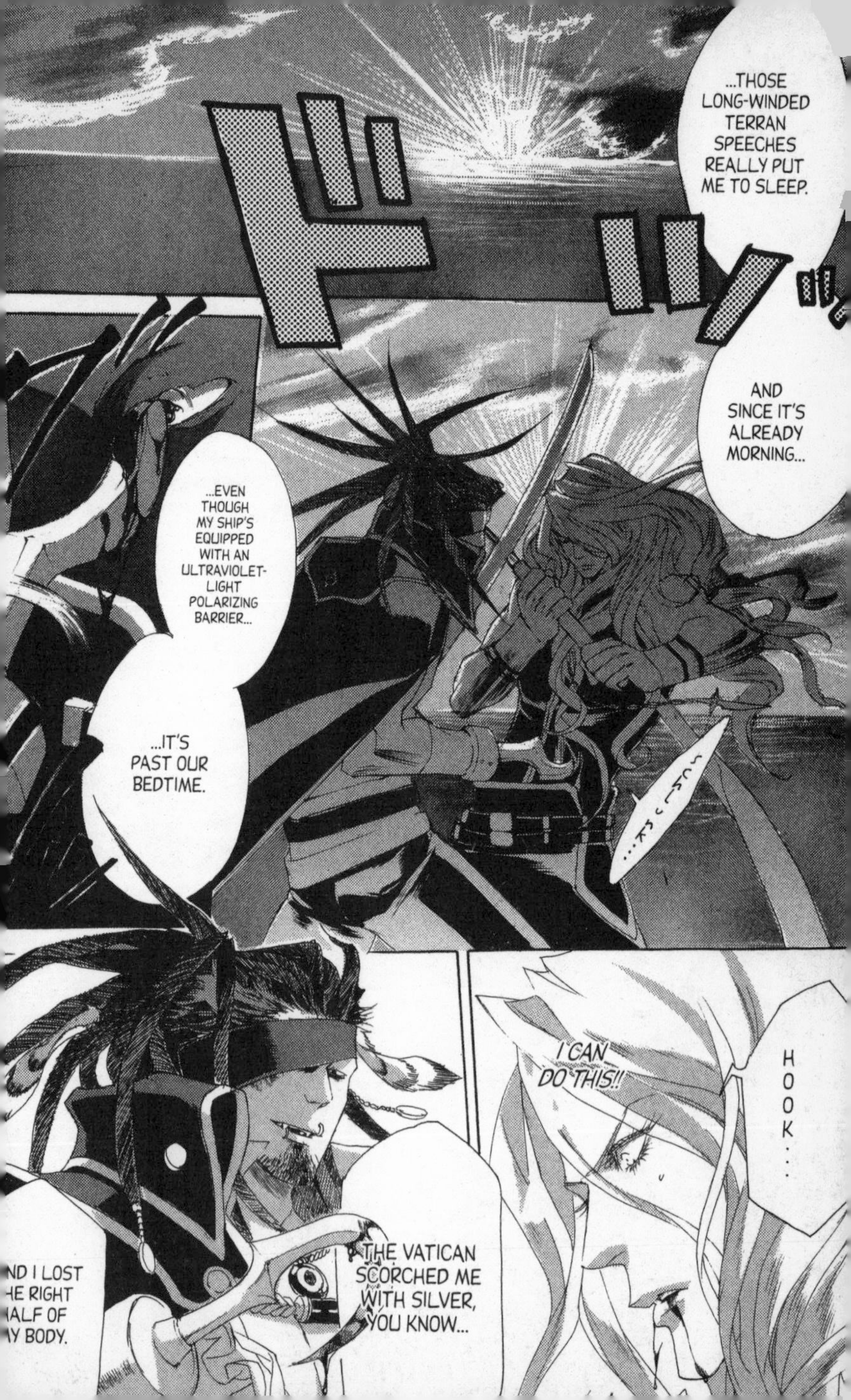
...THOSE LONG-WINDED TERRAN SPEECHES REALLY PUT ME TO SLEEP.
AND SINCE IT'S ALREADY MORNING...
...EVEN THOUGH MY SHIP'S EQUIPPED WITH AN ULTRAVIOLET-LIGHT POLARIZING BARRIER...
...IT'S PAST OUR BEDTIME.
HOOK...
I CAN DO THIS!!
THE VATICAN SCORCHED ME WITH SILVER, YOU KNOW...
ND I LOST HE RIGHT ALF OF Y BODY.

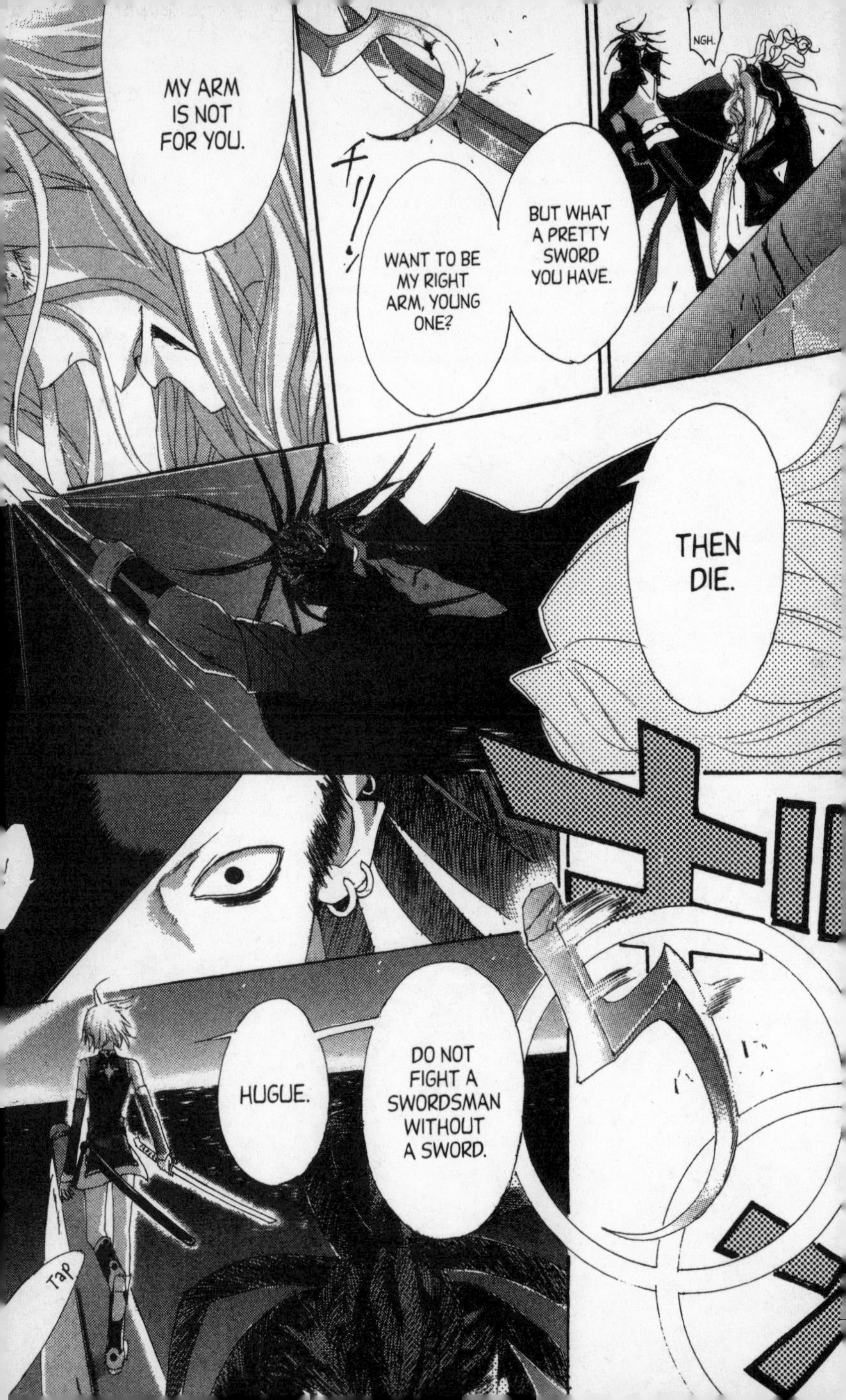
NGH.
BUT WHAT A PRETTY SWORD YOU HAVE.
WANT TO BE MY RIGHT ARM, YOUNG ONE?
MY ARM IS NOT FOR YOU.
THEN DIE.
DO NOT FIGHT A SWORDSMAN WITHOUT A SWORD.
HUGUE.
Tap

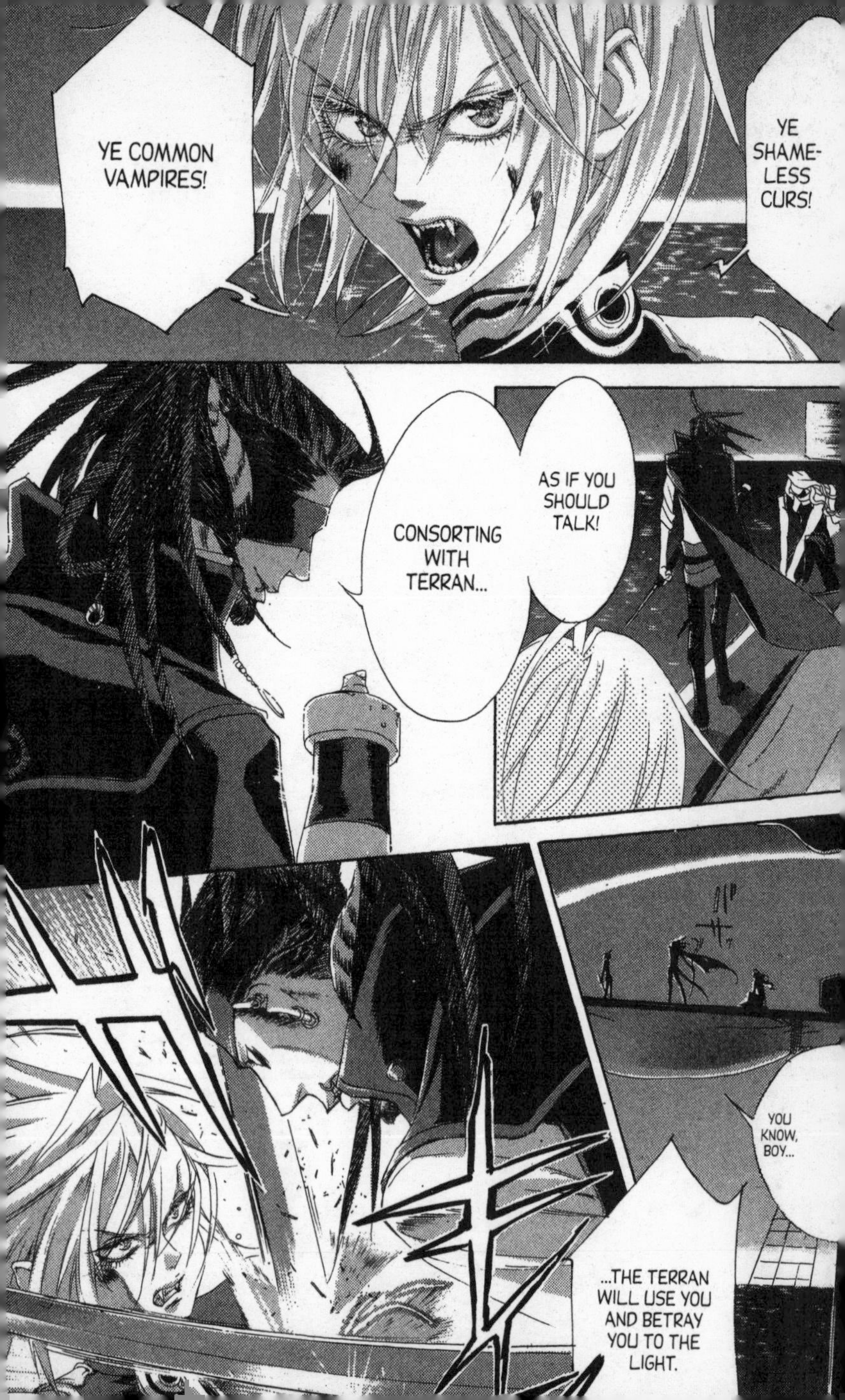
YE SHAME-LESS CURS!
YE COMMON VAMPIRES!
AS IF YOU SHOULD TALK!
CONSORTING WITH TERRAN...
YOU KNOW, BOY...
...THE TERRAN WILL USE YOU AND BETRAY YOU TO THE LIGHT.

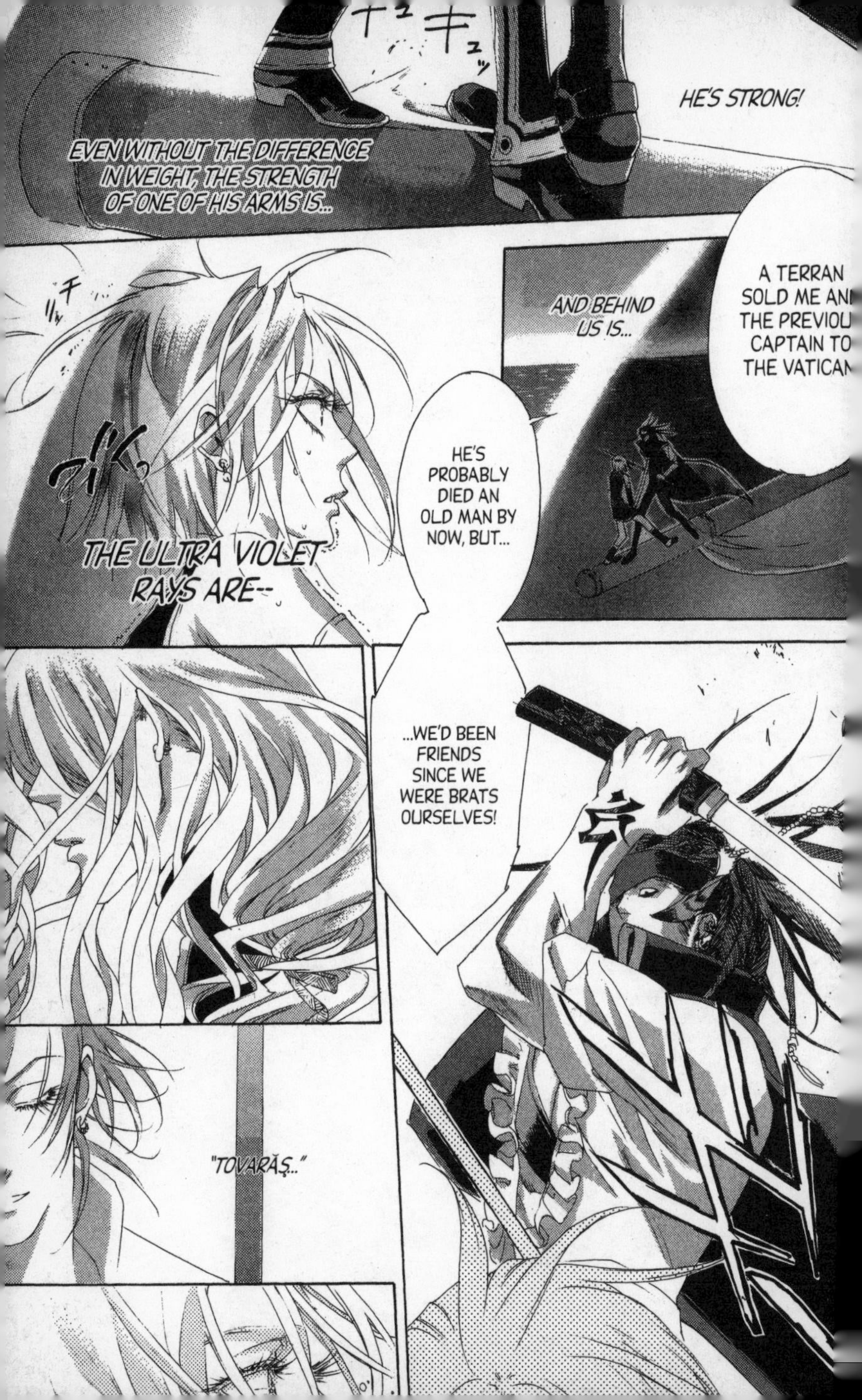

HE'S STRONG!
EVEN WITHOUT THE DIFFERENCE IN WEIGHT, THE STRENGTH OF ONE OF HIS ARMS IS...
A TERRAN SOLD ME AN THE PREVIOU CAPTAIN TO THE VATICAN
AND BEHIND US IS...
HE'S PROBABLY DIED AN OLD MAN BY NOW, BUT...
THE ULTRA VIOLET RAYS ARE--
...WE'D BEEN FRIENDS SINCE WE WERE BRATS OURSELVES!
"TOVARĂŞ..."

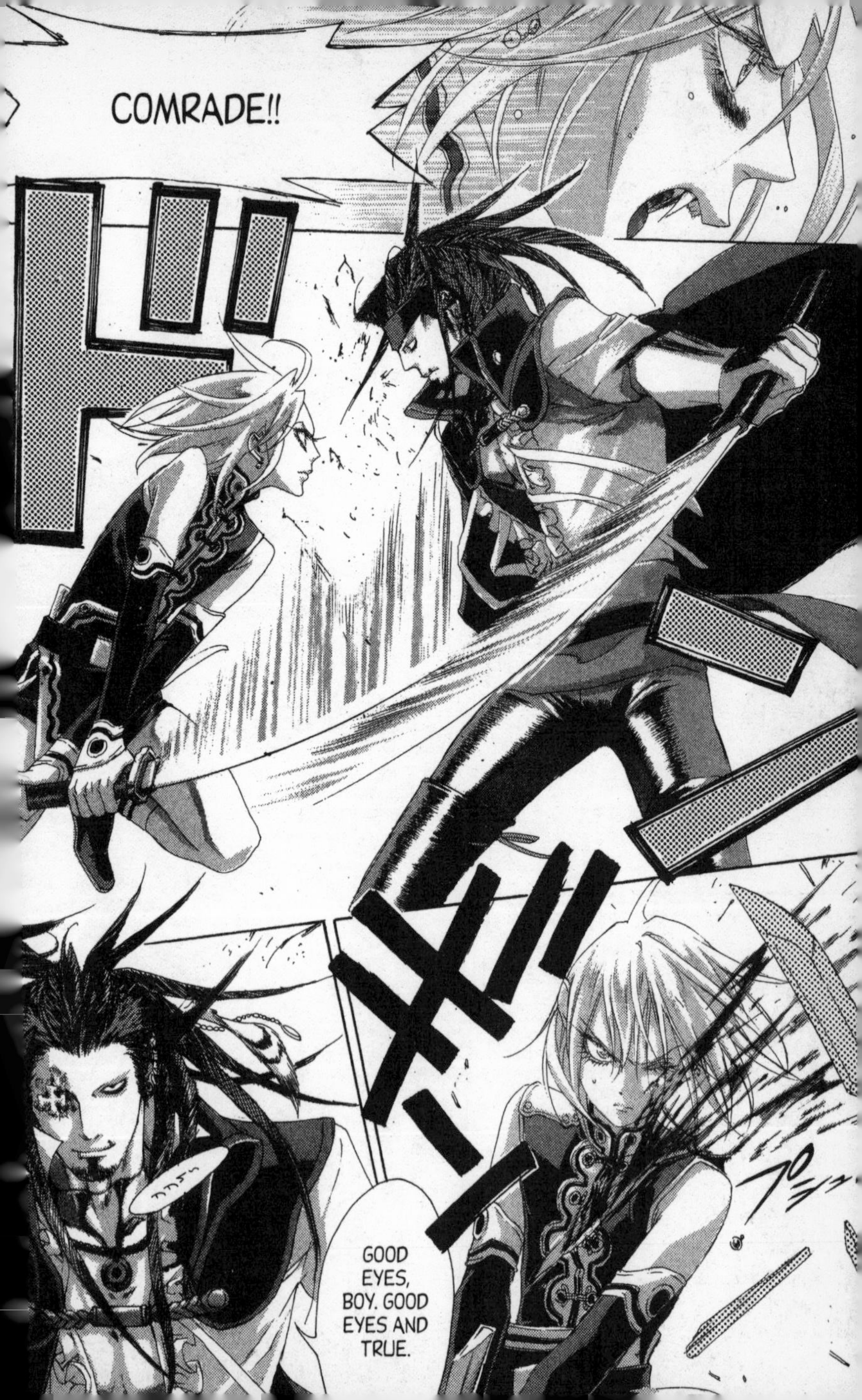
COMRADE!!
GOOD EYES, BOY. GOOD EYES AND TRUE.

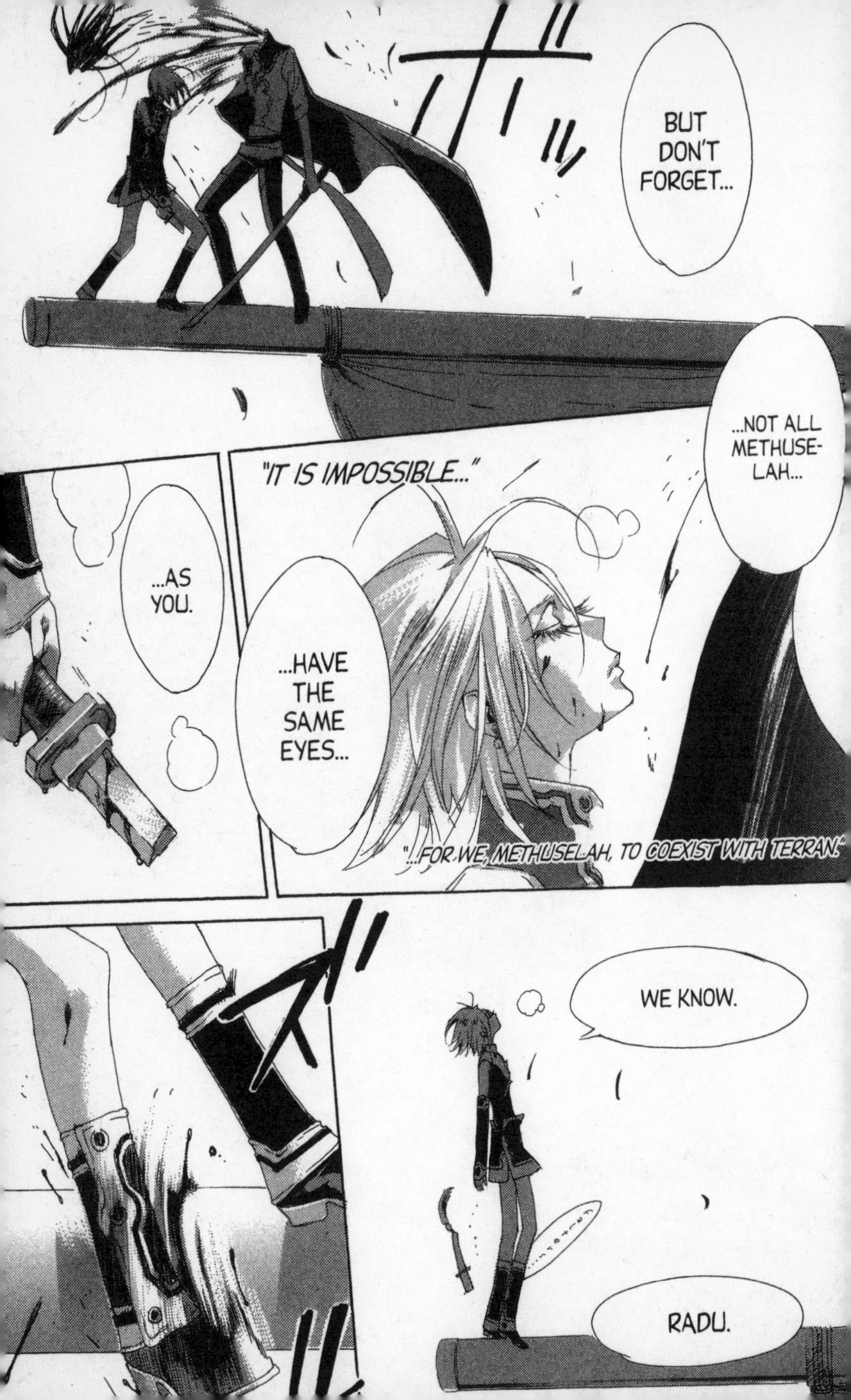
BUT DON'T FORGET...
...NOT ALL METHUSELAH...
"IT IS IMPOSSIBLE..."
...HAVE THE SAME EYES...
"...FOR WE, METHUSELAH, TO COEXIST WITH TERRAN."
...AS YOU.
WE KNOW.
RADU.

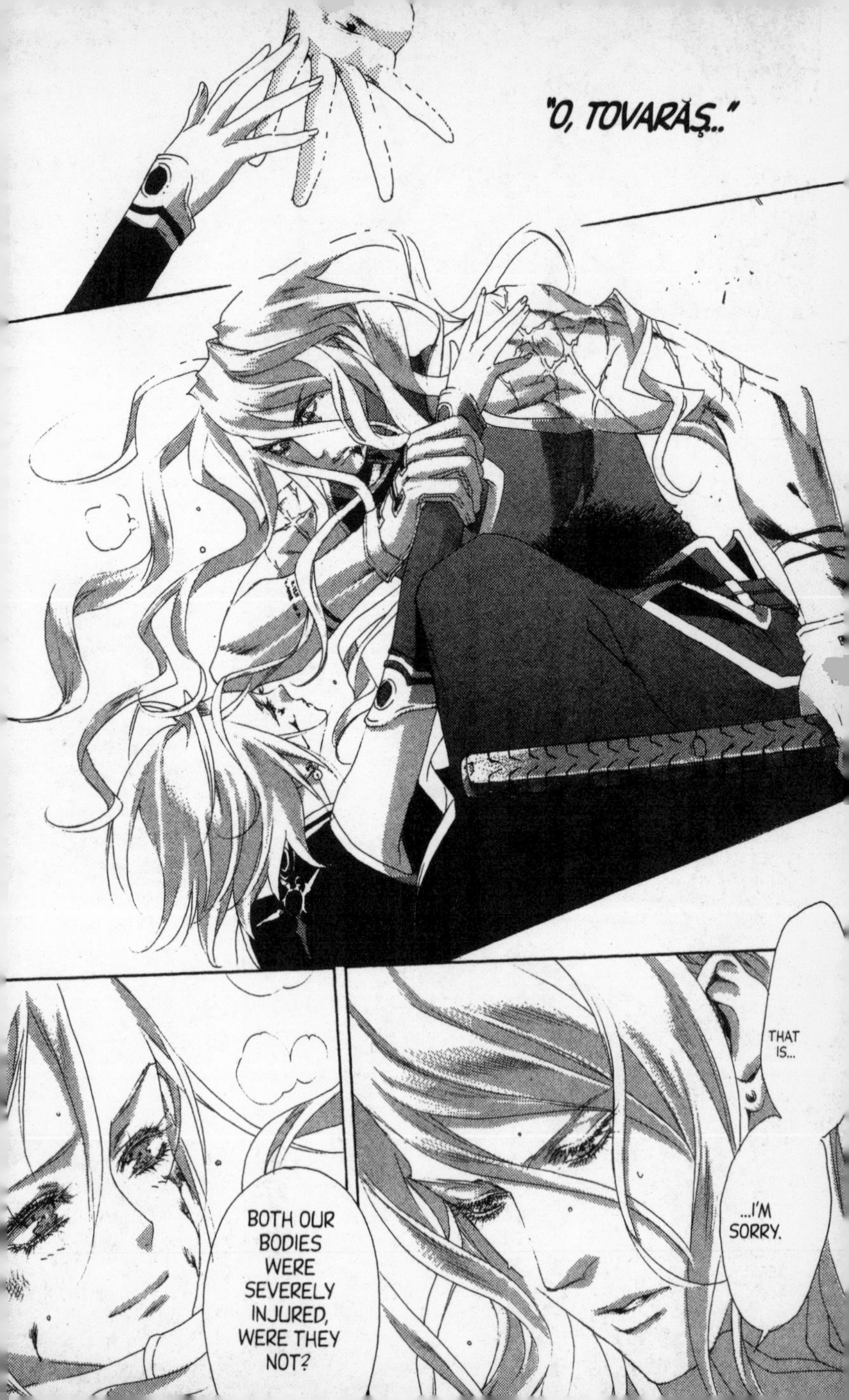
"O, TOVARĂȘ.."
THAT IS...
...I'M SORRY.
BOTH OUR BODIES WERE SEVERELY INJURED, WERE THEY NOT?

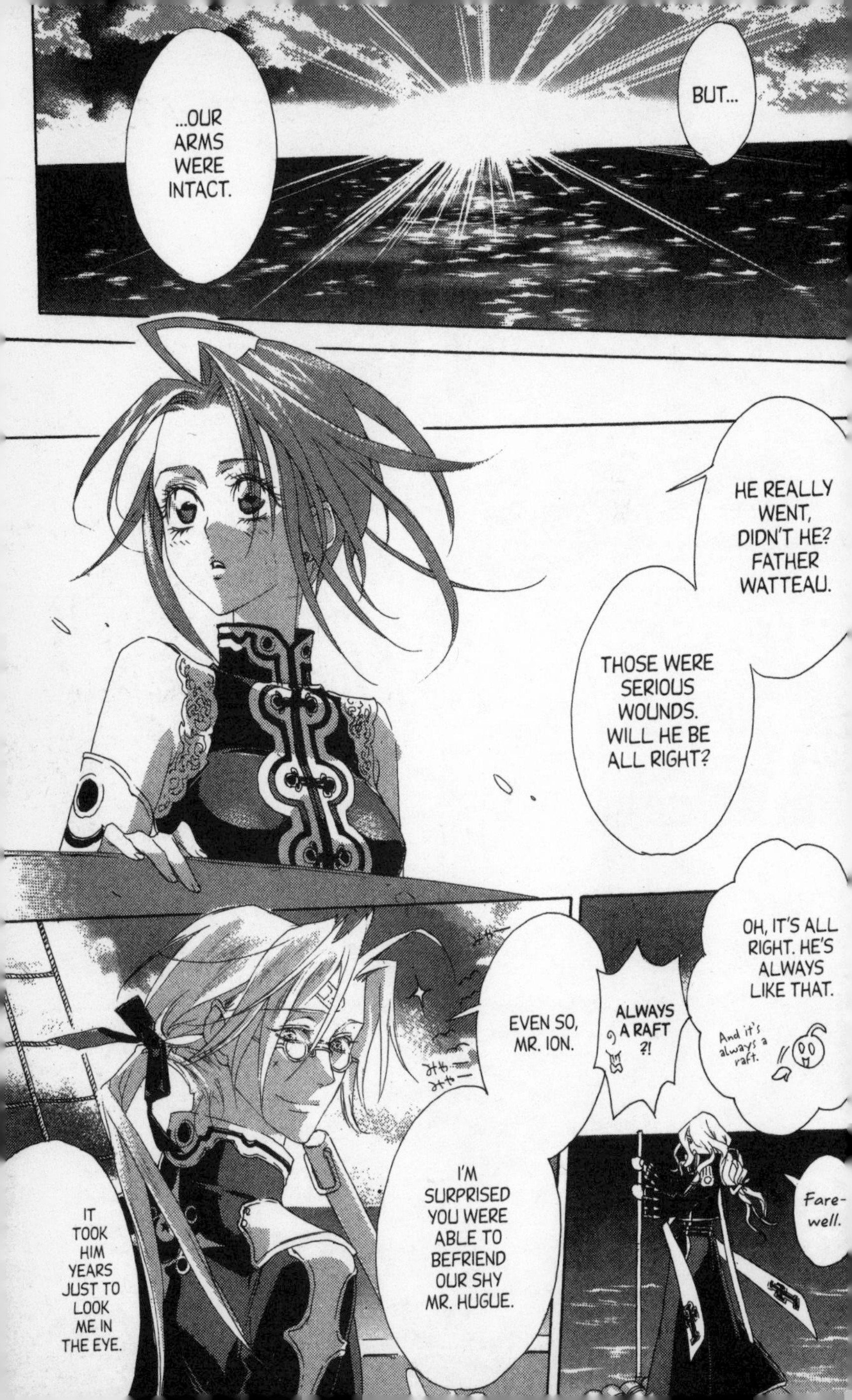
BUT...
...OUR ARMS WERE INTACT.
HE REALLY WENT, DIDN'T HE? FATHER WATTEAU.
THOSE WERE SERIOUS WOUNDS. WILL HE BE ALL RIGHT?
OH, IT'S ALL RIGHT. HE'S ALWAYS LIKE THAT.
And it's always a raft.
ALWAYS A RAFT ?!
Fare-well.
EVEN SO, MR. ION.
I'M SURPRISED YOU WERE ABLE TO BEFRIEND OUR SHY MR. HUGUE.
IT TOOK HIM YEARS JUST TO LOOK ME IN THE EYE.

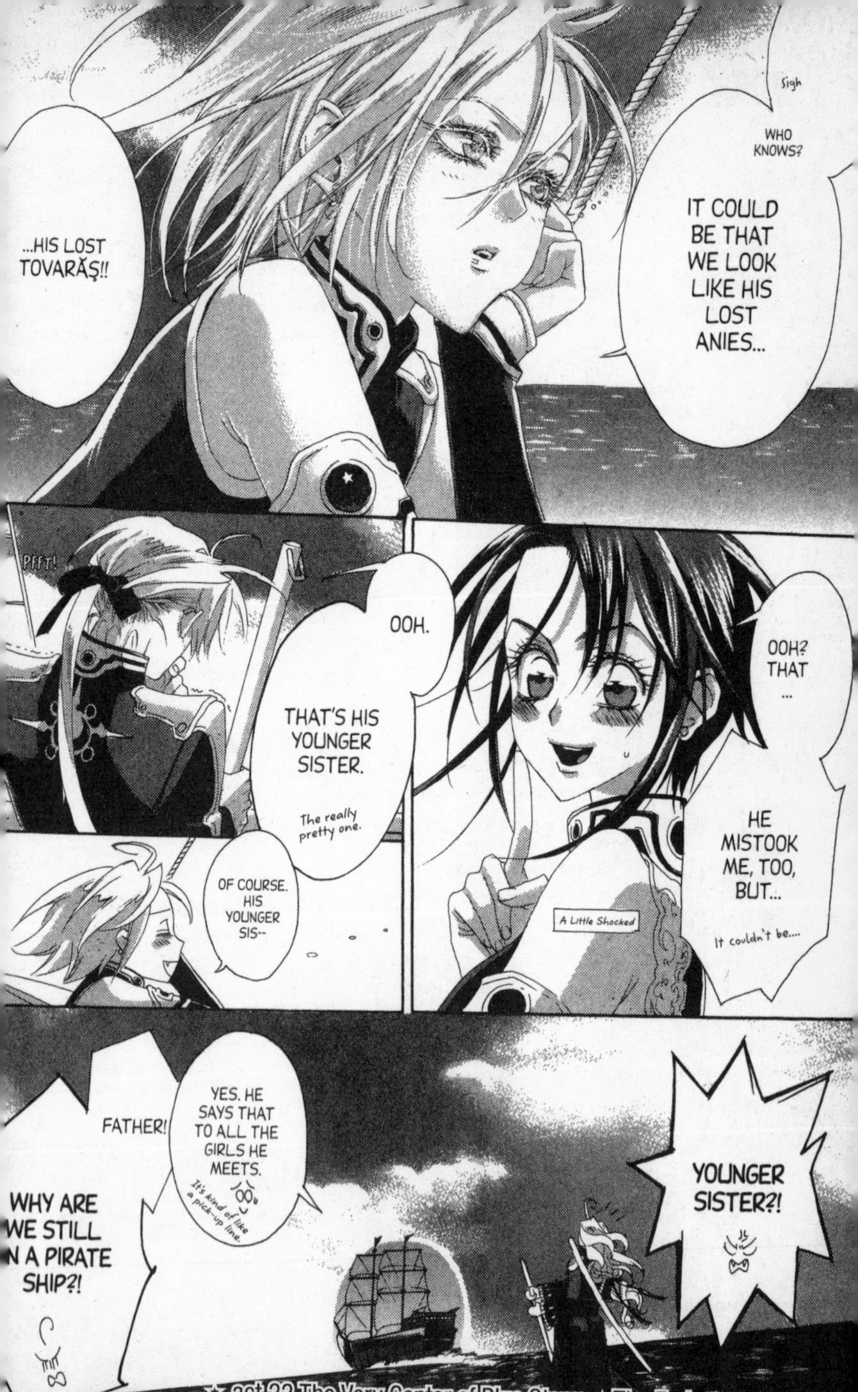
Sigh
WHO KNOWS?
IT COULD BE THAT WE LOOK LIKE HIS LOST ANIES...
...HIS LOST TOVARĂŞ!!
OOH? THAT ...
HE MISTOOK ME, TOO, BUT...
It couldn't be....
A Little Shocked
PFFT!
OOH.
THAT'S HIS YOUNGER SISTER.
The really pretty one.
OF COURSE. HIS YOUNGER SIS--
YOUNGER SISTER?!
YES. HE SAYS THAT TO ALL THE GIRLS HE MEETS.
It's kind of like a pick-up line.
FATHER!
WHY ARE WE STILL N A PIRATE SHIP?!
★ act.22 The Very Center of Blue Storm ★ The End

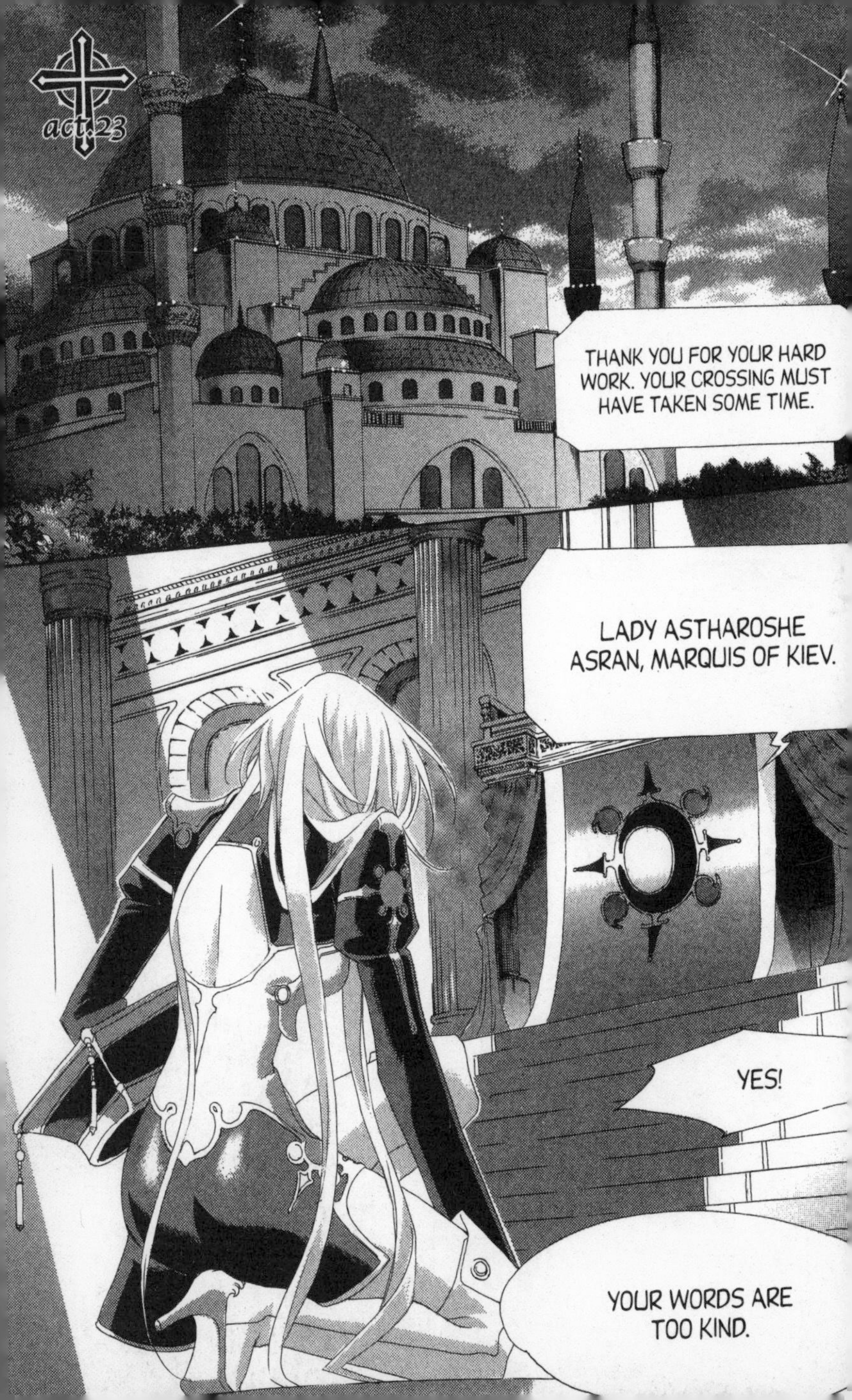
act.23
THANK YOU FOR YOUR HARD WORK. YOUR CROSSING MUST HAVE TAKEN SOME TIME.
LADY ASTHAROSHE ASRAN, MARQUIS OF KIEV.
YES!
YOUR WORDS ARE TOO KIND.

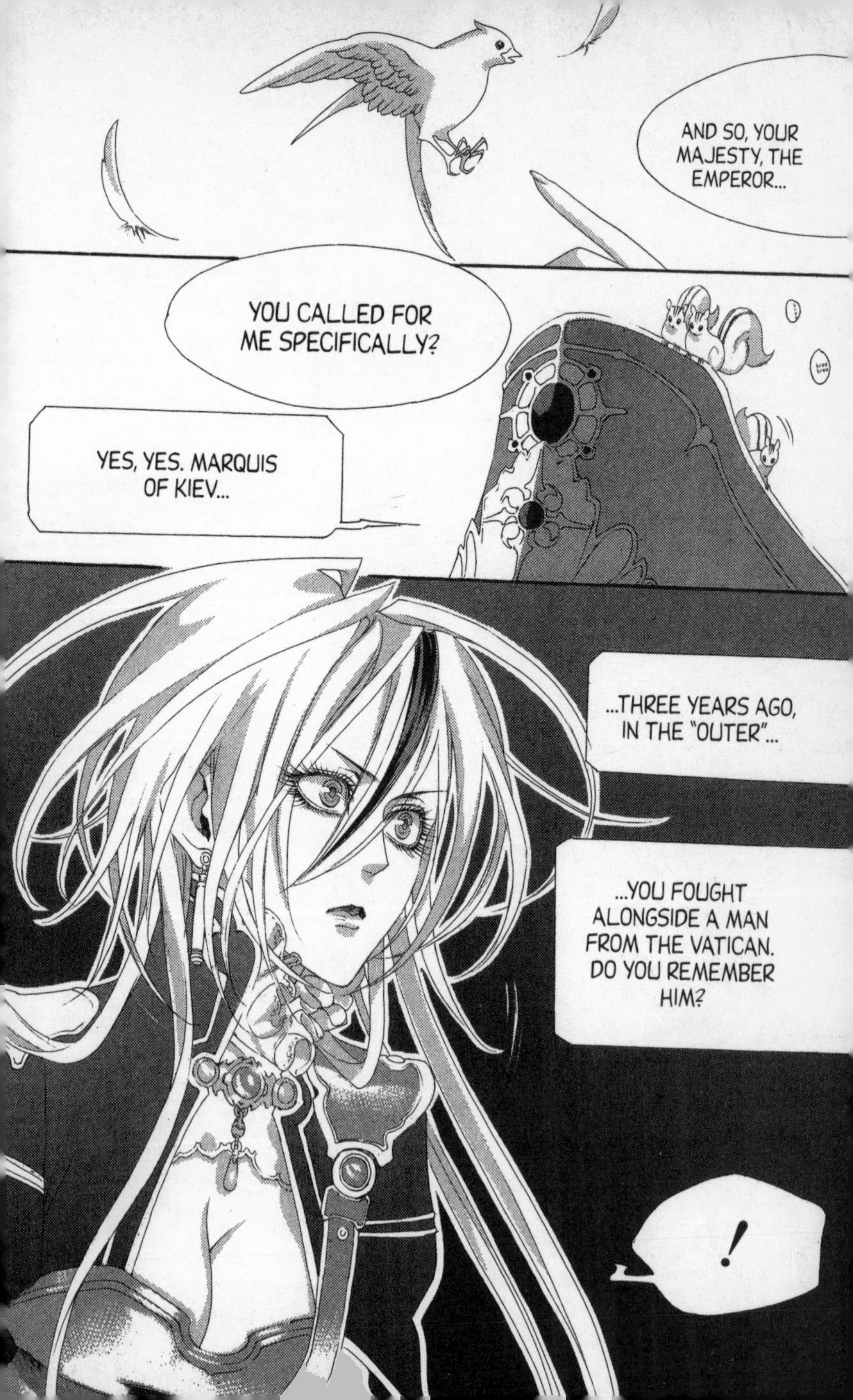
AND SO, YOUR MAJESTY, THE EMPEROR...
YOU CALLED FOR ME SPECIFICALLY?
kree kree
YES, YES. MARQUIS OF KIEV...
...THREE YEARS AGO, IN THE "OUTER"...
...YOU FOUGHT ALONGSIDE A MAN FROM THE VATICAN. DO YOU REMEMBER HIM?
!

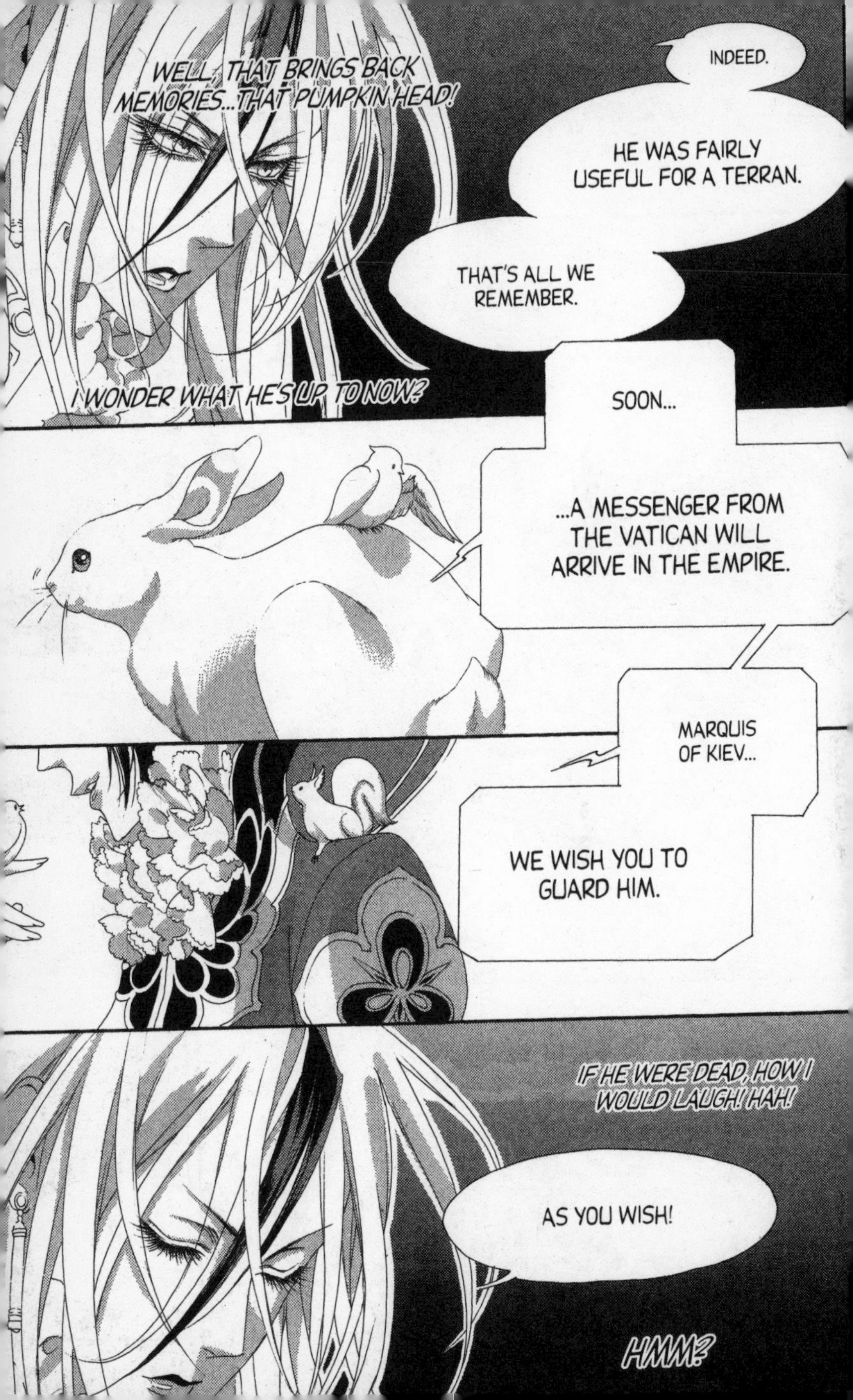
INDEED.
HE WAS FAIRLY USEFUL FOR A TERRAN.
WELL, THAT BRINGS BACK MEMORIES...THAT PUMPKIN HEAD!
THAT'S ALL WE REMEMBER.
I WONDER WHAT HE'S UP TO NOW?
SOON...
...A MESSENGER FROM THE VATICAN WILL ARRIVE IN THE EMPIRE.
MARQUIS OF KIEV...
WE WISH YOU TO GUARD HIM.
IF HE WERE DEAD, HOW I WOULD LAUGH! HAH!
AS YOU WISH!
HMM?

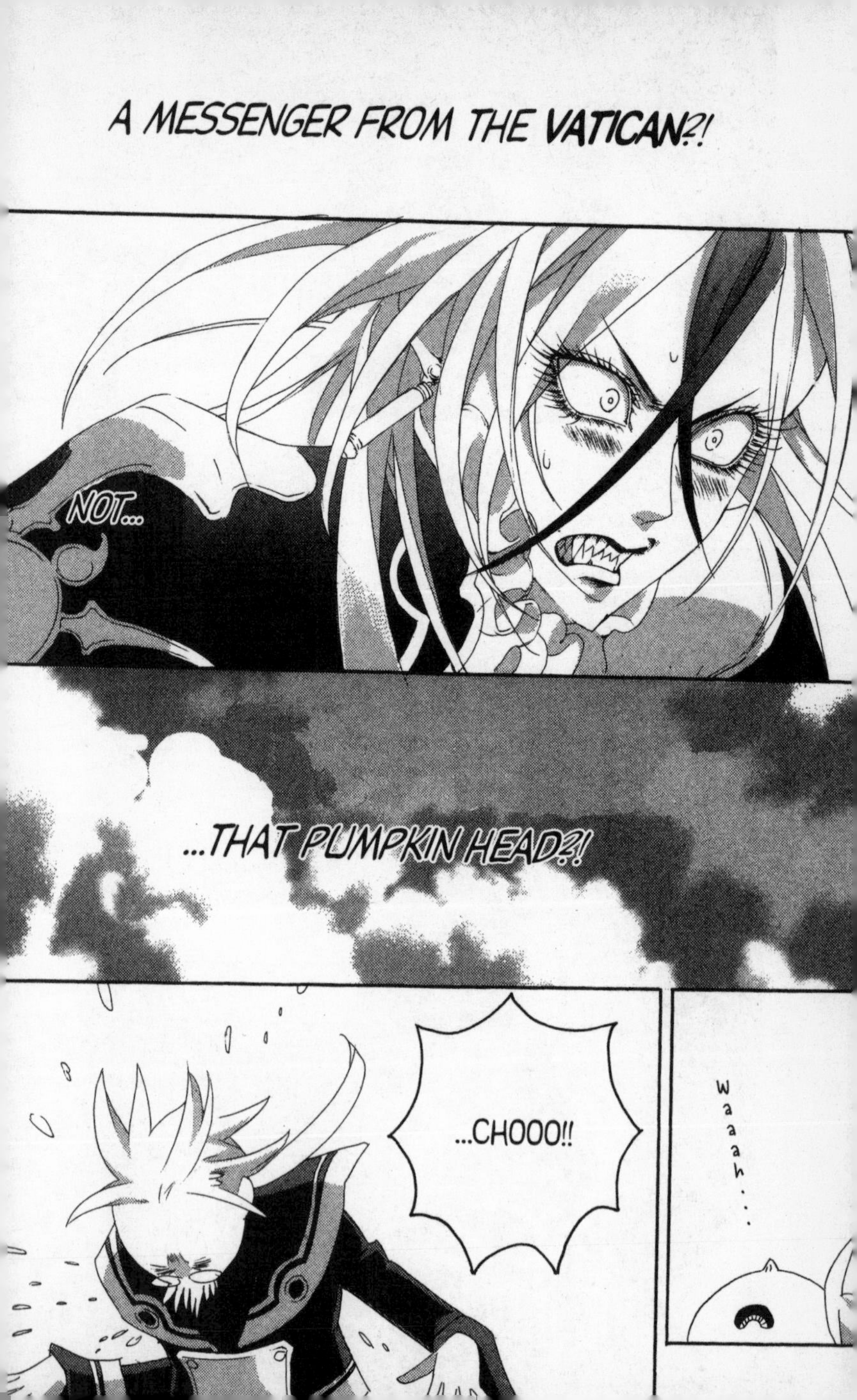
A MESSENGER FROM THE VATICAN?!
NOT...
...THAT PUMPKIN HEAD?!
Waaah...
...CHOOO!!

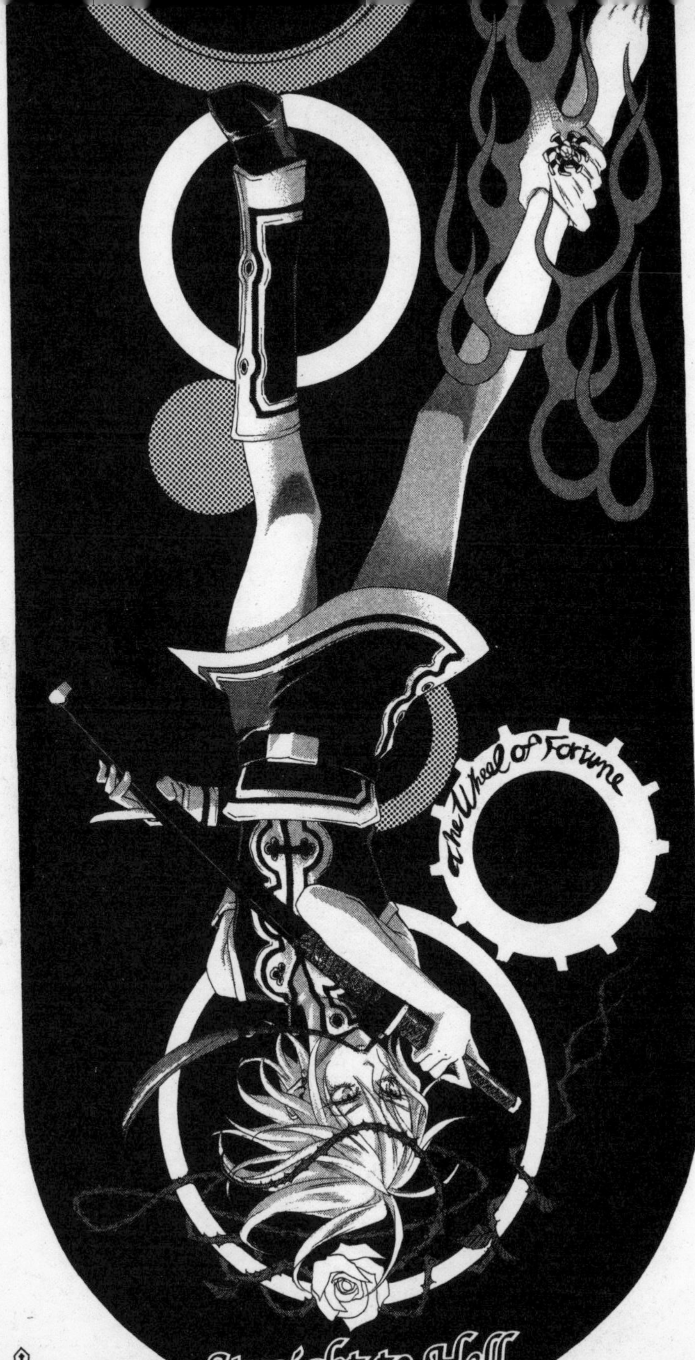
the Wheel of Fortune

act.23 Straight to Hell

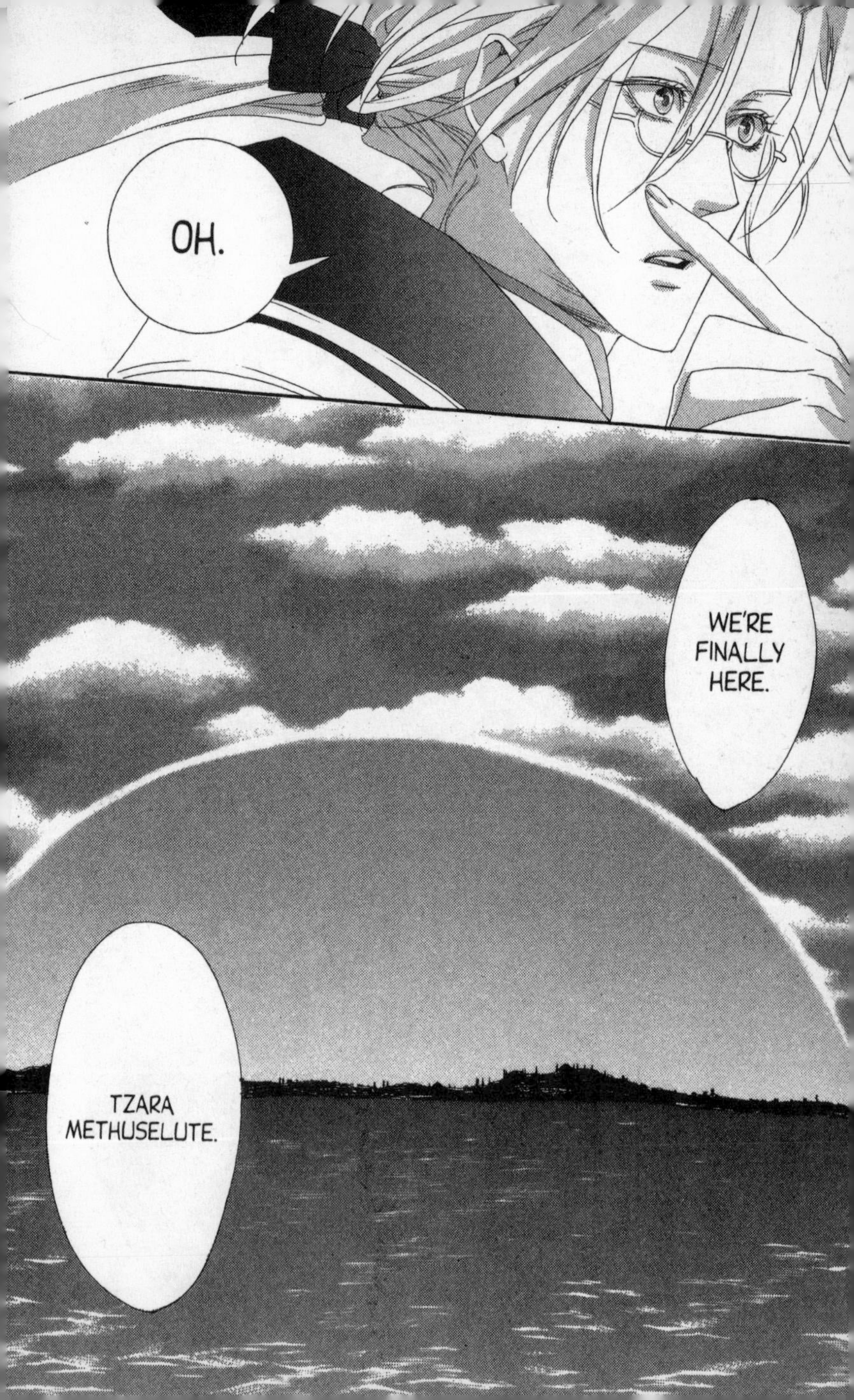
OH.
WE'RE FINALLY HERE.
TZARA METHUSELUTE.

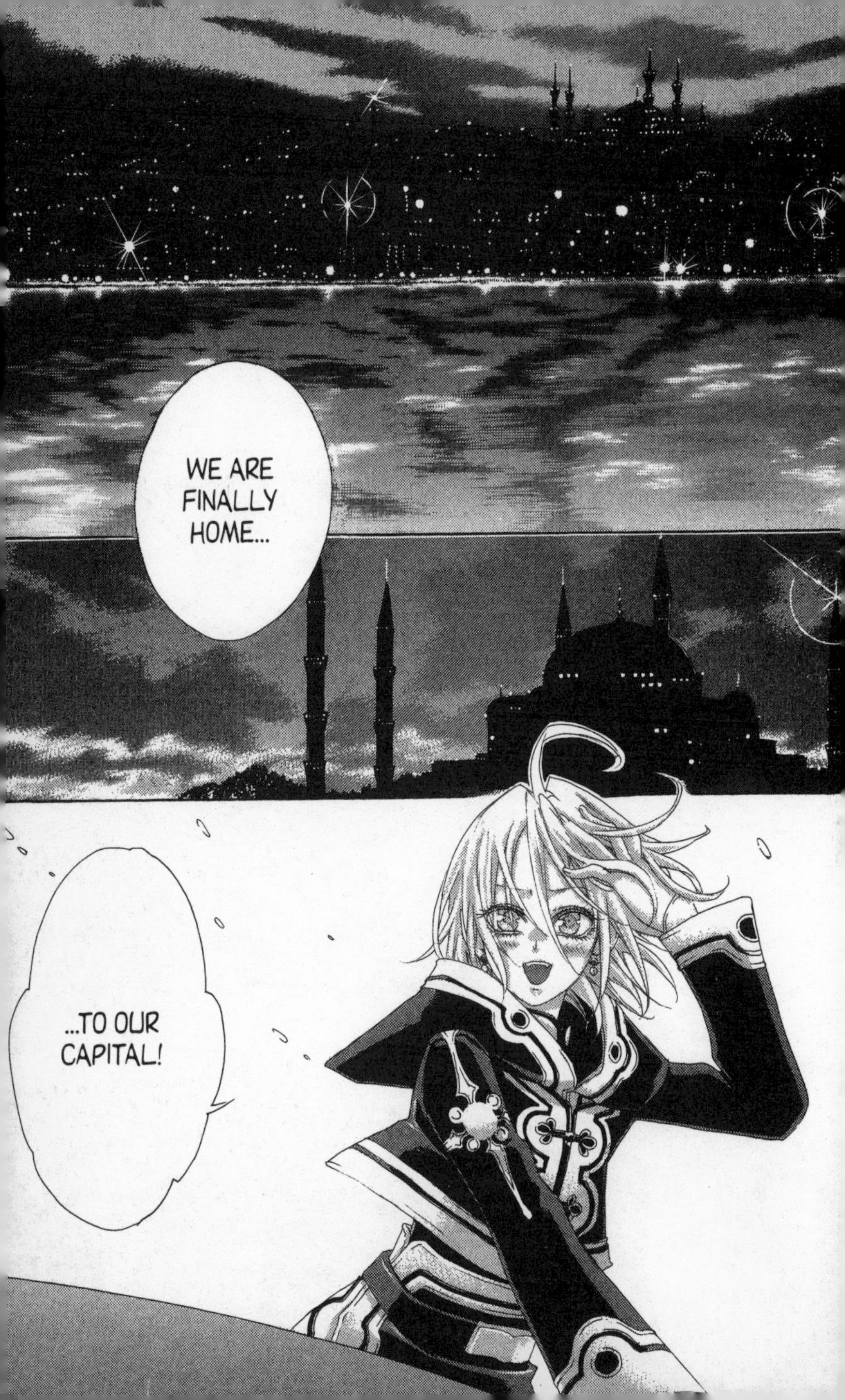
WE ARE FINALLY HOME...
...TO OUR CAPITAL!

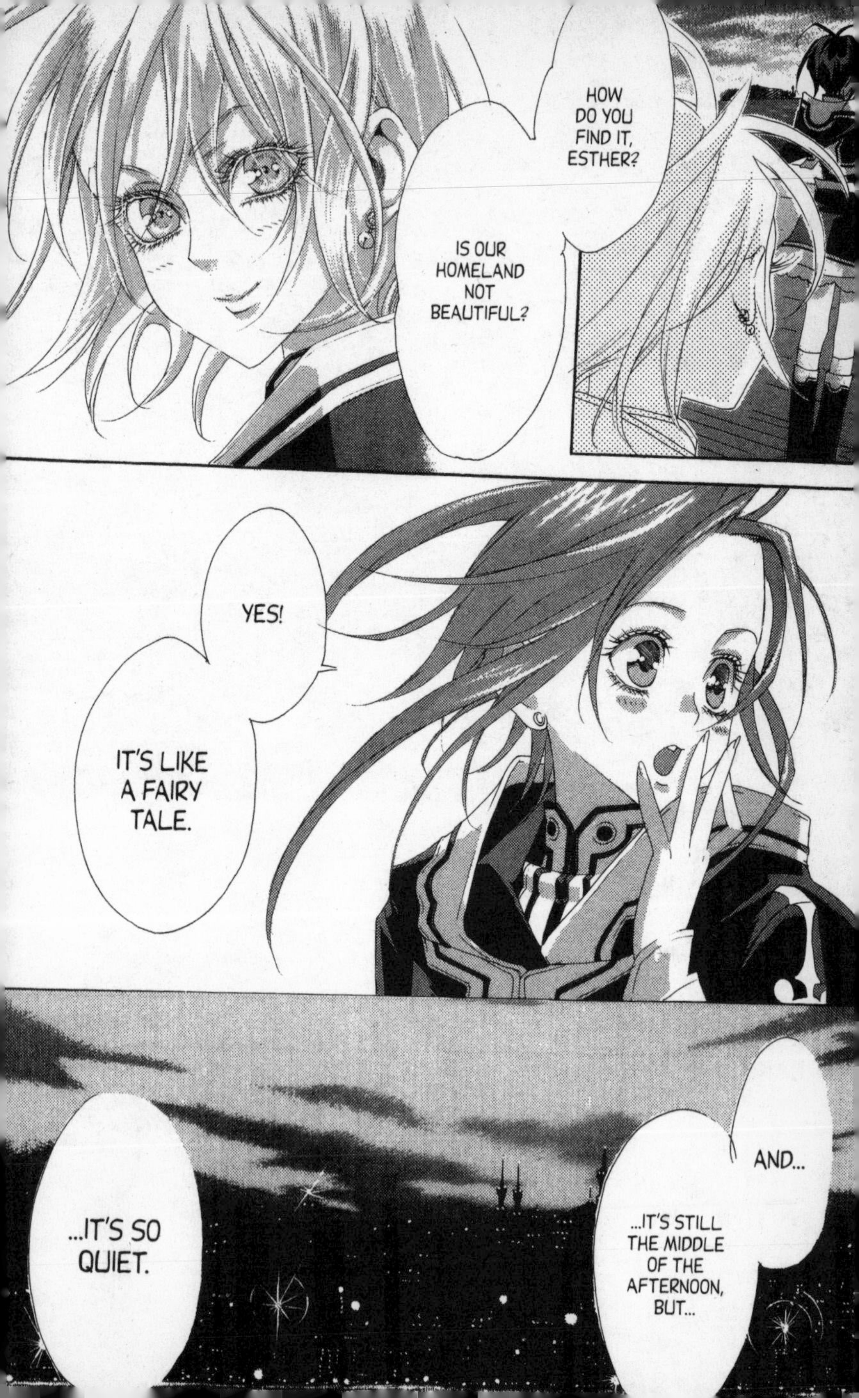
HOW DO YOU FIND IT, ESTHER?
IS OUR HOMELAND NOT BEAUTIFUL?
YES!
IT'S LIKE A FAIRY TALE.
AND...
...IT'S STILL THE MIDDLE OF THE AFTERNOON, BUT...
...IT'S SO QUIET.

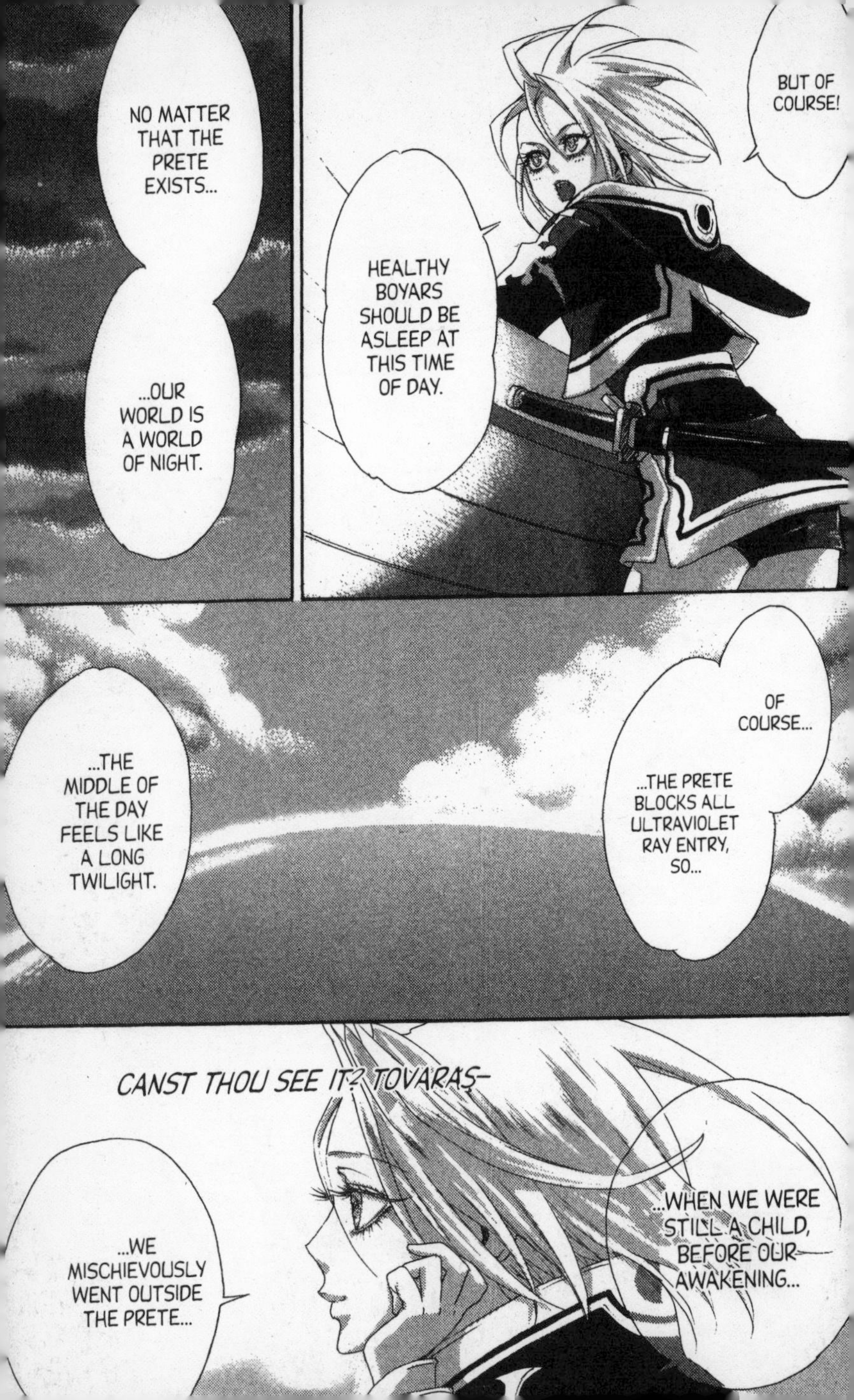
BUT OF COURSE!
HEALTHY BOYARS SHOULD BE ASLEEP AT THIS TIME OF DAY.
NO MATTER THAT THE PRETE EXISTS...
...OUR WORLD IS A WORLD OF NIGHT.
OF COURSE...
...THE PRETE BLOCKS ALL ULTRAVIOLET RAY ENTRY, SO...
...THE MIDDLE OF THE DAY FEELS LIKE A LONG TWILIGHT.
CANST THOU SEE IT? TOVARAS—
...WHEN WE WERE STILL A CHILD, BEFORE OUR AWAKENING...
...WE MISCHIEVOUSLY WENT OUTSIDE THE PRETE...

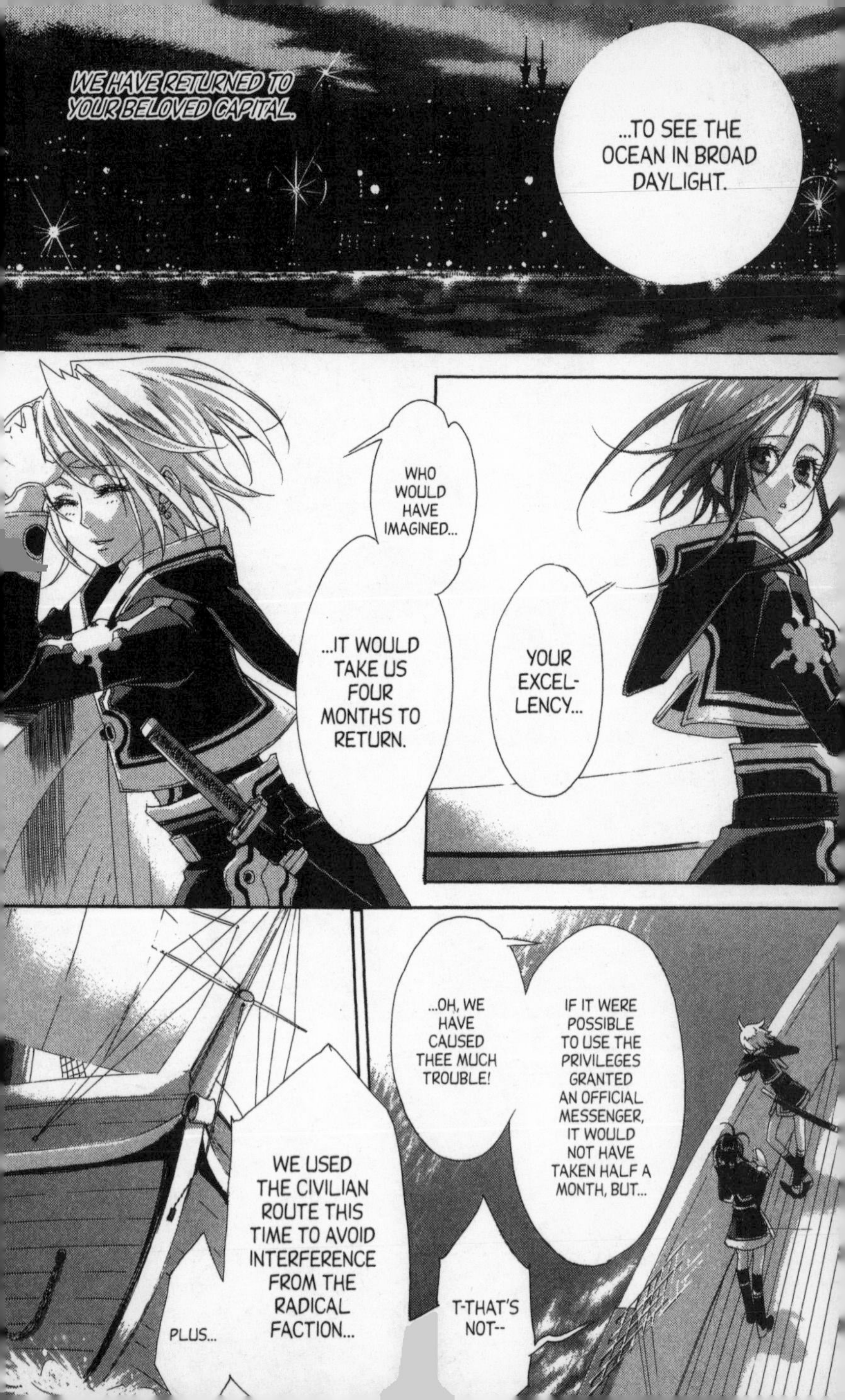
...TO SEE THE OCEAN IN BROAD DAYLIGHT.
WE HAVE RETURNED TO YOUR BELOVED CAPITAL.
YOUR EXCELLENCY...
WHO WOULD HAVE IMAGINED...
...IT WOULD TAKE US FOUR MONTHS TO RETURN.
IF IT WERE POSSIBLE TO USE THE PRIVILEGES GRANTED AN OFFICIAL MESSENGER, IT WOULD NOT HAVE TAKEN HALF A MONTH, BUT...
...OH, WE HAVE CAUSED THEE MUCH TROUBLE!
T-THAT'S NOT--
WE USED THE CIVILIAN ROUTE THIS TIME TO AVOID INTERFERENCE FROM THE RADICAL FACTION...
PLUS...

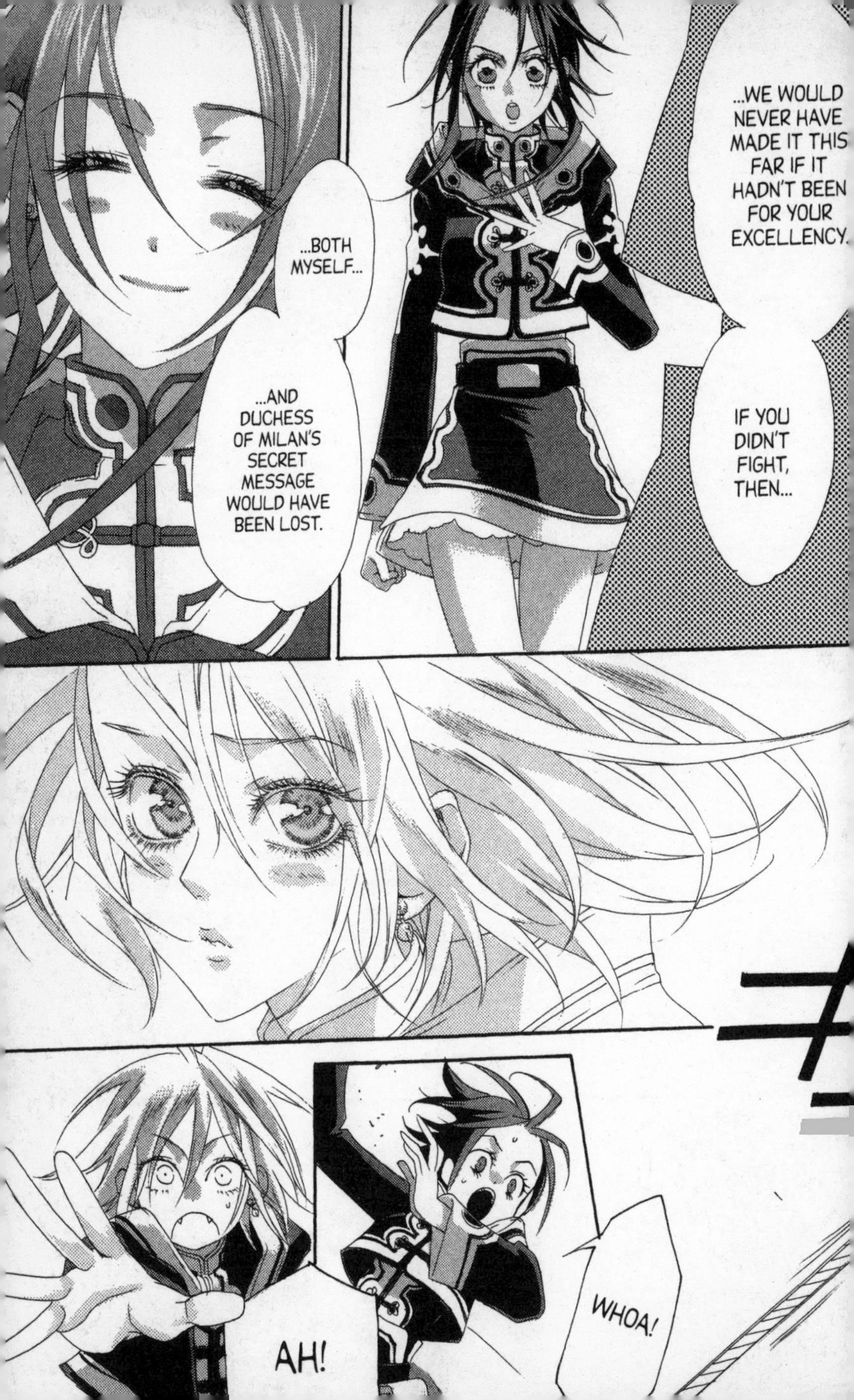
...WE WOULD NEVER HAVE MADE IT THIS FAR IF IT HADN'T BEEN FOR YOUR EXCELLENCY.
IF YOU DIDN'T FIGHT, THEN...
...BOTH MYSELF...
...AND DUCHESS OF MILAN'S SECRET MESSAGE WOULD HAVE BEEN LOST.
WHOA!
AH!

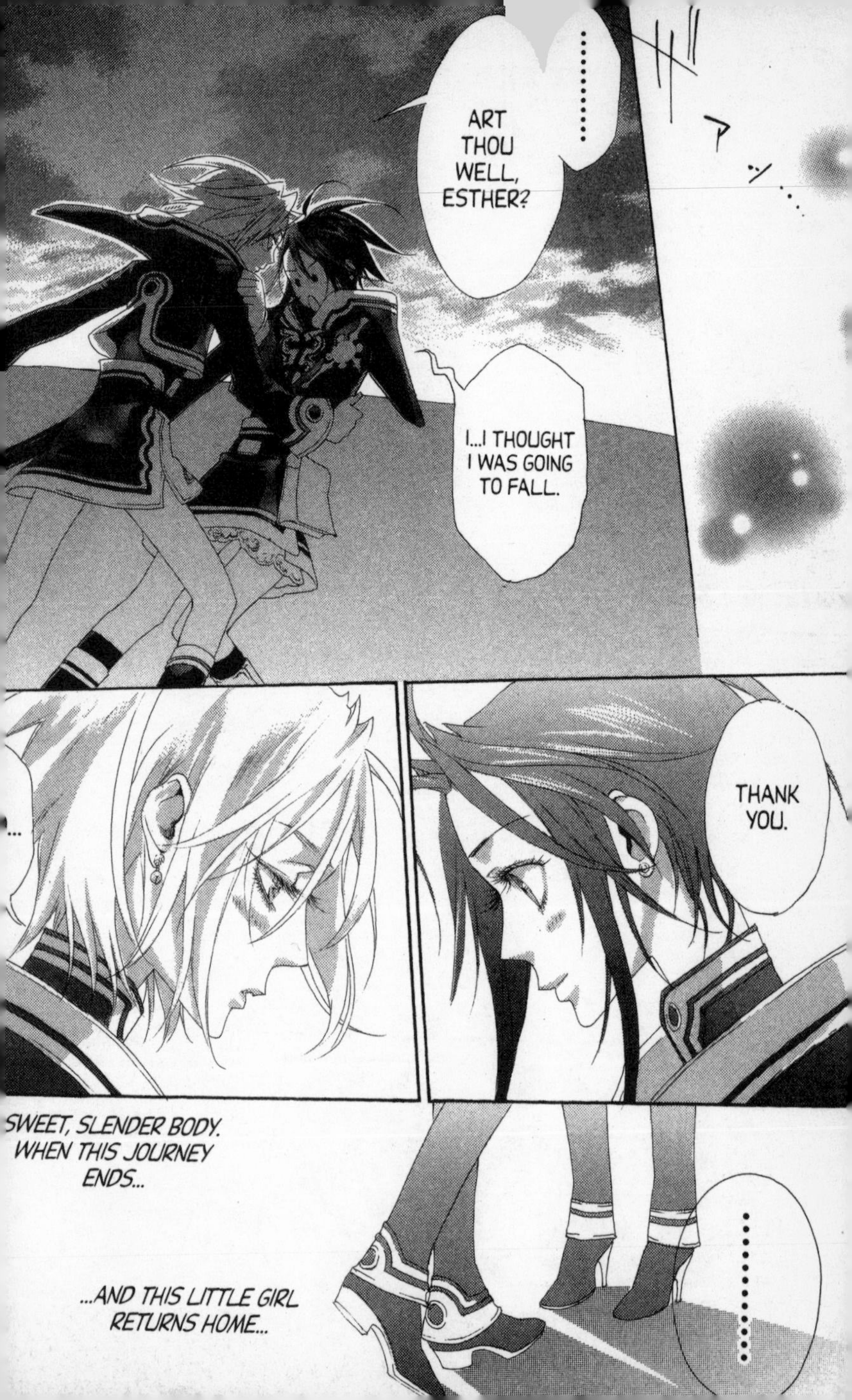
アッ...
......
ART THOU WELL, ESTHER?
I...I THOUGHT I WAS GOING TO FALL.
THANK YOU.
...
......
SWEET, SLENDER BODY. WHEN THIS JOURNEY ENDS...
...AND THIS LITTLE GIRL RETURNS HOME...

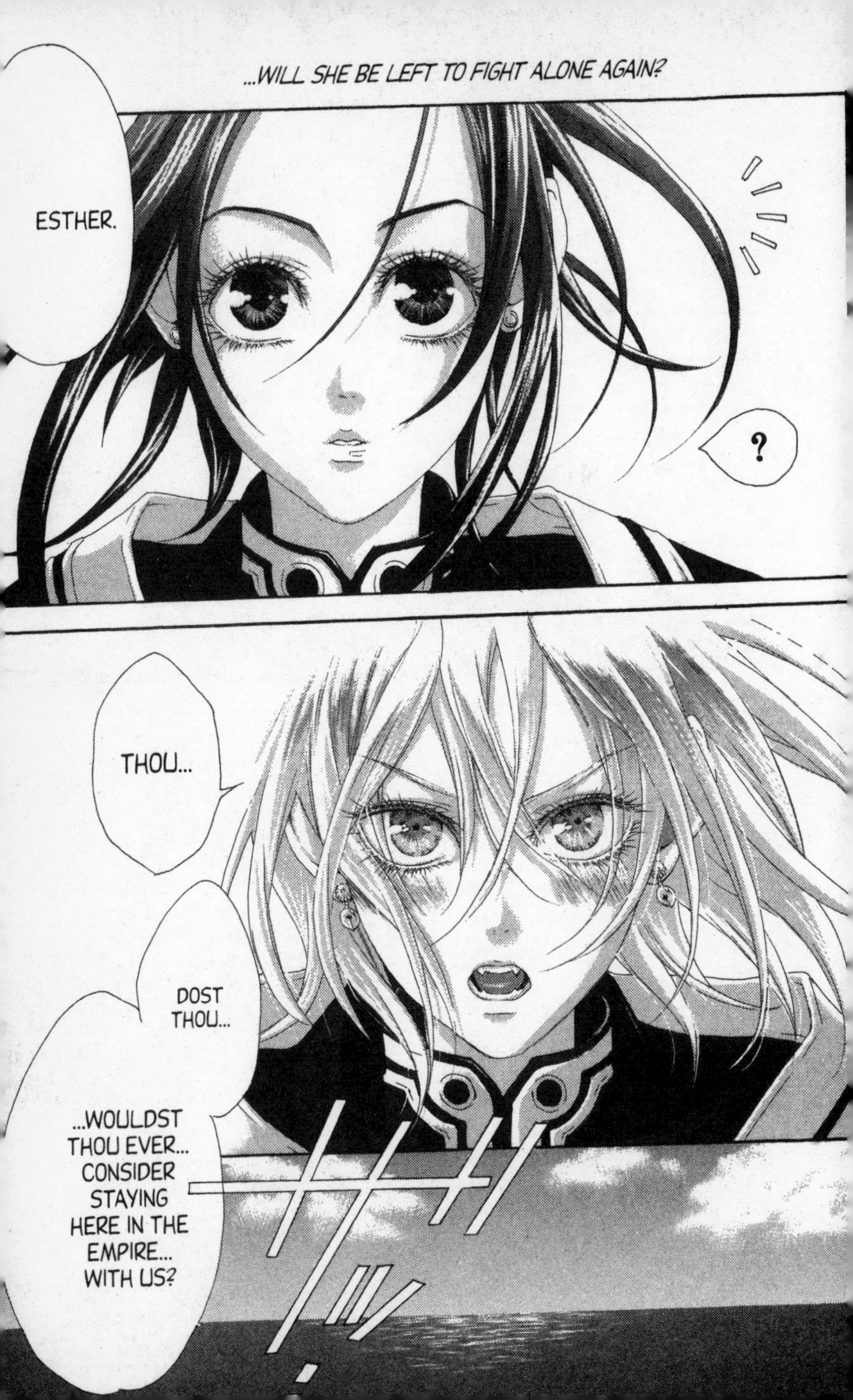
...WILL SHE BE LEFT TO FIGHT ALONE AGAIN?
ESTHER.
?
THOU...
DOST THOU...
...WOULDST THOU EVER... CONSIDER STAYING HERE IN THE EMPIRE... WITH US?

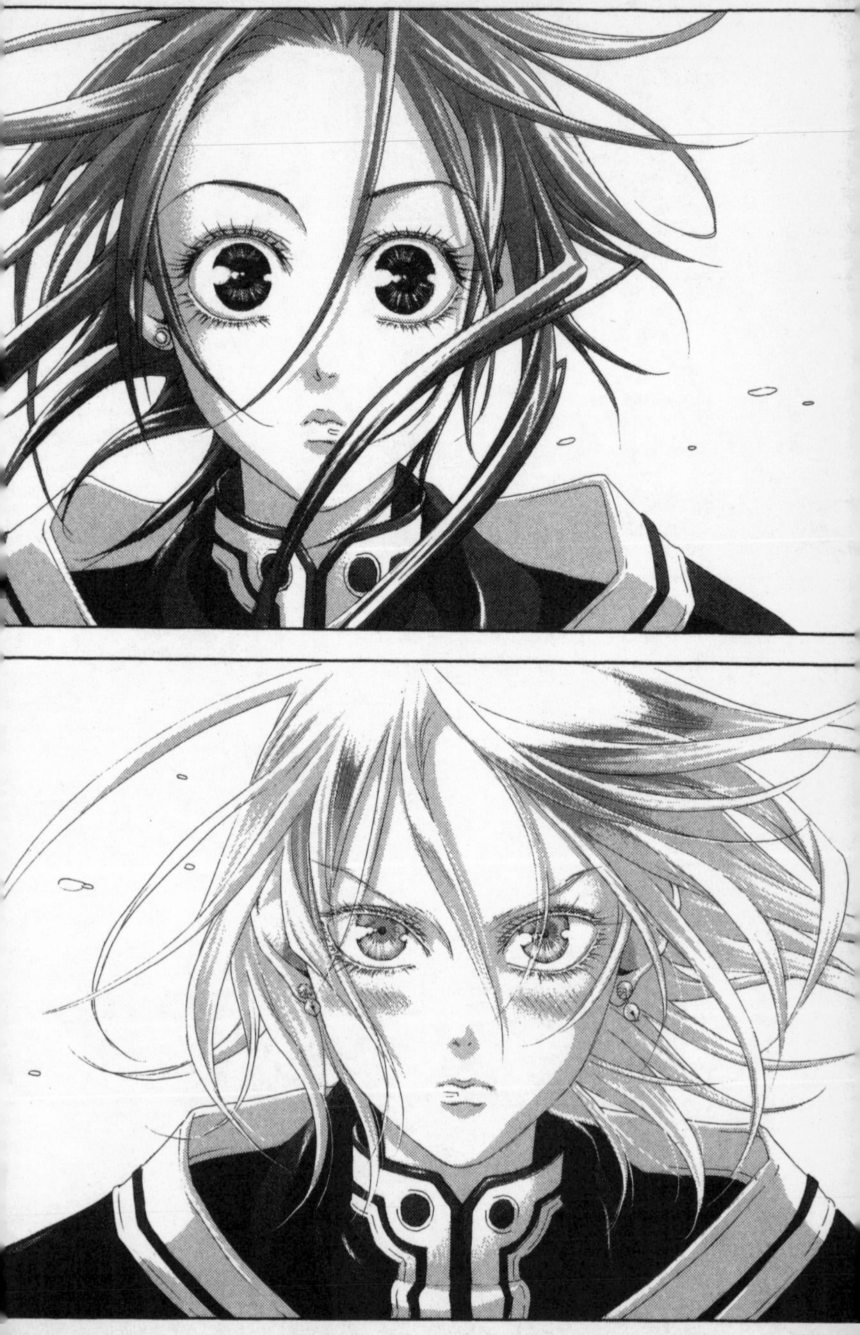

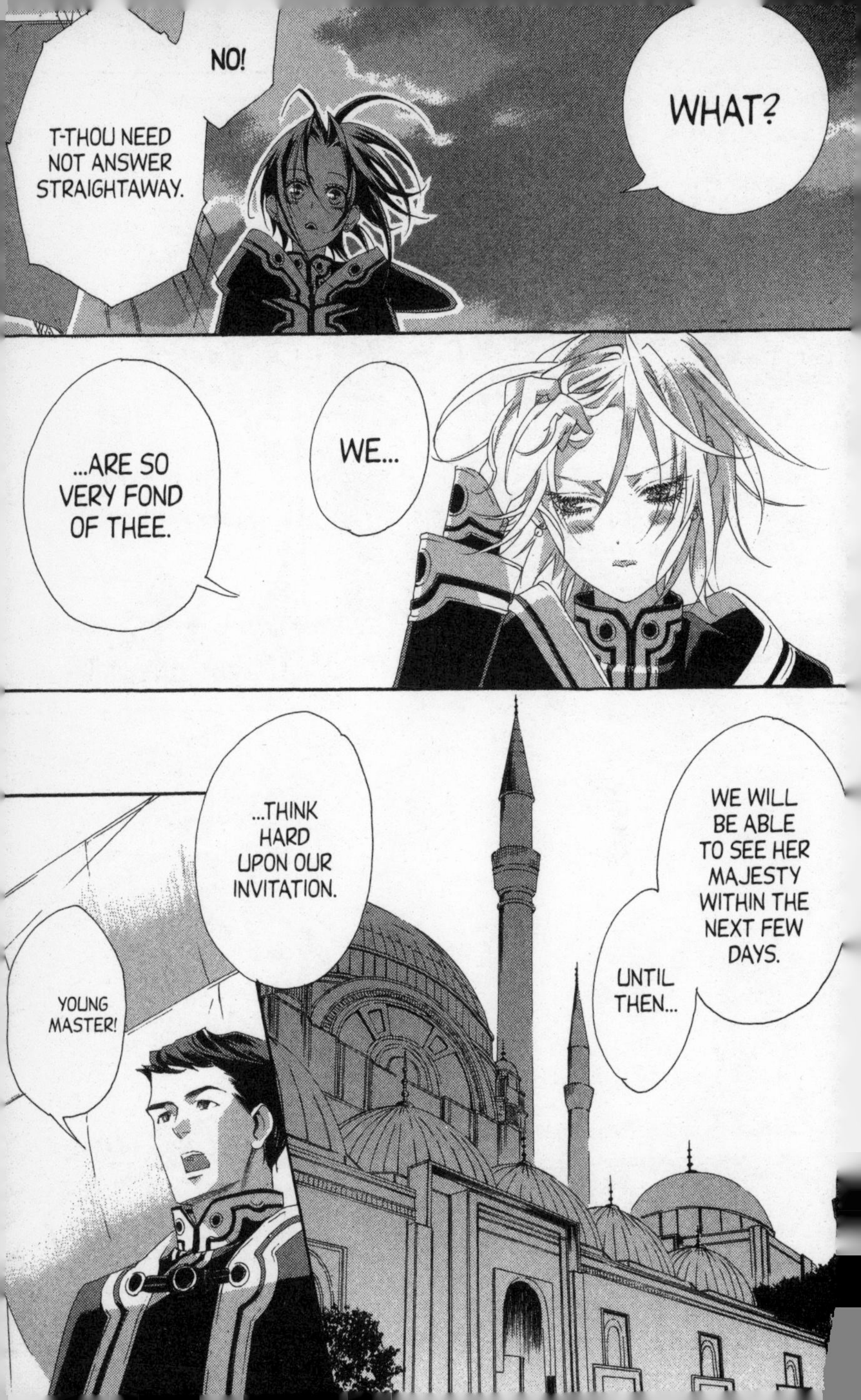
WHAT?
NO!
T-THOU NEED NOT ANSWER STRAIGHTAWAY.
WE...
...ARE SO VERY FOND OF THEE.
WE WILL BE ABLE TO SEE HER MAJESTY WITHIN THE NEXT FEW DAYS.
UNTIL THEN...
...THINK HARD UPON OUR INVITATION.
YOUNG MASTER!

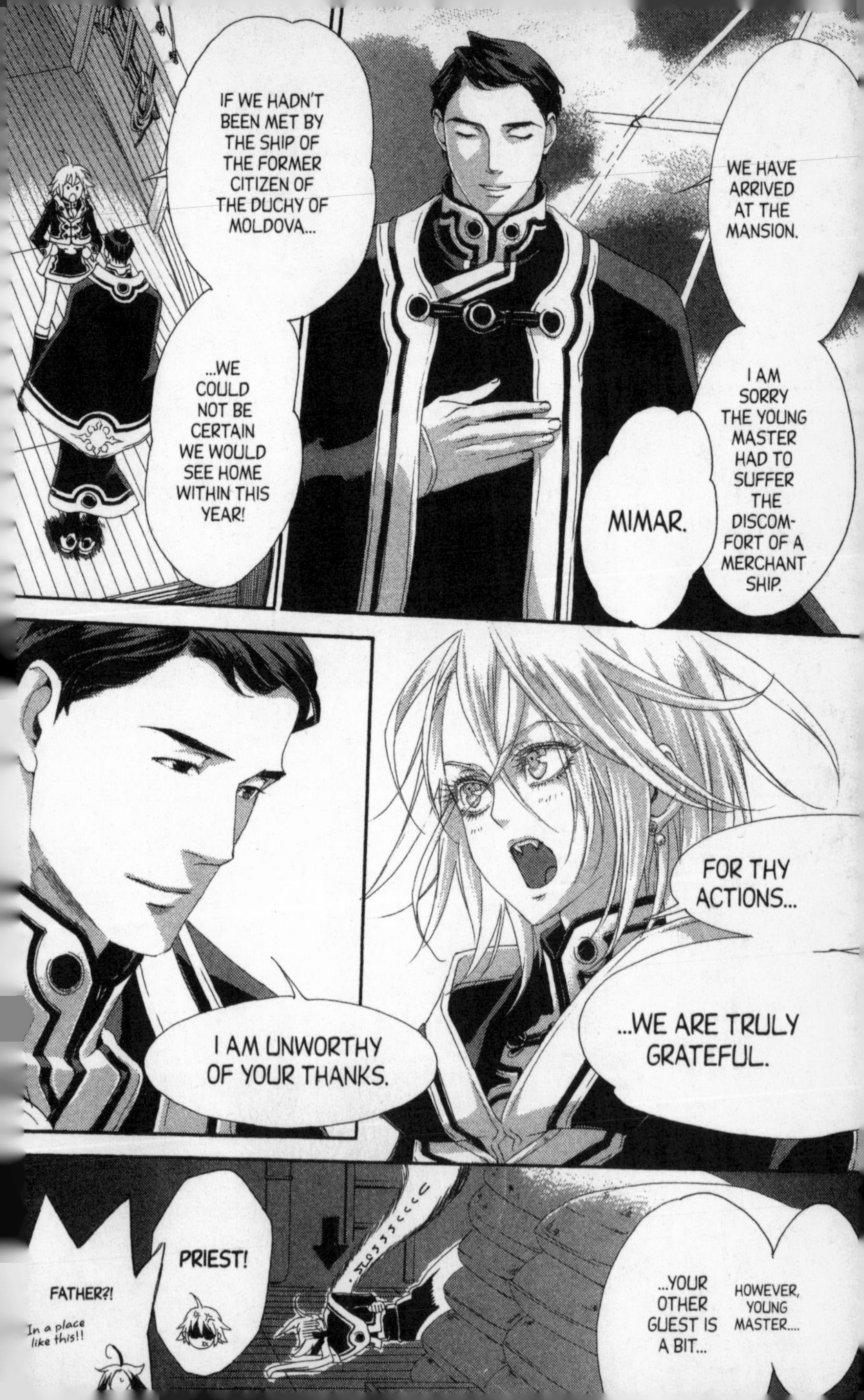
WE HAVE ARRIVED AT THE MANSION.
I AM SORRY THE YOUNG MASTER HAD TO SUFFER THE DISCOMFORT OF A MERCHANT SHIP.
MIMAR.
IF WE HADN'T BEEN MET BY THE SHIP OF THE FORMER CITIZEN OF THE DUCHY OF MOLDOVA...
...WE COULD NOT BE CERTAIN WE WOULD SEE HOME WITHIN THIS YEAR!
FOR THY ACTIONS...
...WE ARE TRULY GRATEFUL.
I AM UNWORTHY OF YOUR THANKS.
HOWEVER, YOUNG MASTER....
...YOUR OTHER GUEST IS A BIT...
PRIEST!
FATHER?!
In a place like this!!

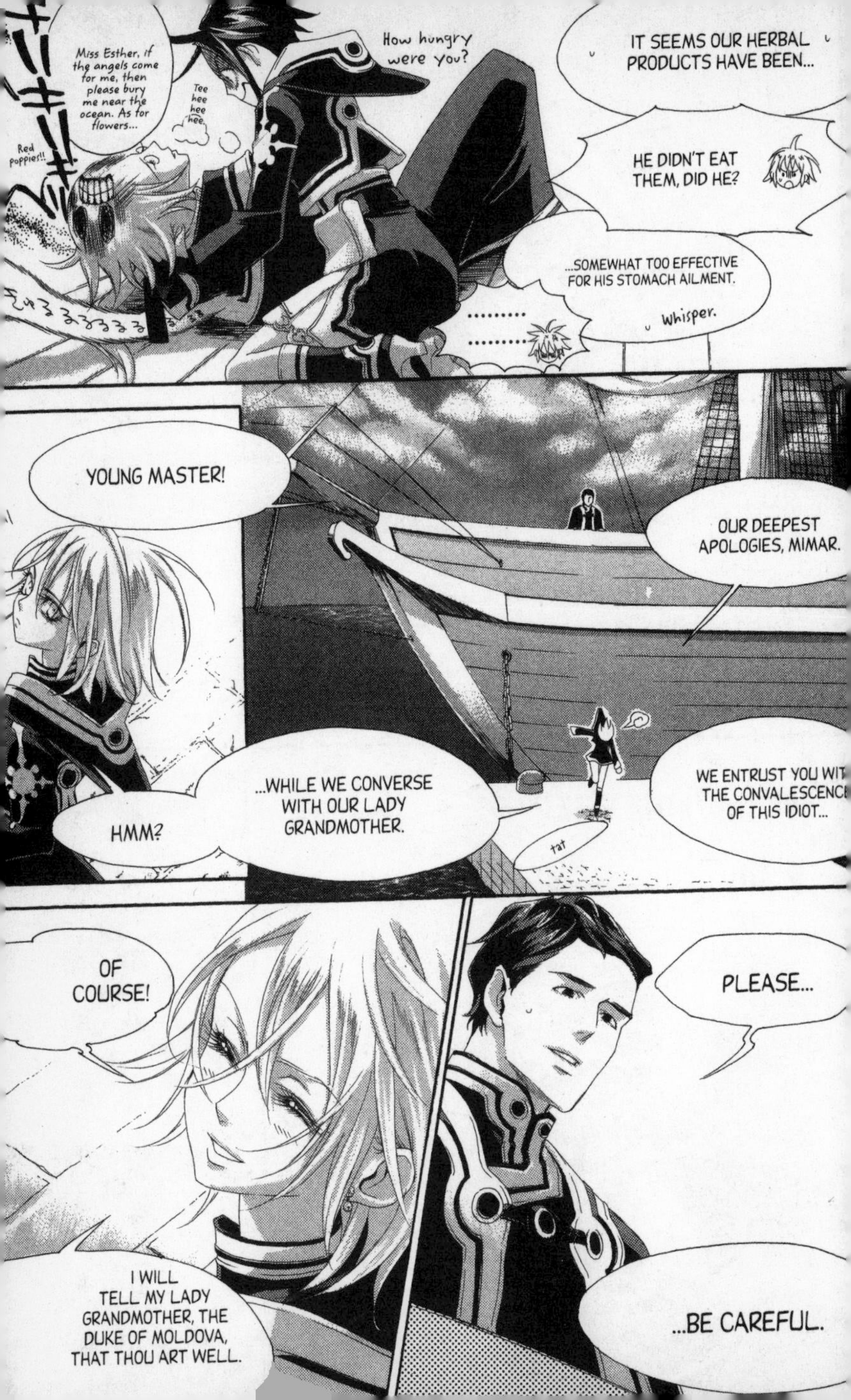

IT SEEMS OUR HERBAL PRODUCTS HAVE BEEN...
HE DIDN'T EAT THEM, DID HE?
...SOMEWHAT TOO EFFECTIVE FOR HIS STOMACH AILMENT.
Whisper.
....
....
How hungry were you?
Tee hee hee hee.
Miss Esther, if the angels come for me, then please bury me near the ocean. As for flowers...
Red poppies!!
OUR DEEPEST APOLOGIES, MIMAR.
WE ENTRUST YOU WIT THE CONVALESCENC OF THIS IDIOT...
...WHILE WE CONVERSE WITH OUR LADY GRANDMOTHER.
tat
YOUNG MASTER!
HMM?
PLEASE...
...BE CAREFUL.
OF COURSE!
I WILL TELL MY LADY GRANDMOTHER, THE DUKE OF MOLDOVA, THAT THOU ART WELL.

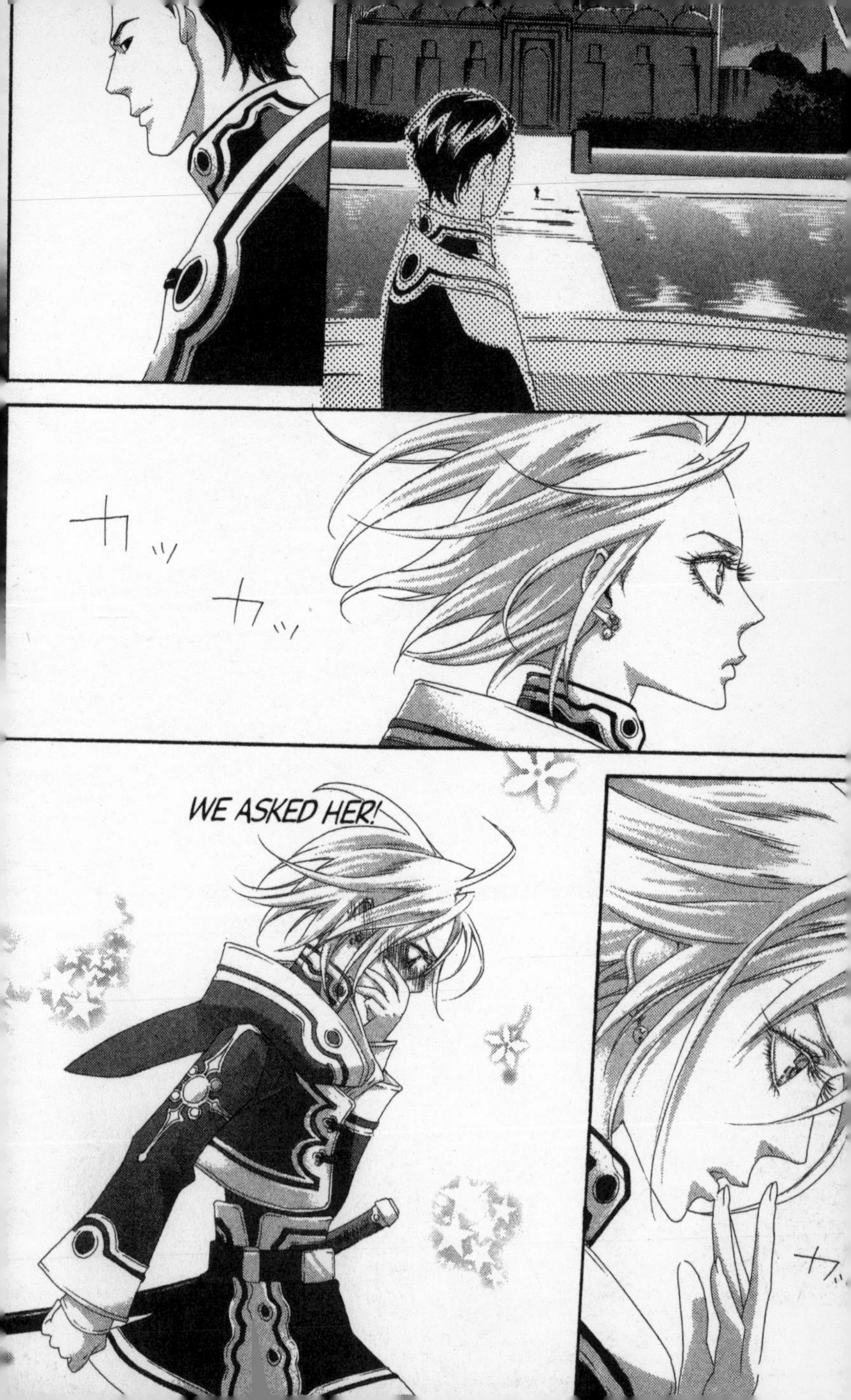
カッ
カッ
WE ASKED HER!

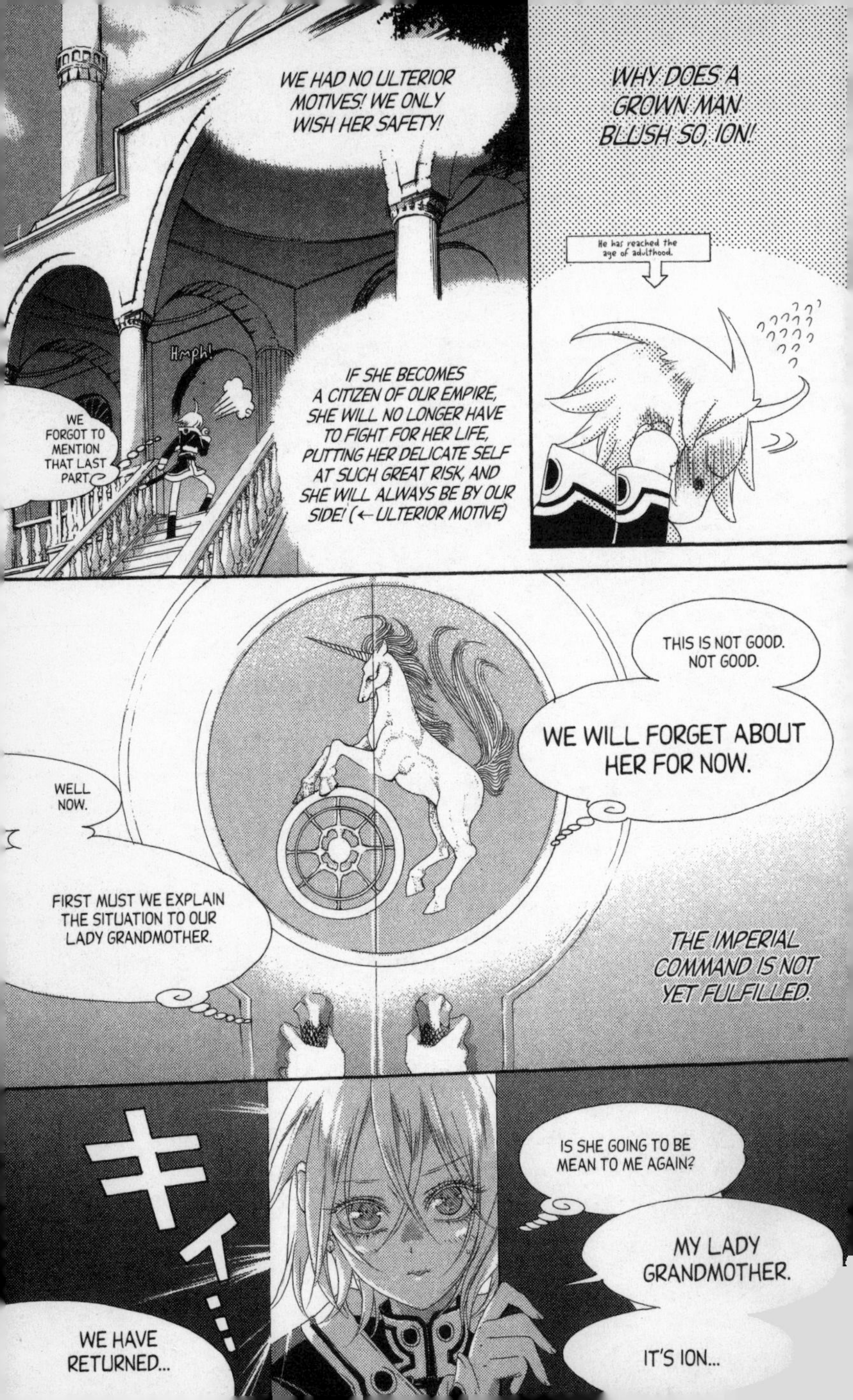
WHY DOES A GROWN MAN BLUSH SO, ION!
He has reached the age of adulthood.
WE HAD NO ULTERIOR MOTIVES! WE ONLY WISH HER SAFETY!
IF SHE BECOMES A CITIZEN OF OUR EMPIRE, SHE WILL NO LONGER HAVE TO FIGHT FOR HER LIFE, PUTTING HER DELICATE SELF AT SUCH GREAT RISK, AND SHE WILL ALWAYS BE BY OUR SIDE! (← ULTERIOR MOTIVE)
Hmph!
WE FORGOT TO MENTION THAT LAST PART
THIS IS NOT GOOD. NOT GOOD.
WE WILL FORGET ABOUT HER FOR NOW.
WELL NOW.
FIRST MUST WE EXPLAIN THE SITUATION TO OUR LADY GRANDMOTHER.
THE IMPERIAL COMMAND IS NOT YET FULFILLED.
IS SHE GOING TO BE MEAN TO ME AGAIN?
MY LADY GRANDMOTHER.
IT'S ION...
キィ...
WE HAVE RETURNED...

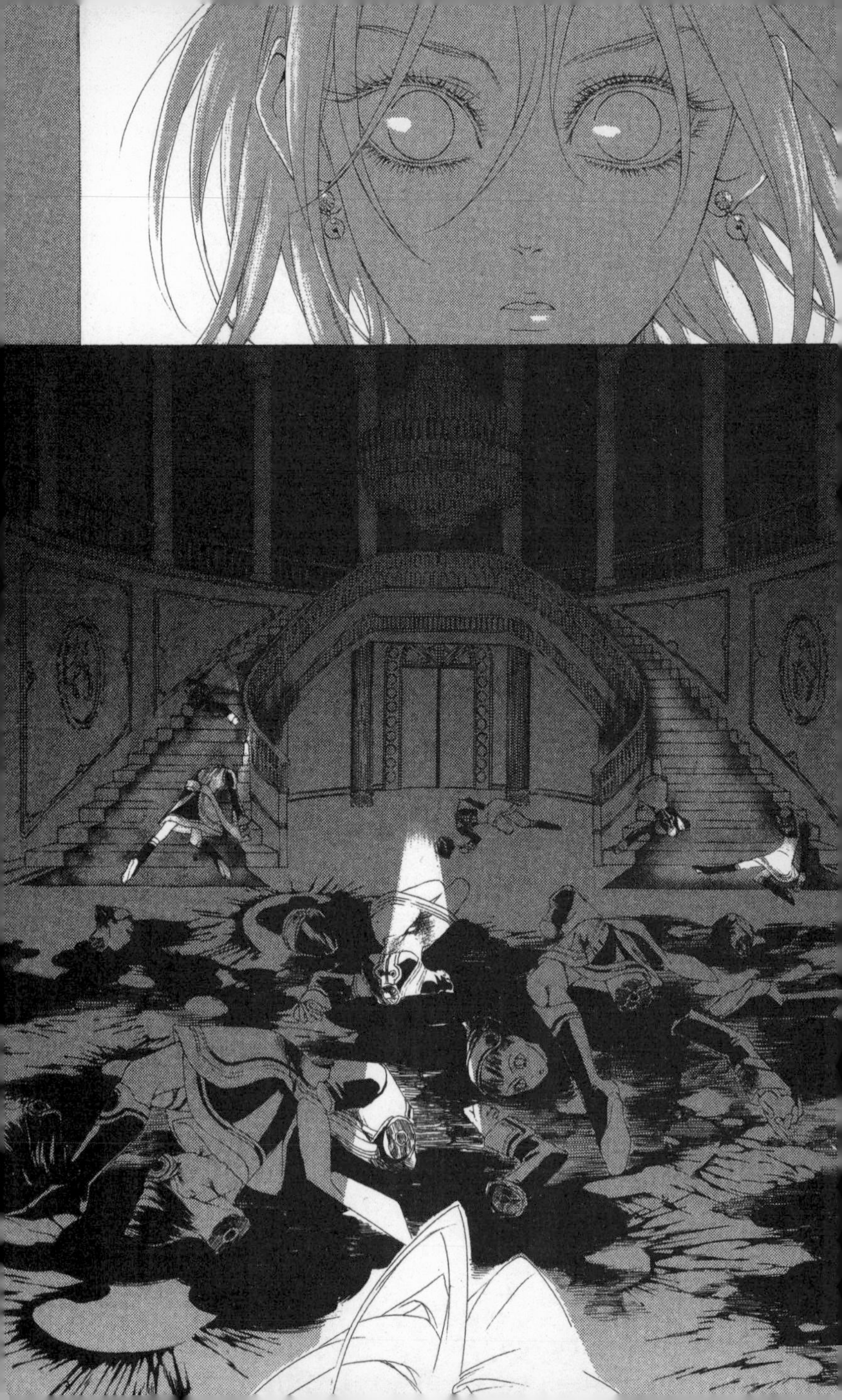

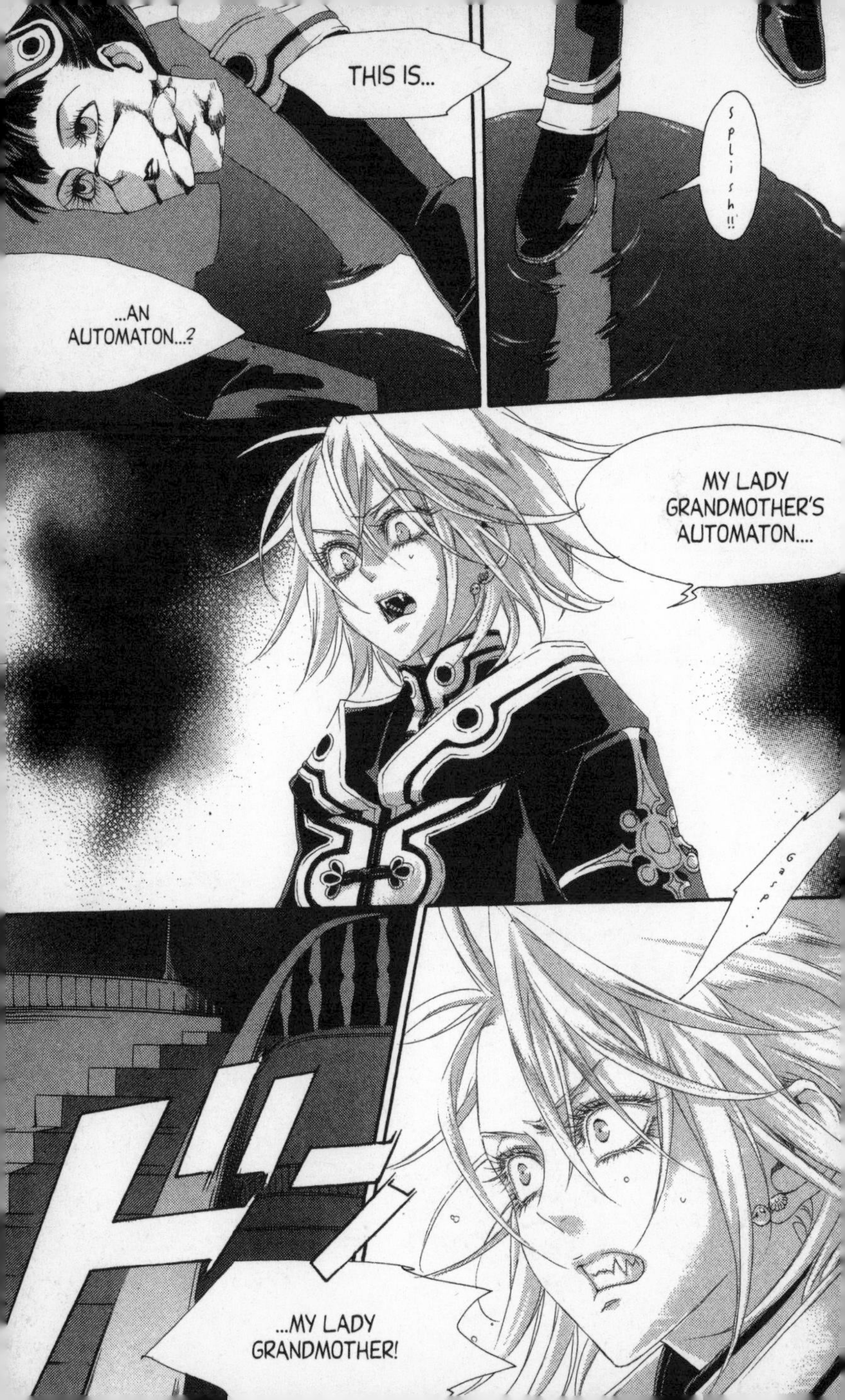
splish!!
THIS IS...
...AN AUTOMATON...?
MY LADY GRANDMOTHER'S AUTOMATON....
Gasp...
...MY LADY GRANDMOTHER!

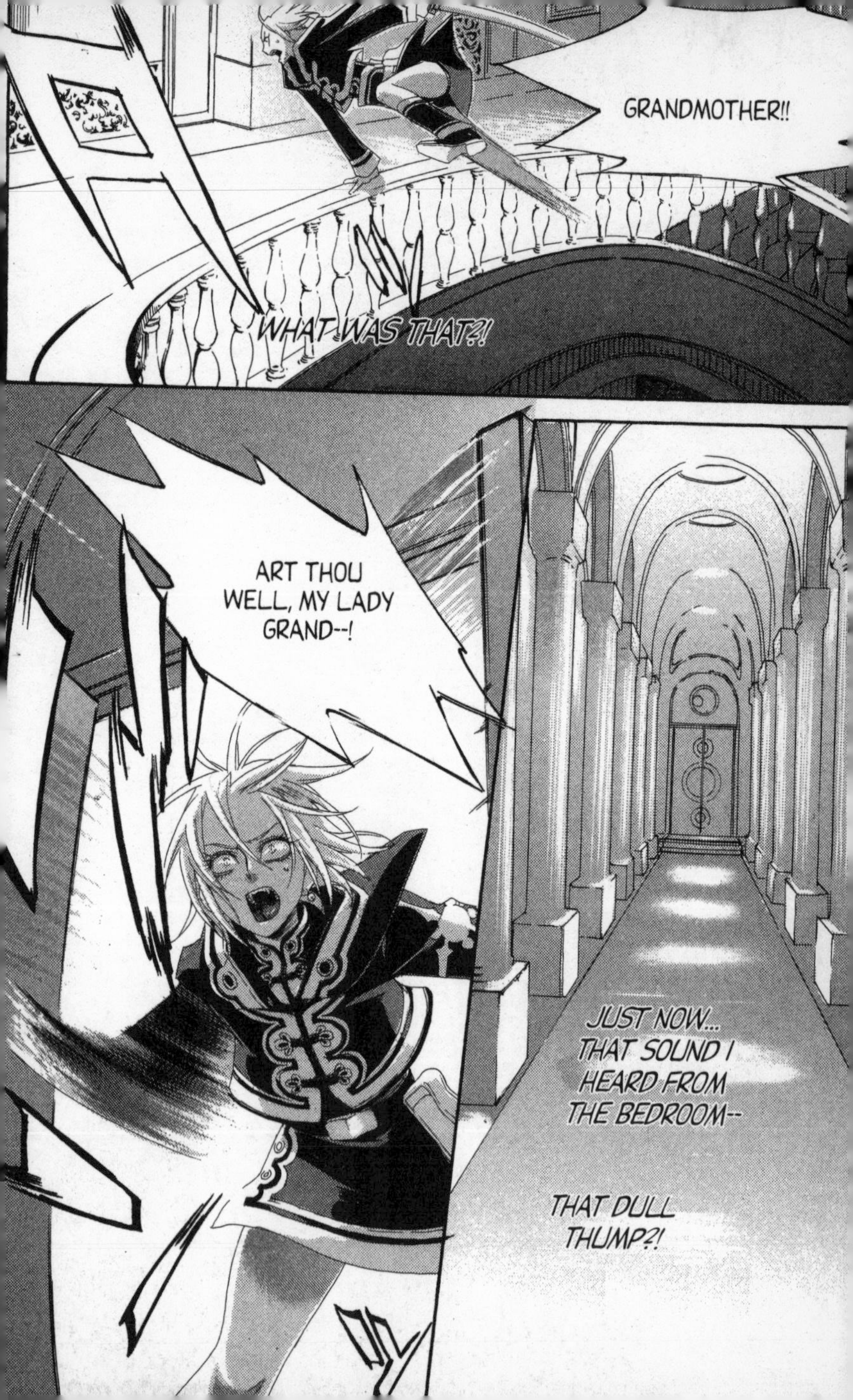
GRANDMOTHER!!
WHAT WAS THAT?!
JUST NOW... THAT SOUND I HEARD FROM THE BEDROOM--
THAT DULL THUMP?!
ART THOU WELL, MY LADY GRAND--!

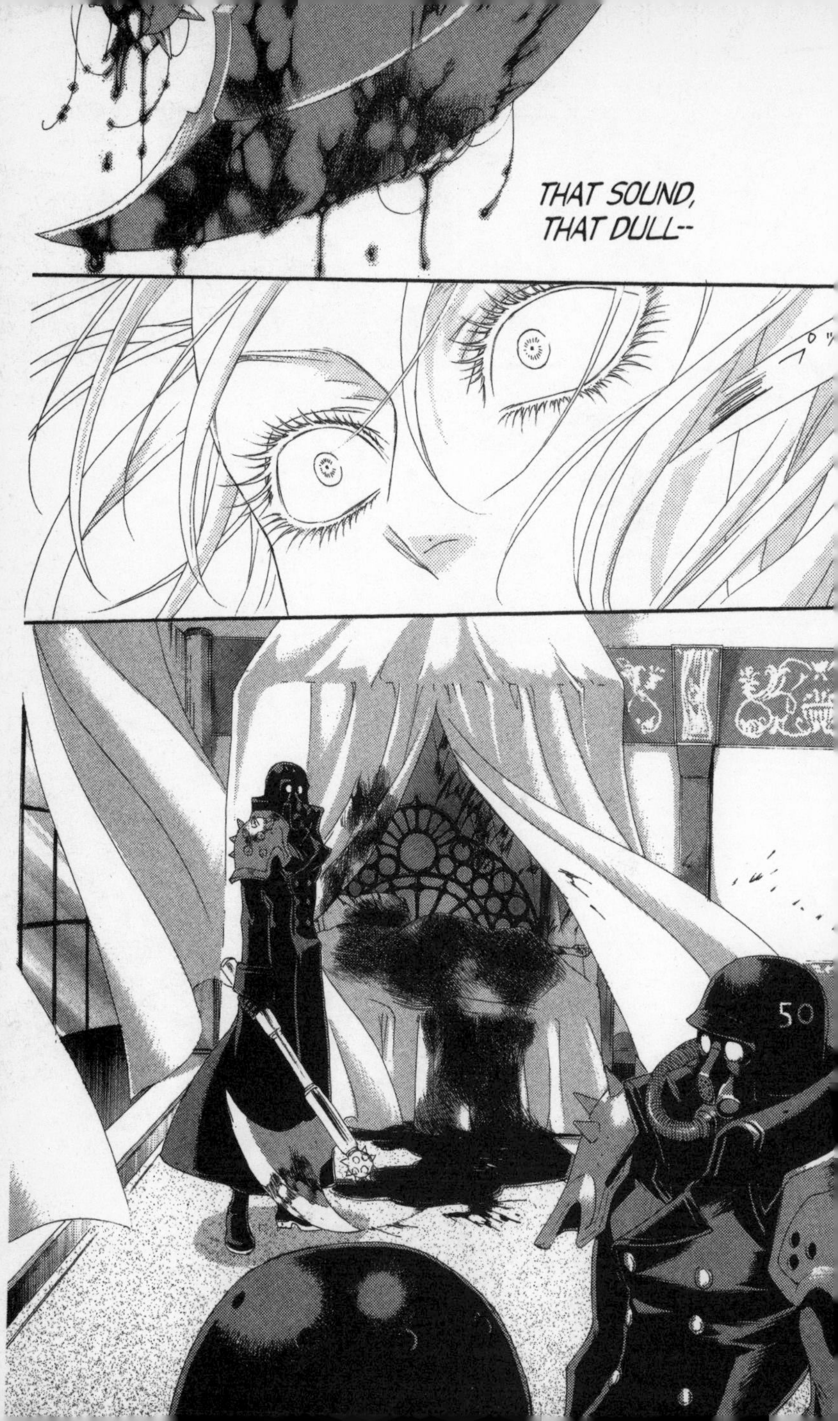
THAT SOUND,
THAT DULL--

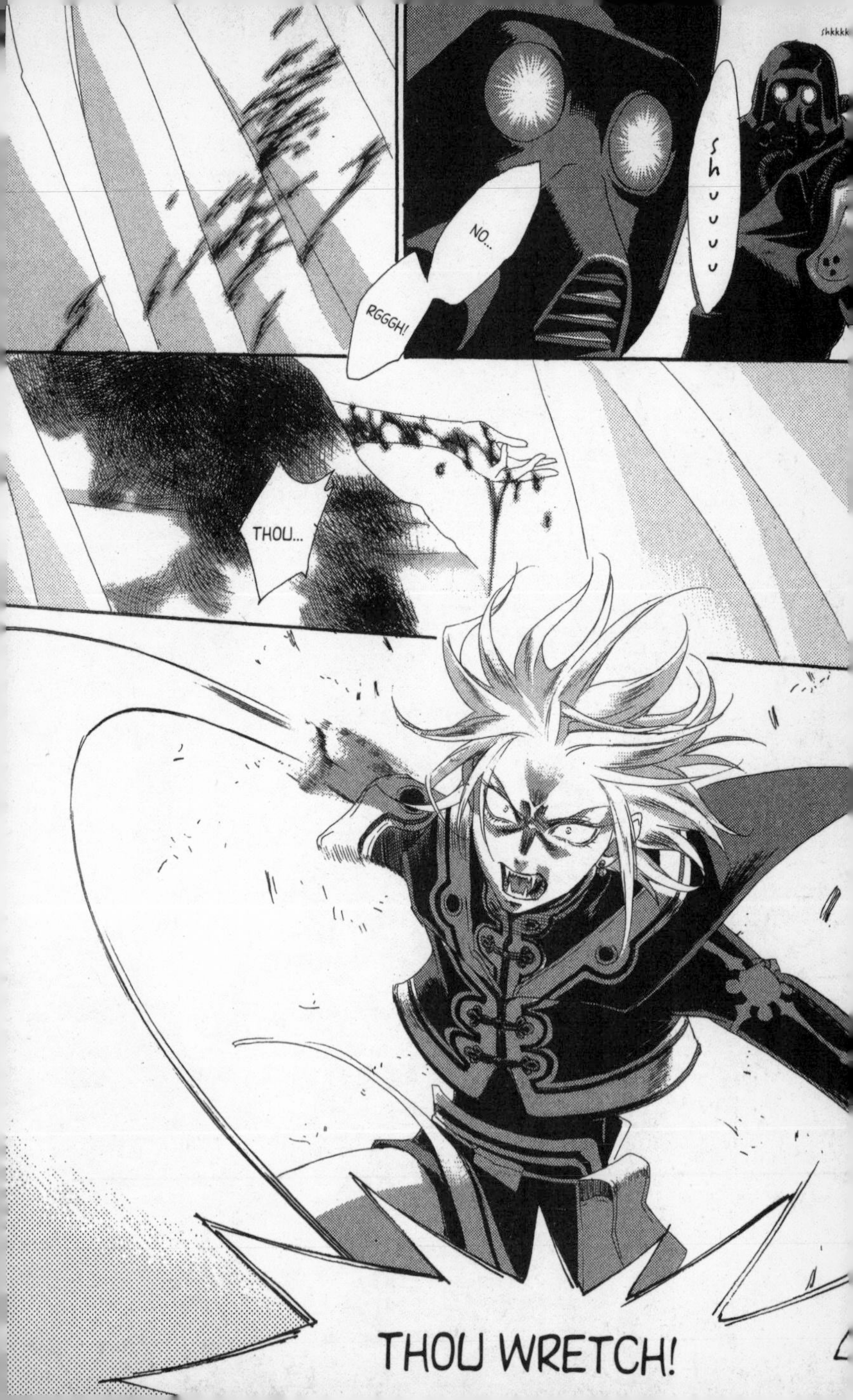
shhkkk
shuuuu
NO...
RGGGH!
THOU...
THOU WRETCH!

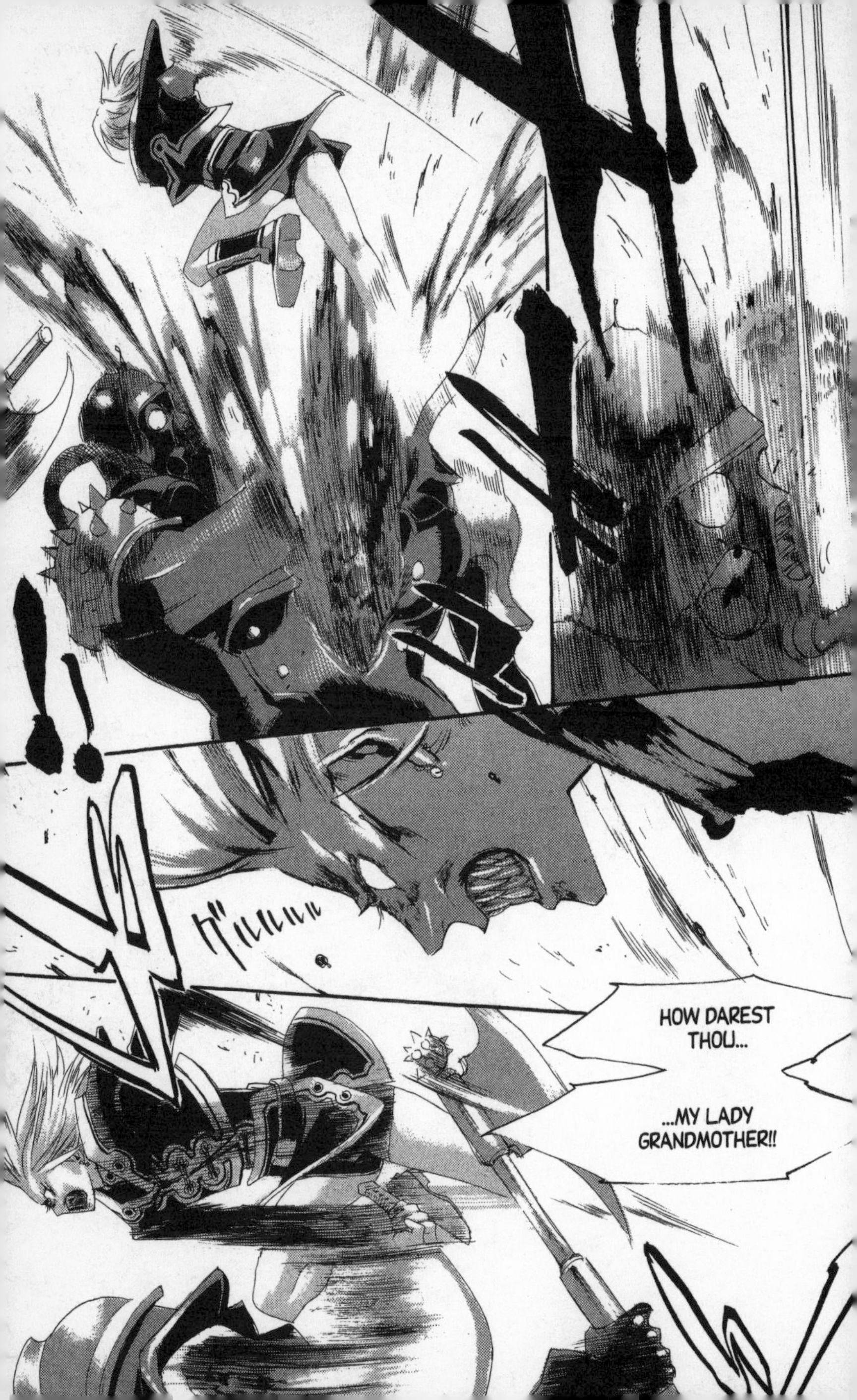
ガルルルル
HOW DAREST THOU...
...MY LADY GRANDMOTHER!!

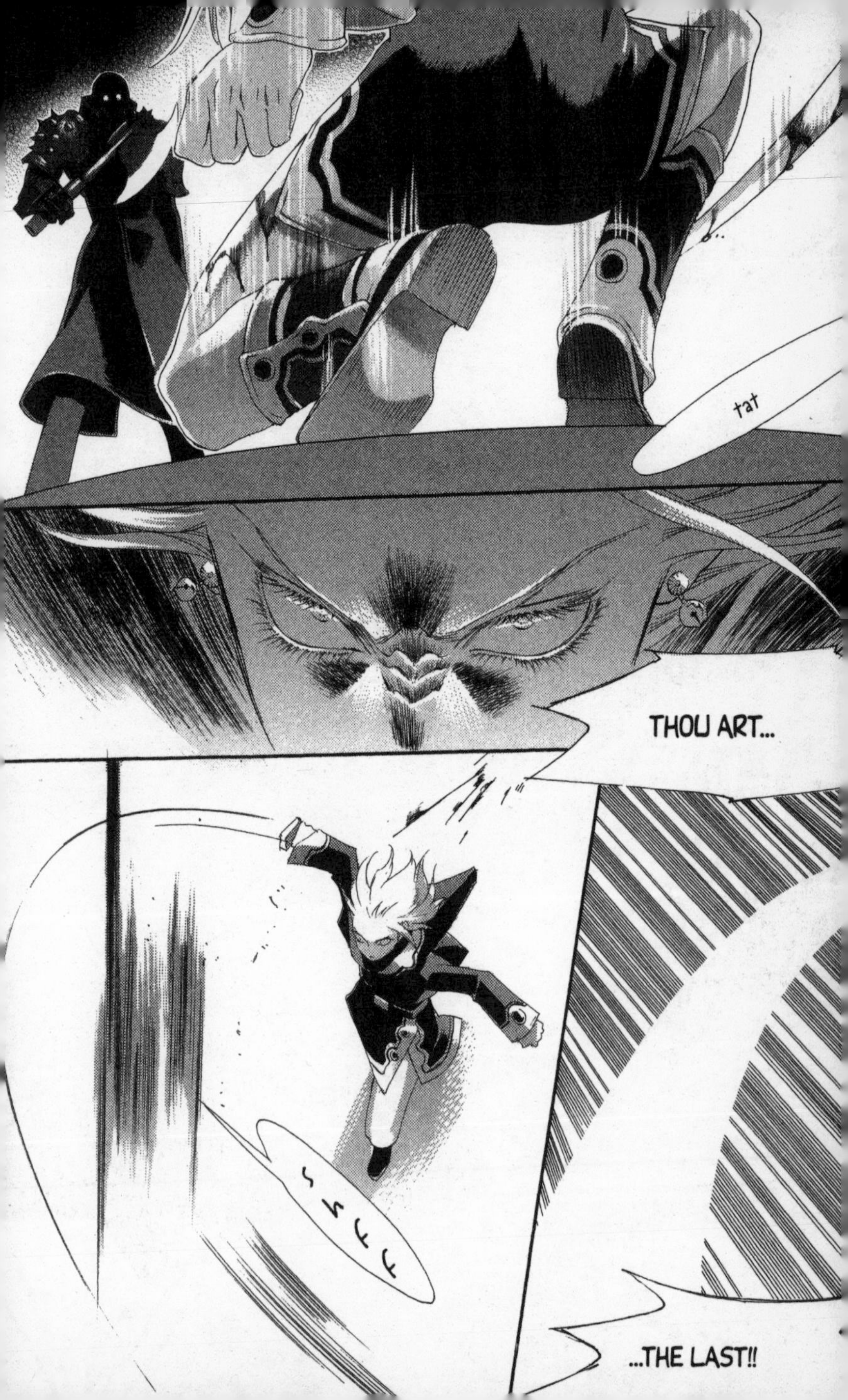
tat
THOU ART...
shff
...THE LAST!!

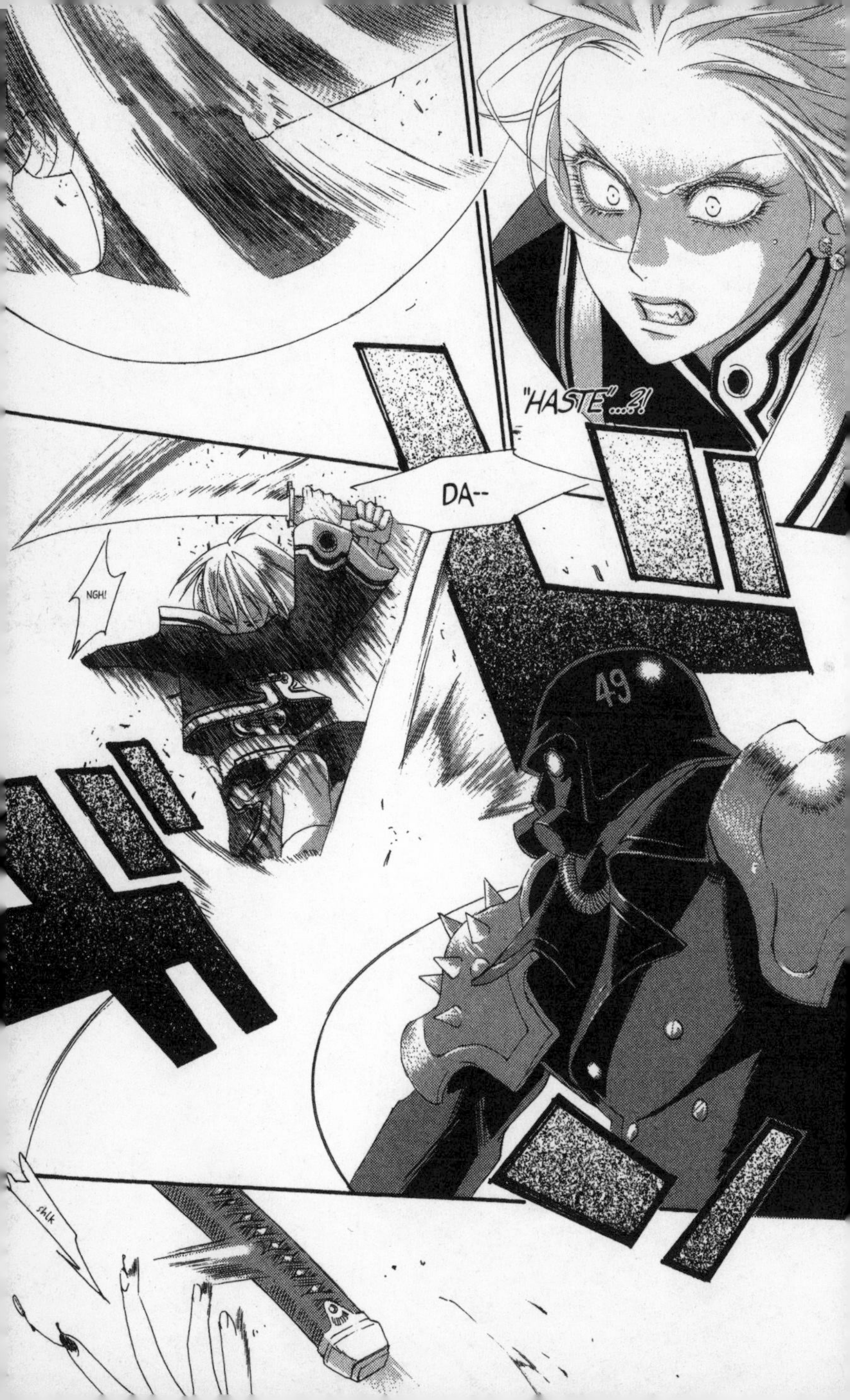
"HASTE"...?!
DA--
NGH!
shlk

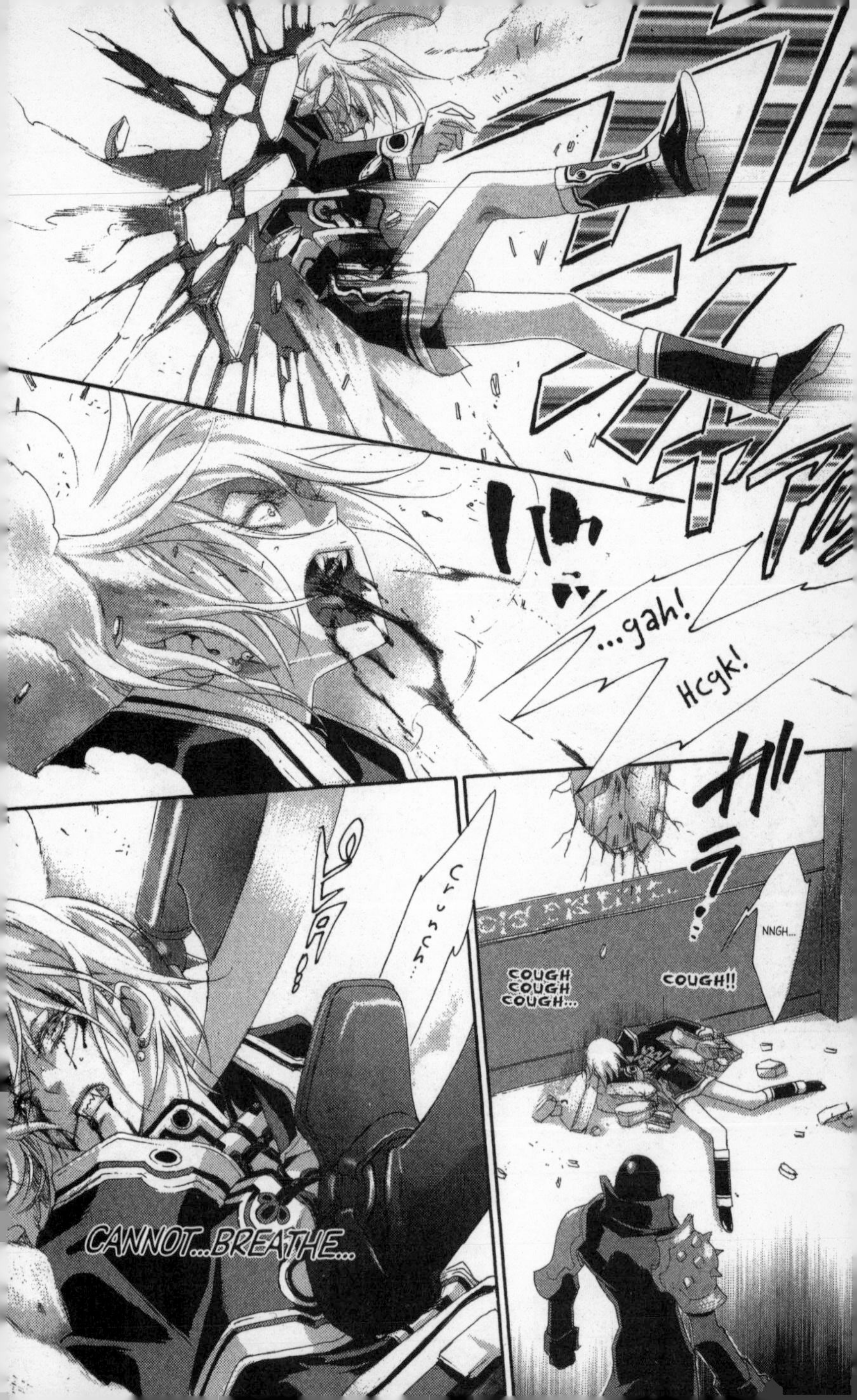
...gah!
Hcgk!
NNGH...
COUGH!!
COUGH
COUGH
COUGH...
Crunch...
CANNOT...BREATHE...

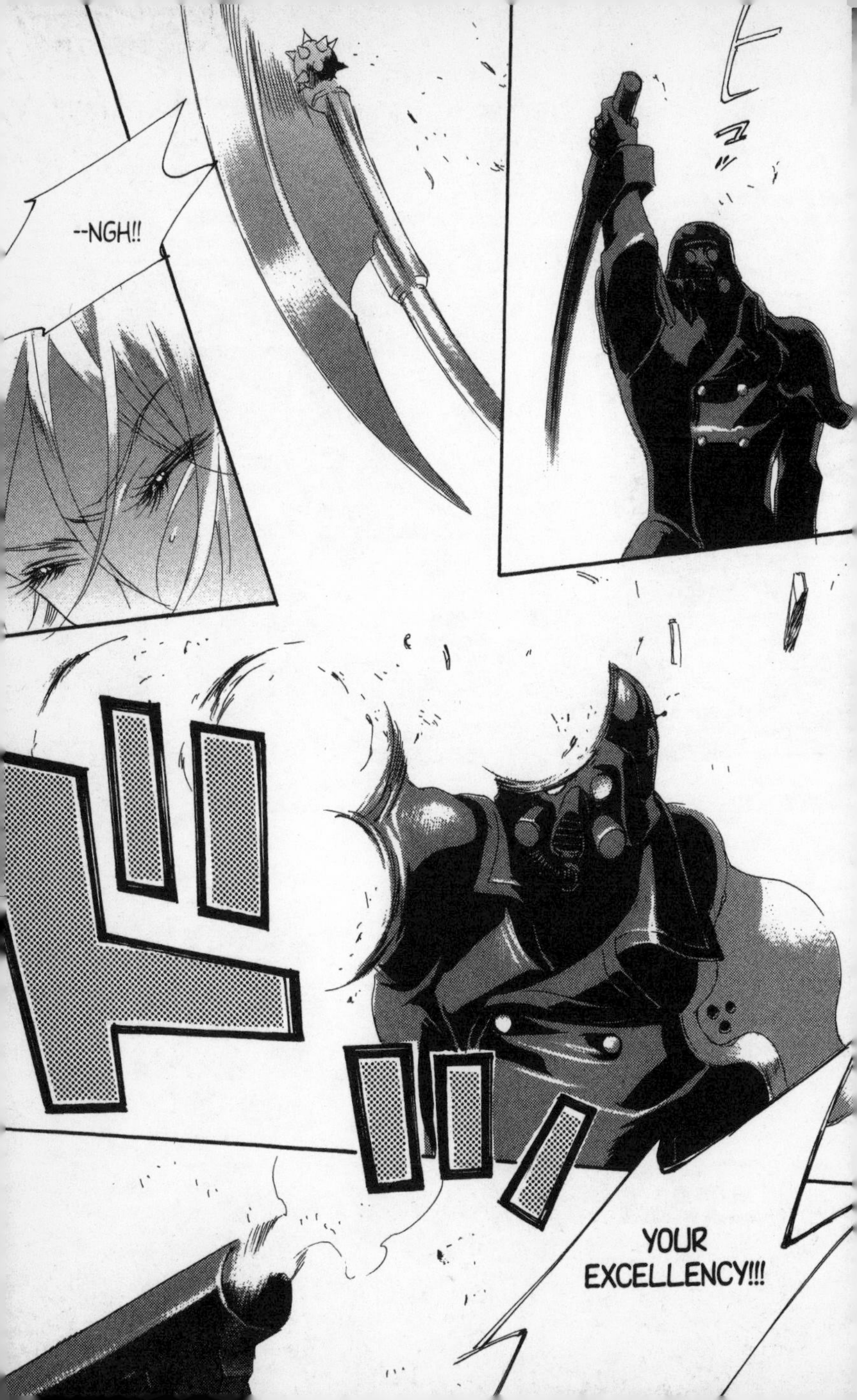
ヒュッ
--NGH!!
ドッ
YOUR EXCELLENCY!!!

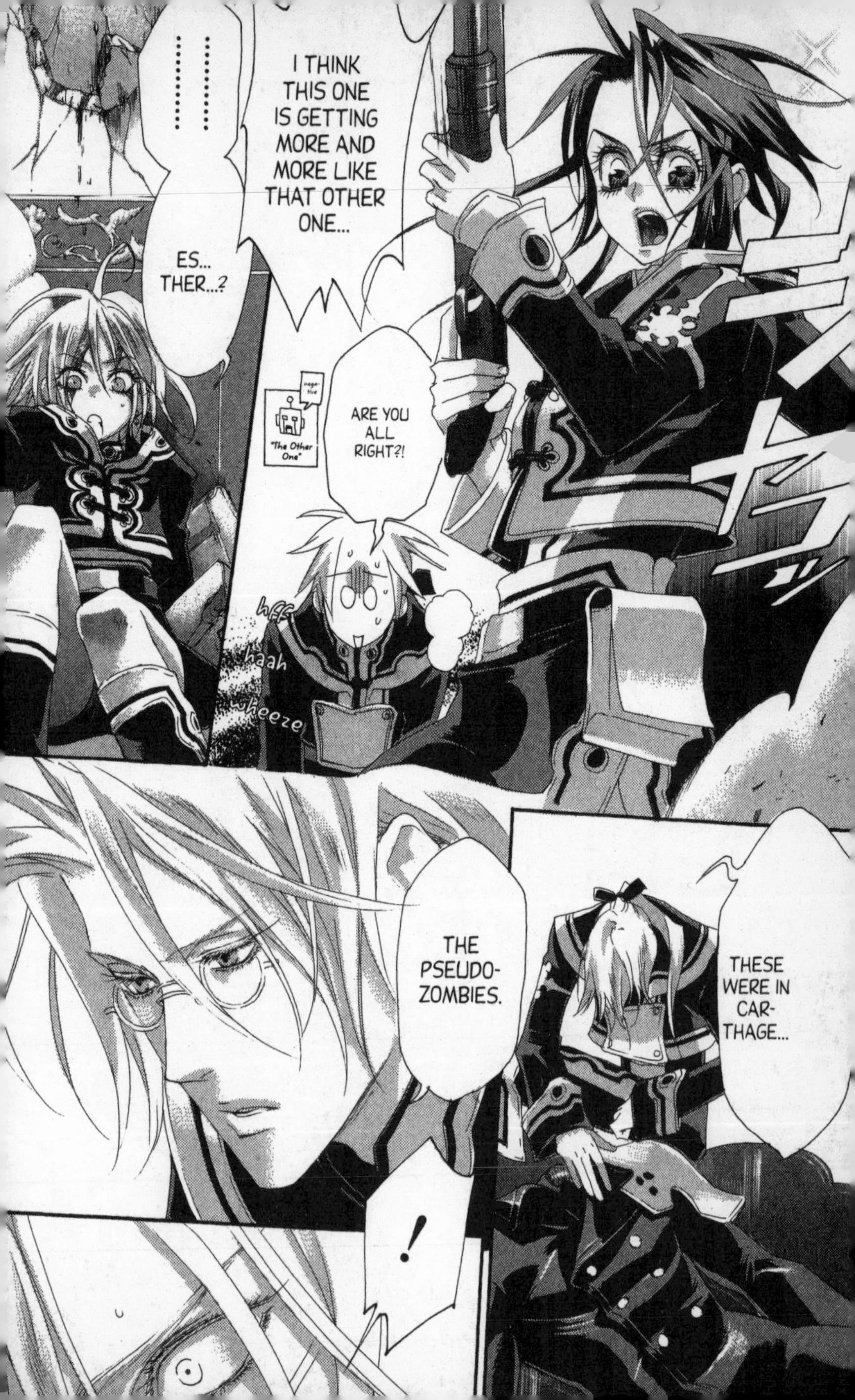
ARE YOU ALL RIGHT?!
hff
haah
wheeze
I THINK THIS ONE IS GETTING MORE AND MORE LIKE THAT OTHER ONE...
nega-tive
"The Other One"
......
ES... THER...?
THESE WERE IN CAR-THAGE...
THE PSEUDO-ZOMBIES.
!

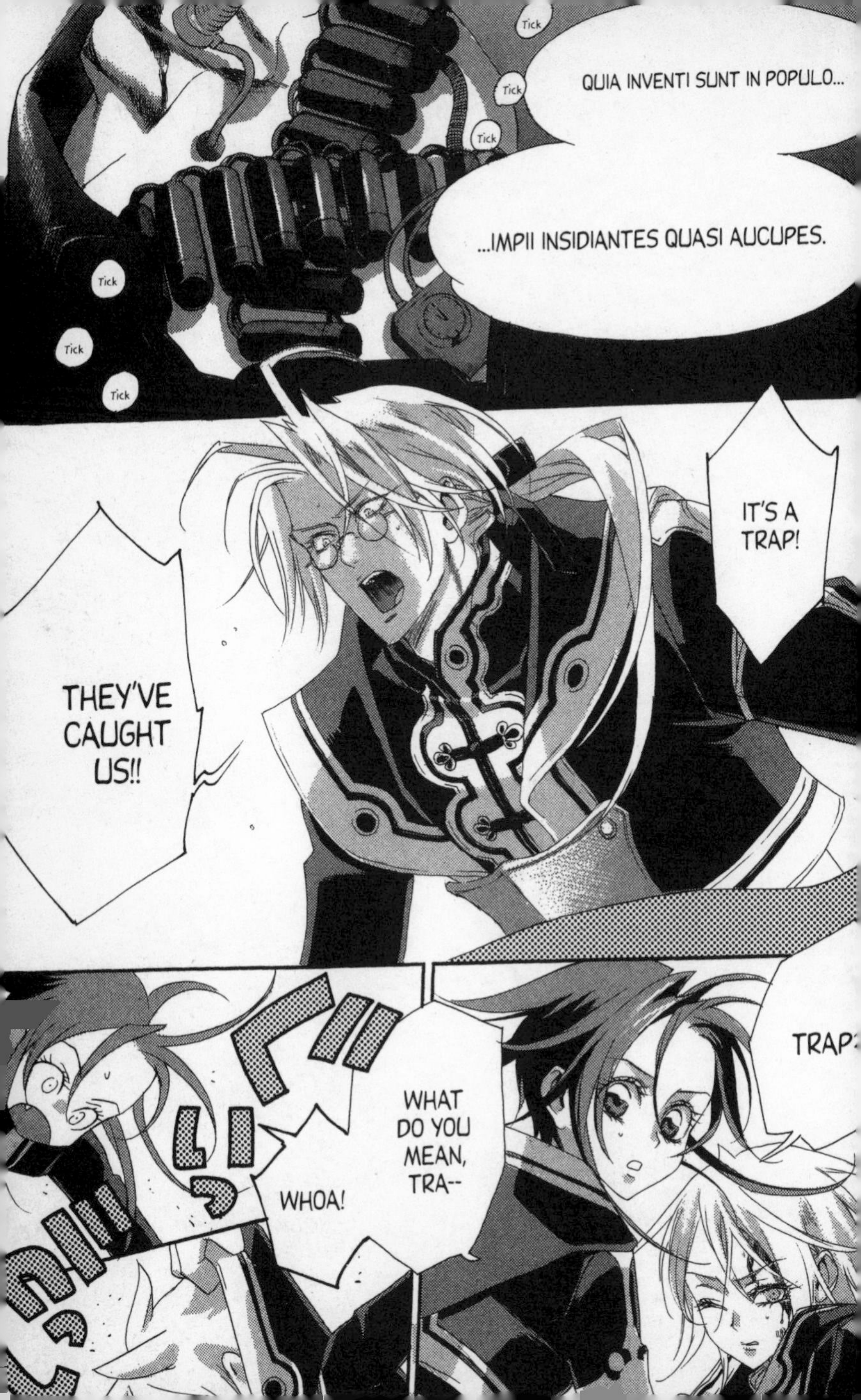
Tick
Tick
Tick
QUIA INVENTI SUNT IN POPULO...
...IMPII INSIDIANTES QUASI AUCUPES.
Tick
Tick
Tick
IT'S A TRAP!
THEY'VE CAUGHT US!!
TRAP?
WHAT DO YOU MEAN, TRA--
WHOA!

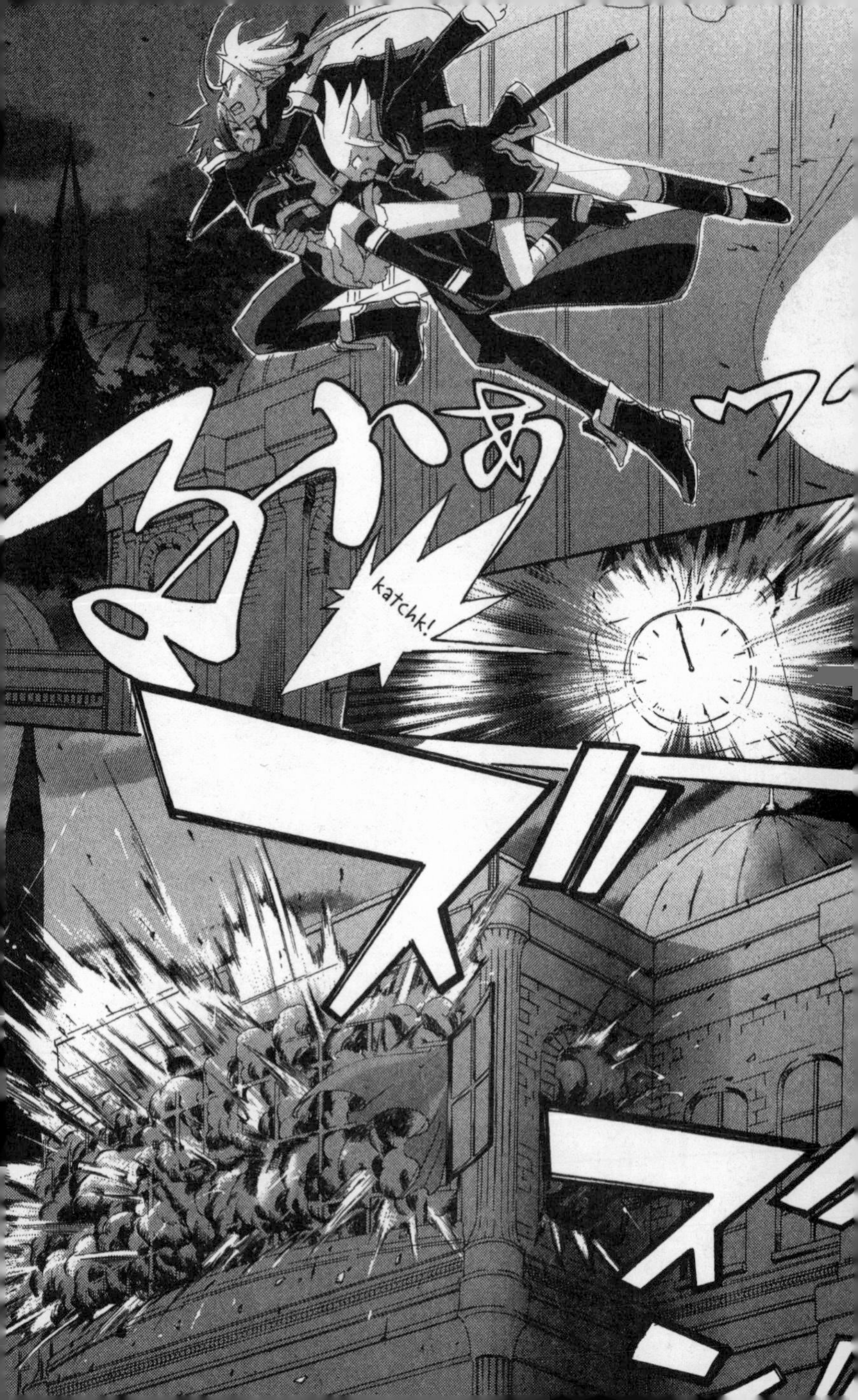
katchk!

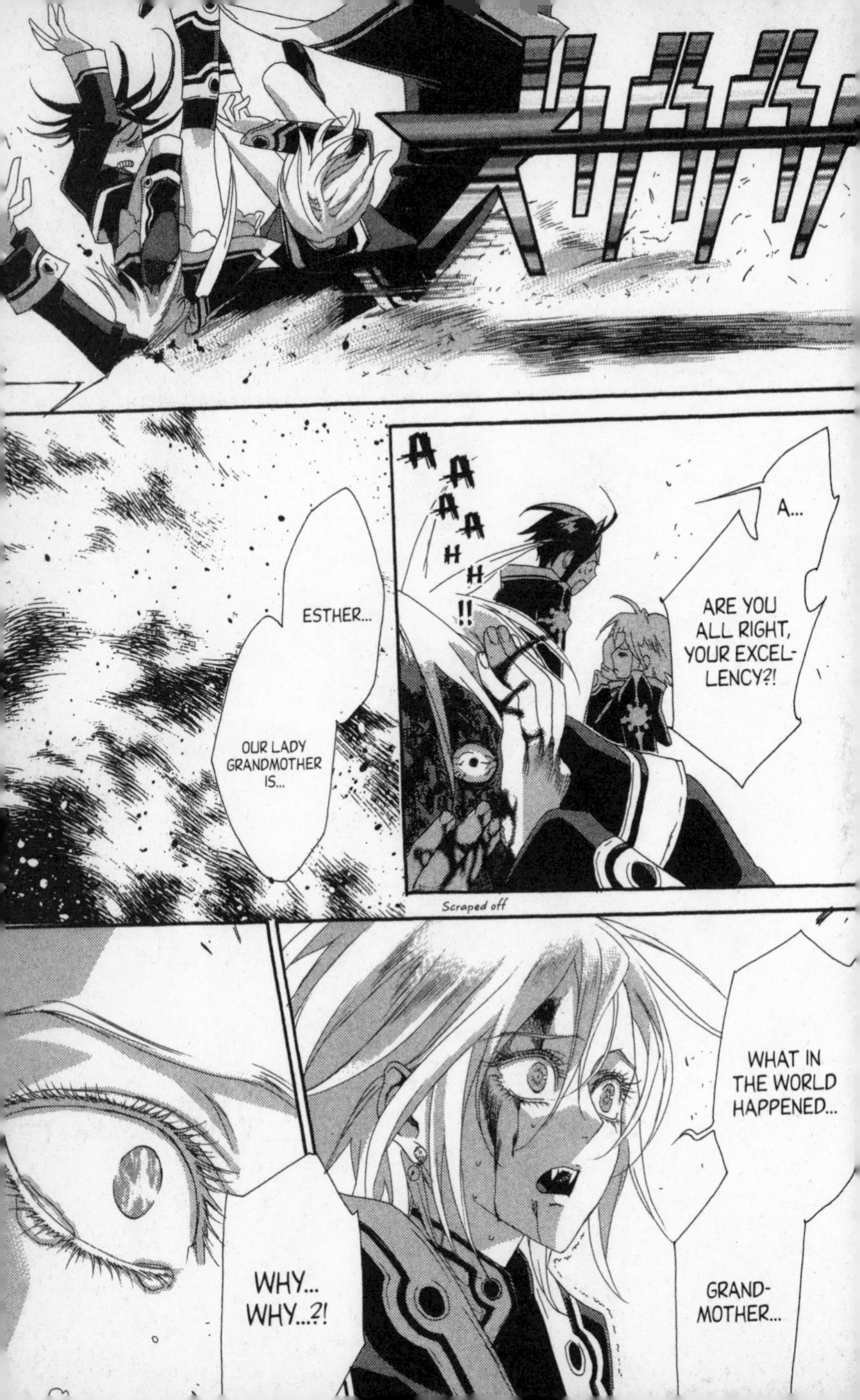
A...
ARE YOU ALL RIGHT, YOUR EXCELLENCY?!
AAAAHH!!
Scraped off
ESTHER...
OUR LADY GRANDMOTHER IS...
WHAT IN THE WORLD HAPPENED...
GRAND-MOTHER...
WHY... WHY...?!

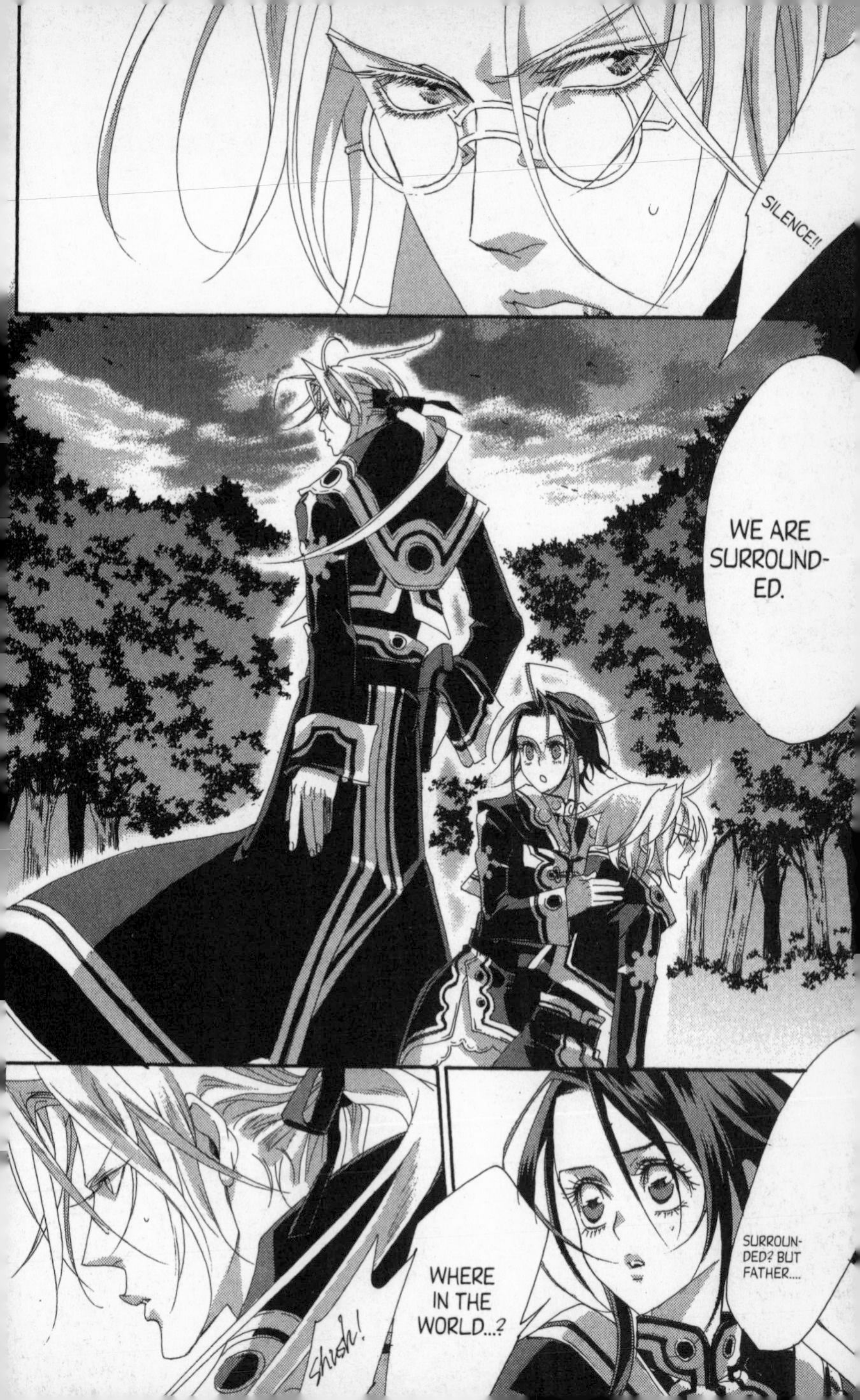
SILENCE!!
WE ARE SURROUNDED.
SURROUNDED? BUT FATHER....
WHERE IN THE WORLD...?
Shush!

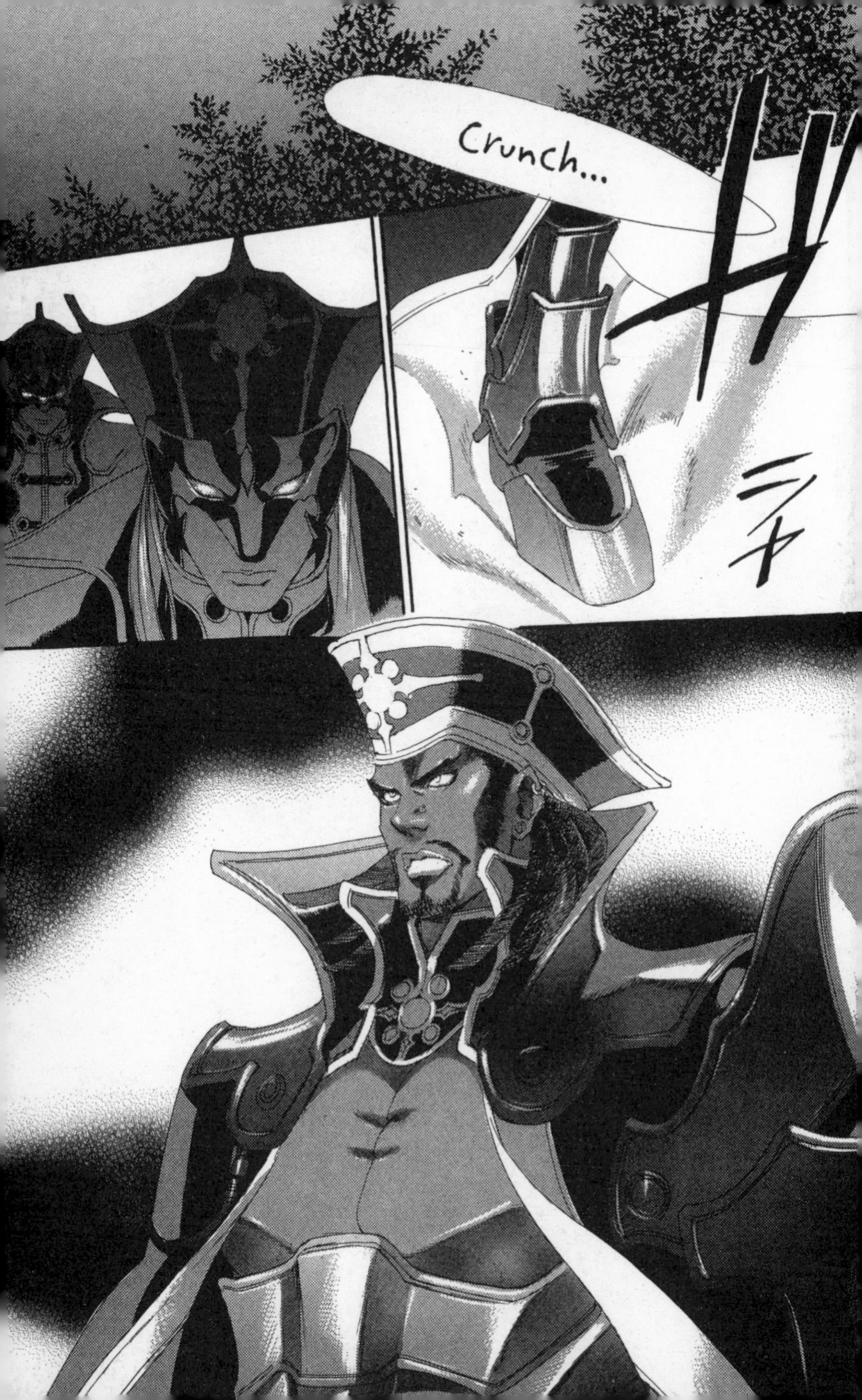
Crunch...

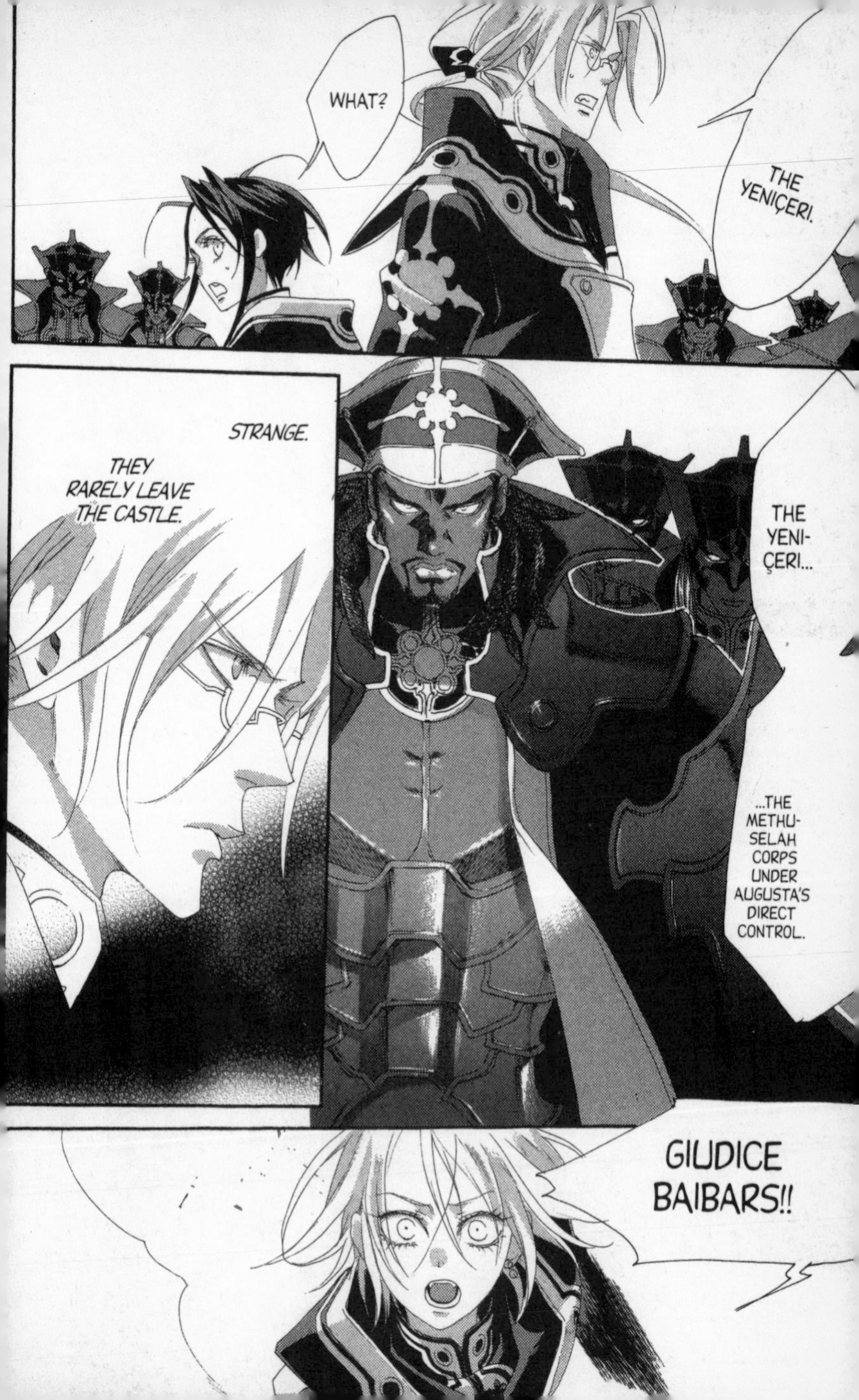
THE YENIÇERI.
WHAT?
THE YENI-ÇERI...
...THE METHU-SELAH CORPS UNDER AUGUSTA'S DIRECT CONTROL.
STRANGE.
THEY RARELY LEAVE THE CASTLE.
GIUDICE BAIBARS!!

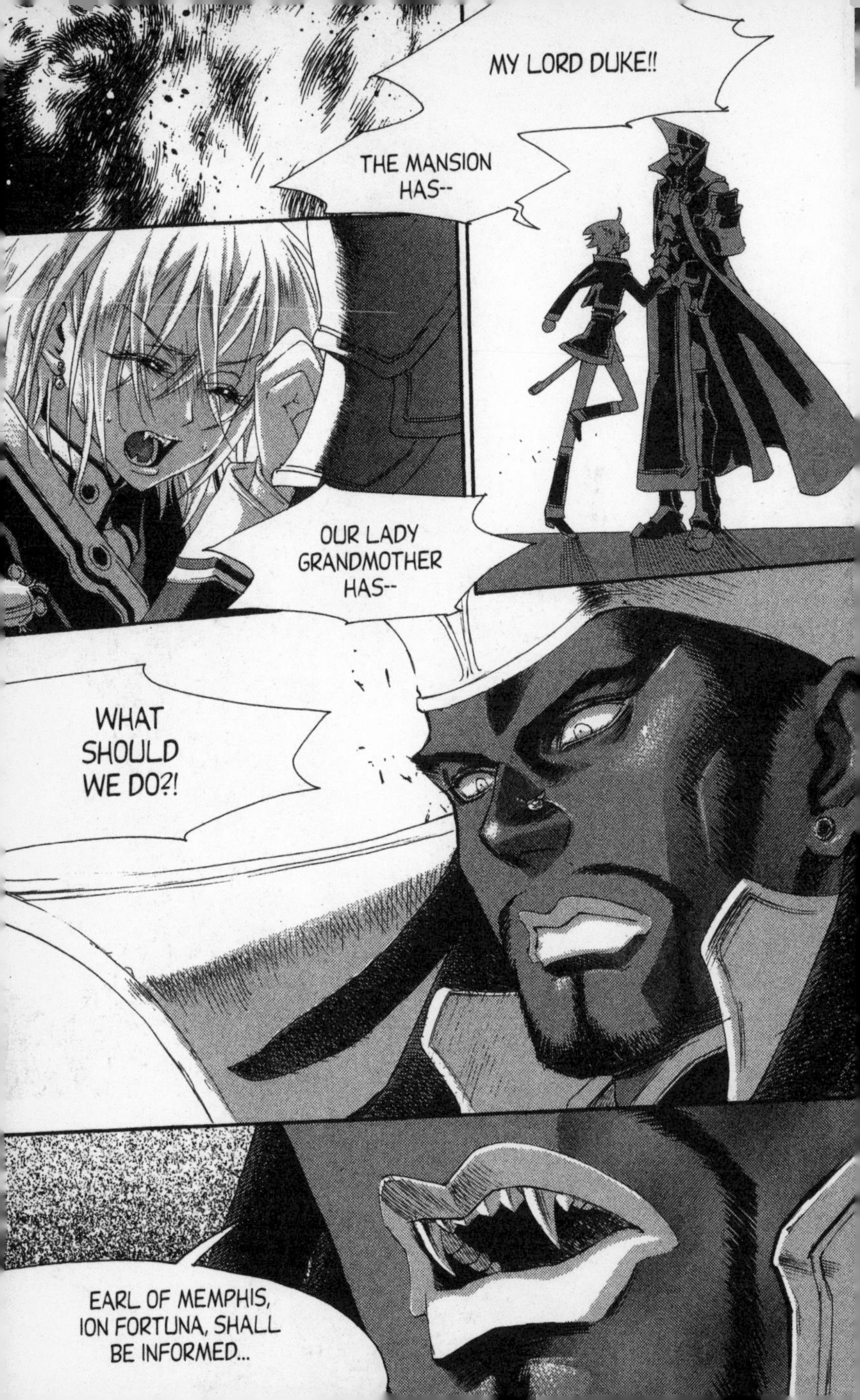
MY LORD DUKE!!
THE MANSION HAS--
OUR LADY GRANDMOTHER HAS--
WHAT SHOULD WE DO?!
EARL OF MEMPHIS, ION FORTUNA, SHALL BE INFORMED...

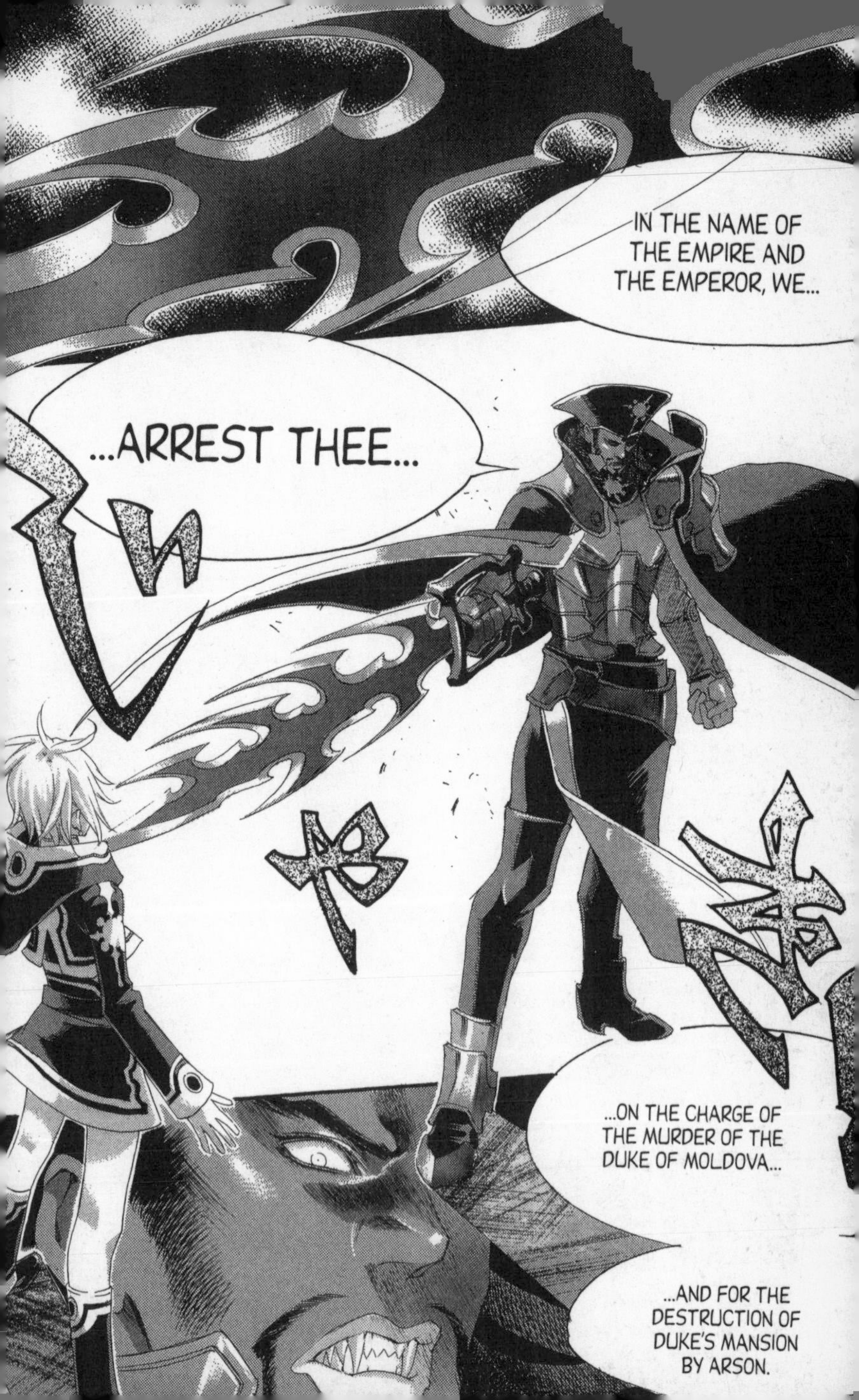
IN THE NAME OF THE EMPIRE AND THE EMPEROR, WE...
...ARREST THEE...
...ON THE CHARGE OF THE MURDER OF THE DUKE OF MOLDOVA...
...AND FOR THE DESTRUCTION OF DUKE'S MANSION BY ARSON.

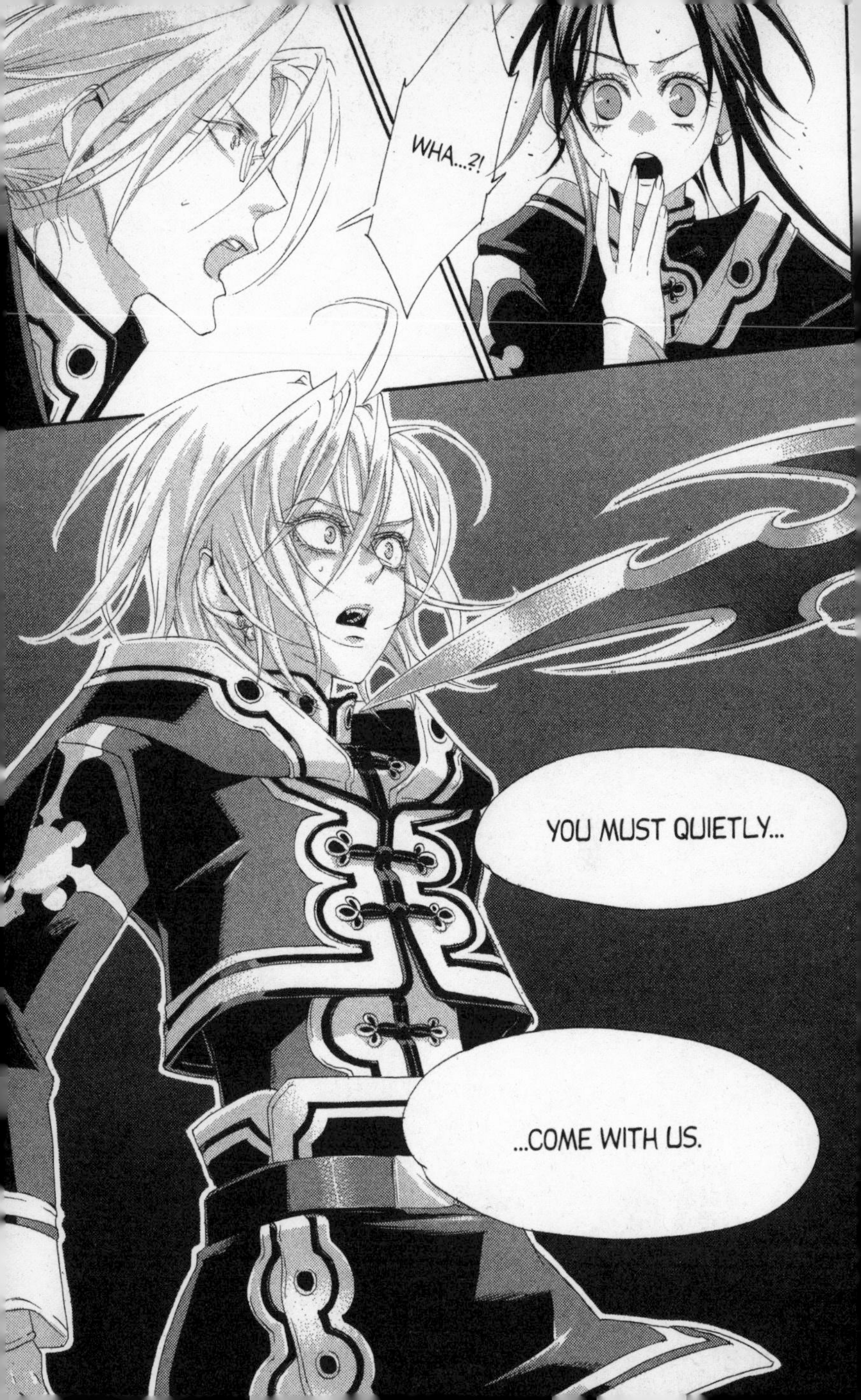
WHA...?!
YOU MUST QUIETLY...
...COME WITH US.

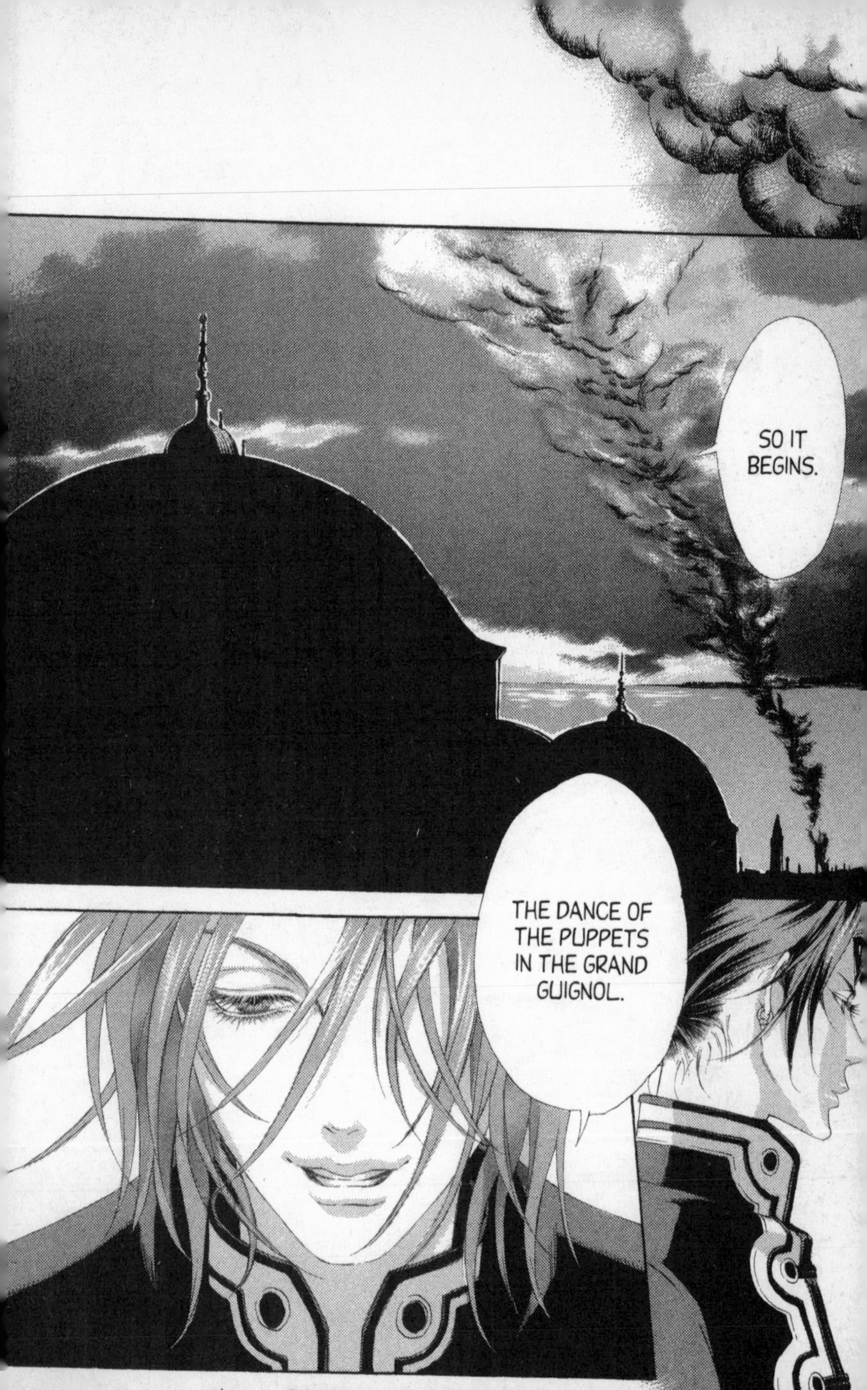
SO IT BEGINS.
THE DANCE OF THE PUPPETS IN THE GRAND GUIGNOL.

★act 23 Straight to Hell★ THE END

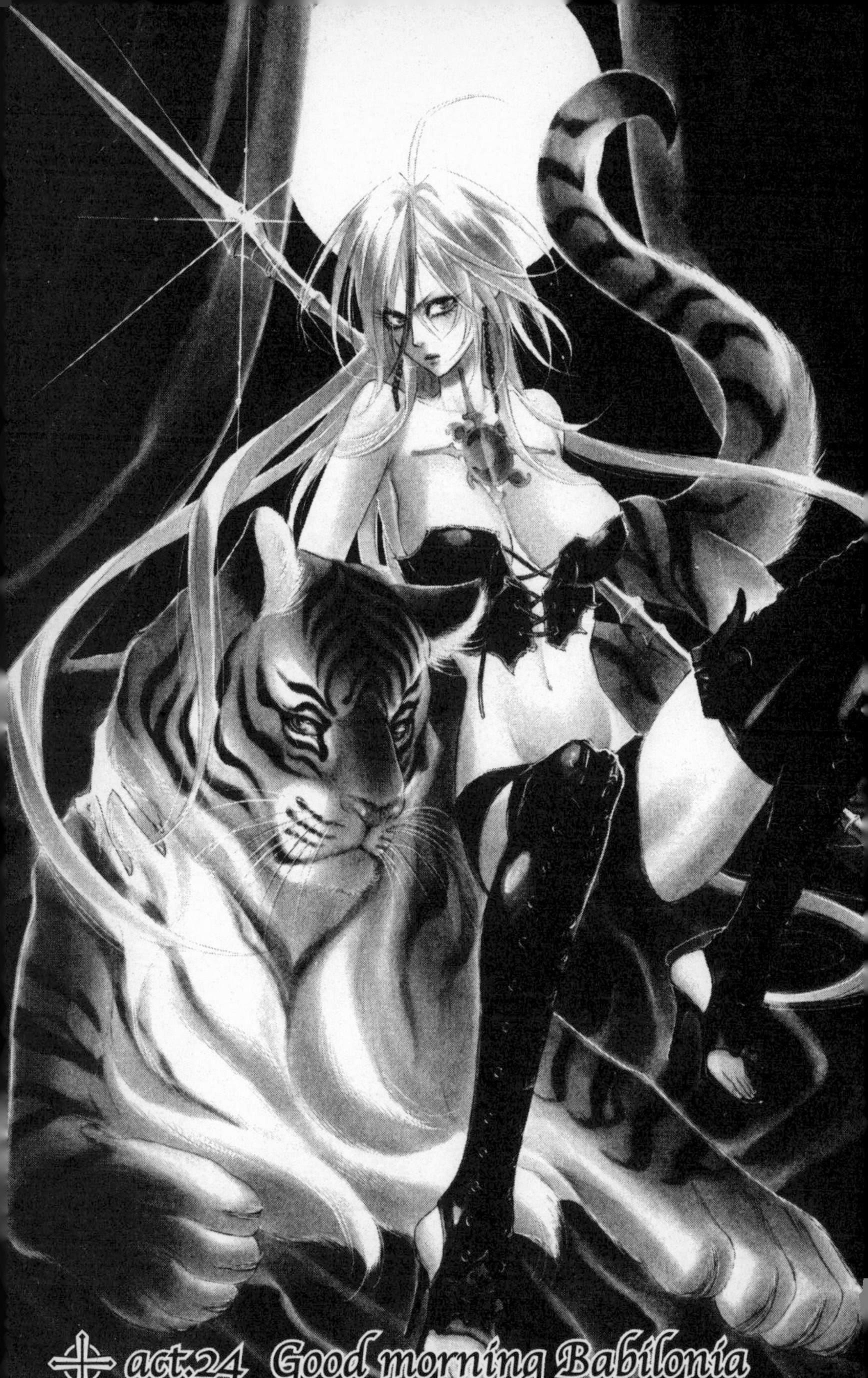

act.24 Good morning Babilonia

TRINITY BLOOD

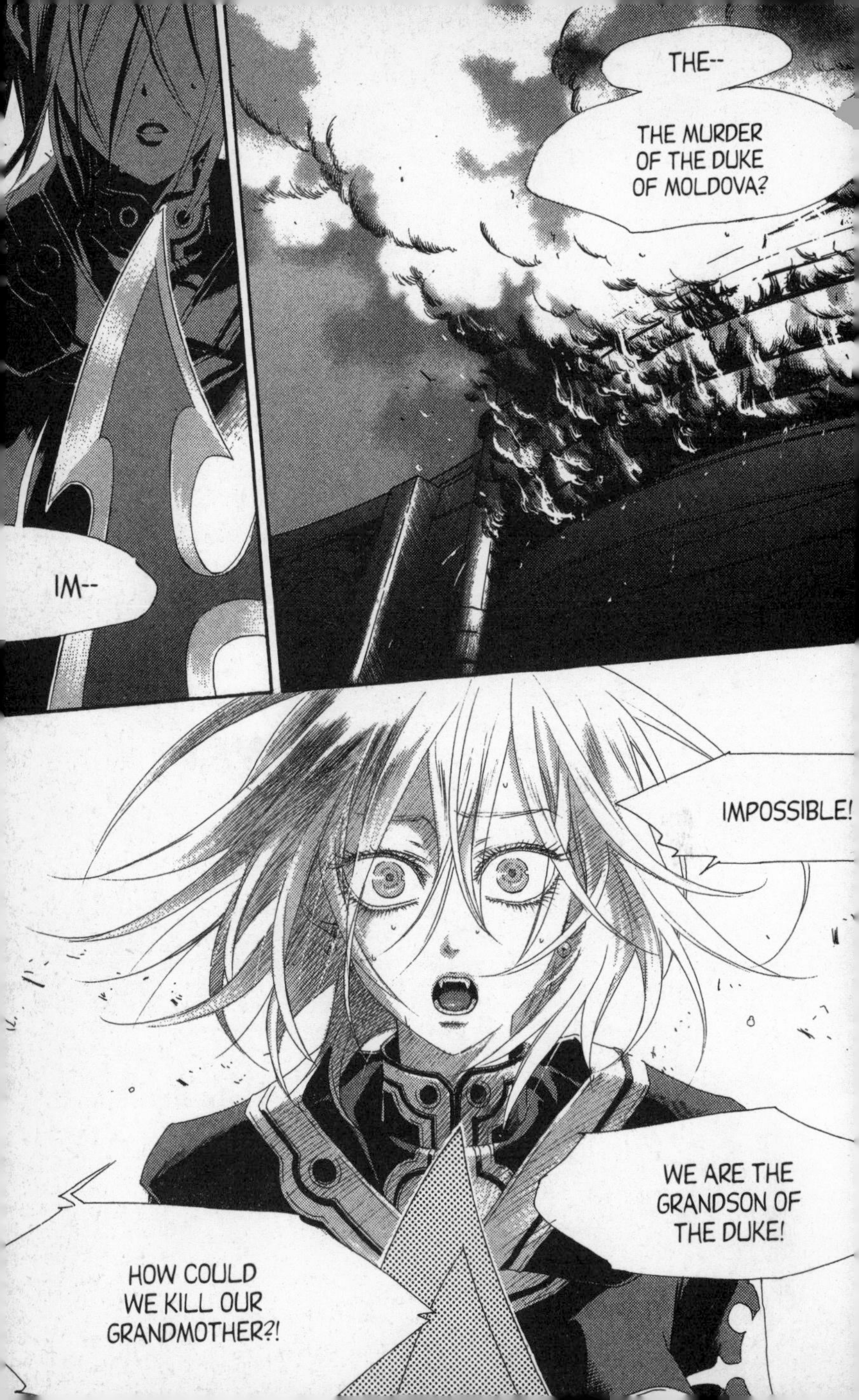
THE--
THE MURDER OF THE DUKE OF MOLDOVA?
IM--
IMPOSSIBLE!
WE ARE THE GRANDSON OF THE DUKE!
HOW COULD WE KILL OUR GRANDMOTHER?!

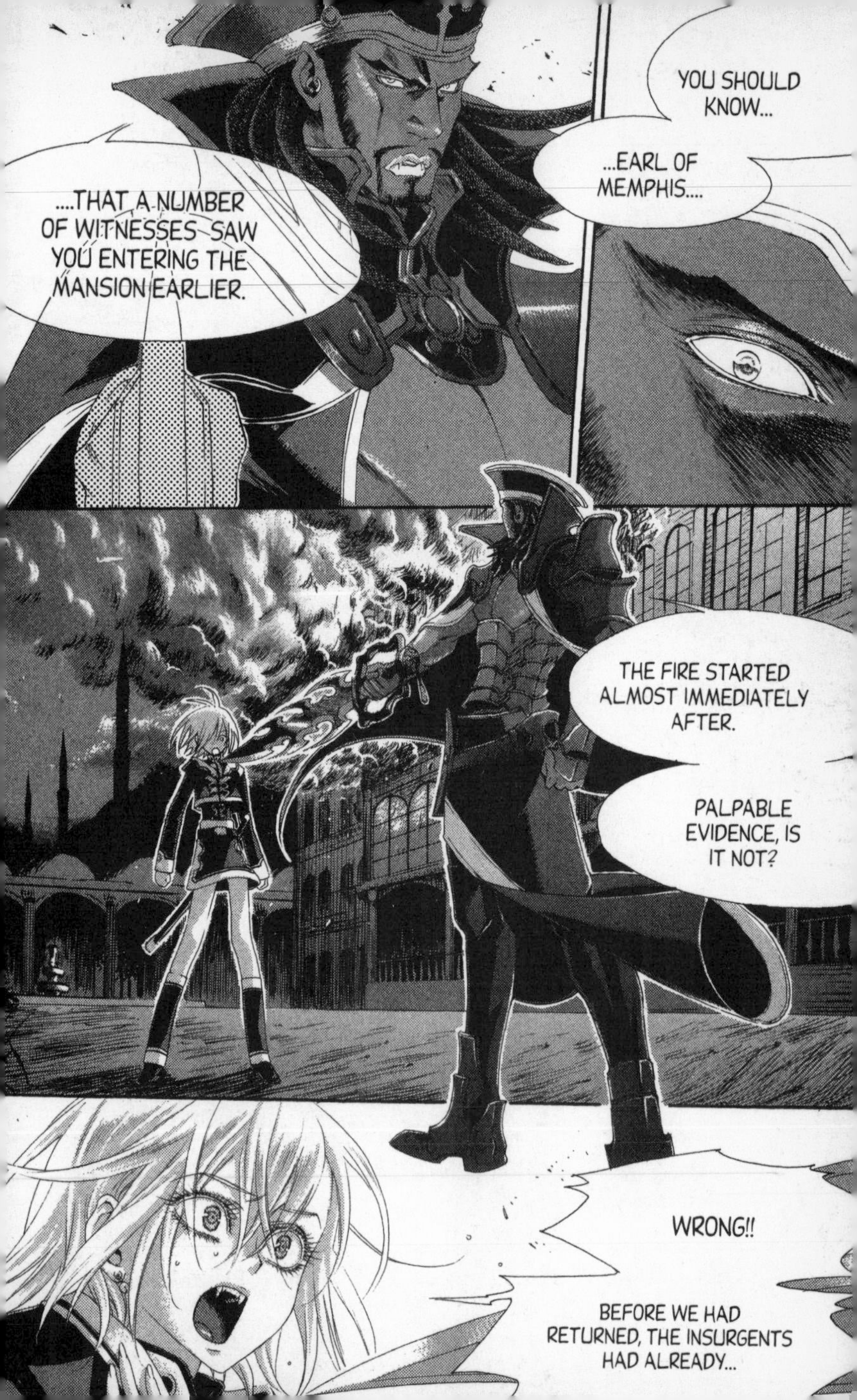
YOU SHOULD KNOW...
...EARL OF MEMPHIS....
....THAT A NUMBER OF WITNESSES SAW YOU ENTERING THE MANSION EARLIER.
THE FIRE STARTED ALMOST IMMEDIATELY AFTER.
PALPABLE EVIDENCE, IS IT NOT?
WRONG!!
BEFORE WE HAD RETURNED, THE INSURGENTS HAD ALREADY...

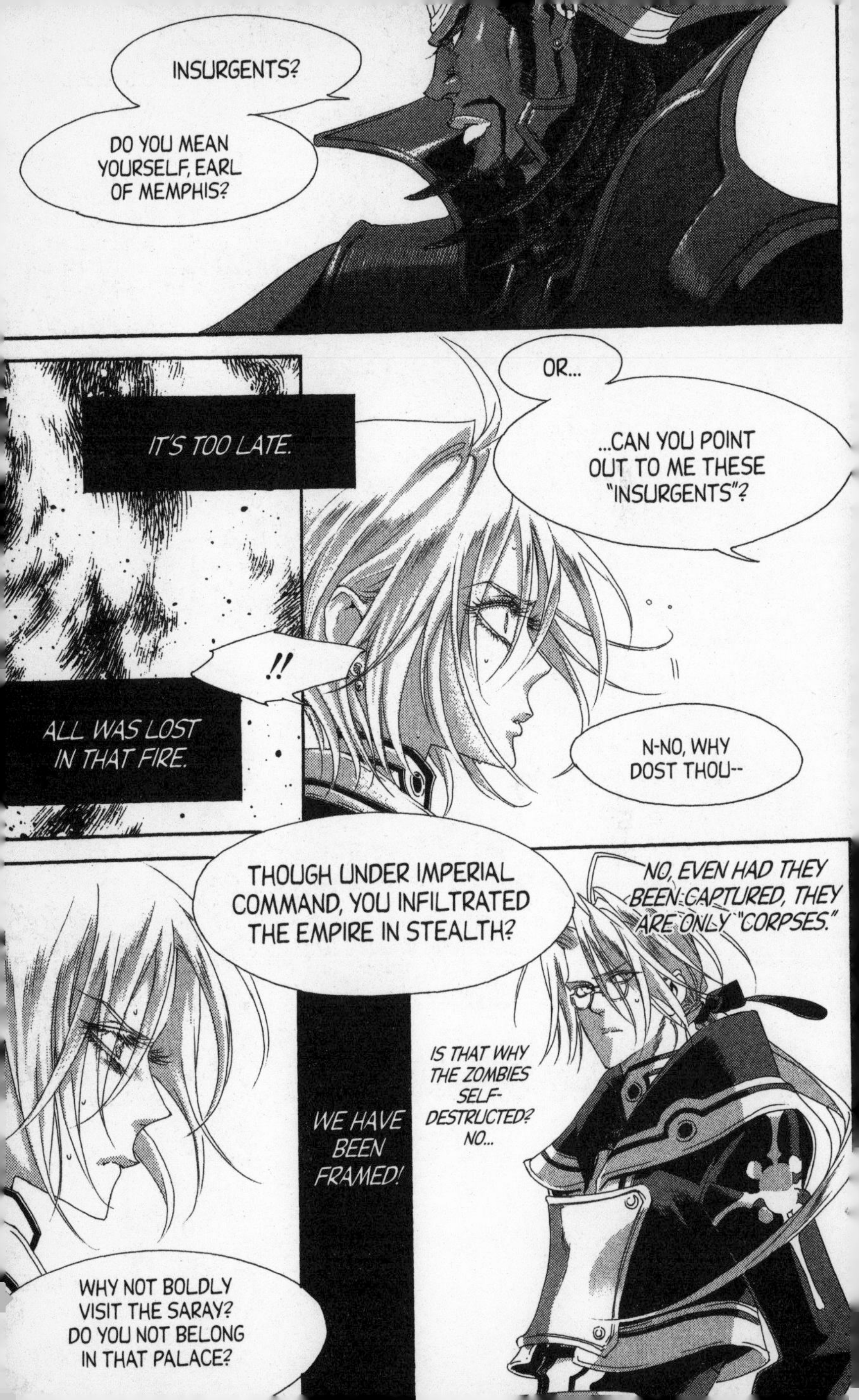
INSURGENTS?
DO YOU MEAN YOURSELF, EARL OF MEMPHIS?
OR...
...CAN YOU POINT OUT TO ME THESE "INSURGENTS"?
!!
N-NO, WHY DOST THOU--
IT'S TOO LATE.
ALL WAS LOST IN THAT FIRE.
NO, EVEN HAD THEY BEEN CAPTURED, THEY ARE ONLY "CORPSES."
IS THAT WHY THE ZOMBIES SELF-DESTRUCTED? NO...
WE HAVE BEEN FRAMED!
THOUGH UNDER IMPERIAL COMMAND, YOU INFILTRATED THE EMPIRE IN STEALTH?
WHY NOT BOLDLY VISIT THE SARAY? DO YOU NOT BELONG IN THAT PALACE?

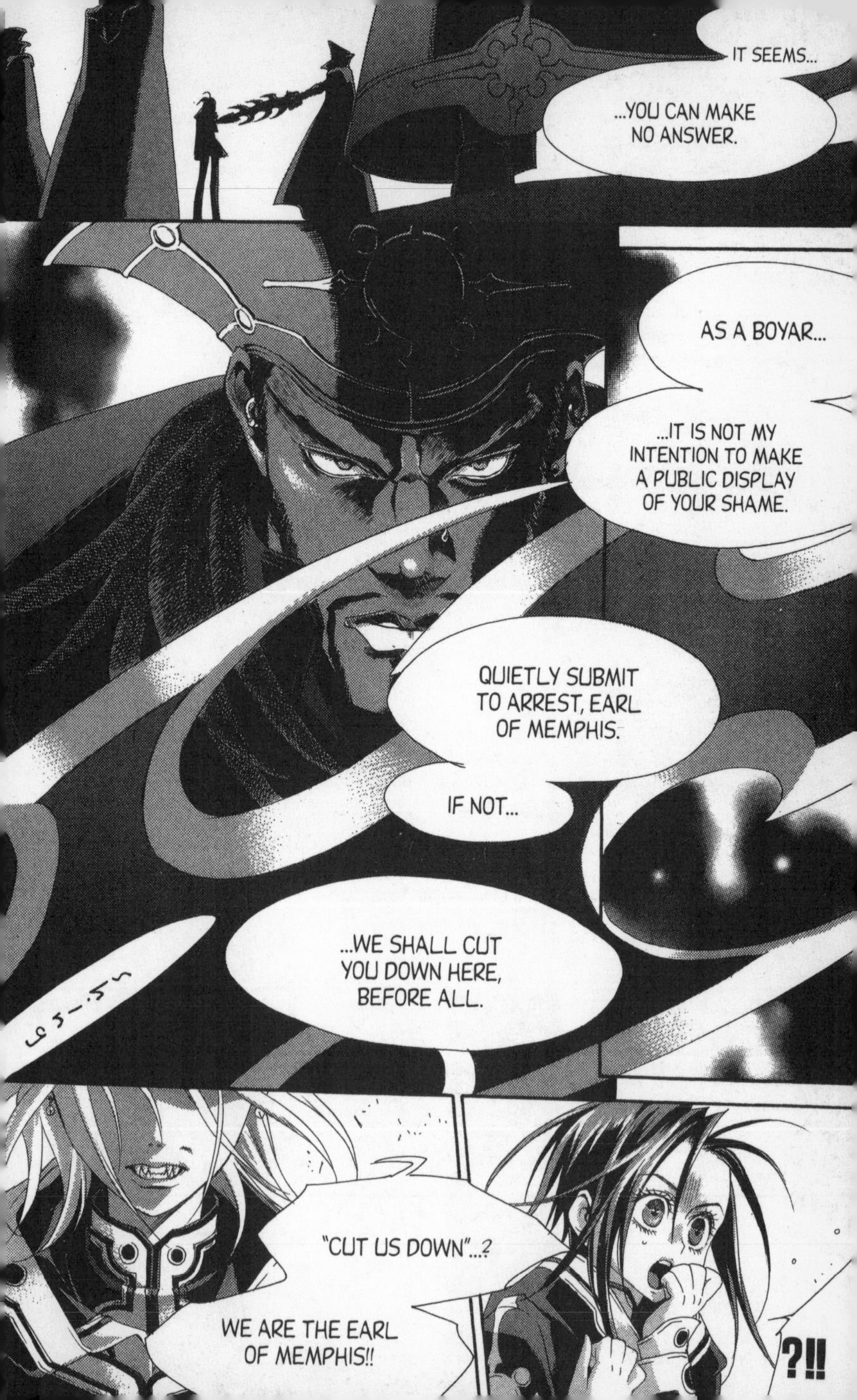
IT SEEMS...
...YOU CAN MAKE NO ANSWER.
AS A BOYAR...
...IT IS NOT MY INTENTION TO MAKE A PUBLIC DISPLAY OF YOUR SHAME.
QUIETLY SUBMIT TO ARREST, EARL OF MEMPHIS.
IF NOT...
...WE SHALL CUT YOU DOWN HERE, BEFORE ALL.
"CUT US DOWN"...?
WE ARE THE EARL OF MEMPHIS!!
?!!

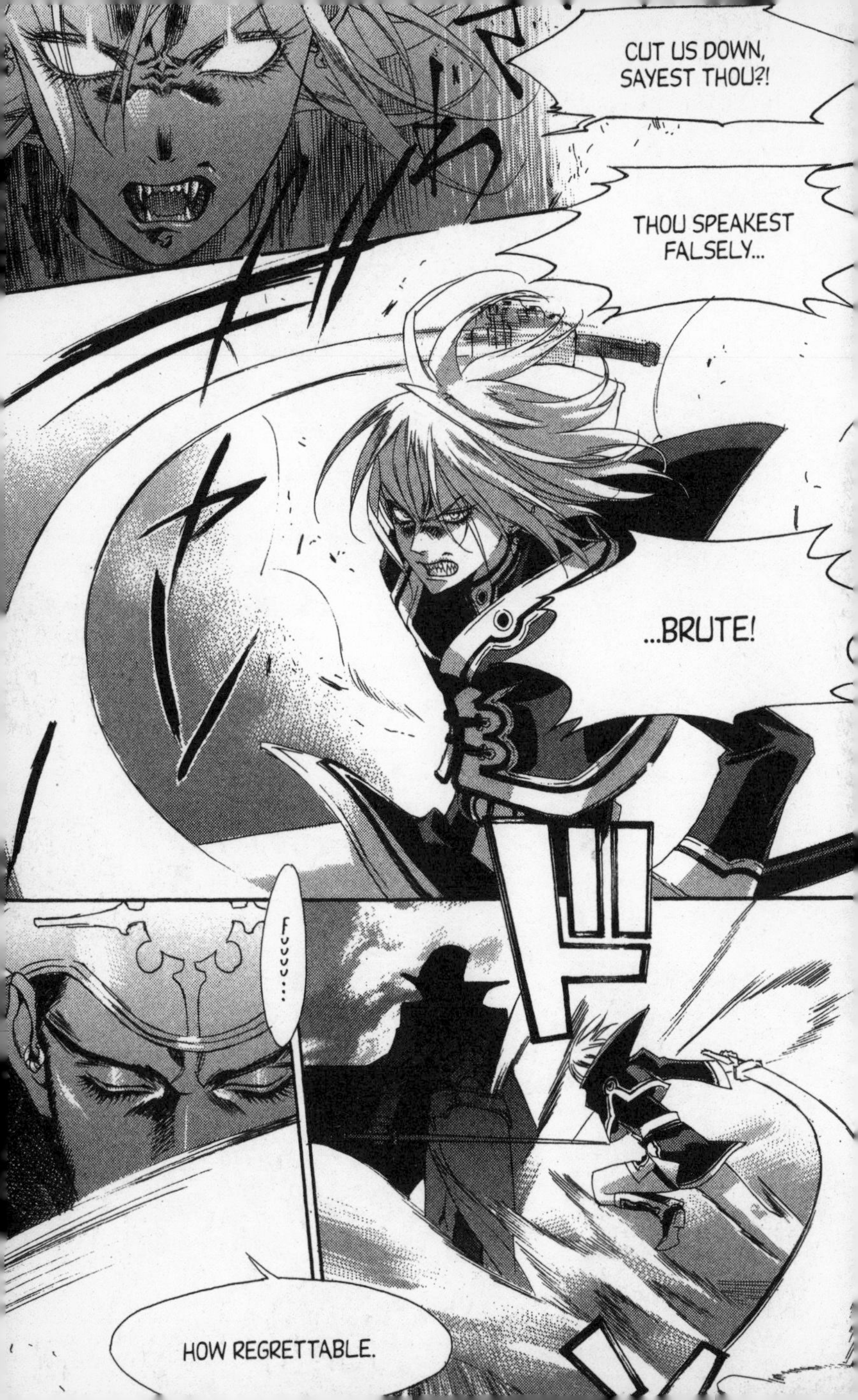
CUT US DOWN, SAYEST THOU?!
THOU SPEAKEST FALSELY...
...BRUTE!
Fuuuu...
HOW REGRETTABLE.

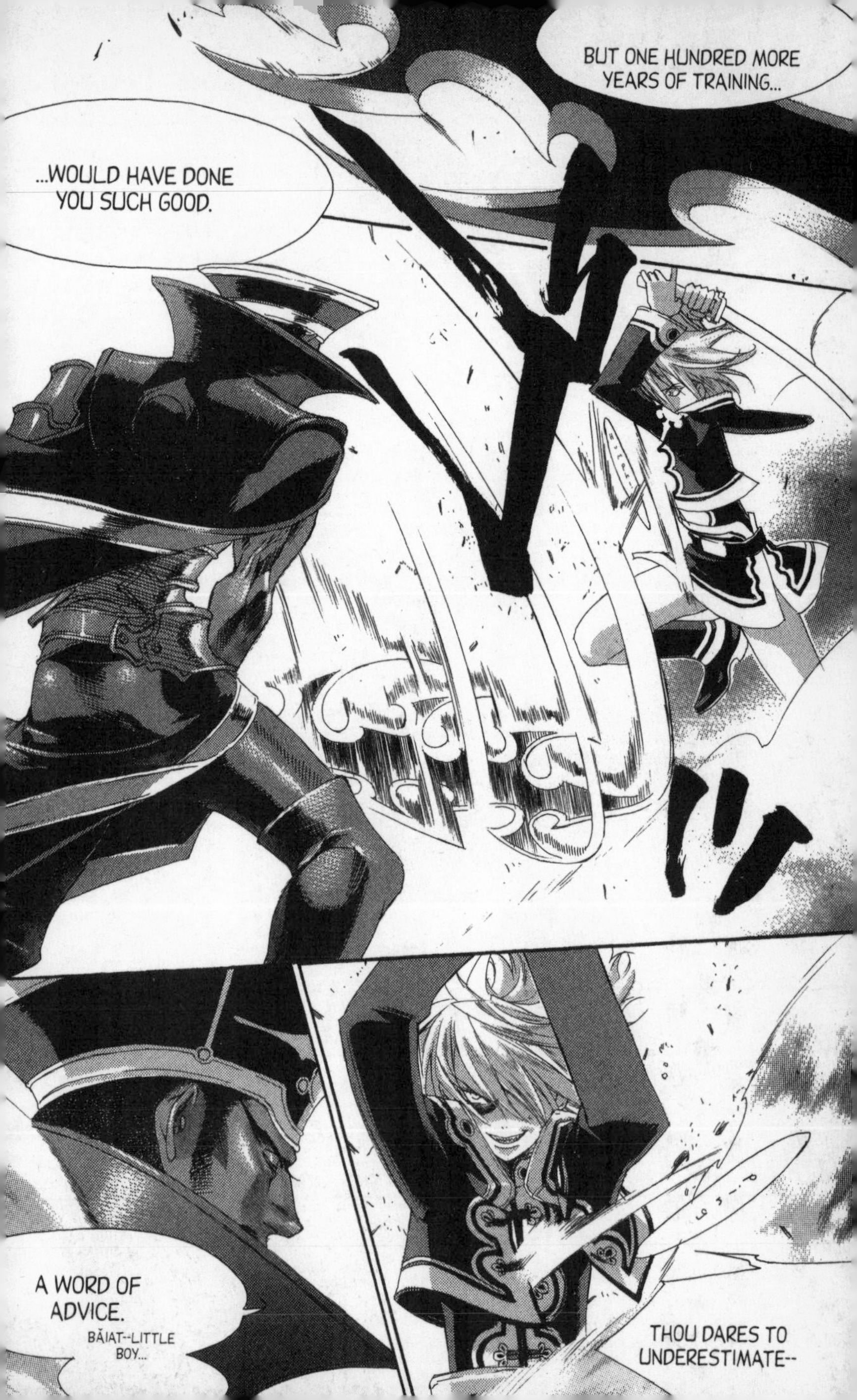
BUT ONE HUNDRED MORE YEARS OF TRAINING...
...WOULD HAVE DONE YOU SUCH GOOD.
THOU DARES TO UNDERESTIMATE--
A WORD OF ADVICE.
BĂIAT--LITTLE BOY...

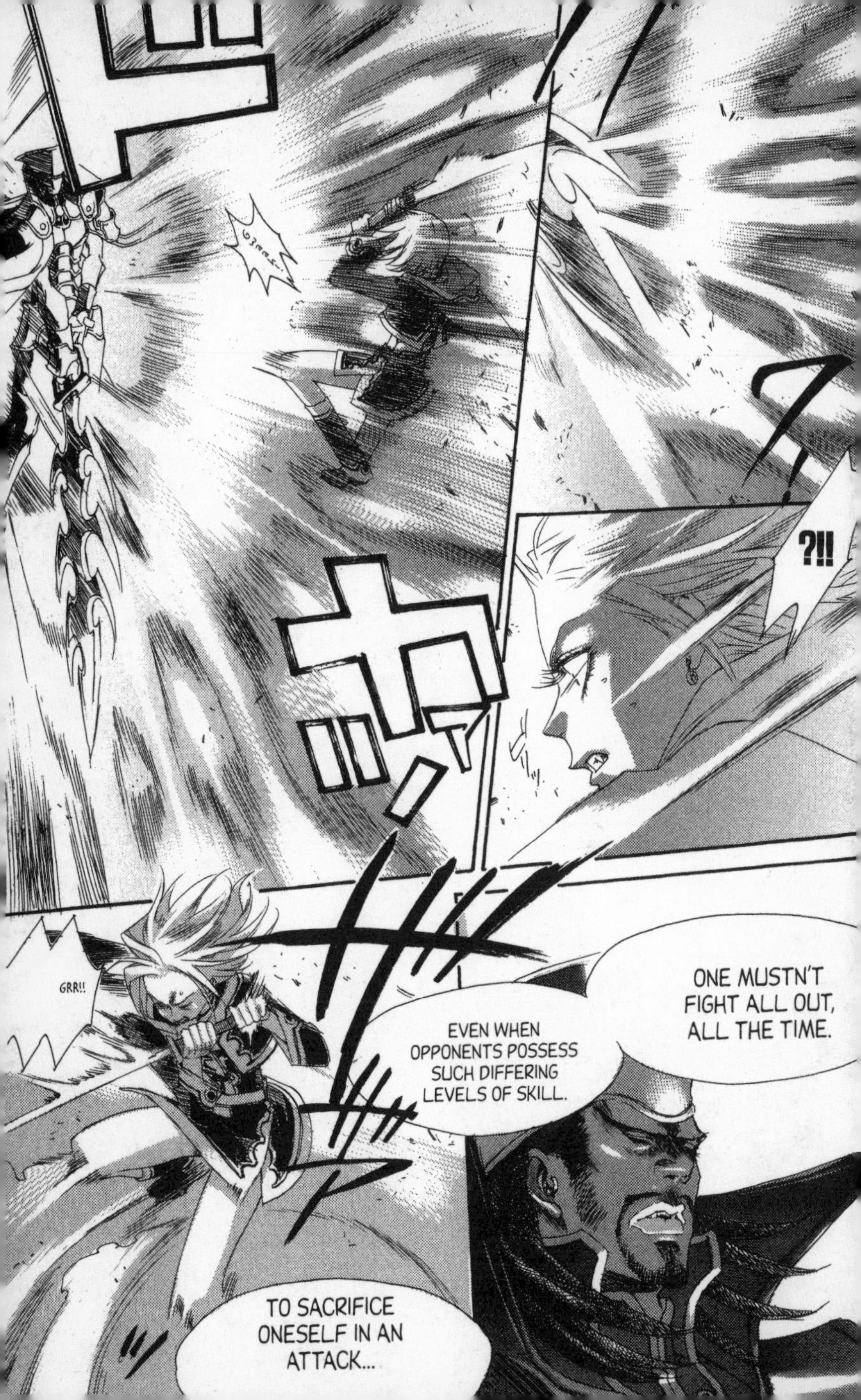
?!!
ONE MUSTN'T FIGHT ALL OUT, ALL THE TIME.
EVEN WHEN OPPONENTS POSSESS SUCH DIFFERING LEVELS OF SKILL.
GRR!!
TO SACRIFICE ONESELF IN AN ATTACK...

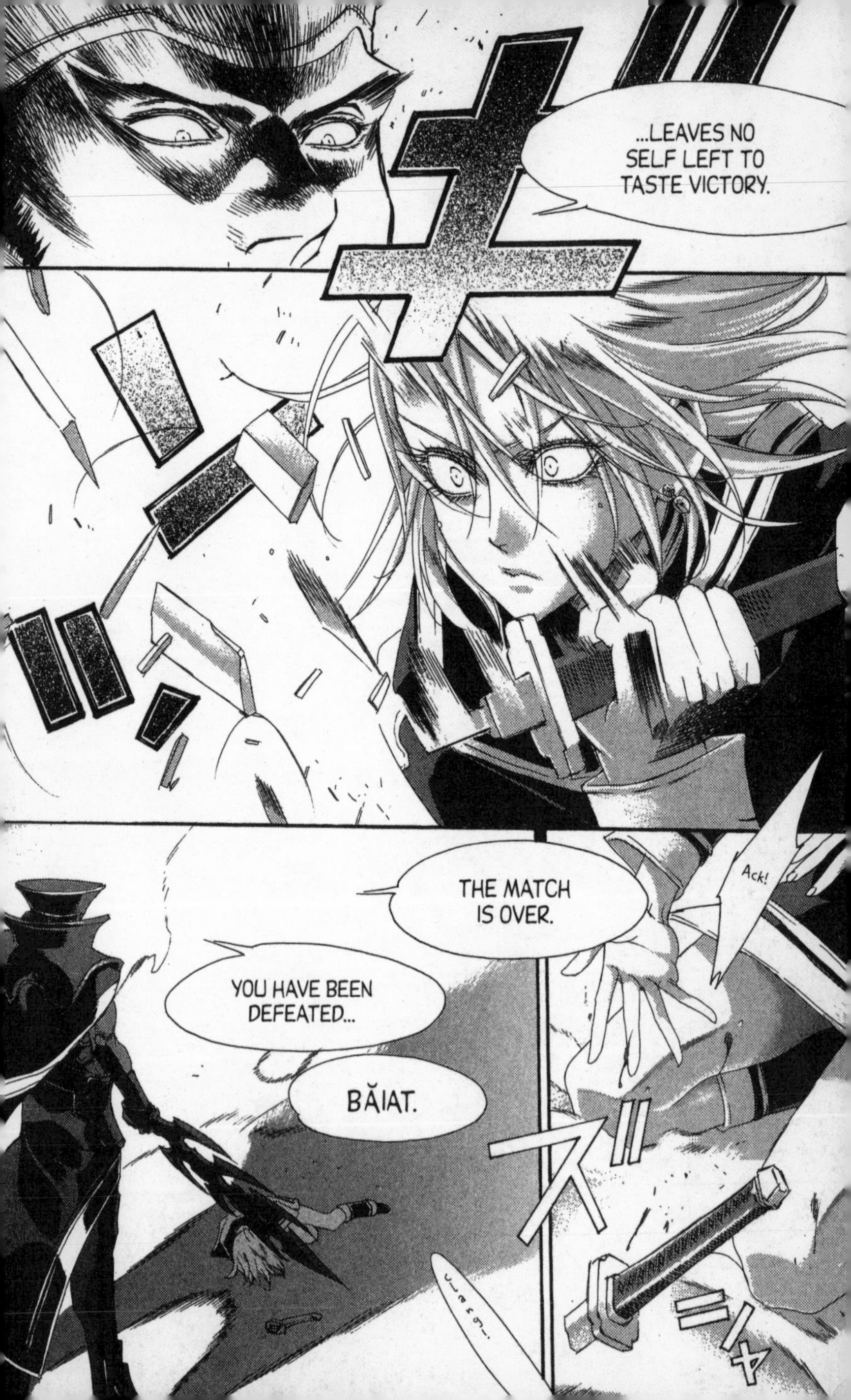

...LEAVES NO SELF LEFT TO TASTE VICTORY.
Ack!
THE MATCH IS OVER.
YOU HAVE BEEN DEFEATED...
BĂIAT.

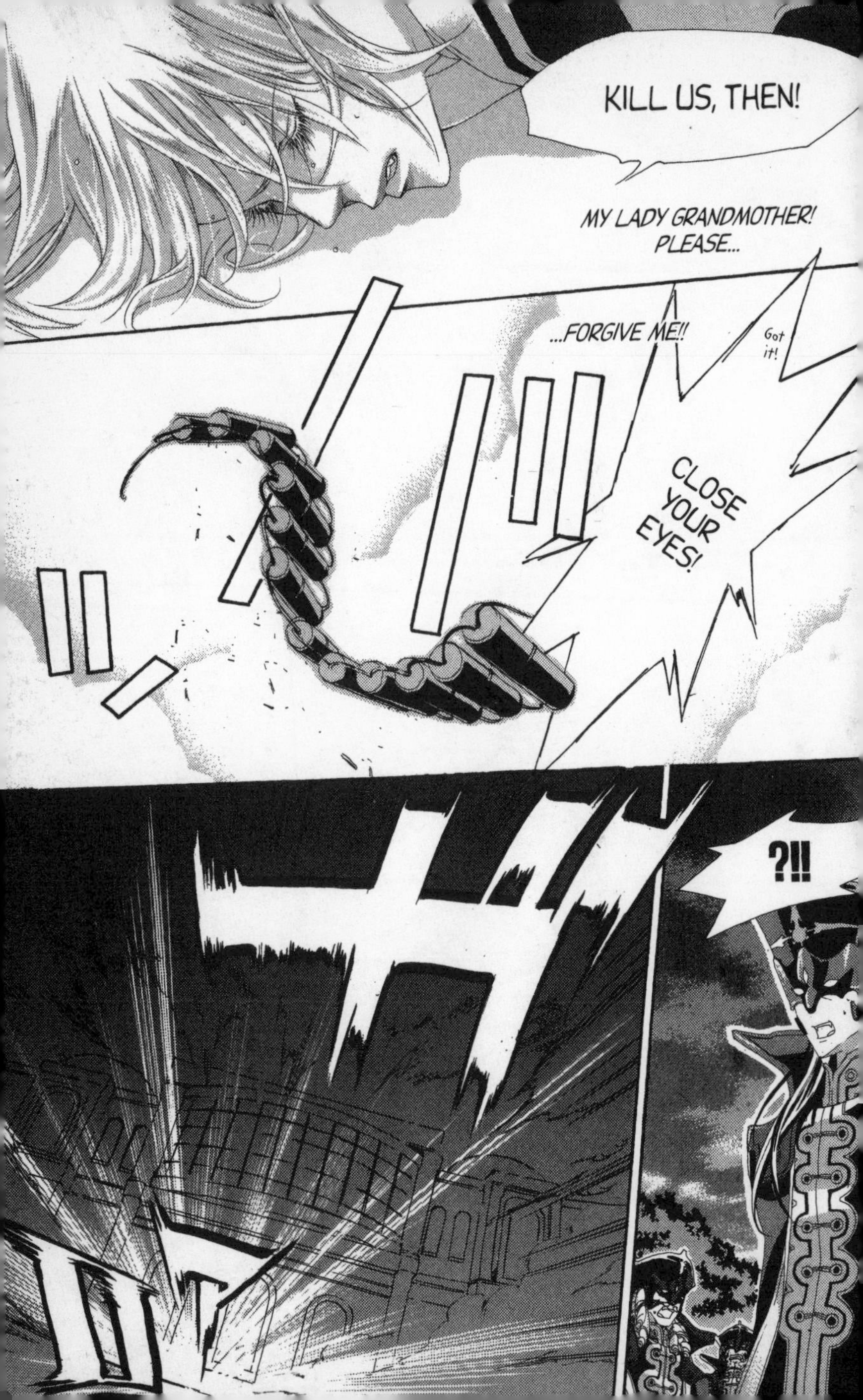
KILL US, THEN!
MY LADY GRANDMOTHER! PLEASE...
...FORGIVE ME!!
Got it!
CLOSE YOUR EYES!
?!!

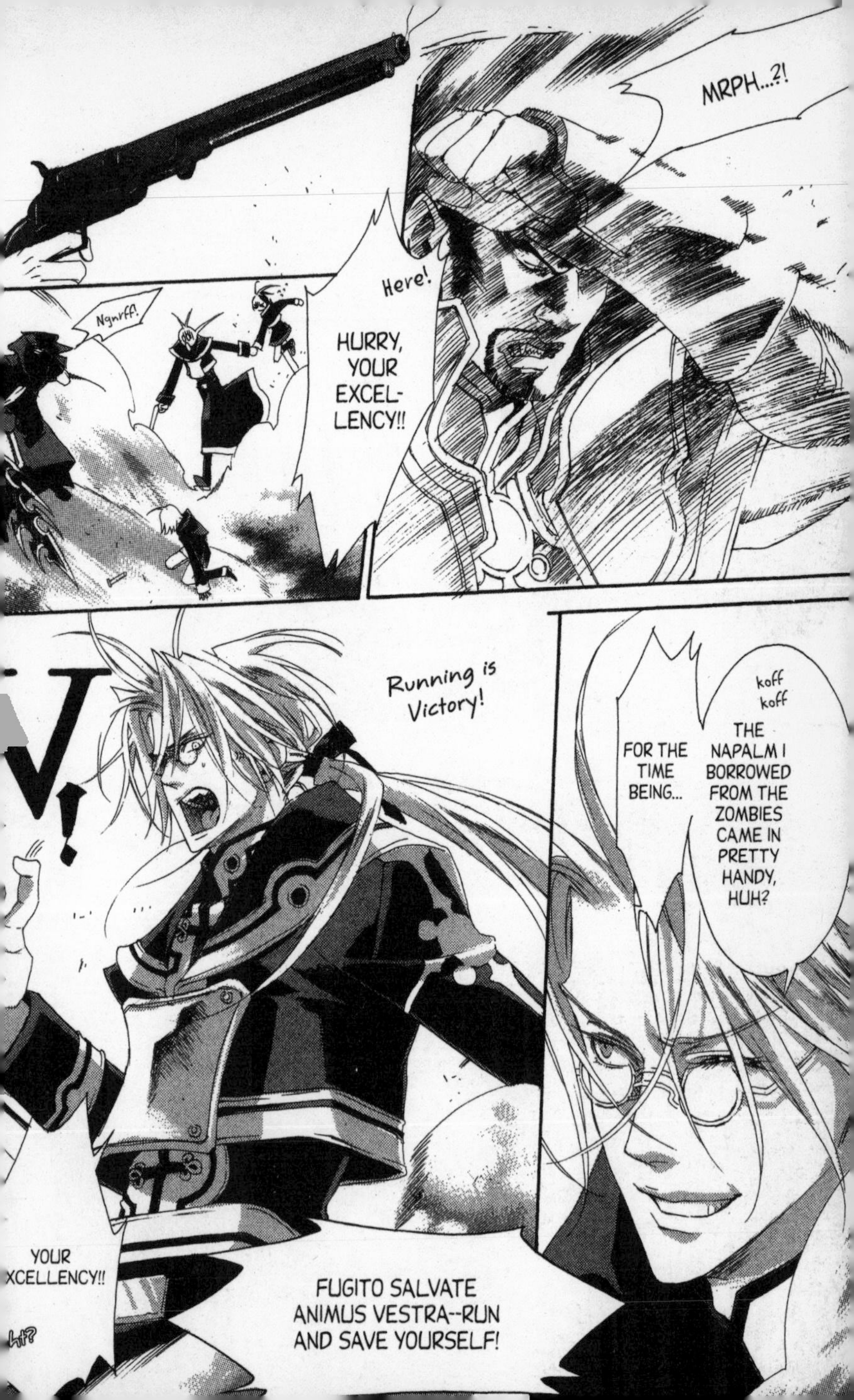
MRPH...?!
Here!
HURRY, YOUR EXCEL- LENCY!!
Ngnrff!
koff koff
THE NAPALM I BORROWED FROM THE ZOMBIES CAME IN PRETTY HANDY, HUH?
FOR THE TIME BEING...
Running is Victory!
YOUR XCELLENCY!!
FUGITO SALVATE ANIMUS VESTRA--RUN AND SAVE YOURSELF!

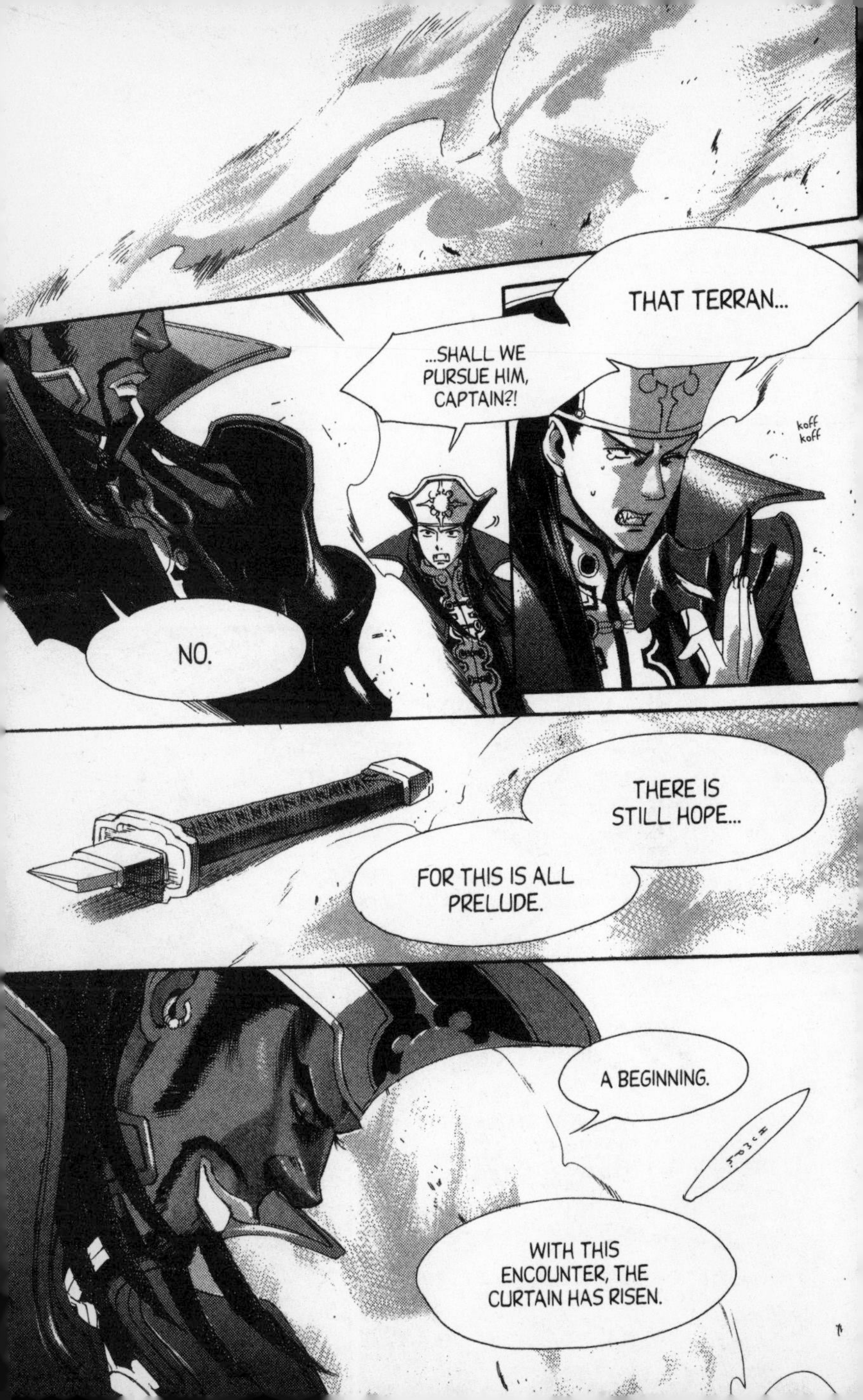
THAT TERRAN...
koff koff
...SHALL WE PURSUE HIM, CAPTAIN?!
NO.
THERE IS STILL HOPE...
FOR THIS IS ALL PRELUDE.
A BEGINNING.
WITH THIS ENCOUNTER, THE CURTAIN HAS RISEN.

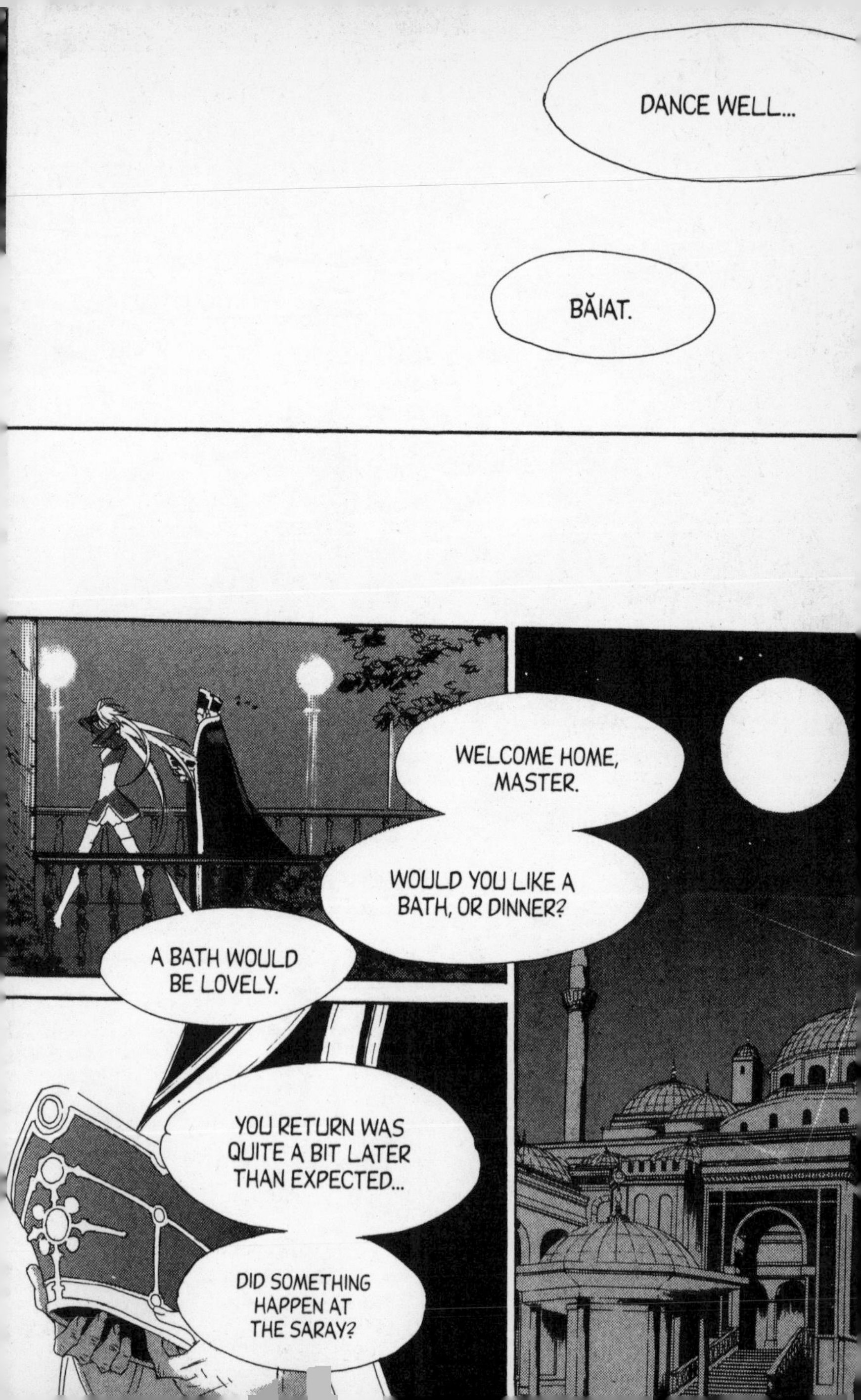
DANCE WELL...
BĂIAT.
WELCOME HOME, MASTER.
WOULD YOU LIKE A BATH, OR DINNER?
A BATH WOULD BE LOVELY.
YOU RETURN WAS QUITE A BIT LATER THAN EXPECTED...
DID SOMETHING HAPPEN AT THE SARAY?

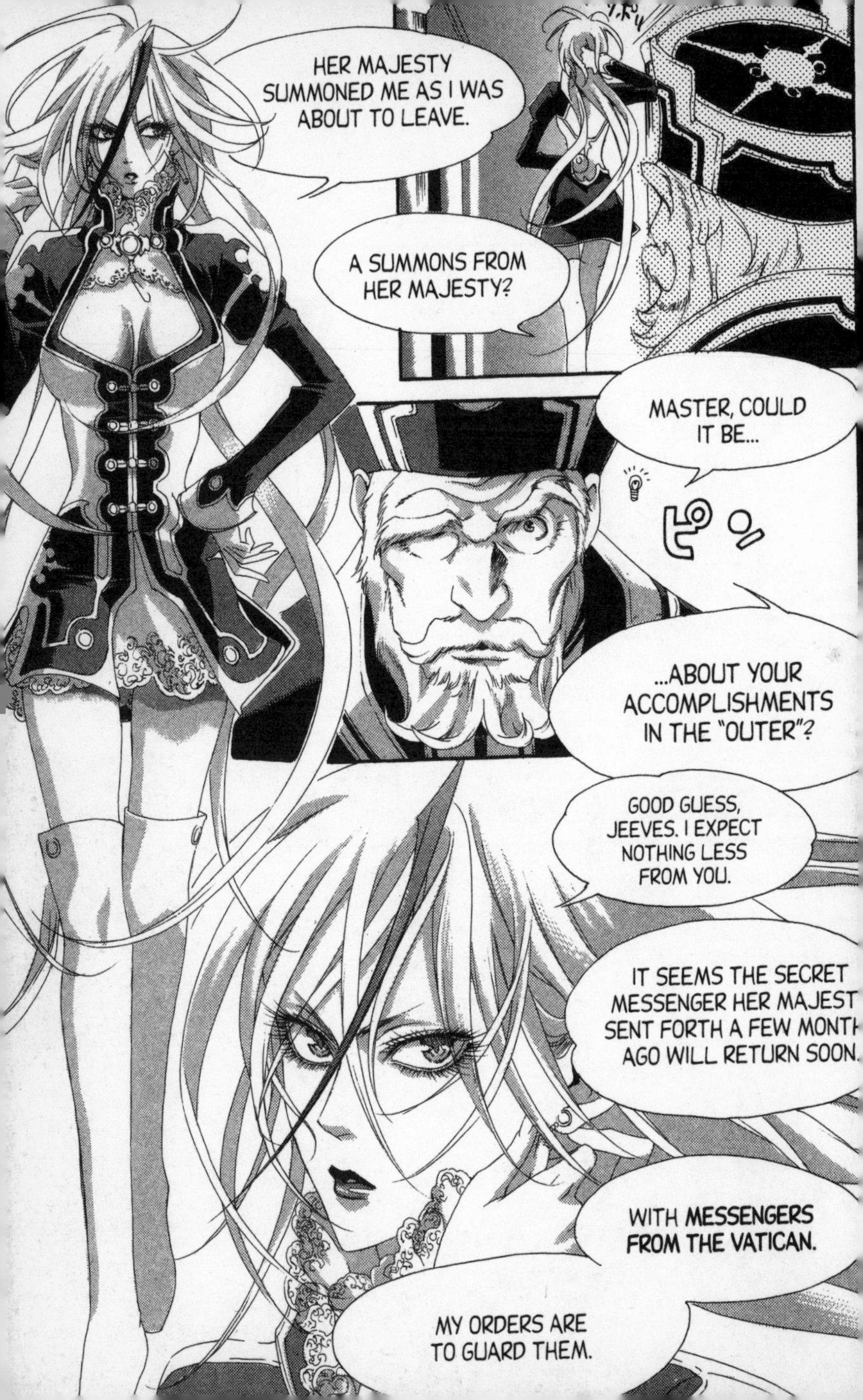
HER MAJESTY SUMMONED ME AS I WAS ABOUT TO LEAVE.
A SUMMONS FROM HER MAJESTY?
MASTER, COULD IT BE...
...ABOUT YOUR ACCOMPLISHMENTS IN THE "OUTER"?
GOOD GUESS, JEEVES. I EXPECT NOTHING LESS FROM YOU.
IT SEEMS THE SECRET MESSENGER HER MAJEST SENT FORTH A FEW MONTH AGO WILL RETURN SOON.
WITH **MESSENGERS FROM THE VATICAN.**
MY ORDERS ARE TO GUARD THEM.

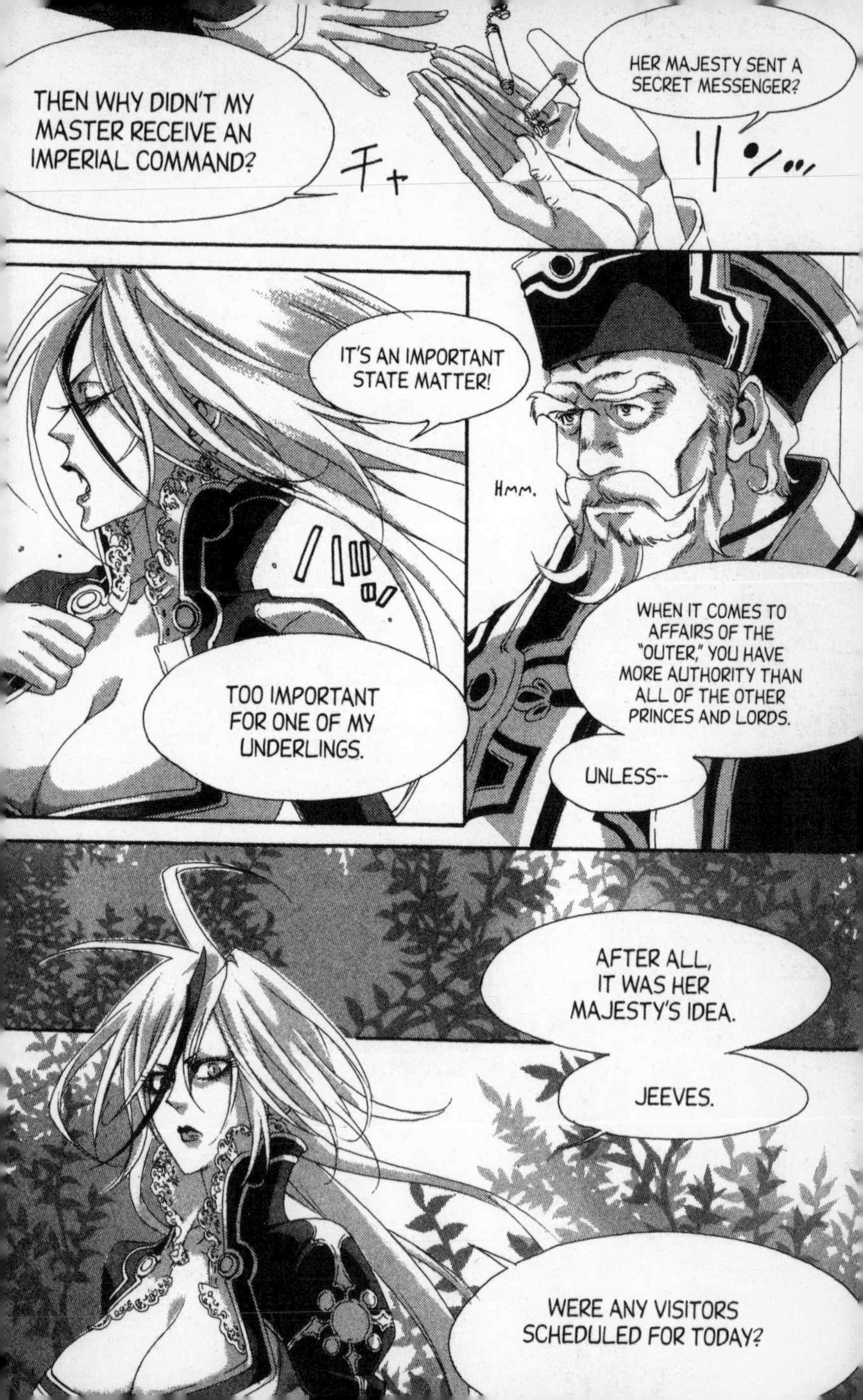
HER MAJESTY SENT A SECRET MESSENGER?
THEN WHY DIDN'T MY MASTER RECEIVE AN IMPERIAL COMMAND?
チャ
HMM.
WHEN IT COMES TO AFFAIRS OF THE "OUTER," YOU HAVE MORE AUTHORITY THAN ALL OF THE OTHER PRINCES AND LORDS.
UNLESS--
IT'S AN IMPORTANT STATE MATTER!
TOO IMPORTANT FOR ONE OF MY UNDERLINGS.
AFTER ALL, IT WAS HER MAJESTY'S IDEA.
JEEVES.
WERE ANY VISITORS SCHEDULED FOR TODAY?

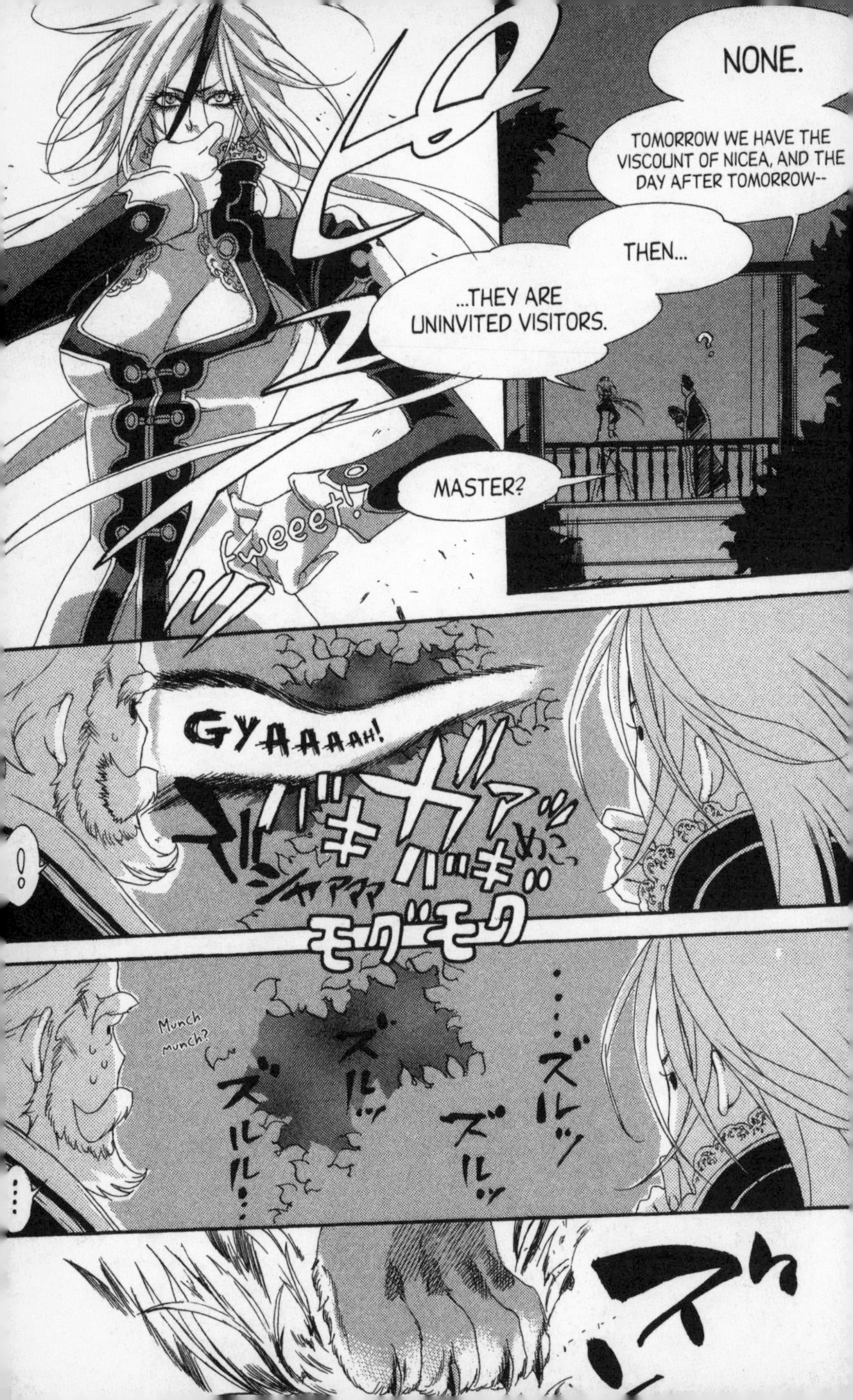
NONE.
TOMORROW WE HAVE THE VISCOUNT OF NICEA, AND THE DAY AFTER TOMORROW--
THEN...
...THEY ARE UNINVITED VISITORS.
?
MASTER?
weeeet!
GYAAAAH!
モグモグ
!
Munch munch?
....

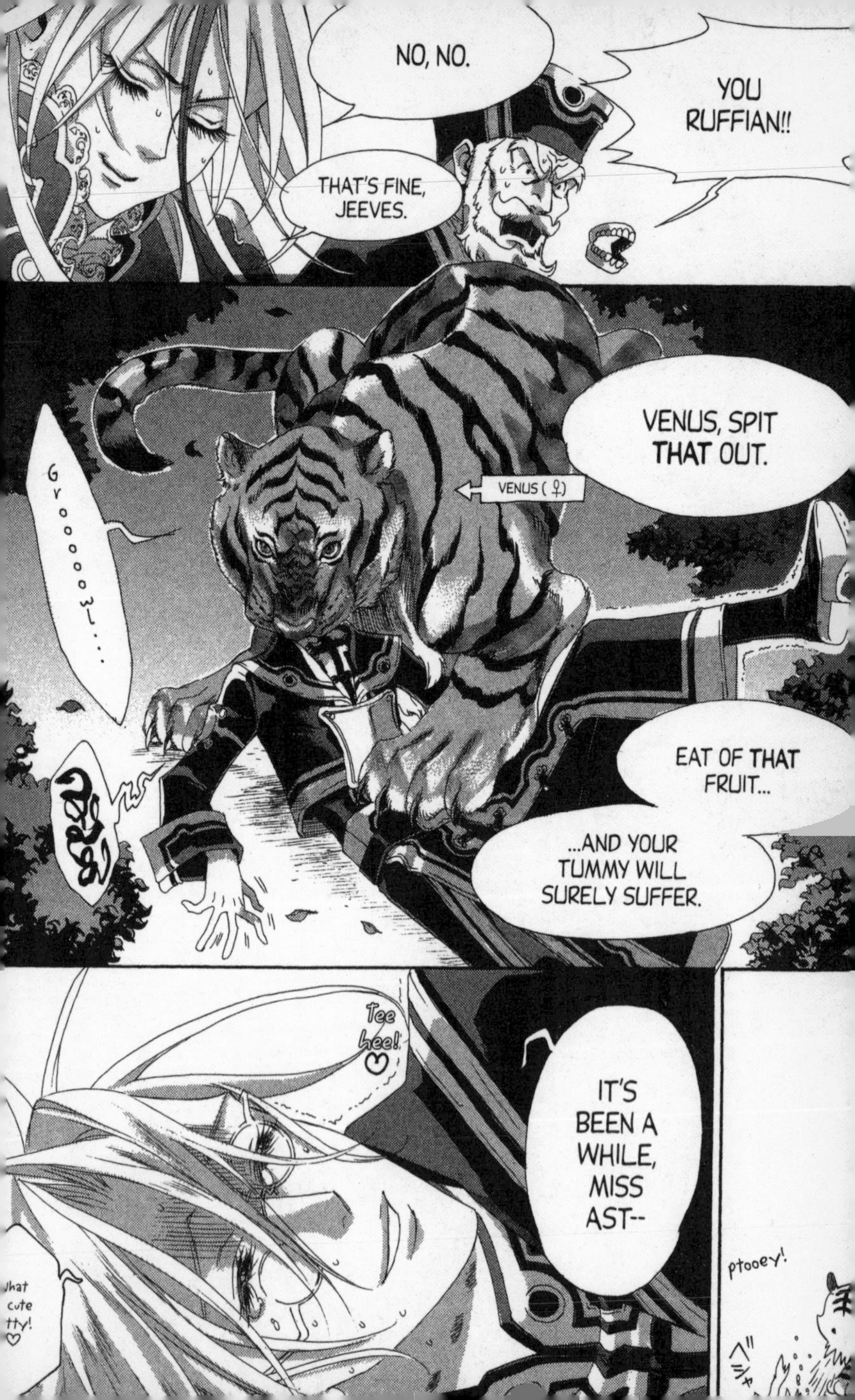
YOU RUFFIAN!!
NO, NO.
THAT'S FINE, JEEVES.
VENUS, SPIT THAT OUT.
VENUS (♀)
EAT OF THAT FRUIT...
...AND YOUR TUMMY WILL SURELY SUFFER.
Groooowl...
ptooey!
IT'S BEEN A WHILE, MISS AST--
Tee hee! ♡

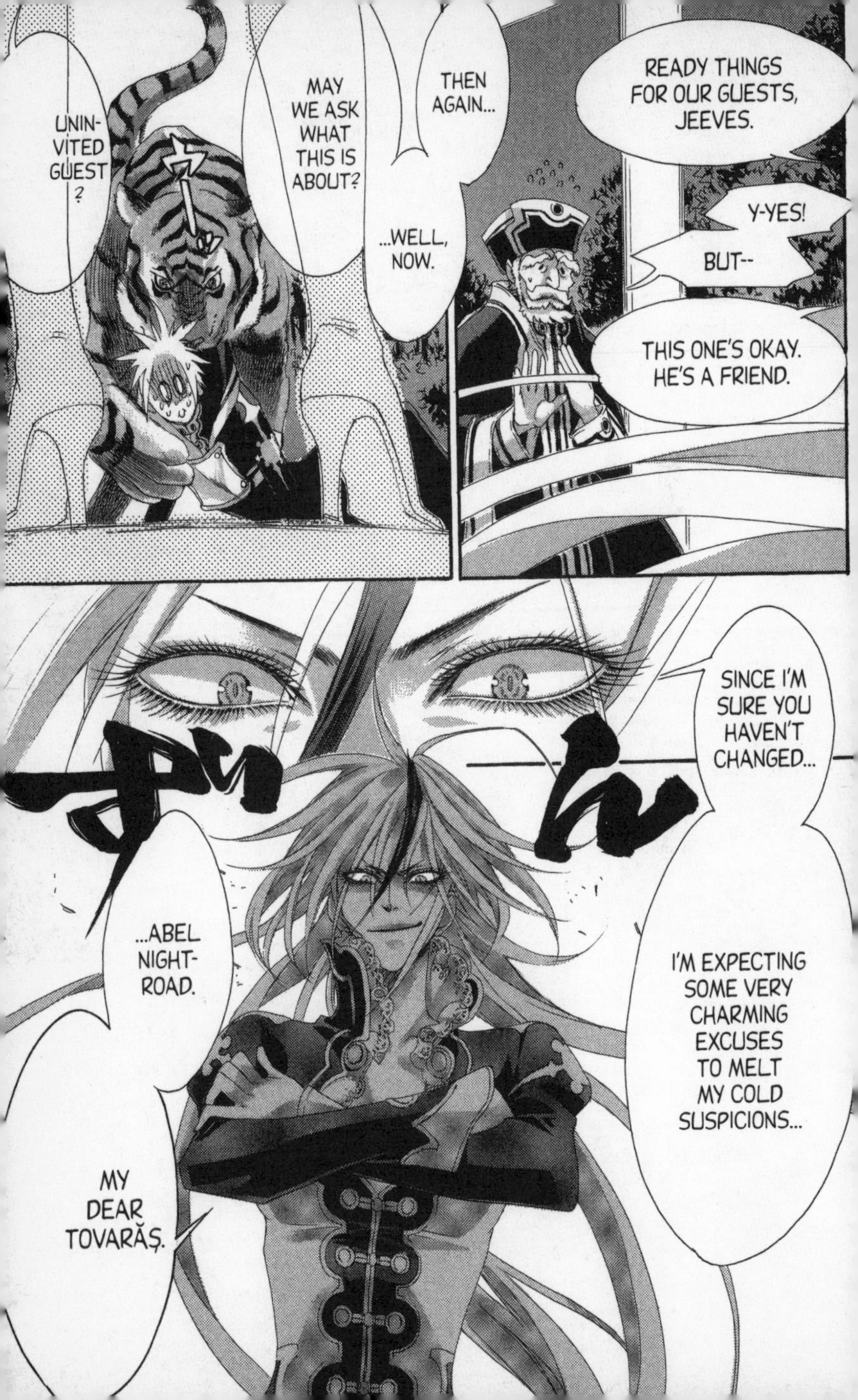
READY THINGS FOR OUR GUESTS, JEEVES.
Y-YES!
BUT--
THIS ONE'S OKAY. HE'S A FRIEND.
THEN AGAIN...
...WELL, NOW.
MAY WE ASK WHAT THIS IS ABOUT?
UNIN-VITED GUEST?
SINCE I'M SURE YOU HAVEN'T CHANGED...
I'M EXPECTING SOME VERY CHARMING EXCUSES TO MELT MY COLD SUSPICIONS...
...ABEL NIGHT-ROAD.
MY DEAR TOVARĂȘ.

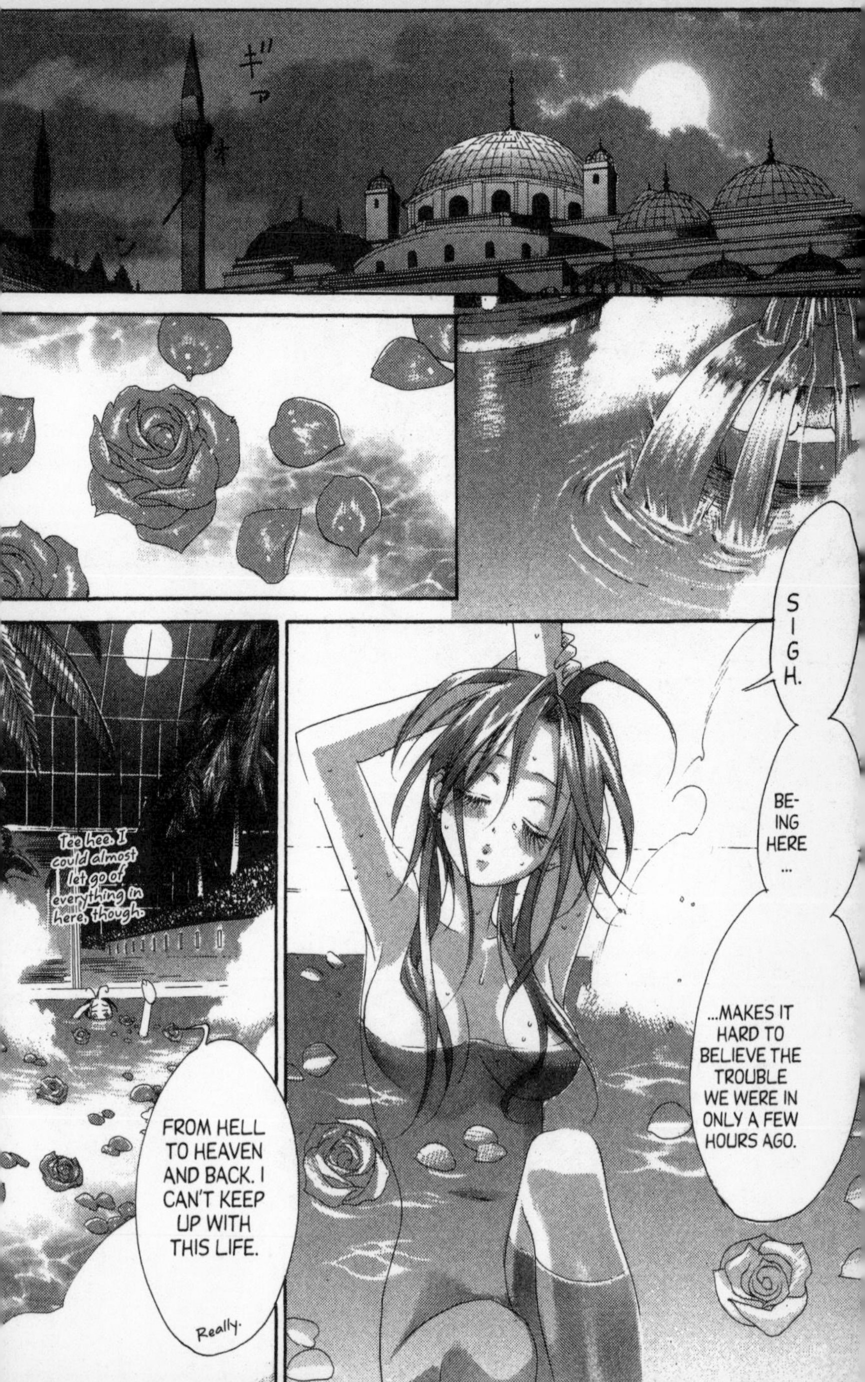
SIGH.
BE-ING HERE...
...MAKES IT HARD TO BELIEVE THE TROUBLE WE WERE IN ONLY A FEW HOURS AGO.
Tee hee. I could almost let go of everything in here, though.
FROM HELL TO HEAVEN AND BACK. I CAN'T KEEP UP WITH THIS LIFE.
Really.

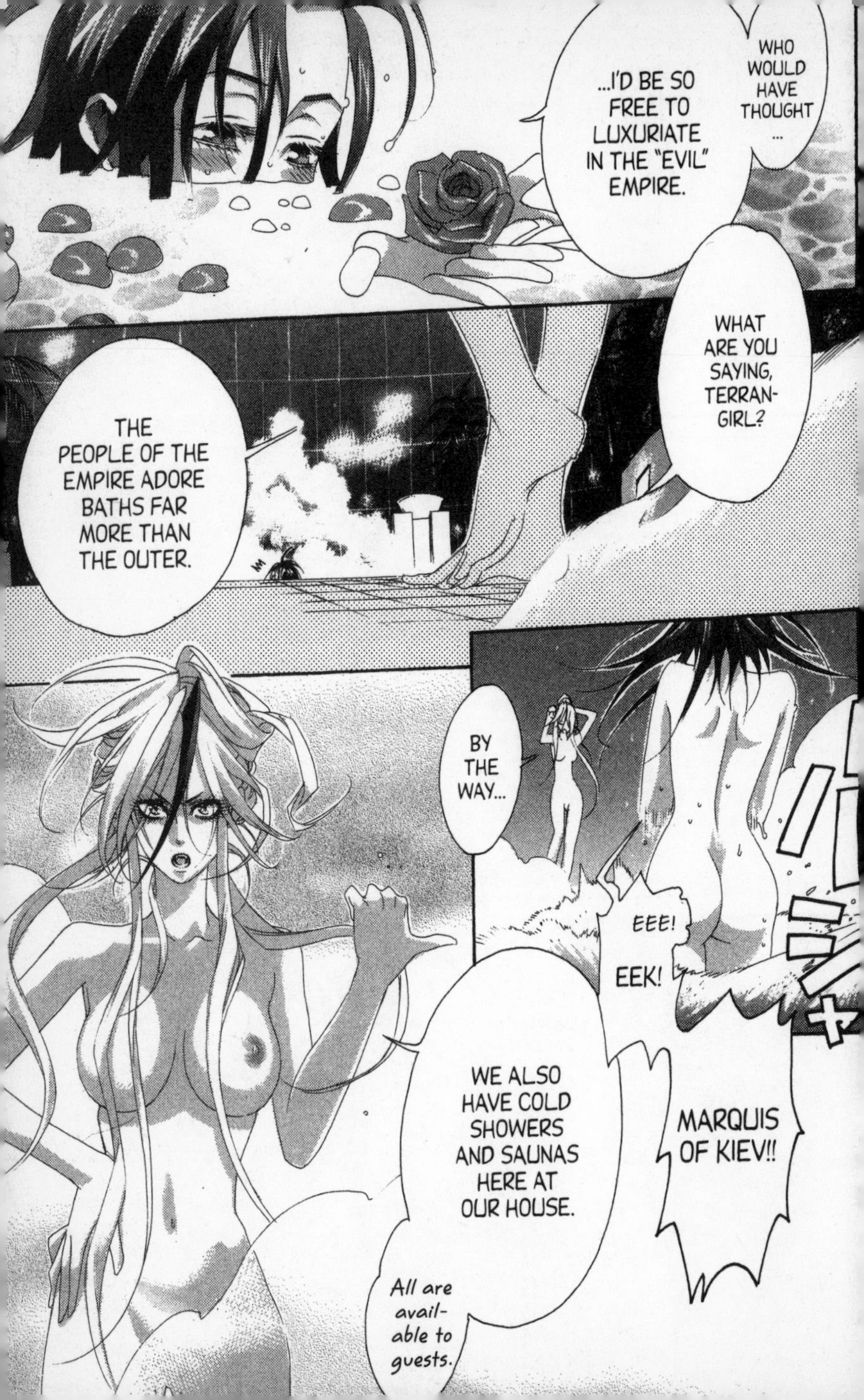
WHO WOULD HAVE THOUGHT ...
...I'D BE SO FREE TO LUXURIATE IN THE "EVIL" EMPIRE.
WHAT ARE YOU SAYING, TERRAN-GIRL?
THE PEOPLE OF THE EMPIRE ADORE BATHS FAR MORE THAN THE OUTER.
BY THE WAY...
EEE!
EEK!
MARQUIS OF KIEV!!
WE ALSO HAVE COLD SHOWERS AND SAUNAS HERE AT OUR HOUSE.
All are available to guests.

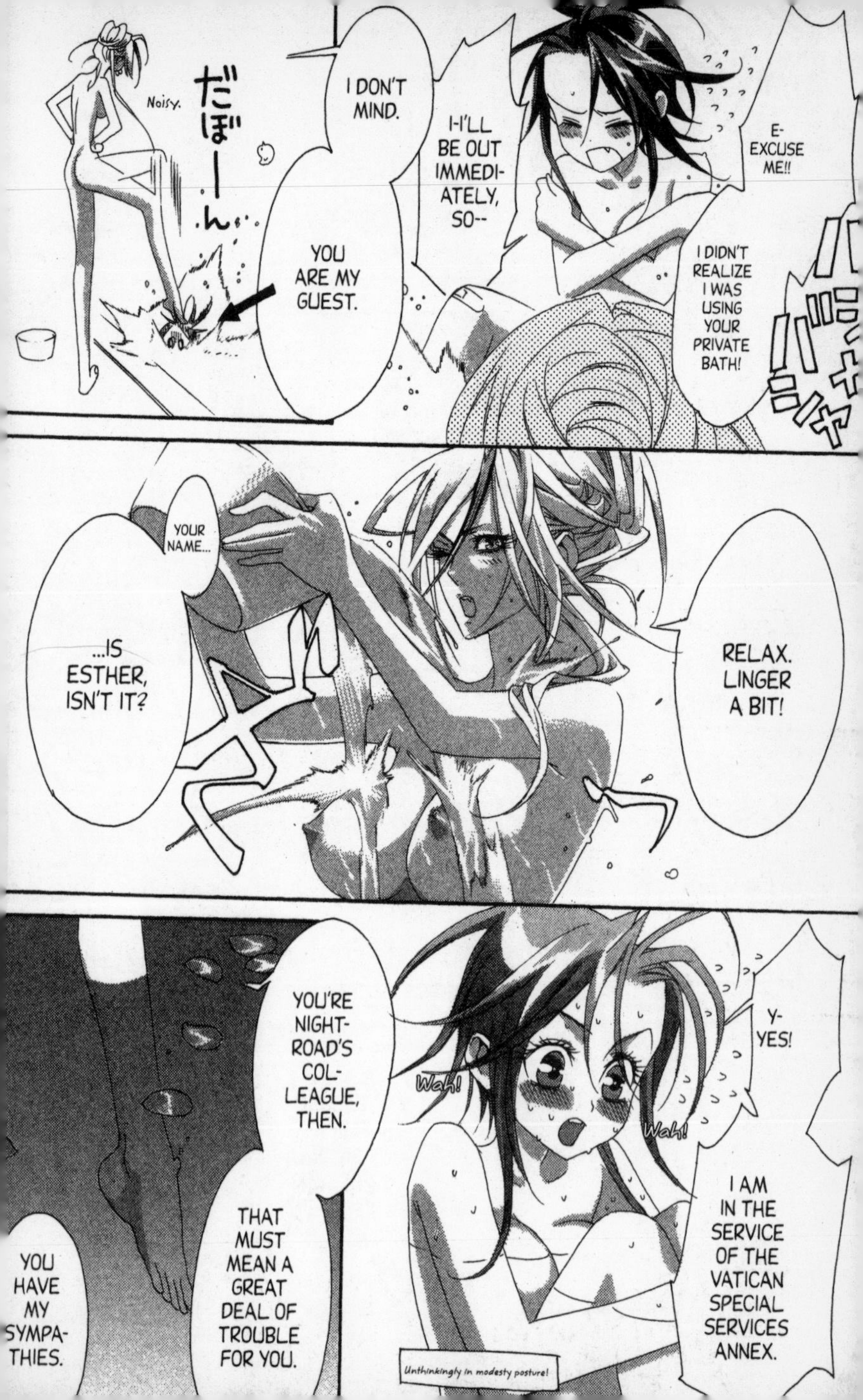
E-EXCUSE ME!!
I DIDN'T REALIZE I WAS USING YOUR PRIVATE BATH!
I-I'LL BE OUT IMMEDIATELY, SO--
I DON'T MIND.
YOU ARE MY GUEST.
だぼーん
Noisy.
RELAX. LINGER A BIT!
YOUR NAME...
...IS ESTHER, ISN'T IT?
Y-YES!
Wah!
Wah!
I AM IN THE SERVICE OF THE VATICAN SPECIAL SERVICES ANNEX.
Unthinkingly in modesty posture!
YOU'RE NIGHTROAD'S COLLEAGUE, THEN.
THAT MUST MEAN A GREAT DEAL OF TROUBLE FOR YOU.
YOU HAVE MY SYMPATHIES.

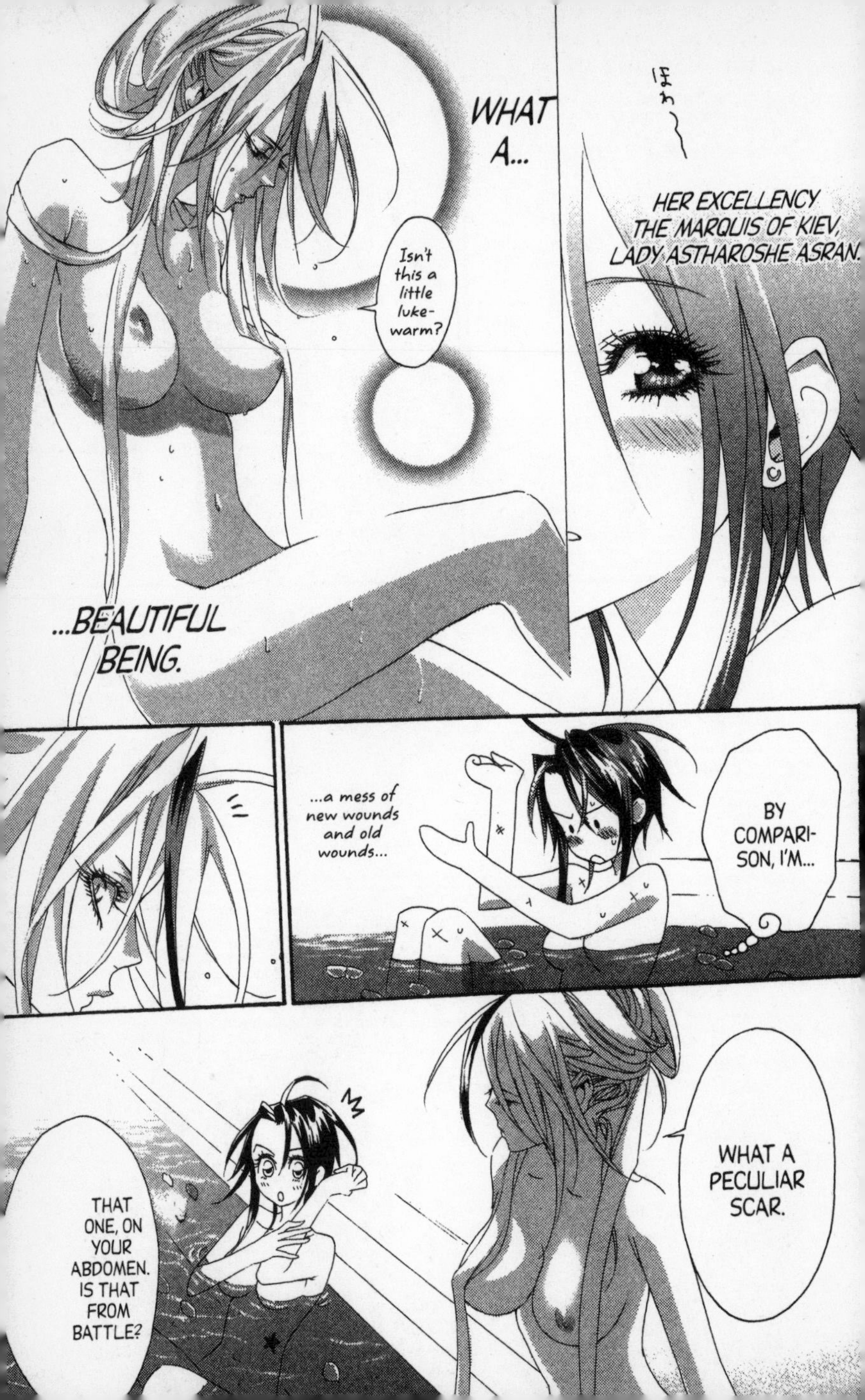
ほわ〜
HER EXCELLENCY THE MARQUIS OF KIEV, LADY ASTHAROSHE ASRAN.
WHAT A...
Isn't this a little luke-warm?
...BEAUTIFUL BEING.
BY COMPARI-SON, I'M...
...a mess of new wounds and old wounds...
WHAT A PECULIAR SCAR.
THAT ONE, ON YOUR ABDOMEN. IS THAT FROM BATTLE?

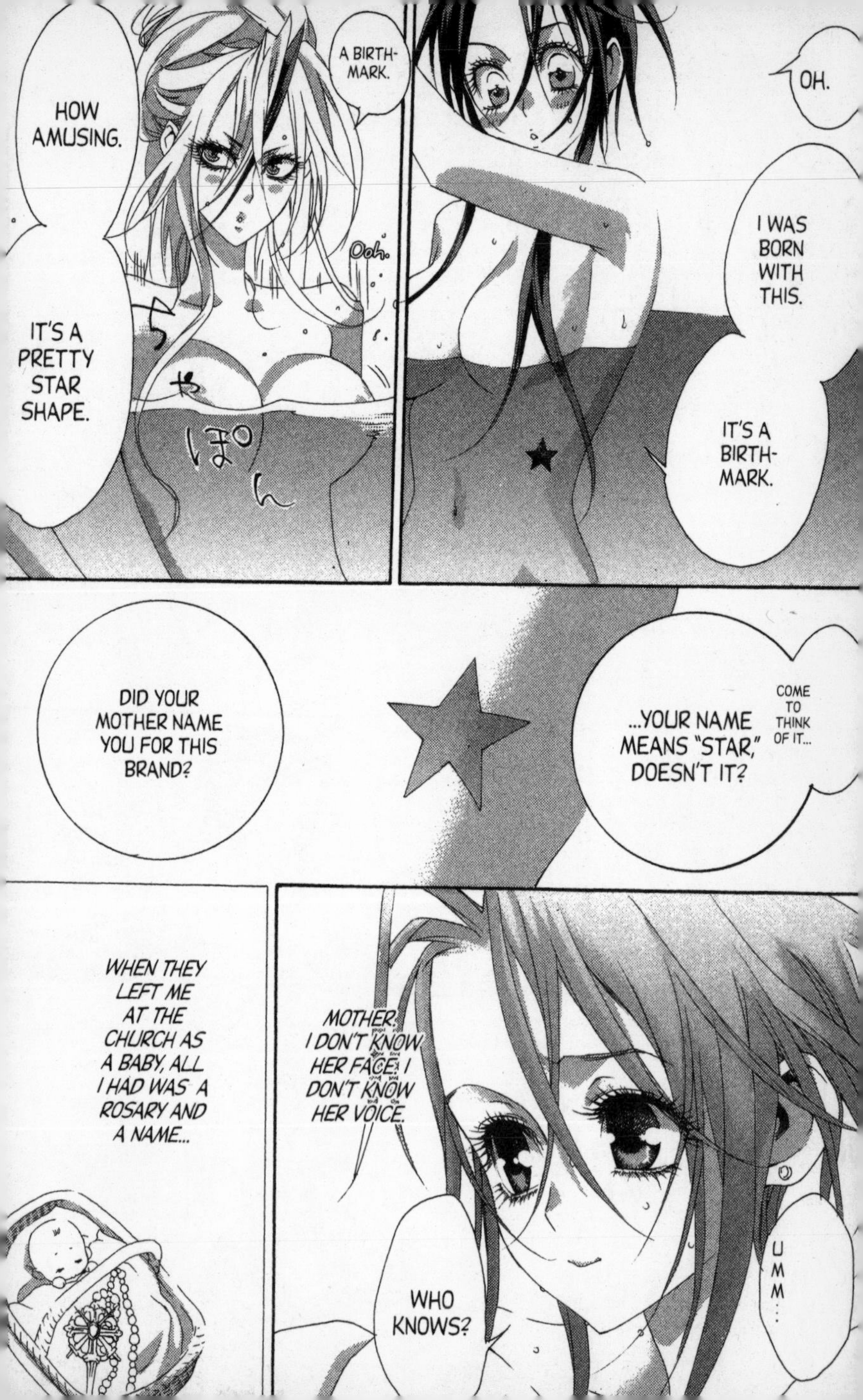
OH.
I WAS BORN WITH THIS.
IT'S A BIRTH-MARK.
A BIRTH-MARK.
Ooh.
HOW AMUSING.
ちゃぽん
IT'S A PRETTY STAR SHAPE.
COME TO THINK OF IT...
...YOUR NAME MEANS "STAR," DOESN'T IT?
DID YOUR MOTHER NAME YOU FOR THIS BRAND?
UMM...
WHO KNOWS?
MOTHER. I DON'T KNOW HER FACE. I DON'T KNOW HER VOICE.
WHEN THEY LEFT ME AT THE CHURCH AS A BABY, ALL I HAD WAS A ROSARY AND A NAME...

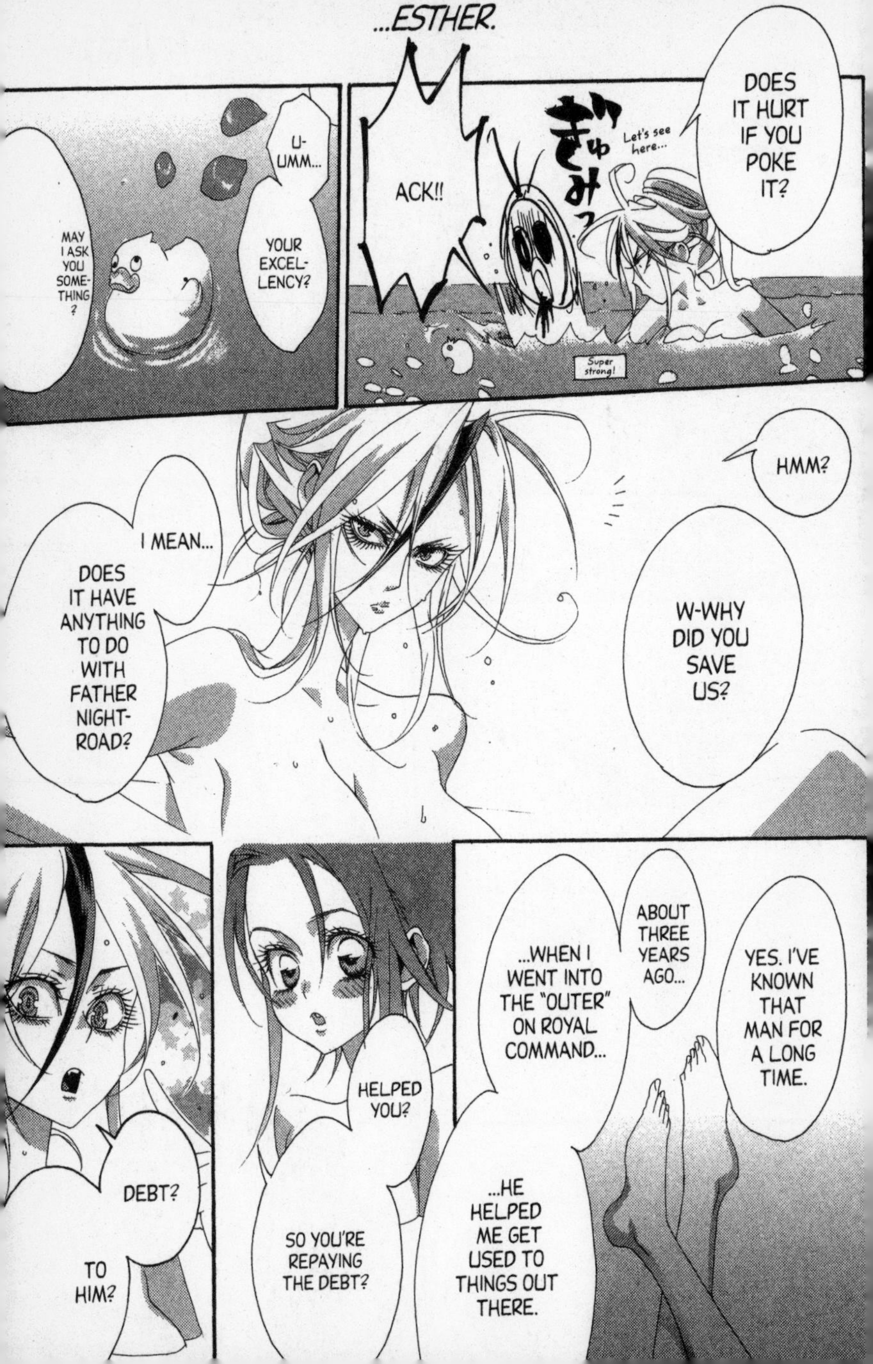
...ESTHER.
DOES IT HURT IF YOU POKE IT?
Let's see here...
ACK!!
Super strong!
U-UMM... YOUR EXCEL-LENCY?
MAY I ASK YOU SOME-THING?
HMM?
W-WHY DID YOU SAVE US?
I MEAN... DOES IT HAVE ANYTHING TO DO WITH FATHER NIGHT-ROAD?
YES. I'VE KNOWN THAT MAN FOR A LONG TIME.
ABOUT THREE YEARS AGO...
...WHEN I WENT INTO THE "OUTER" ON ROYAL COMMAND...
...HE HELPED ME GET USED TO THINGS OUT THERE.
HELPED YOU?
SO YOU'RE REPAYING THE DEBT?
DEBT?
TO HIM?

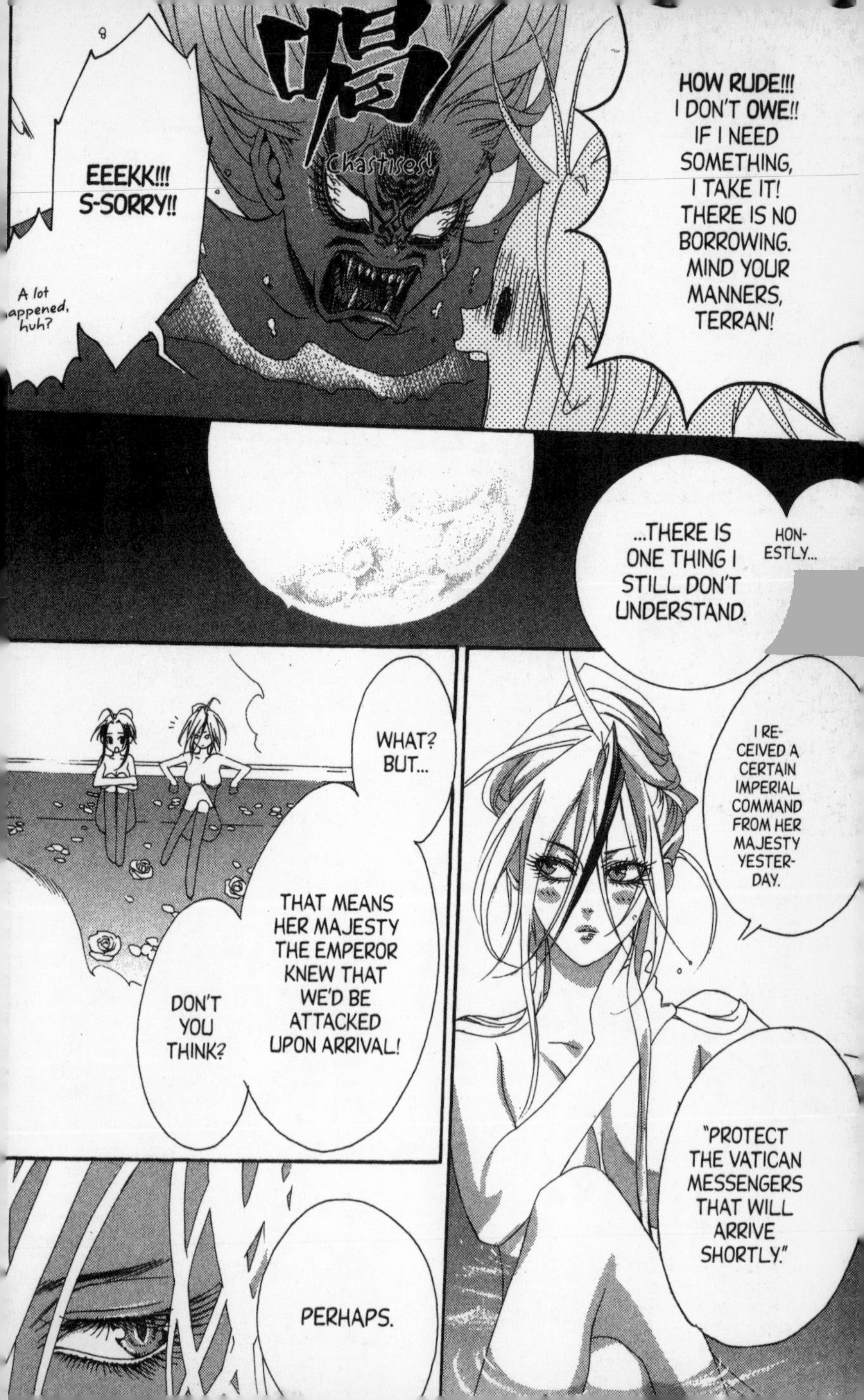
HOW RUDE!!! I DON'T OWE!! IF I NEED SOMETHING, I TAKE IT! THERE IS NO BORROWING. MIND YOUR MANNERS, TERRAN!
Chastises!
EEEKK!!! S-SORRY!!
A lot happened, huh?
HON-ESTLY...
...THERE IS ONE THING I STILL DON'T UNDERSTAND.
I RECEIVED A CERTAIN IMPERIAL COMMAND FROM HER MAJESTY YESTERDAY.
"PROTECT THE VATICAN MESSENGERS THAT WILL ARRIVE SHORTLY."
WHAT? BUT...
THAT MEANS HER MAJESTY THE EMPEROR KNEW THAT WE'D BE ATTACKED UPON ARRIVAL!
DON'T YOU THINK?
PERHAPS.

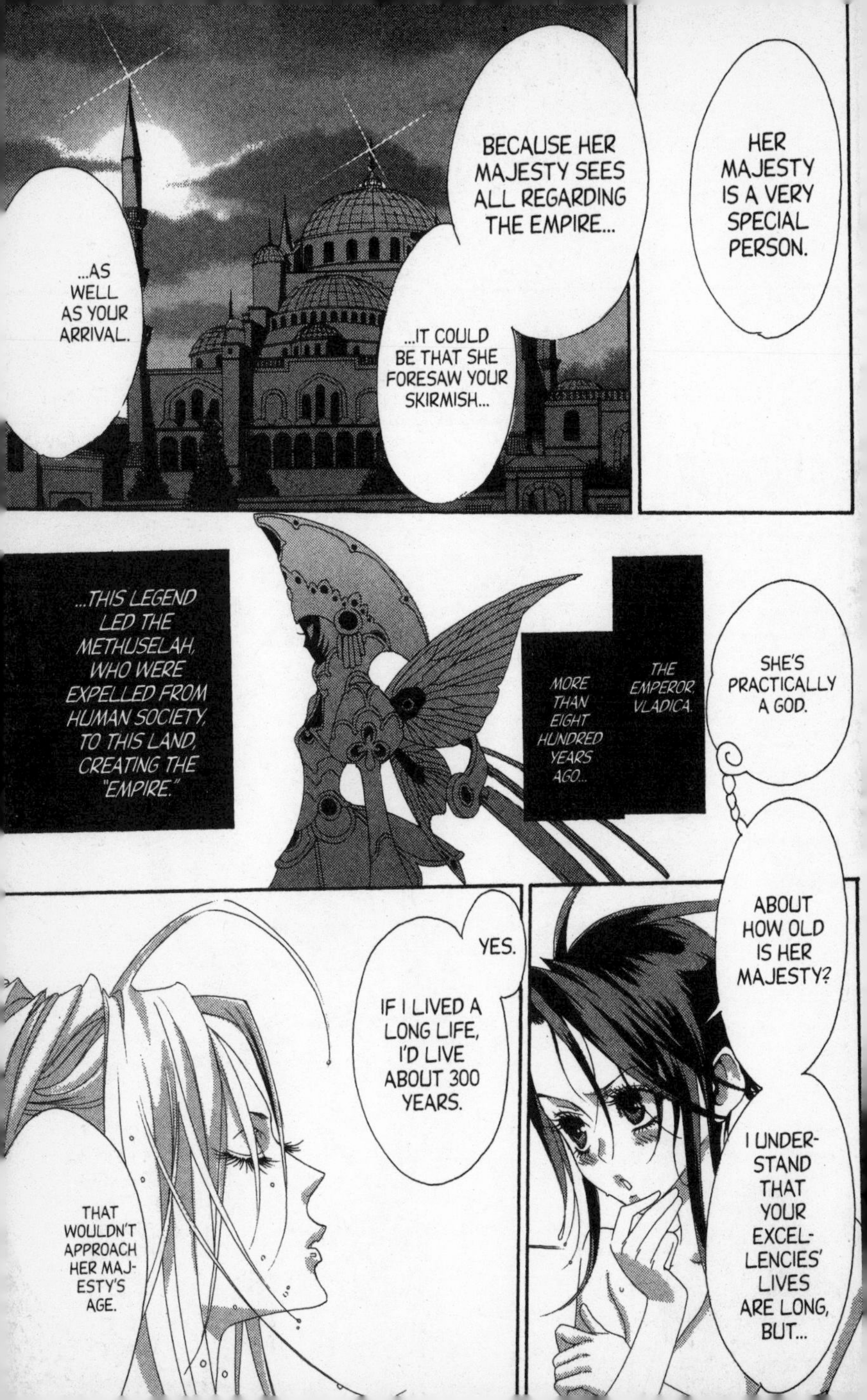
HER MAJESTY IS A VERY SPECIAL PERSON.
BECAUSE HER MAJESTY SEES ALL REGARDING THE EMPIRE...
...IT COULD BE THAT SHE FORESAW YOUR SKIRMISH...
...AS WELL AS YOUR ARRIVAL.
SHE'S PRACTICALLY A GOD.
THE EMPEROR, VLADICA.
MORE THAN EIGHT HUNDRED YEARS AGO...
...THIS LEGEND LED THE METHUSELAH, WHO WERE EXPELLED FROM HUMAN SOCIETY, TO THIS LAND, CREATING THE "EMPIRE."
ABOUT HOW OLD IS HER MAJESTY?
I UNDERSTAND THAT YOUR EXCELLENCIES' LIVES ARE LONG, BUT...
YES.
IF I LIVED A LONG LIFE, I'D LIVE ABOUT 300 YEARS.
THAT WOULDN'T APPROACH HER MAJESTY'S AGE.

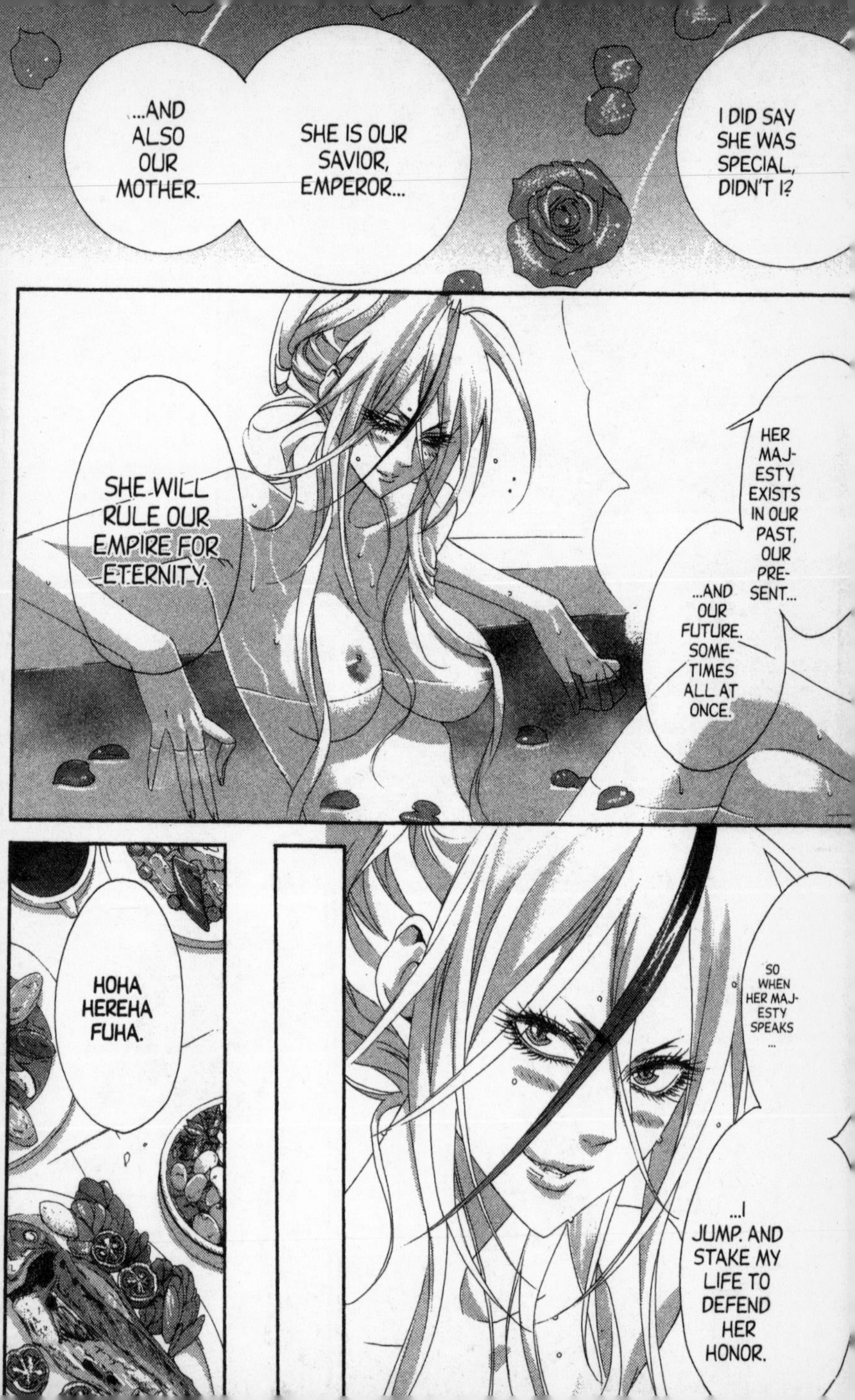
I DID SAY SHE WAS SPECIAL, DIDN'T I?
SHE IS OUR SAVIOR, EMPEROR...
...AND ALSO OUR MOTHER.
HER MAJ-ESTY EXISTS IN OUR PAST, OUR PRE-SENT...
...AND OUR FUTURE. SOME-TIMES ALL AT ONCE.
SHE WILL RULE OUR EMPIRE FOR ETERNITY.
SO WHEN HER MAJ-ESTY SPEAKS...
...I JUMP. AND STAKE MY LIFE TO DEFEND HER HONOR.
HOHA HEREHA FUHA.

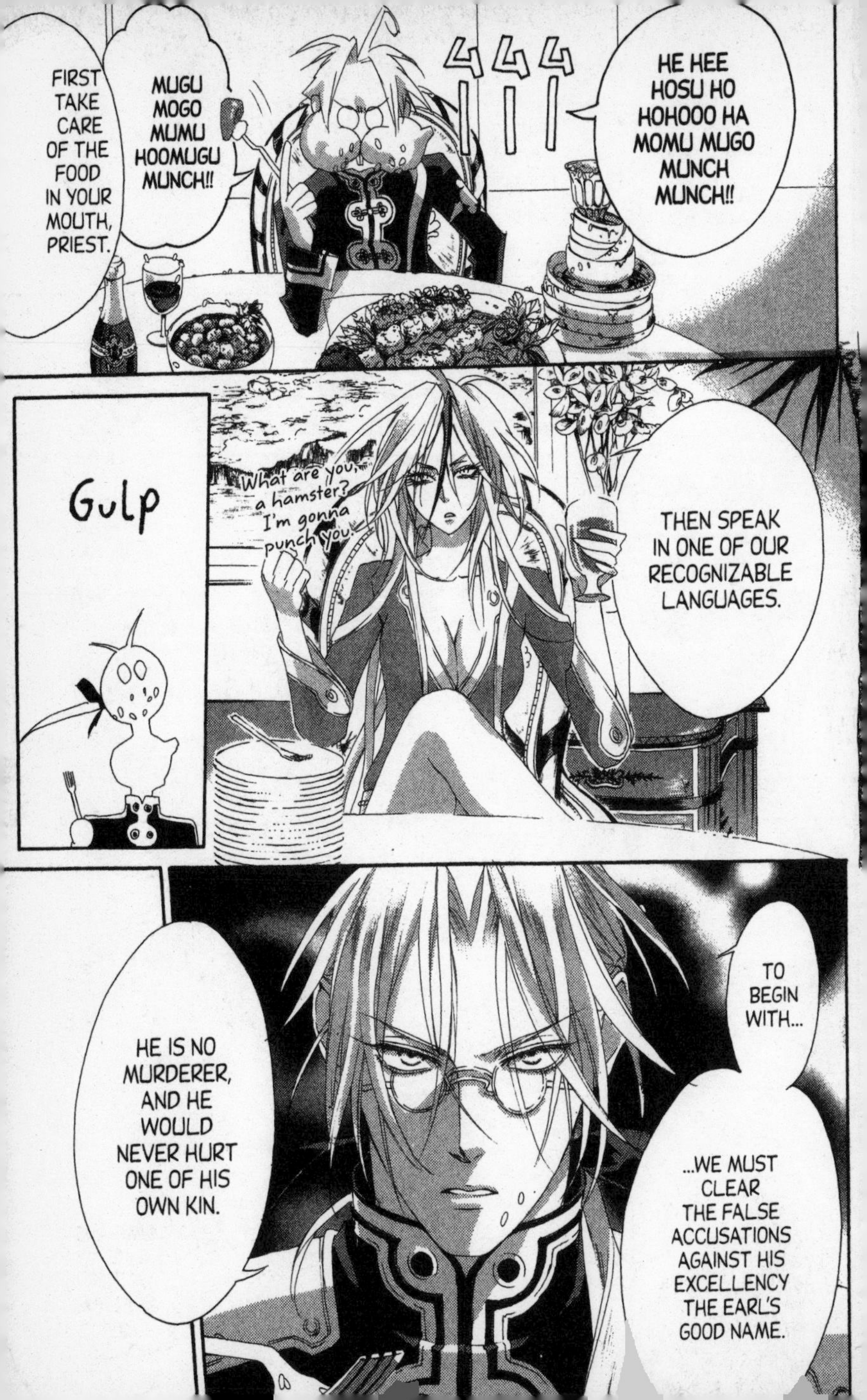
HE HEE HOSU HO HOHOOO HA MOMU MUGO MUNCH MUNCH!!
MUGU MOGO MUMU HOOMUGU MUNCH!!
FIRST TAKE CARE OF THE FOOD IN YOUR MOUTH, PRIEST.
THEN SPEAK IN ONE OF OUR RECOGNIZABLE LANGUAGES.
What are you, a hamster? I'm gonna punch you.
Gulp
TO BEGIN WITH...
...WE MUST CLEAR THE FALSE ACCUSATIONS AGAINST HIS EXCELLENCY THE EARL'S GOOD NAME.
HE IS NO MURDERER, AND HE WOULD NEVER HURT ONE OF HIS OWN KIN.

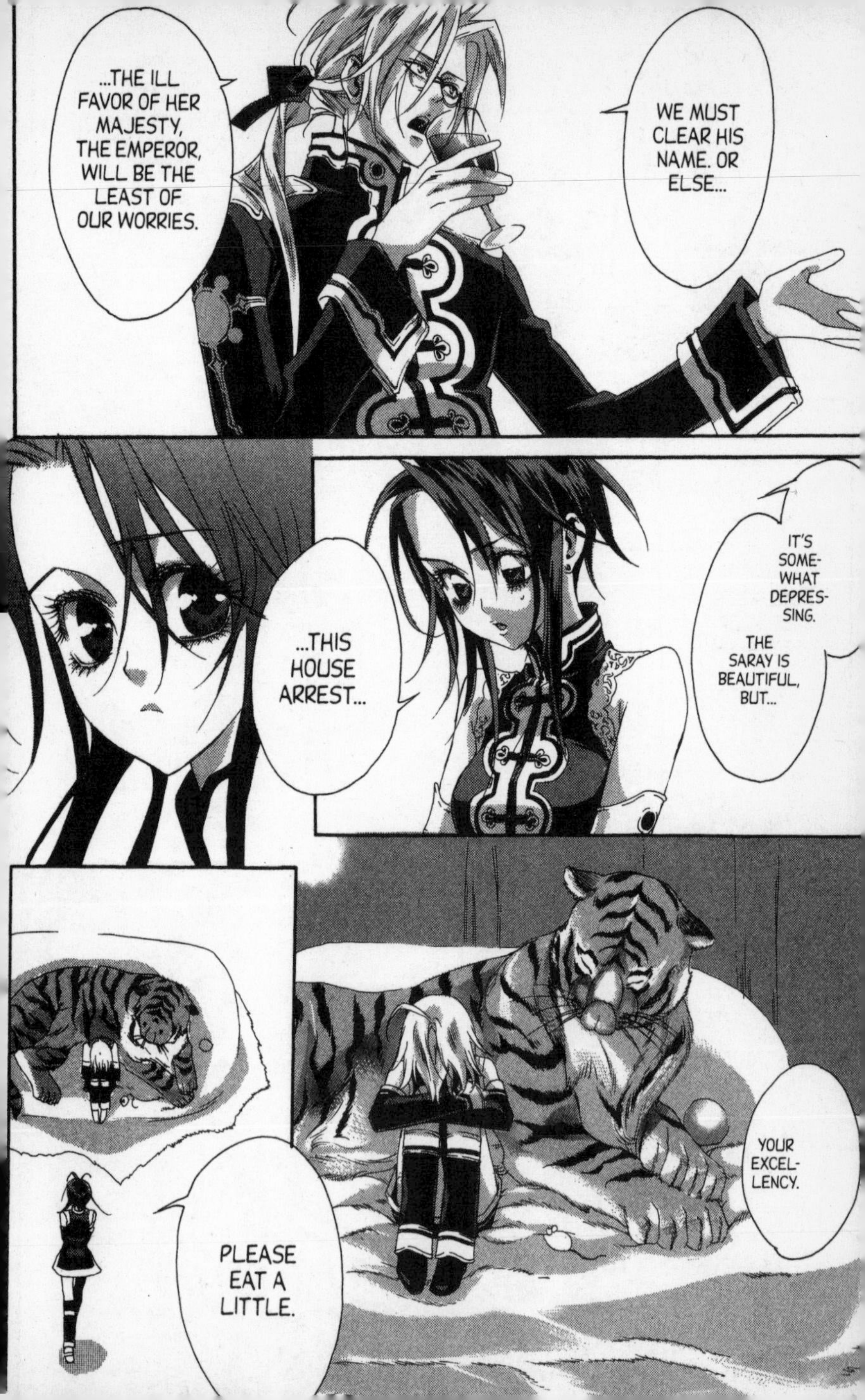
WE MUST CLEAR HIS NAME. OR ELSE...
...THE ILL FAVOR OF HER MAJESTY, THE EMPEROR, WILL BE THE LEAST OF OUR WORRIES.
IT'S SOME-WHAT DEPRES-SING.
THE SARAY IS BEAUTIFUL, BUT...
...THIS HOUSE ARREST...
YOUR EXCEL-LENCY.
PLEASE EAT A LITTLE.

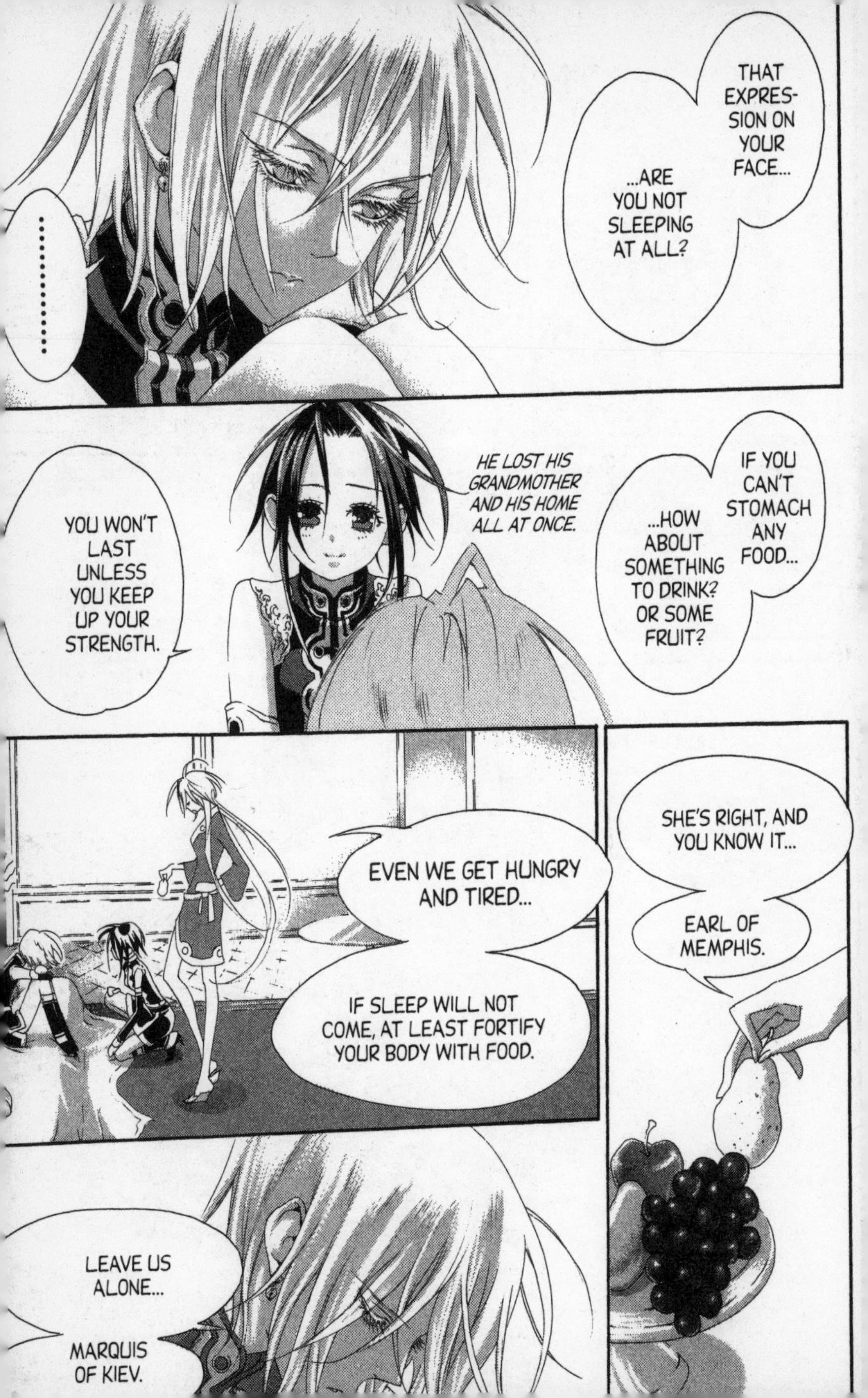
THAT EXPRES-SION ON YOUR FACE...
...ARE YOU NOT SLEEPING AT ALL?
......
IF YOU CAN'T STOMACH ANY FOOD...
...HOW ABOUT SOMETHING TO DRINK? OR SOME FRUIT?
HE LOST HIS GRANDMOTHER AND HIS HOME ALL AT ONCE.
YOU WON'T LAST UNLESS YOU KEEP UP YOUR STRENGTH.
SHE'S RIGHT, AND YOU KNOW IT...
EARL OF MEMPHIS.
EVEN WE GET HUNGRY AND TIRED...
IF SLEEP WILL NOT COME, AT LEAST FORTIFY YOUR BODY WITH FOOD.
LEAVE US ALONE...
MARQUIS OF KIEV.

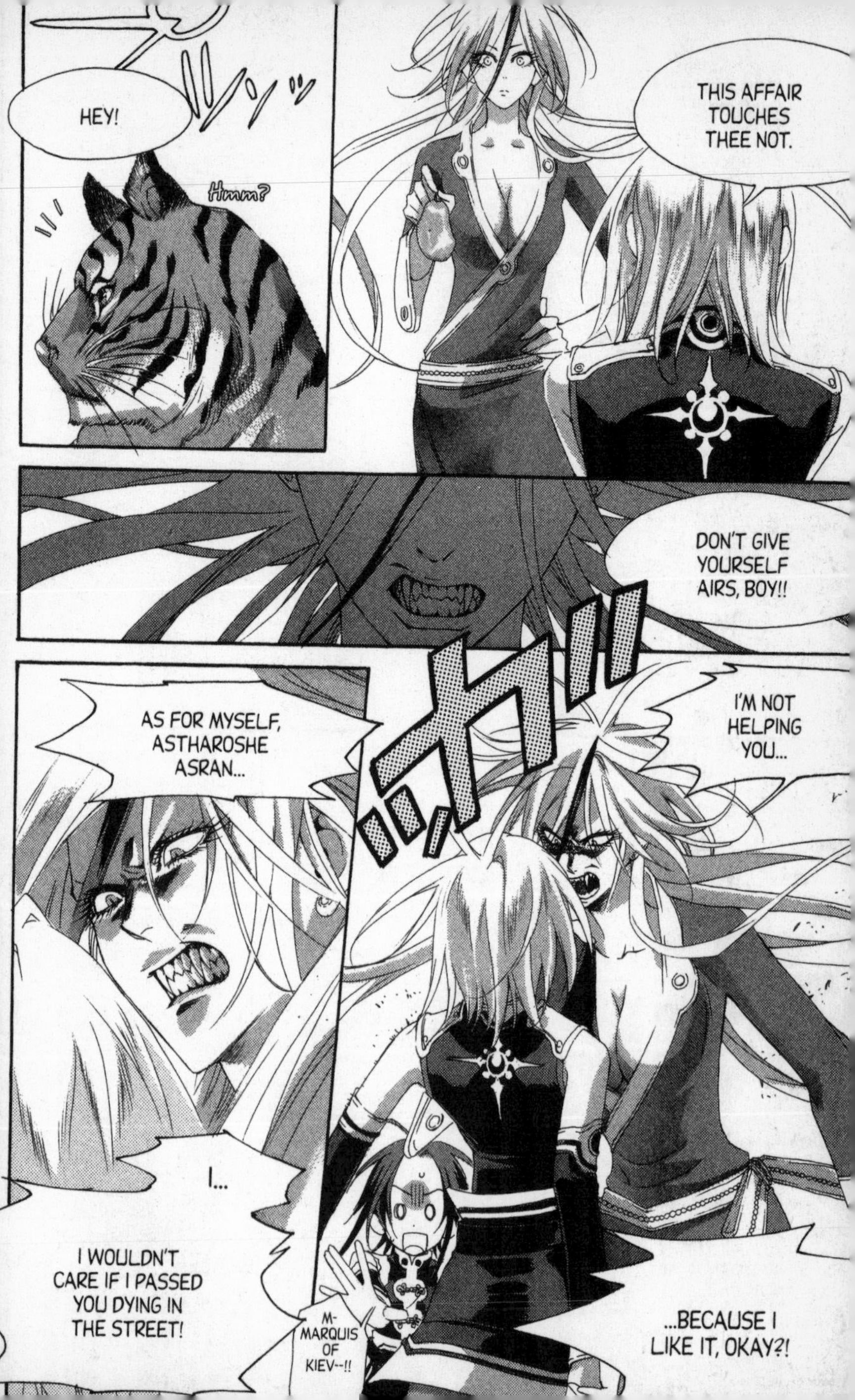
THIS AFFAIR TOUCHES THEE NOT.
HEY!
Hmm?
DON'T GIVE YOURSELF AIRS, BOY!!
I'M NOT HELPING YOU...
...BECAUSE I LIKE IT, OKAY?!
M-MARQUIS OF KIEV--!!
AS FOR MYSELF, ASTHAROSHE ASRAN...
I...
I WOULDN'T CARE IF I PASSED YOU DYING IN THE STREET!

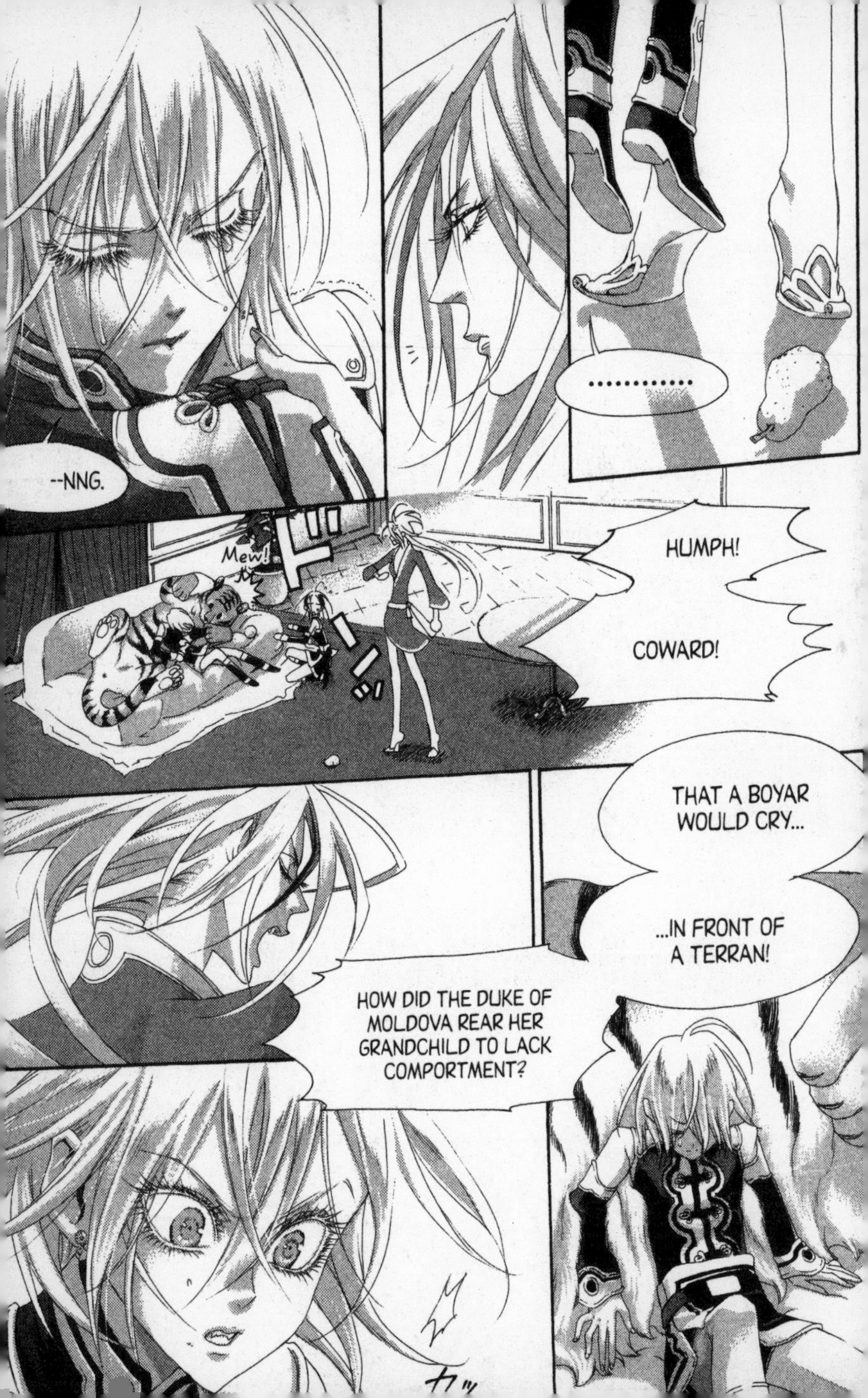
....
--NNG.
Mew!
HUMPH!
COWARD!
THAT A BOYAR WOULD CRY...
...IN FRONT OF A TERRAN!
HOW DID THE DUKE OF MOLDOVA REAR HER GRANDCHILD TO LACK COMPORTMENT?

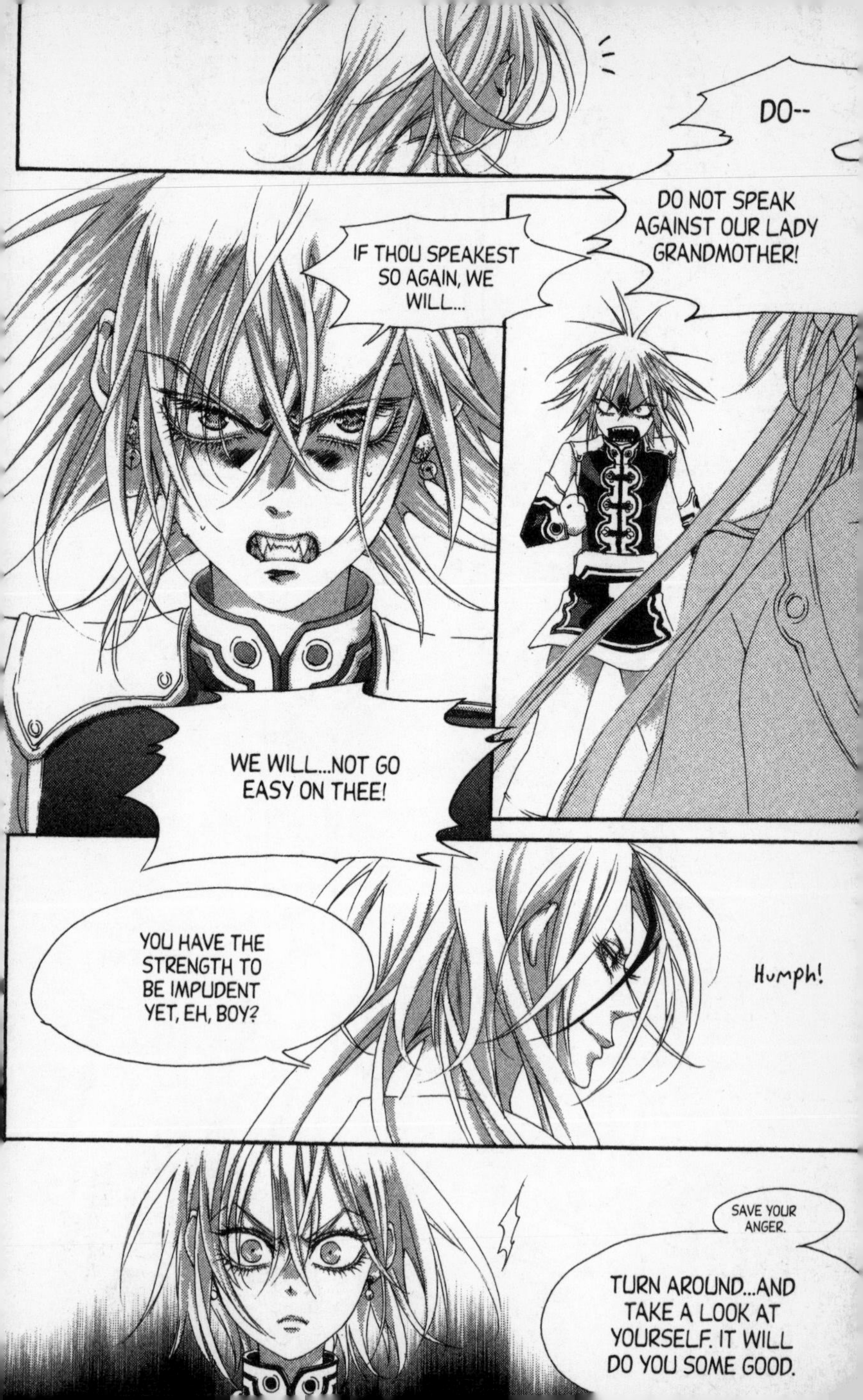
DO--
DO NOT SPEAK AGAINST OUR LADY GRANDMOTHER!
IF THOU SPEAKEST SO AGAIN, WE WILL...
WE WILL...NOT GO EASY ON THEE!
Humph!
YOU HAVE THE STRENGTH TO BE IMPUDENT YET, EH, BOY?
SAVE YOUR ANGER.
TURN AROUND...AND TAKE A LOOK AT YOURSELF. IT WILL DO YOU SOME GOOD.

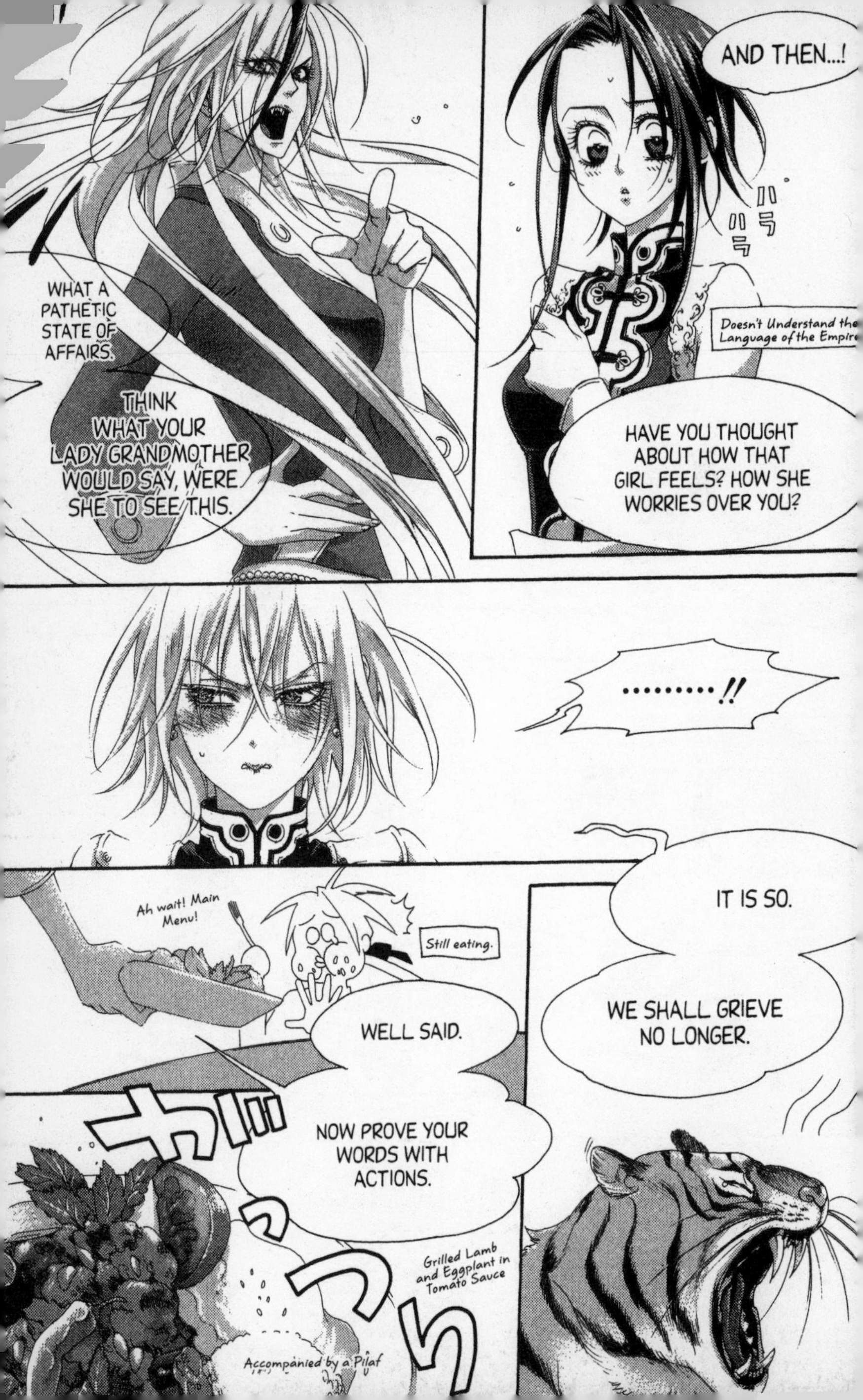
AND THEN...!
ハラハラ
Doesn't Understand the Language of the Empire
HAVE YOU THOUGHT ABOUT HOW THAT GIRL FEELS? HOW SHE WORRIES OVER YOU?
WHAT A PATHETIC STATE OF AFFAIRS.
THINK WHAT YOUR LADY GRANDMOTHER WOULD SAY, WERE SHE TO SEE THIS.
..........!!
IT IS SO.
WE SHALL GRIEVE NO LONGER.
Still eating.
Ah wait! Main Menu!
WELL SAID.
NOW PROVE YOUR WORDS WITH ACTIONS.
Grilled Lamb and Eggplant in Tomato Sauce
Accompanied by a Pilaf

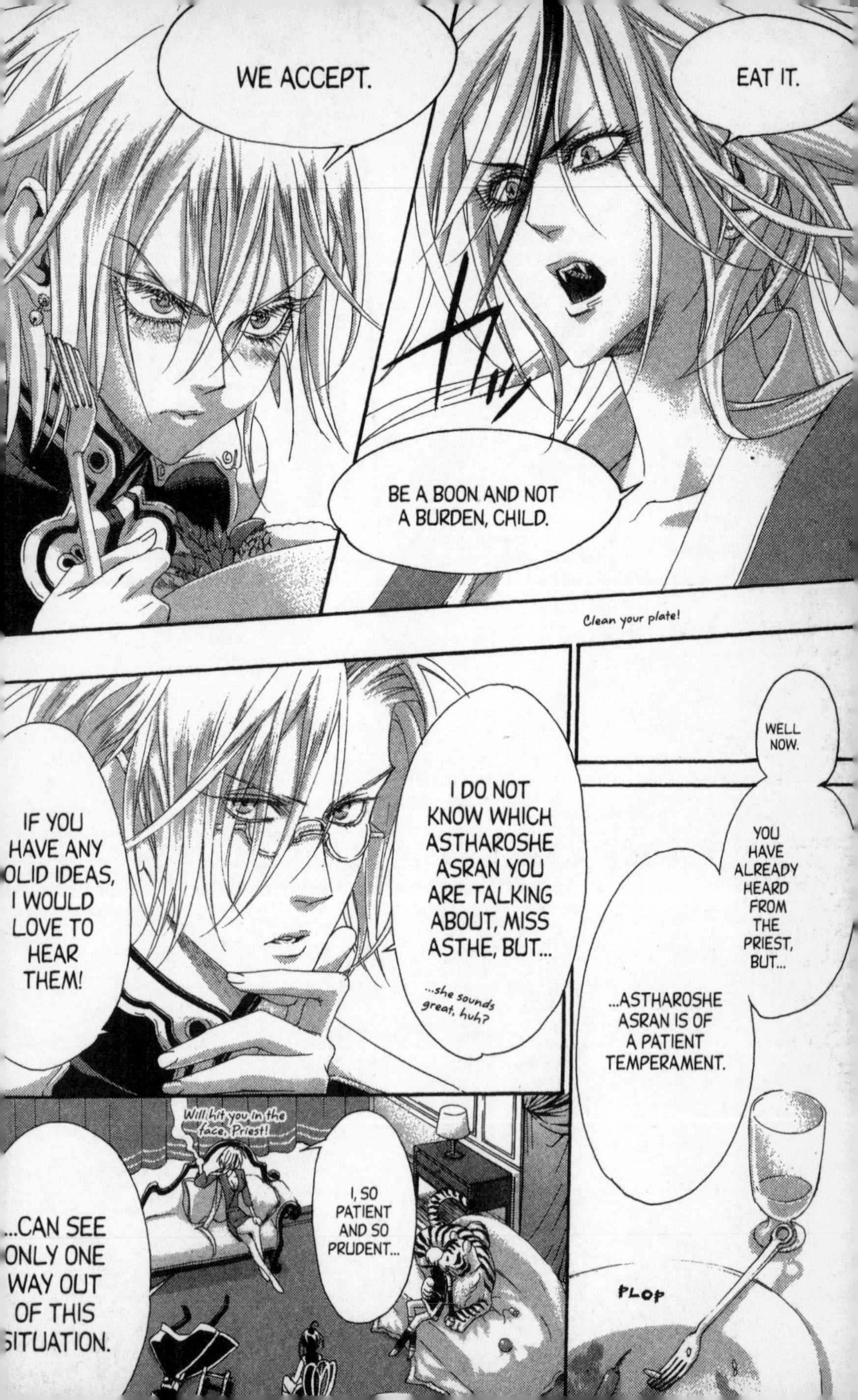

EAT IT.
BE A BOON AND NOT A BURDEN, CHILD.
WE ACCEPT.
Clean your plate!
WELL NOW.
YOU HAVE ALREADY HEARD FROM THE PRIEST, BUT...
...ASTHAROSHE ASRAN IS OF A PATIENT TEMPERAMENT.
PLOP
I DO NOT KNOW WHICH ASTHAROSHE ASRAN YOU ARE TALKING ABOUT, MISS ASTHE, BUT...
...she sounds great, huh?
IF YOU HAVE ANY OLID IDEAS, I WOULD LOVE TO HEAR THEM!
I, SO PATIENT AND SO PRUDENT...
Will hit you in the face, Priest!
...CAN SEE ONLY ONE WAY OUT OF THIS SITUATION.

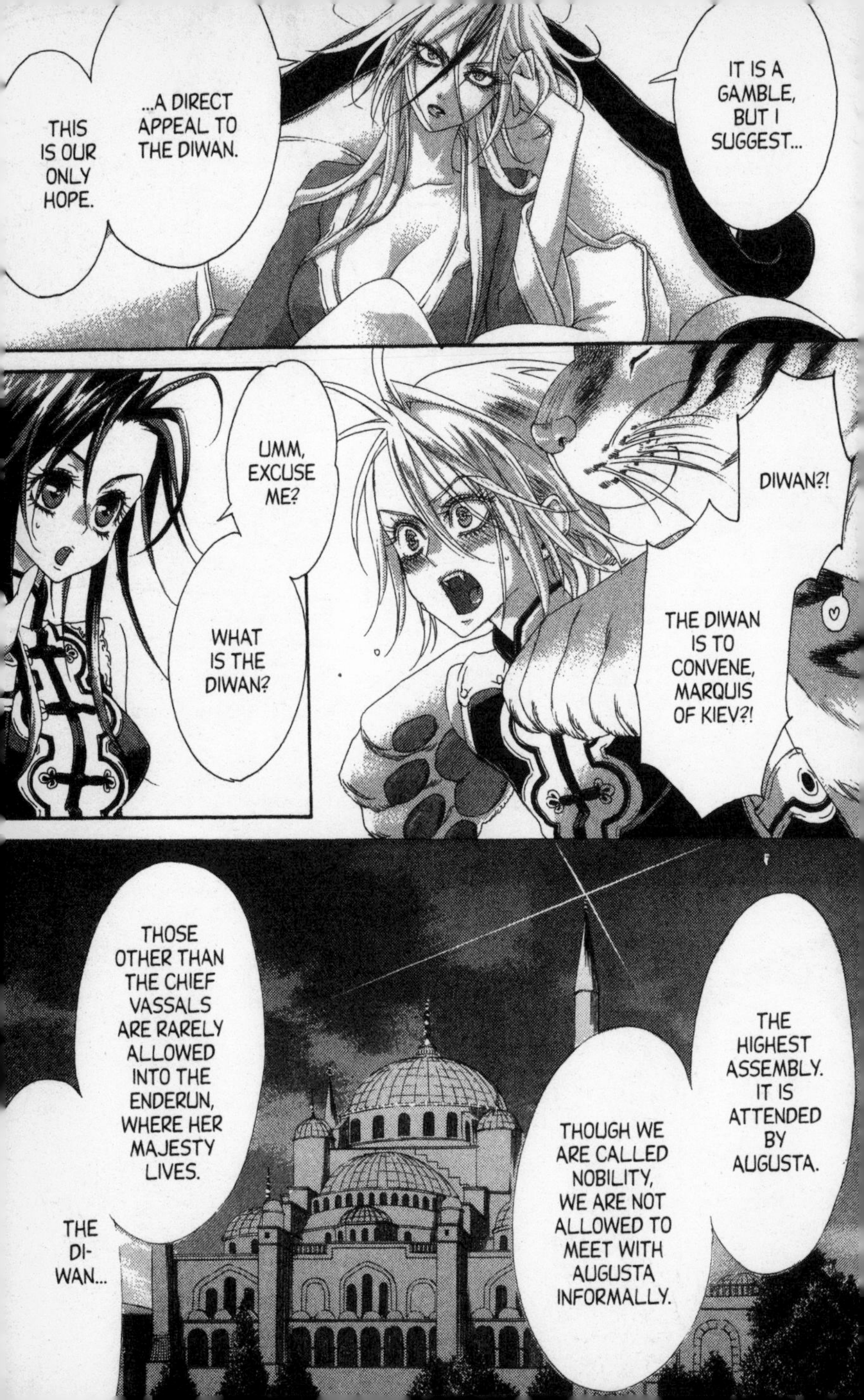
IT IS A GAMBLE, BUT I SUGGEST...
...A DIRECT APPEAL TO THE DIWAN.
THIS IS OUR ONLY HOPE.
DIWAN?!
THE DIWAN IS TO CONVENE, MARQUIS OF KIEV?!
UMM, EXCUSE ME?
WHAT IS THE DIWAN?
THE HIGHEST ASSEMBLY. IT IS ATTENDED BY AUGUSTA.
THOUGH WE ARE CALLED NOBILITY, WE ARE NOT ALLOWED TO MEET WITH AUGUSTA INFORMALLY.
THOSE OTHER THAN THE CHIEF VASSALS ARE RARELY ALLOWED INTO THE ENDERUN, WHERE HER MAJESTY LIVES.
THE DI-WAN...

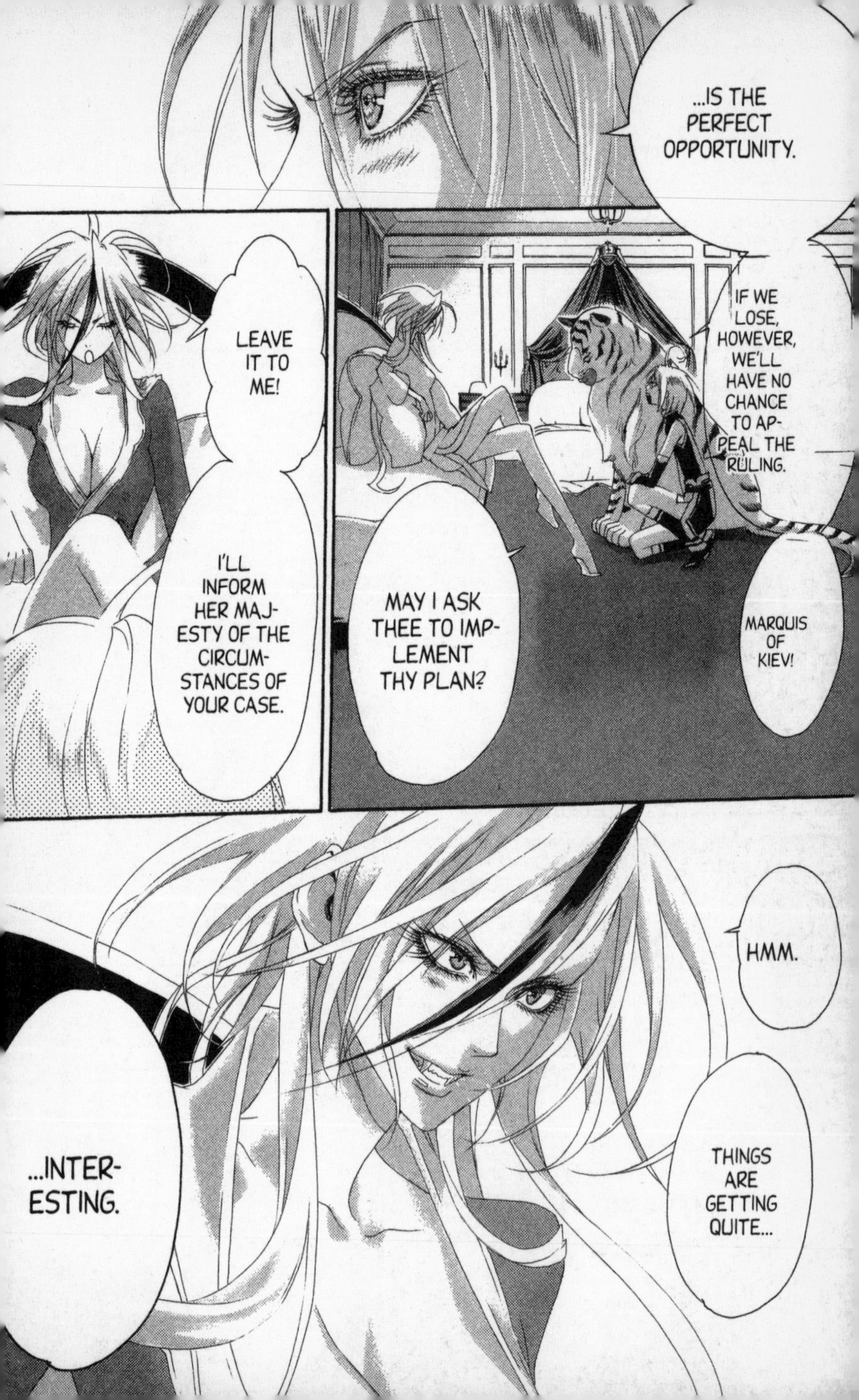
...IS THE PERFECT OPPORTUNITY.
IF WE LOSE, HOWEVER, WE'LL HAVE NO CHANCE TO AP-PEAL THE RULING.
MARQUIS OF KIEV!
MAY I ASK THEE TO IMP-LEMENT THY PLAN?
LEAVE IT TO ME!
I'LL INFORM HER MAJ-ESTY OF THE CIRCUM-STANCES OF YOUR CASE.
HMM.
THINGS ARE GETTING QUITE...
...INTER-ESTING.

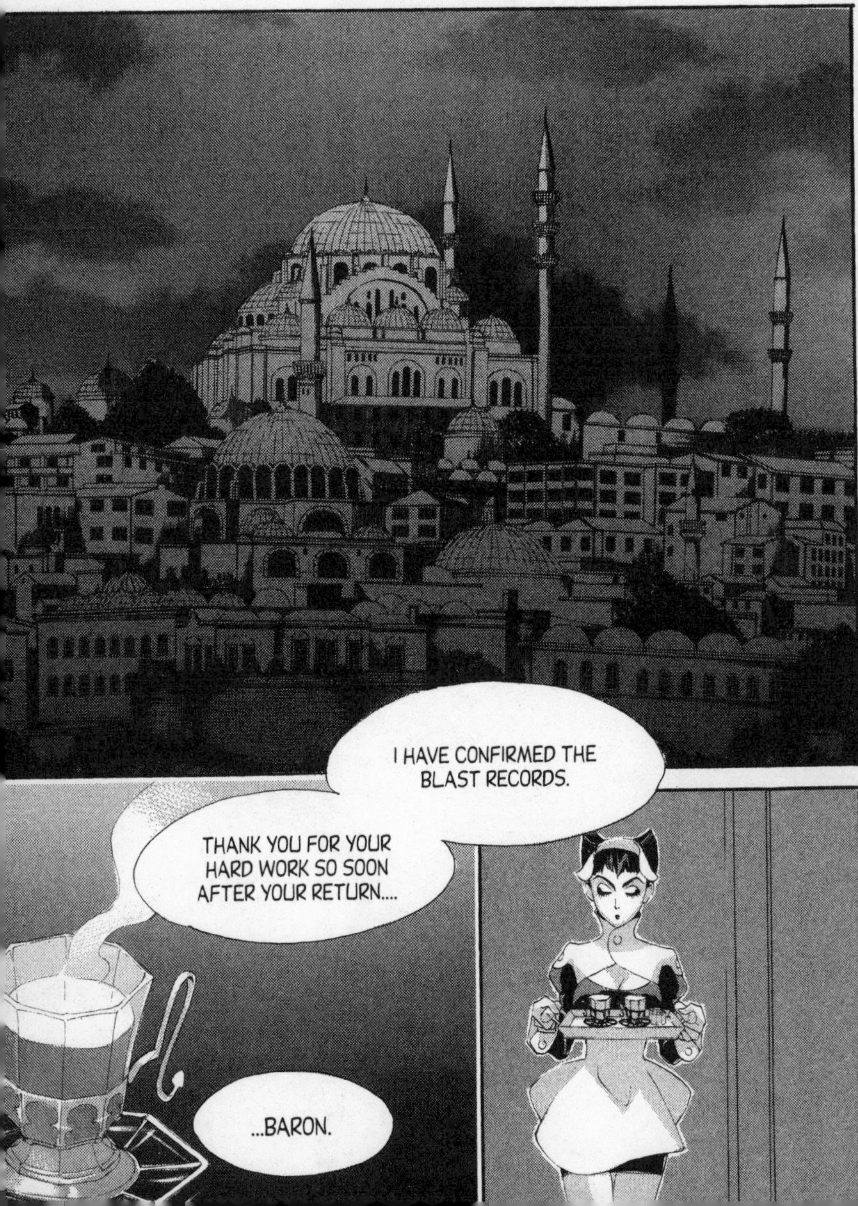
I HAVE CONFIRMED THE BLAST RECORDS.
THANK YOU FOR YOUR HARD WORK SO SOON AFTER YOUR RETURN....
...BARON.

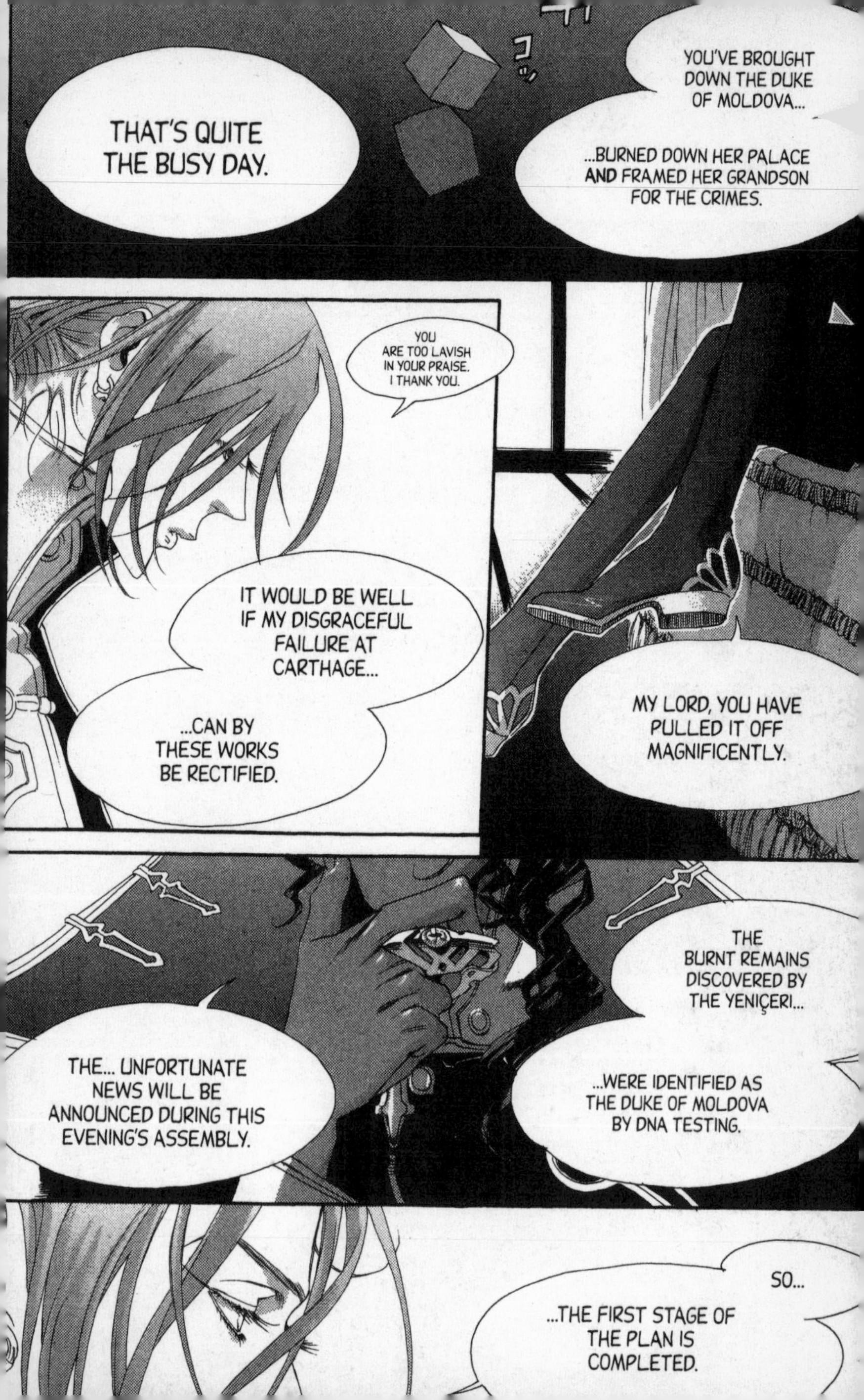
YOU'VE BROUGHT DOWN THE DUKE OF MOLDOVA...
...BURNED DOWN HER PALACE AND FRAMED HER GRANDSON FOR THE CRIMES.
THAT'S QUITE THE BUSY DAY.
MY LORD, YOU HAVE PULLED IT OFF MAGNIFICENTLY.
YOU ARE TOO LAVISH IN YOUR PRAISE. I THANK YOU.
IT WOULD BE WELL IF MY DISGRACEFUL FAILURE AT CARTHAGE...
...CAN BY THESE WORKS BE RECTIFIED.
THE BURNT REMAINS DISCOVERED BY THE YENIÇERI...
...WERE IDENTIFIED AS THE DUKE OF MOLDOVA BY DNA TESTING.
THE... UNFORTUNATE NEWS WILL BE ANNOUNCED DURING THIS EVENING'S ASSEMBLY.
SO...
...THE FIRST STAGE OF THE PLAN IS COMPLETED.

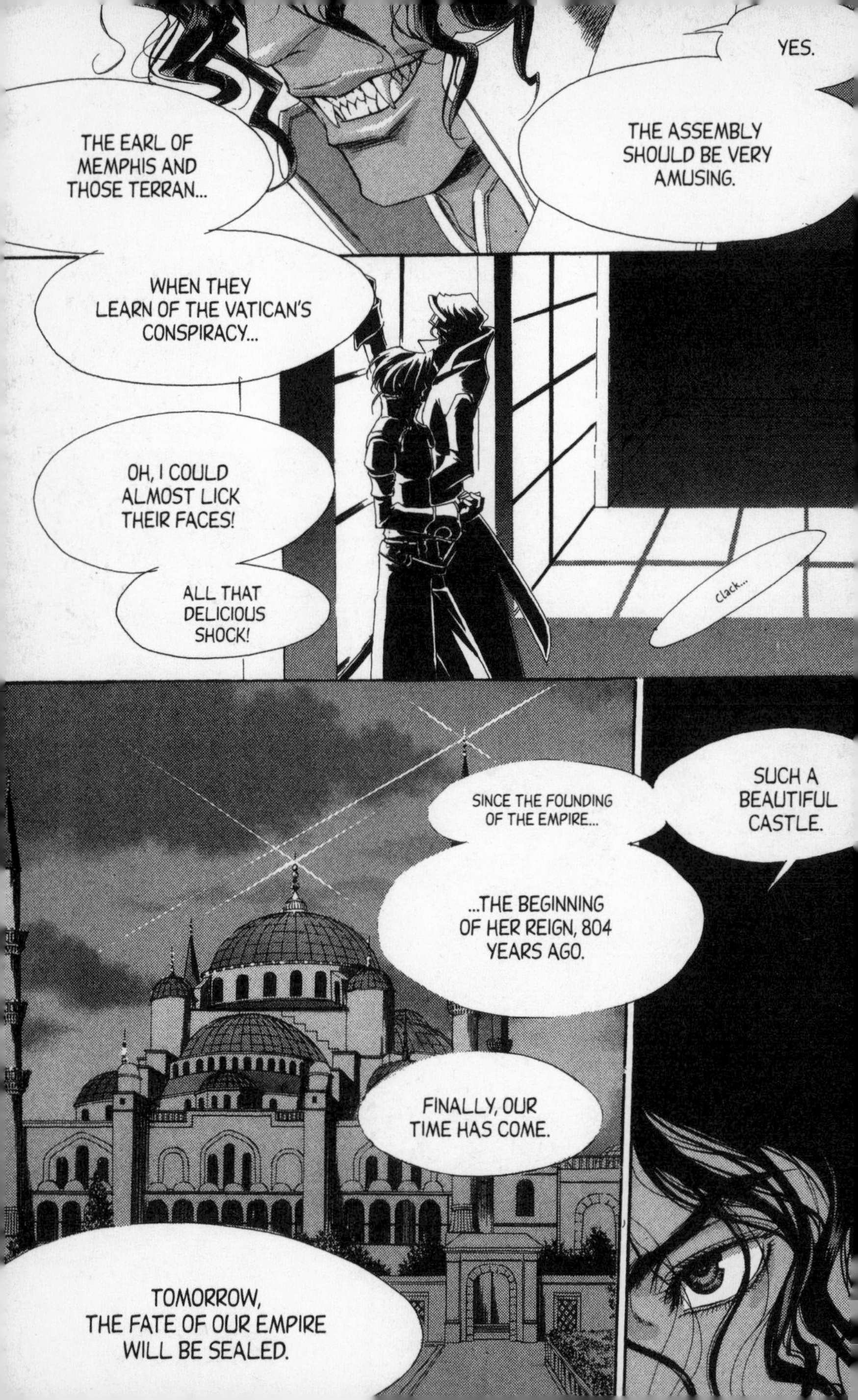
YES.
THE ASSEMBLY SHOULD BE VERY AMUSING.
THE EARL OF MEMPHIS AND THOSE TERRAN...
WHEN THEY LEARN OF THE VATICAN'S CONSPIRACY...
OH, I COULD ALMOST LICK THEIR FACES!
ALL THAT DELICIOUS SHOCK!
Clack...
SUCH A BEAUTIFUL CASTLE.
SINCE THE FOUNDING OF THE EMPIRE...
...THE BEGINNING OF HER REIGN, 804 YEARS AGO.
FINALLY, OUR TIME HAS COME.
TOMORROW, THE FATE OF OUR EMPIRE WILL BE SEALED.

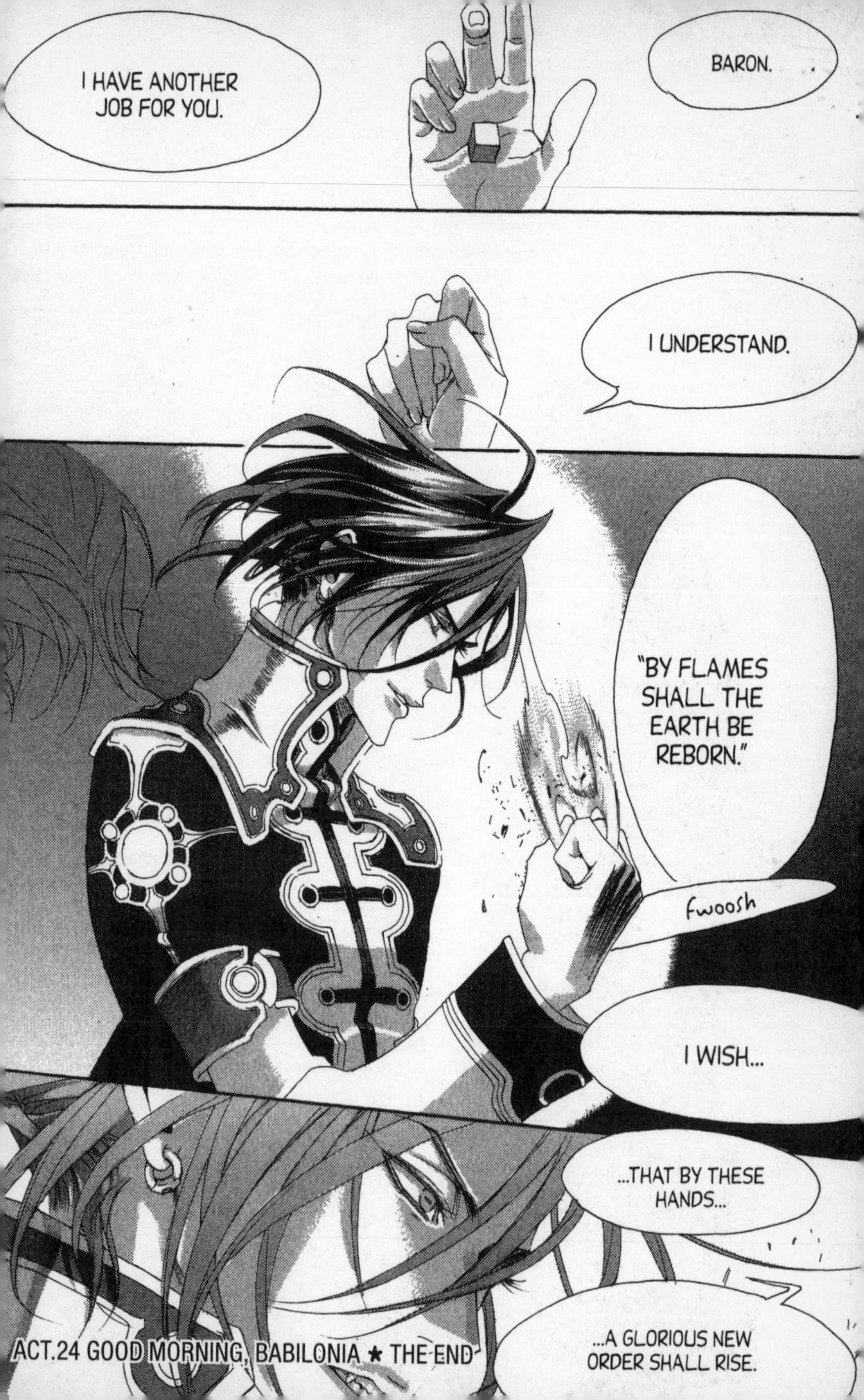
BARON.
I HAVE ANOTHER JOB FOR YOU.
I UNDERSTAND.
"BY FLAMES SHALL THE EARTH BE REBORN."
fwoosh
I WISH...
...THAT BY THESE HANDS...
...A GLORIOUS NEW ORDER SHALL RISE.
ACT.24 GOOD MORNING, BABILONIA ★ THE END

(犬) Dog: It's the year of the dog(2006), but I wasn't able to get out my New Year's cards this year either. Dog. Dog. Dog. I love dogs. I especially like the big ones. I drew Tres-kun for the first time in a while. I think Tres-kun looks like those small Shiba dogs with their round black eyebrows.

About the Original Story:

The chapter titles for the manga always come from movie titles, but just this once I've called a chapter "The Very Center of Blue storm" (or the eye of the storm), from the lyrics of the theme song of a certain pioneering kendo anime. When you put swords in a story, they've got to come back again and again. The pirates appeared because there was a slight mention of a scary episode where pirates attack the smuggling ship they used from Carthage in the original work. Though there wasn't any mention at all of Hugue drifting in. Hugue is one of those characters I like because he's interesting and mysterious and, even though they call him a samurai, he's not at all uptight.

About the Tiger:

When I found out that Asthe kept a cat in the original work, I thought, "If I'm going to draw Miss Asthe's house, then I'll put in a cat." "A normal cat's cute, but I'll make it a celebrity-like saber cat with a name like 'Trinity.'" But then I couldn't decide between a leopard and an Amur (or Siberian) Tiger. It made a very big appearance, though, didn't it? I like tigers. Among animals, I like them the best, tied with dogs and wolves. And lions, too. Though they're hard to draw. Those long noses... and fluffy chests. They're great!

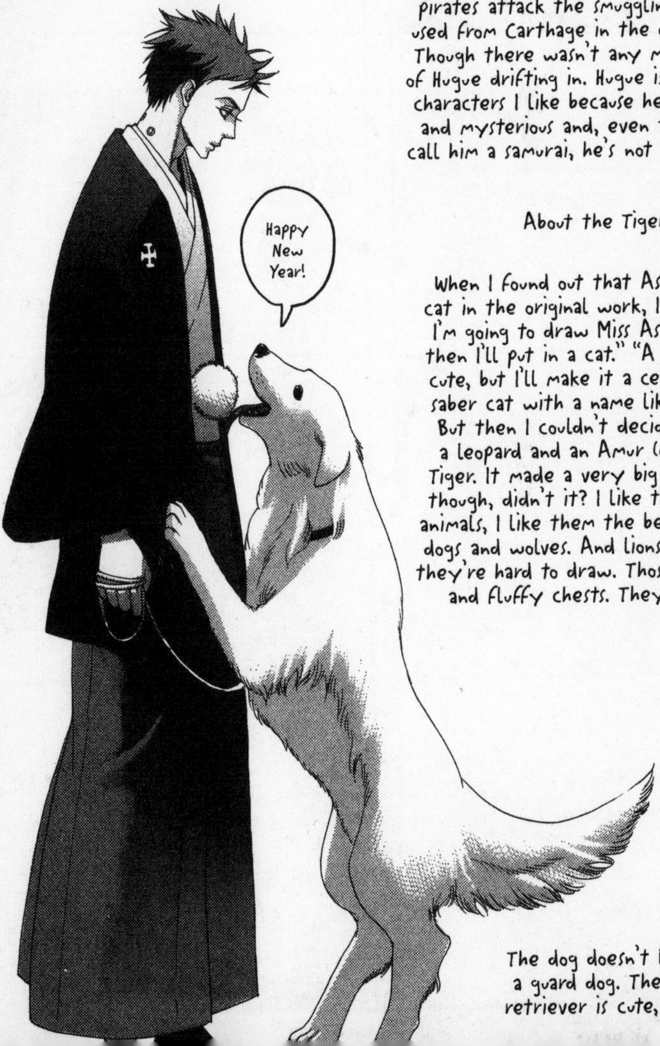
Happy New Year!

The dog doesn't look like a guard dog. The golden retriever is cute, isn't it?

Things Can't Stay the Way They Are!!

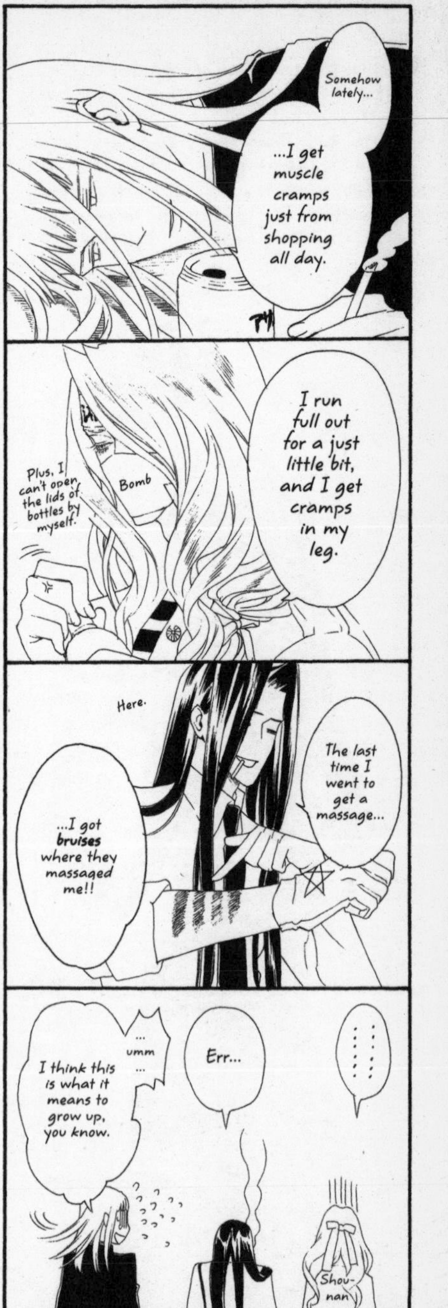
Somehow lately...
...I get muscle cramps just from shopping all day.
I run full out for a just little bit, and I get cramps in my leg.
Plus, I can't open the lids of bottles by myself.
Bomb
Here.
The last time I went to get a massage...
...I got **bruises** where they massaged me!!
Err...
...
... umm ...
I think this is what it means to grow up, you know.
Shou-nan

BUT...

Director = Kyujyo Professor = Father Samurai = Tsukasa-kun Magician = Masaki-kun

I do respect you...but...!!

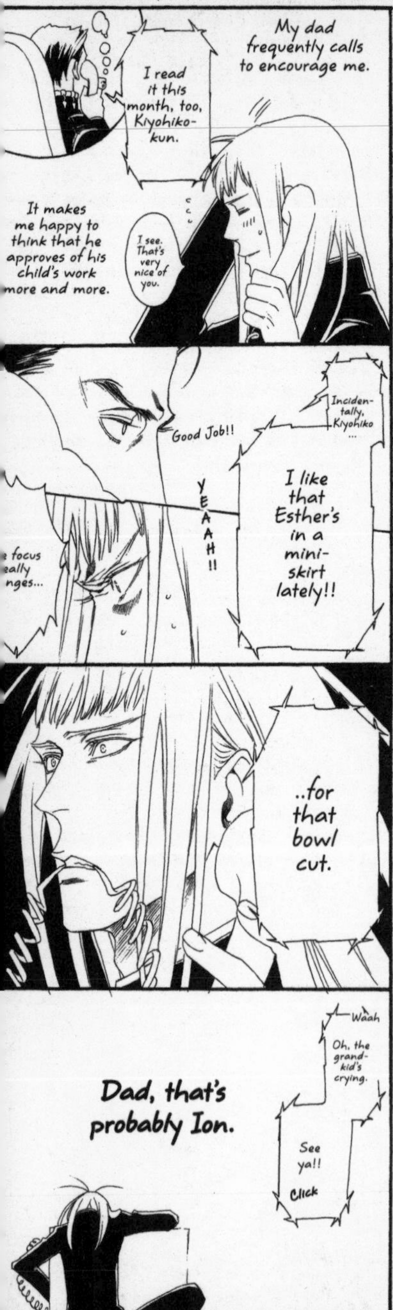
My dad frequently calls to encourage me.
I read it this month, too, Kiyohiko-kun.
It makes me happy to think that he approves of his child's work more and more.
I see. That's very nice of you.
Incidentally, Kiyohiko...
I like that Esther's in a mini-skirt lately!!
Good Job!!
YEAAH!!
..for that bowl cut.
Waah
Oh, the grand-kid's crying.
See ya!!
Click
Dad, that's probably Ion.

You're wrong.

It's Not a Skirt, It's a Waistband.

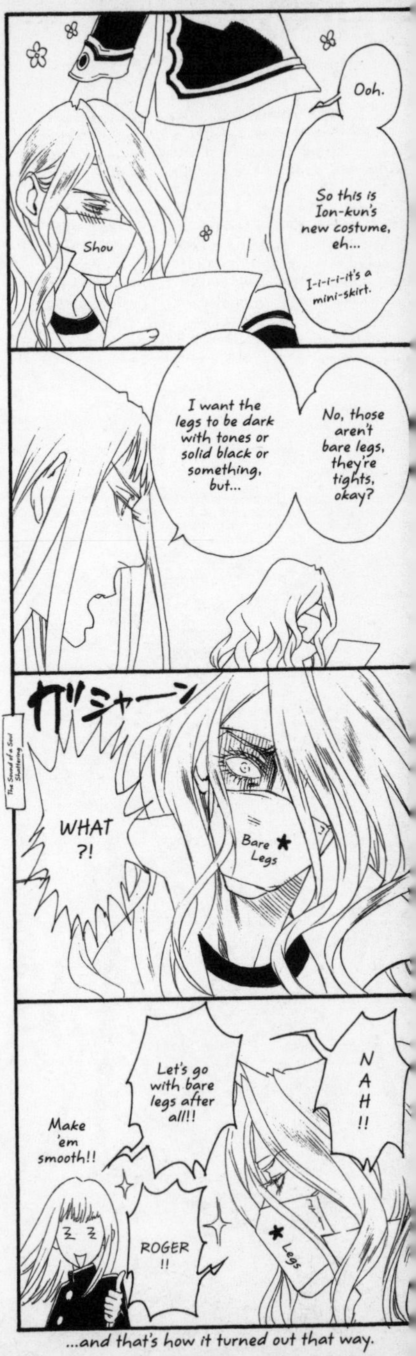
Ooh.
So this is Ion-kun's new costume, eh...
I-i-i-i-it's a mini-skirt.
Shou
No, those aren't bare legs, they're tights, okay?
I want the legs to be dark with tones or solid black or something, but...
ガッシャーン
The Sound of a Soul Shattering
WHAT ?!
Bare ★ Legs
NAH!!
Let's go with bare legs after all!!
Make 'em smooth!!
ROGER !!
★ Legs

...and that's how it turned out that way.

When we get to the carnage and climax scenes, we all go into chorus mode. Usually it's D•gon Ball stuff. It's kind of sad that we can all sing this...

If someone shouts this, then we all unconditionally start singing the full chorus intensely.

↓

SPARKING!! <-- vocal instrumental

↓

La lala la la la laaalala ~~

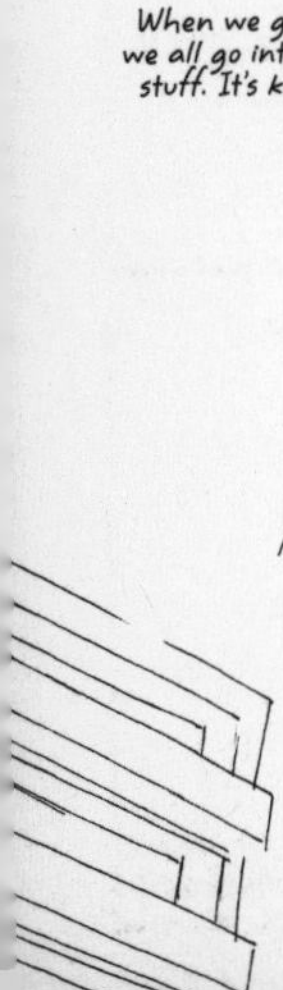

We're totally not calm, though.

Outro

It's the 6th volume! Hello. Thank you. I've come this far, the cover is Hugue and Kyujyo is starting to get afraid of how far they're letting me go. Plus, it's already the new year!! It looks like the curtain's risen for another stormy year. I caught a bad cold, I bought the anime DVDs all at the same time again and then it snows! Then I heard the original story from Volume 2 will be turned into a drama CD and...it's scary!! Really, I don't have the words to express my gratitude. I'm shaking. Speaking of shaking, it's cold!! In the 5th volume I was all talking about it being the end of summer and whatnot but now it's cold!!

It's winter and I hate it. I wish there were no such thing as winter, right?! Everyone, try hard and let's welcome spring. It looks like it won't be possible for Kyujyo, no, I'll be all right...then, I'll be happy if we meet again in the next volume. Nonstop! Kiyo Kyujyo.

Thanks

Tsukasa "Our race will, hereon after be abbreviated" **Kyouka:** Public Morals Monitor

Akira "I will share my future with you, hereon after will be abbreviated" **Ootaki** P.E. Monitor

I will nominate the "shrimp-like butt" for the first half of '06 "Wise Sayings Collection." It's already too late for me, isn't it...a tearful death is so difficult in this transient world.

Really, I'm sorry to make such a huge fuss all the time. I feel bad about it. But it's like that, isn't it, you know? Like that thing to keep the tension high all the time (abbreviated).

Shouko "We are tied together with a strong bond, hereon after will be abbreviated" **Kitamura:** Rabbit Monitor

Thank you for the shrimp!! All of them are jumping, bouncing, reducing, increasing and are really healthy, you know. It's like that isn't it; shrimp are cute, too! I think I'll have to add them to my favorite animals, like "Dogs, wolves, tigers, lions, shrimp."

Kazutoshi "Honestly, you like small boobs, too, right?" **Masataka:** Bodyguard

I'm sorry about last time when I called you all of a sudden when you were busy, had you stay with me until the end, and on top of that I got you addicted to Nadia and barged into your house! Let's bug each other again!

Mayuko-chan, Nagisa-chan Hitomi-chan

Editor "A...Amigo...?"
Saori-sama

Thank you always and always! I'm sorry I'm always keep sexually harassing you. I really make trouble for you all the time. The cold medicine made me happy. I'll get my act together more in 2006, so best regards!! Thank you for 2005.

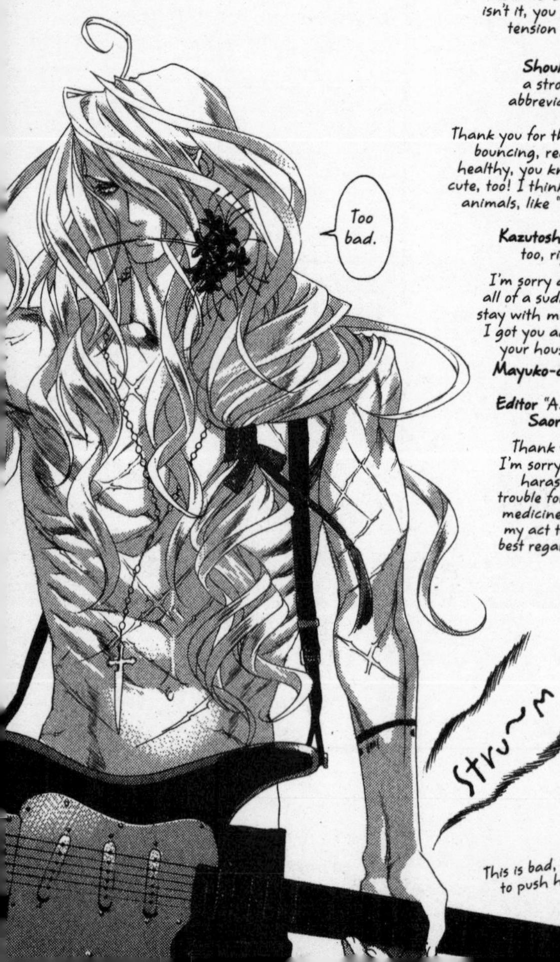
Too bad.
Stru~m

This is bad, I just want to push him over!!

Guitar Samurai
(Old joke!)

IN THE NEXT VOLUME OF

TRINITY BLOOD™

Astharoshe and Abel prepare to present their case to the Diwan, but the royal court is full of backstabbing intrigue, conspiracy and unpleasant surprises! Meanwhile Ion and Esther get lost in the Methuselah capital, meet a strange young tea-seller, and learn the horrifying truth that Radu may not be dead after all...

EDITOR'S NOTES:

THIS VOLUME OF TRINITY BLOOD SURPRISED ME BY BEING ONE OF THE HARDEST TO WORK ON SO FAR. IT'S NOT A TEXT-HEAVY SERIES OVERALL (IN SPITE OF SOME MICROSCOPIC ASIDES), BUT IT'S FULL OF OBSCURE REFERENCES, AND THERE IS THE ADDED TASK OF TRYING TO KEEP THE MANGA VERSION CONSISTENT WITH BOTH THE NOVELS AND THE ANIME. THIS VOLUME WAS PARTICULARLY DIFFICULT THOUGH, BECAUSE IN ADDITION TO MOVING THE SETTING TO BYZANTIUM, THROWING NEW REFERENCES INTO THE MIX, THERE TURNED OUT TO BE LENGTHY PASSAGES IN BOTH LATIN AND ROMANIAN. YIKES! AS ANY FIRST-YEAR JAPANESE-LANGUAGE STUDENT KNOWS, IT'S HARD ENOUGH TO FIGURE OUT ENGLISH WORDS WRITTEN IN JAPANESE, LET ALONE A LANGUAGE THAT YOU'RE NOT FLUENT IN!

FOR THESE PASSAGES, THE TEXT WAS ORIGINALLY WRITTEN IN JAPANESE WITH "SUBTITLES" ABOVE THE TEXT IN KATAKANA, THE WRITING SYSTEM USED PRIMARILY FOR LOAN WORDS, SOUNDING OUT THE ORIGINAL LANGUAGE. IF YOU READ MANGA IN JAPANESE, YOU'LL OFTEN SEE THIS KIND OF SUBTITLING TECHNIQUE IF A SENTENCE HAS A DOUBLE MEANING, A WEIRD PUN, OR IF THE SPEAKER IS BEING INTENTIONALLY OBTUSE. IT CAME IN HANDY HERE SINCE WHENEVER WE WERE CONFUSED ABOUT WHAT THE LATIN SHOULD BE, WE COULD REFER TO THE JAPANESE, AND SEARCH FOR A MATCHING BIBLICAL PHRASE (THIS IS HARDER THAN IT SOUNDS, BUT IT AT LEAST GAVE US A WAY TO DOUBLE-CHECK A FEW THINGS). IT WAS NOT AS EASY WITH THE ROMANIAN, AND SO I'D LIKE TO GIVE OUR TRANSLATOR SOME EXTRA PROPS FOR ALL HER NOTES ON THIS SCRIPT. WHEW!

AS AN EDITOR, I GENERALLY AVOID ADDING FOOTNOTES TO MANGA, SINCE IT CAN BREAK UP THE FLOW FOR THE READER, AND CAN OFTEN BE AVOIDED BY WORKING THE TRANSLATION INTO THE DIALOGUE ITSELF. WE DID THIS FOR SOME OF THE SHORTER ROMANIAN PHRASES, FOR INSTANCE. HOWEVER, THE ENTIRE FIGHT SCENE BETWEEN ION AND BAIBARS IS SUPPOSED TO BE IN ROMANIAN, AS INDICATED BY THE HORIZONTAL BALLOONS (JAPANESE IS USUALLY WRITTEN VERTICALLY, SO THE MANGA SHORT-HAND FOR FOREIGN LANGUAGES IS OFTEN TO CHANGE THE ORIENTATION OF THE TEXT), BUT THE ONLY WORDS ACTUALLY IN THE "SUBTITLED" ROMANIAN WERE THE FINAL WORDS OF THE BATTLE. UNFORTUNATELY, MY ROMANIAN IS PRACTICALLY NON-EXISTENT, AND ALAS, WHILE THERE ARE MANY LANGUAGES SPOKEN HERE AT THE TP OFFICES, ROMANIAN IS NOT ONE OF THEM. WHILE I TRUST THAT OUR HARD-WORKING TRANSLATOR DID HER RESEARCH, I DIDN'T FEEL COMFORTABLE RUNNING THE ROMANIAN LINES AS ACTUAL DIALOGUE WITHOUT AN EXTERNAL CONFIRMATION. THEY ARE HERE, FOR YOUR READING PLEASURE, THOUGH: "UMIL PĂREA URA. LUPTA ESTE GATA. TĂU VOI INTRA GRABĂ... BĂIAT." PRACTICE THOSE UP FOR THE NEXT TIME YOU COSPLAY AS A GIANT YENICERI GUARD.

OUR TRANSLATOR ALSO WENT ABOVE AND BEYOND BY LEAVING COPIOUS NOTES IN THE SCRIPT SOURCING THE LATIN BIBLE PASSAGES. AGAIN, IT SEEMED DISTRACTING TO FOOTNOTE THEM (ESPECIALLY SINCE THEY OCCUR DURING DRAMATIC BATTLE SEQUENCES), AND THEY WERE TOO LONG TO COMFORTABLY TRANSLATE WITHIN THE SENTENCE, SO IN THIS CASE, I DECIDED TO LEAVE THEM IN THE ORIGINAL LATIN. THEY DON'T CONTRIBUTE DIRECTLY TO THE PLOT, BUT THE PASSAGES ARE LOVELY AND POETIC, AND THE LATIN ADDS TO THE MOOD OF THE SCENE (WHEREAS BAIBAR'S UNTRANSLATED LINES WOULD HAVE JUST BEEN CONFUSING).

ANYWAY, FOR THOSE OF YOU WHO ARE CURIOUS, THEY ARE AS FOLLOWS:

CRUSNIK-ABEL'S LINE: A VARIATION ON THE PRAYER FOR THE DECEASED, ENDING IN THE FAMILIAR, "ASHES TO ASHES, DUST TO DUST."

HUGUE'S LINE: OMNES ENIM, QUI ACCEPERINT GLADIUM, GLADIO PERIBUNT: "THOSE WHO LIVE BY THE SWORD, DIE BY THE SWORD." MATTHEW 26:52

ABEL'S SECOND LINE: QUIA INVENTI SUNT IN POPULO MEO IMPII INSIDIANTES QUASI AUCUPES: "AS FLOWERS SET TRAPS FOR BIRDS, [WICKED MEN] SET TRAPS TO CATCH US." ECCLESIASTES 5:26

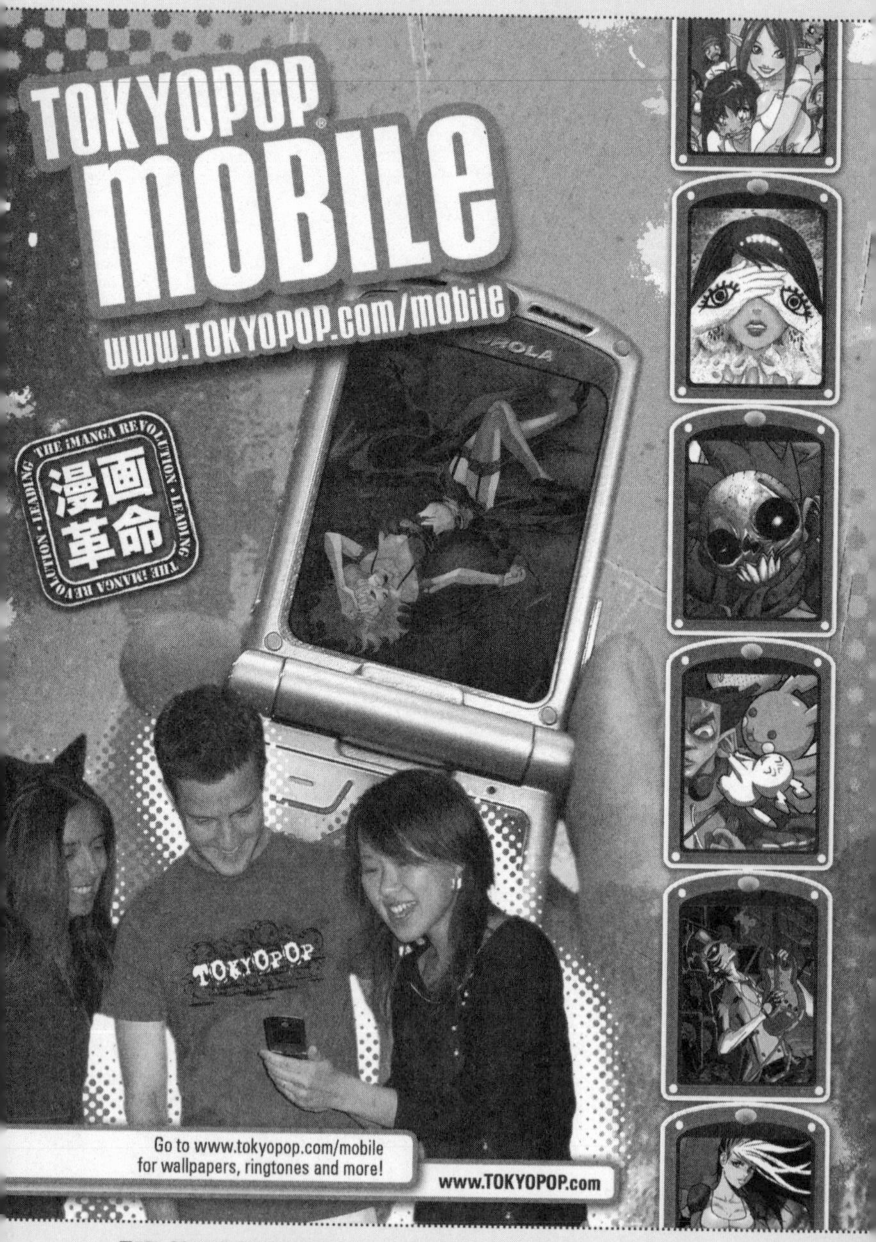
TOKYOPOP®
MOBILE
www.TOKYOPOP.com/mobile
THE iMANGA REVOLUTION · LEADING THE iMANGA REVOLUTION · LEADING
漫画革命
TOKYOPOP
Go to www.tokyopop.com/mobile
for wallpapers, ringtones and more!
www.TOKYOPOP.com

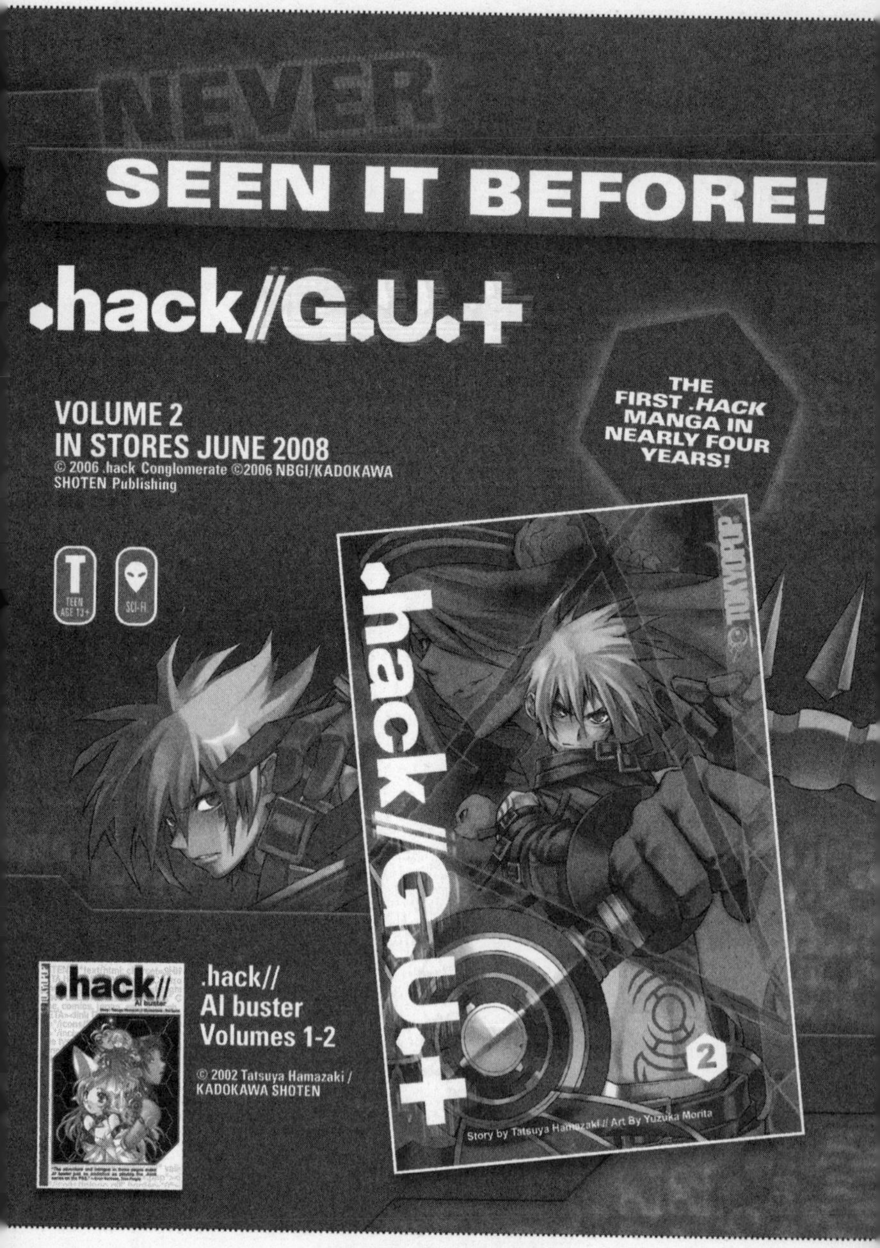
NEVER
SEEN IT BEFORE!
.hack//G.U.+
THE FIRST .HACK MANGA IN NEARLY FOUR YEARS!
VOLUME 2
IN STORES JUNE 2008
© 2006 .hack Conglomerate ©2006 NBGI/KADOKAWA SHOTEN Publishing
T TEEN AGE 13+
SCI-FI
.hack//G.U.+
2
Story by Tatsuya Hamazaki // Art By Yuzuka Morita
TOKYOPOP
.hack//
AI buster
.hack//
AI buster
Volumes 1-2
© 2002 Tatsuya Hamazaki / KADOKAWA SHOTEN

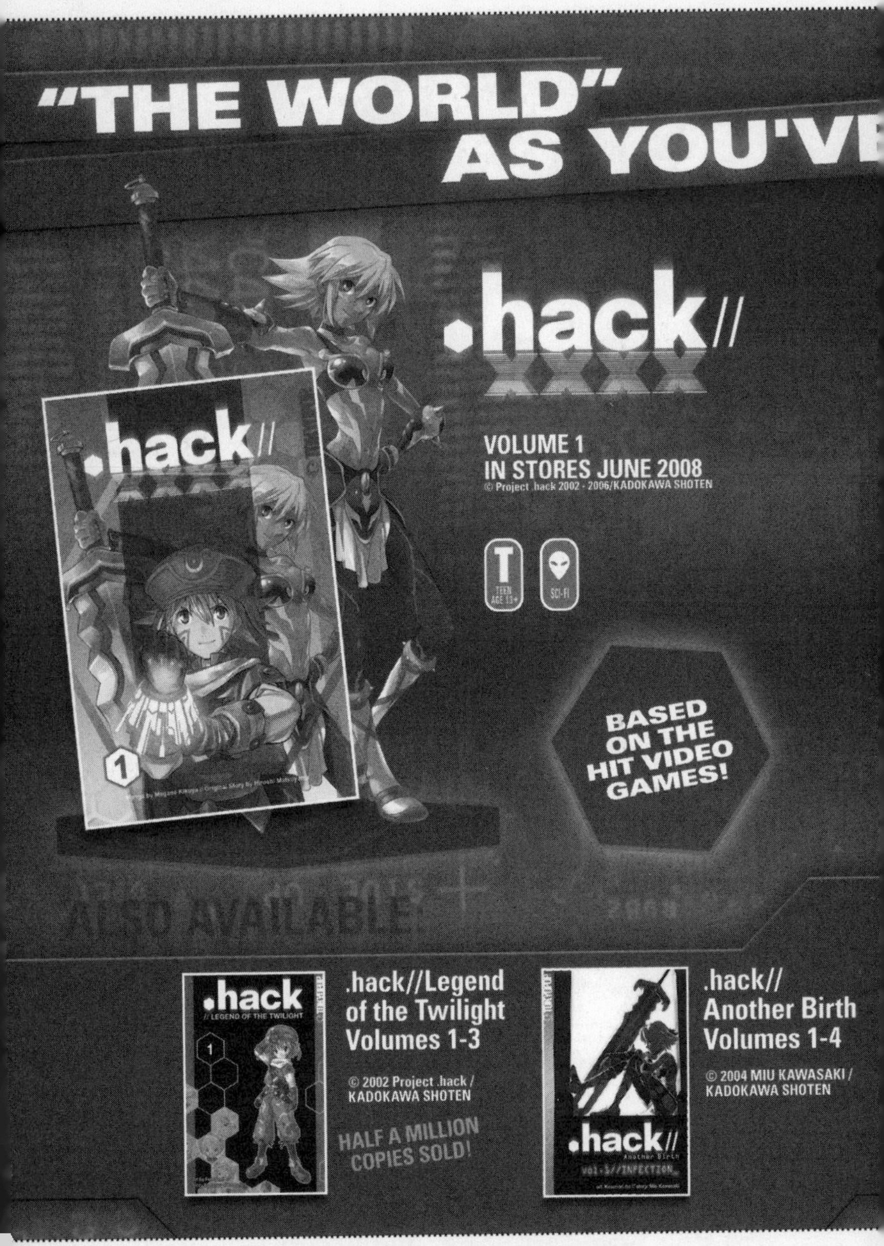
"THE WORLD"
AS YOU'VE
.hack//
XXXX
VOLUME 1
IN STORES JUNE 2008
© Project .hack 2002 - 2006/KADOKAWA SHOTEN
T
TEEN AGE 13+
SCI-FI
BASED ON THE HIT VIDEO GAMES!
ALSO AVAILABLE
.hack//Legend of the Twilight
Volumes 1-3
© 2002 Project .hack / KADOKAWA SHOTEN
HALF A MILLION COPIES SOLD!
.hack//
Another Birth
Volumes 1-4
© 2004 MIU KAWASAKI / KADOKAWA SHOTEN

FOR MORE INFORMATION VISIT:

STOP!

This is the back of the book.
You wouldn't want to spoil a great ending!

This book is printed "manga-style," in the authentic Japanese right-to-left format. Since none of the artwork has been flipped or altered, readers get to experience the story just as the creator intended. You've been asking for it, so TOKYOPOP® delivered: authentic, hot-off-the-press, and far more fun!

DIRECTIONS

If this is your first time reading manga-style, here's a quick guide to help you understand how it works.

It's easy... just start in the top right panel and follow the numbers. Have fun, and look for more 100% authentic manga from TOKYOPOP®!

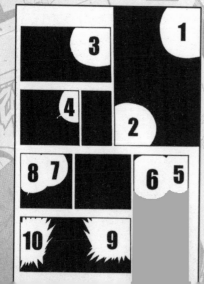